# LUCKY'S
# CHOICE

# Lucky's Choice

## THE LAST RIDERS, #7

JAMIE BEGLEY

Lucky's Choice

Young Ink Press Publication
YoungInkPress.com

Copyright © 2015 by Jamie Begley

Edited by C&D Editing and Hot Tree Editing
Cover Art by Young Ink Press

All rights reserved.

*Connect with Jamie,*
*JamieBegley@ymail.com*
*www.facebook.com/AuthorJamieBegley*
*www.JamieBegley.net*

ISBN: 0692505679
ISBN-13: 9780692505670

*For my mother,*
*God willing, we will be together again.*

# PROLOGUE

"Harder, Lucky, harder." Jenna's hands gripped his ass, pulling him against her more tightly.

Lucky hoped the kitchen table he was fucking her on held up to the strain of the hard thrusts he was driving into Jenna's clenching pussy. As he stood, watching his cock delve into her, her hips arched to take him deeper while he held on to the edge of the table to keep it from scooting across the floor. Then her hands fell to the side, nearly knocking a dessert plate off the table.

Why did women always try to cook and bake for him? Whenever he went anywhere, women were always attempting to show off their cooking skills. All but one—Willa.

Her name flashing through his mind nearly sucked the life out of his dick before another image materialized—her curvy body underneath his on the table instead of Jenna.

Lucky watched as Jenna ran a finger through the vanilla icing, lifting it to her peaked nipple.

"Help yourself," she teased.

Lucky bent over her, licking at the frosting until it melted against her flesh.

"Delicious," he said, licking the last dollop away before straightening.

He felt his cock jerk as he came in the condom he insisted he wore with Jenna or any woman when he fucked them.

"Better than Willa's frosting?"

Lucky leaned over her again, licking her nipple. "Much better."

"The next time she brings a cake to a church dinner, I can tell her you said my frosting was better," Jenna gloated.

Lucky felt his dick go limp at her words while his temper soared. He circled his hand around her throat, gripping it tightly enough to get his message across without inflicting any actual pain. "You won't open your fucking mouth to her if you expect to see me again. You get me?"

Jenna's eyes widened. "Yes, Lucky."

Lucky released her, moving away. He angrily took off the condom, throwing it into the trashcan before shoving his dick back into his jeans and zipping them closed.

Jenna shakily sat up on the table, holding her throat. "Shit, Lucky, I was only kidding."

"Don't act like I hurt you. I've held you tighter when you're coming," he snapped.

Jenna climbed off the table and picked up her shorts and top. "I didn't expect you to get so fucking pissed off at a joke. Why do you care what Willa thinks?" Her eyes narrowed on him.

"I don't give a fuck what anyone thinks about me, but I do care when someone deliberately tries to hurt someone else. The better question is why do you want to hurt Willa?"

"It was only a fucking joke!"

Lucky stared back at her, knowing the woman was lying.

"Whatever problem you have with Willa, leave me out of it. I won't be happy if you drag me into the middle of it."

"How can I put you in the middle unless there's something between you and Willa?"

"The only thing between me and Willa is that I used to be her pastor." Lucky gave her a hard look. "Let's get one thing straight, Jenna; there's nothing between me and Willa. She would tell you herself she doesn't even consider me a friend. There's also nothing going on between you and me other than when I want an easy lay," he said crudely.

Jenna's face whitened at his blunt words. "I thought you've been coming around a lot lately—"

"I've been coming around because I like what you've been giving me. When I get tired of it, I'll quit coming around. Don't make more out of it than there is...You'll be disappointed."

"I need to get cleaned up for work." Jenna started to move past him, but Lucky caught her arm.

"I don't want to hurt you, Jenna, but I'm not going to tell you there's something going on between us when there isn't."

Jenna gave an abrupt nod. "Don't worry, Lucky. I got the message," she snapped, jerking away then turning to go toward her bedroom.

Lucky sighed when he heard the bedroom door slam shut. Then he went to the front door.

He had made no promises to Jenna. She had built more between them in her own mind than there was to the reality of them fucking.

Lucky walked down the sidewalk of Jenna's house to his motorcycle, seeing Willa standing in the side yard with the children she had been fostering since their parents' deaths.

Lucky refused to acknowledge the discomfort he felt from her seeing him. He had seen her earlier when she had gone inside her house as he'd parked his bike in Jenna's driveway, and he had sensed her eyes on him. Giving her a casual wave, he had still gone inside Jenna's house.

The shy woman always turned a bright red when she saw him, and she avoided catching his gaze, as if she had convinced herself that, if she didn't look at him, she would miraculously become invisible.

"What the fuck!" Lucky came to a stop when he drew closer to his bike. Someone had spray-painted *'Blasphemer'* across it in bold red, and anger scored his soul at the insult.

Lucky had lived the last few years undercover as a pastor in Treepoint, Kentucky, and one of the things he had looked forward to while he had tried to bust an inter-state drug trafficking ring had been his motorcycle.

When he looked up, he saw Willa staring at him furtively.

"Did you see who did this?" Lucky heard the accusation in his own voice, but it was too late to regain his temper as Willa paled. He was having a shit time with women so far today.

Willa walked toward him, the five children following behind her.

"Is something wrong...?" Her words trailed off as her eyes caught sight of his bike.

"We just came outside. Chrissy and Caroline saw a stray cat when they were playing outside earlier. They wanted to feed it..."

Lucky's eyes went to the tabby cat at the side of Willa's house that was contentedly eating tuna from a can. Then he studied the children. "Are you sure you didn't hear or see anything?"

"Jenna's house is closer to your bike. It would be easily seen from her living room window. If you didn't see anything, why would we?" Willa said.

Lucky's face turned red in embarrassment and anger at her logic. "Because I'm not the one who's constantly looking out the window."

Once again, Willa was the one turning bright red. "I'll go get something to clean the paint off."

She hurried inside her house, leaving him alone with five kids staring at him with varying expressions—from the overtly hostile glares of the two older girls to the three younger ones scowling at him.

"We didn't see who touched your bike," Leanne stated, staring him directly in the eyes.

Lucky knew the children fairly well from when he had been undercover as pastor. Leanne and Sissy were sisters; their mother Georgia had been a member of his congregation who had recently been killed when she was incarcerated for setting a fire in The Last Rider's clubhouse. Shade and his wife Lily could have easily died if not for the precautions that Viper, the club president, had taken.

"I just asked if anyone had seen anything, Leanne. Maybe one of you put the other up to doing it?"

A firestorm was unleashed at his words.

"We don't put each other up to doing stuff that will get us in trouble!" Sissy snapped. The oldest girl, at seventeen, had been hit the hardest by her mother's death.

Lucky guiltily admitted to himself that he was wrong. This wasn't a prank a kid would play.

"What does the word mean?" Charlie, the eight-year-old, questioned as he held his younger sister Caroline's hand while his other sister, Chrissy, stared at him, sucking her thumb.

The three younger children Willa was fostering were Lewis's, Georgia's brother, who had also been raising his nieces after her death. Lewis had been determined to marry Willa to help care for his large family. The sick bastard had gotten his wish; he just wasn't around to benefit from it. Willa had shot and killed him when he had come to her house in a rage and attacked not only her but also Rachel, who had tried to help her.

"It means that Pastor Dean isn't acting like a pastor anymore." Sissy smirked at him.

Lucky knew her age and recent difficulties were responsible for her attitude, but it didn't keep him from snarling back at her. "You have a problem with me, Sissy?"

"I have a problem with you treating Willa the way you just did."

"Willa needs to learn to take up for herself. She doesn't need another person taking up for her. Certainly not a seventeen-year-old."

Caroline's foot kicked out, striking him in the leg.

"Stop it!" Lucky had long since lost control of the embarrassing situation.

He noticed Shade was parking his bike on the street as Willa rushed out of the house. Great, all he needed was an audience to his embarrassment.

"You a-hole!" Sissy yelled.

"Sissy!" Willa moved between Lucky and the girl, handing Lucky a towel and a plastic bottle.

"What am I supposed to do with this?" Lucky snapped, staring at the items in his hand.

"I thought you could use them to clean it off." Willa pointed at his bike.

Shade got off his bike, moving to Lucky's motorcycle, while Willa grabbed the items back from Lucky's hands.

"I'll clean it for you." Willa was about to spray the words with the cleaning solution when Shade stopped her.

"What happened?"

"Lucky thinks one of the children or I did this while he was inside Jenna's house. I told him they didn't, that they were playing in the backyard, but he doesn't believe me." Willa's lashes blinked furiously, trying to hold back the tears brimming in her eyes.

Lucky was now flushing a guilty shade of red as Shade stared back at him angrily.

"I didn't say they did. They"—Lucky pointed at Charlie and Sissy—"were both out front when I came outside, and Willa was going inside her house when I got here two hours ago. I was just trying to ask if they had seen who did it."

"That wasn't the way it sounded to me," Willa said.

"Then I'm sorry." Lucky pointed at his bike. "I was just angry when I saw that. Maybe I overreacted."

Willa ignored his apology, again moving to clean the word written across the entire frame of Lucky's bike.

"Don't touch it, Willa." Shade stopped her. "I'm going to call Knox and get him to come take pictures and see if he can find any prints."

A frightened look came to her eyes as she stared at the children behind his back. "That's not necessary. I can pay for the damages."

"Why would you pay for something you're not responsible for?" Lucky snapped.

Willa always worried about others more than herself.

"I don't want you thinking we did it. There's no need for a police report."

"I'll take care of it," Lucky said as the front door of Jenna's house opened and she walked out, dressed in her uniform of a short, black skirt and a red, silky blouse. She used to work at Mick's until King's new restaurant opened, and then she had been hired to work there. He wished she didn't have to leave for work; he didn't need her putting her two cents in to make Willa feel even worse.

"I thought you left," Jenna said, coming to Lucky's side and placing an arm around his waist.

"I was side-tracked," Lucky replied without moving away. He had already put her in her place before he had left her house. However, if Evie was right about Willa having a thing for him, then it was kinder to let her know she wasn't his type by showing who was.

That plan kind of backfired, though, and Lucky cursed himself when a hurt look flashed briefly across Willa's face.

"Who…?" Jenna finally noticed the bike sitting in her driveway then looked accusingly at the children. "You fucking brats. You need to have the—"

"Shut up, Jenna!" Lucky interrupted. "They didn't do it."

"Then who?" Her eyes went to Willa. "You jealous bitch." Her hand flew out, smacking Willa across the face before Lucky or Shade could stop her.

Willa cried out, her hand going to her cheek. Lucky grabbed Jenna back while Shade stepped forward, fury storming through his eyes at Jenna's unnecessary violence toward Willa.

"Go to work, Jenna. I'll deal with you later," Lucky said harshly.

Jenna paled as Lucky let go of her roughly, causing her to stumble. Nodding her head, she went to her car and got inside, but not without shooting a retributive look toward Willa as she drove away.

"If she touches Willa again, we're going to have a problem," Shade warned. "She's a friend of Lily's."

Lucky didn't need Shade's warning; he planned to deal with Jenna himself when she got off work.

"I'll talk to her tonight," Lucky promised before reaching out to pry Willa's hand away from her face, but Willa jerked away from his touch.

"Since you don't want my help cleaning the paint off, there's no need for us to be here. Shade, go ahead and call Knox. I'll talk to him when he comes. Let's go, kids." Willa bustled the kids inside her house, the flaming red handprint on her cheek standing out starkly.

Lucky winced at the sound of her front door closing. Any other woman would have slammed it shut, yet the quiet sound of the door closing was a testament to the embarrassment the woman had just suffered. Not only did he feel like an ass, but Shade had been there to witness the fuck-up.

"Don't say a fucking thing," Lucky warned between clenched teeth.

Shade remained silent as he took out his phone, calling Knox and asking him to come to Jenna's house.

Willa was hurt, Shade was pissed off, and his bike was going to have to be repainted. His afternoon fuck session with Jenna hadn't been worth any of the hassle.

As soon as he hung up, he told Lucky, "I have to get back to the hospital." Then he slid the phone back into his pocket and nodded at Willa's house where the two older girls were staring out the curtained windows. "You going to send Knox over there?"

"No, they didn't see anything. If they had, they would have said something."

"They didn't do it. Whoever trashed mine and Razer's bikes did this."

"I figured that out too late. I let my temper get away from me when I saw that word," Lucky confessed. When Shade didn't say anything, Lucky added, "I'll stop by in a day or two to apologize since I don't think she wants to hear anything I have to say right now."

"I don't think that woman wants to ever see you again, much less hear anything you have to say," Shade said wryly.

"I won't be getting a cupcake from her anytime soon; that's for sure," Lucky agreed glumly.

"I've had Jenna's pussy and Willa's cupcakes. I know which one I would've chosen, but you were never the smartest brother in the club."

Lucky had to silently agree with him, even if he hated it when the fucker was right.

# CHAPTER ONE

"May I get you something to drink?" Willa jumped at Rachel's voice behind her.

"No, thanks." Willa turned to face the woman who had talked her into coming to Lily's baby shower despite her intention to stay away.

Willa felt an unwanted flash of envy at Rachel's red hair. Her hand unwittingly went to her own lackluster brown hair to make sure it was still in a neat knot at the nape of her neck, wishing belatedly that she had left it loose.

"The cake is beautiful, Willa. You outdid yourself."

Willa smiled, blushing. She had taken extra time to make the cake special for Lily who was being released from the hospital after being kidnapped by her adoptive father. The State Police had led a search for several days to find the town's former pastor before releasing a statement that they had found evidence that Saul Cornett had managed to escape the country.

Not only had Lily and her husband Shade had to deal with her kidnapping, but their home had been wrecked by a storm that had swept through the town. The baby shower today was to replace the items that had been destroyed.

Willa had never been in The Last Riders' clubhouse before. She had somehow expected broken-down furniture and beer cans sitting around; instead, it was clean and furnished with leather furniture that actually looked very comfortable. There was a bar at one end of the room and a pool table with several other tables with chairs positioned around the room.

Winter came down the stairs from the upper floor, approaching her and Rachel. The wife of Viper, the club president, looked pretty in a blue maxi dress that showed off her slim figure.

Willa always felt huge and graceless when she was near the other woman. Not only did she outweigh Winter by over eighty pounds, but her own five-foot-eight height made Winter seem even more diminutive.

She was angry at herself for her envy of other women that went to the extent of constantly trying to reinvent her own appearance. Her hair had gone through several color changes recently from blonde to different shades of red to finally admitting defeat and returning to her plain brown hair color. Her makeover attempts hadn't stopped at hair, either. Trying to transform her large body into their dainty sizes had been another failed attempt.

"How are you coping with the children?" Winter questioned, her friendly gaze making Willa feel even guiltier for yearning to be as attractive as they were to the men who filled the motorcycle club.

Willa couldn't explain to herself why she felt that way, though. The Lord knew she wouldn't be able to handle the attention from the alarmingly lethal-looking bikers.

"It's been a transition for them," Willa admitted carefully, not revealing how difficult it had been to go from living a solitary life to one filled with tantrums and broken china, some of which didn't stem from the toddlers she was caring for until a relative could be located. The older children were proving to be the bigger challenge.

"I'm sure it has been," Winter said sympathetically.

Willa glanced away from Winter's astute gaze. The school had notified her two days ago that, unless Sissy quit missing school so often, she would be moved to the alternative school where Winter was the principal as well as a member of the committee that placed problematic children in the school. As a result, Winter was probably more knowledgeable about Sissy's academic failings than Willa was as her foster parent. However, she didn't say anything about the child in front of Rachel, which Willa was grateful for.

The problem was that Willa had never had any idea Sissy hadn't been in school. Although she had dropped her off each day with Leanne at the high school, the girl had been sneaking out and skipping. Leanne had known, yet hadn't told on her sister.

When Willa had confronted Sissy, the girl had gone upstairs to her room, locking Willa out, and now Willa was at a loss on how to deal with the girl.

"Cash needs some help. Excuse me." Rachel left, going to her husband's side as he haphazardly stacked baby presents on the bar.

"Any advice on how to deal with Sissy would be appreciated. I'm ashamed to admit I'm not handling her very well," Willa confessed to Winter as soon as Rachel moved away.

"Be patient. If you like, I could try to talk to her," Winter offered.

"I'll take any help I can get. I'm afraid, if she gets into anymore trouble, Child Services will reconsider my ability to foster the children. The sheriff and the state are trying to find Georgia and Lewis's half-brother. As soon as they find him, I won't have to be so worried about having them broken apart." That fear had been keeping her awake at night.

"Don't worry; I'm sure it won't be much longer." Winter touched her arm, and Willa instinctively drew away.

"Hi, Willa." Evie and King stopped as they passed through the crowded room.

"Hello," Willa responded, suddenly becoming aware the women in the group were trying to make her feel comfortable. It wasn't going to happen with Dean—or Lucky, as everyone was calling him now—in the room. She forced herself to keep her eyes averted from where he was standing, dressed in jeans and a T-shirt like the rest of the men except King, who wore his usual slacks and dress shirt.

"Your cakes are selling well at the restaurant, Willa. We need to talk about increasing our order." King was one of the few men who had the power to get under her guard and make her feel relaxed.

"I can't. I can hardly keep up with the orders I have now." Willa bit her lip, not wanting to disappoint her most lucrative customer.

"You could take the diner off your list. I could buy what you're selling them," King offered with a suave smile that had Willa considering the option for a brief second.

Willa shook her head regretfully. "That wouldn't be fair. I've sold my cakes and pies to them for years."

"I would pay you more," King tempted.

Willa could definitely understand how he had managed to steal his wife Evie away from the men of The Last Riders.

"It isn't about the money," Willa refused. "If I have any openings during the week, I can make a few extra desserts. We can do it on a week by week basis."

King grinned. "I'll take what I can get."

Evie leaned against her husband's side. "Isn't that the truth?"

Willa blushed from witnessing the sexually heated look between them. Thankfully, Shade brought Lily into the room at that moment, providing a welcome distraction.

Whenever she saw Shade and Lily together, it brought a lump to her throat. She was fortunate to have seen several extremely happy marriages in her own family, but what Lily and Shade shared was beyond explanation. Their love was a gift. It was special. It also reinforced her own sense of loneliness.

She had thought she would have been married by now with a couple of children, not alone and taking care of five children who belonged to two people who had made her childhood and adulthood miserable.

She had originally taken in the children as her penance for taking the life of Lewis, the father of the three younger children and the guardian of Leanne and Sissy, his sister Georgia's children, but it had evolved into her having a genuine care for all of them.

Willa stayed toward the back of the crowd as Lily began to open her presents while Shade held his small son in his arms. The harsh, azure-eyed man was smiling down at his wife indulgently.

Unable to keep watching without feeling envious, Willa moved to the large table set up with drinks where Bliss, an attractive blonde, was watching with a pained expression she was unable to disguise. Willa could sympathize with her. She constantly wanted what she couldn't have. Every night, she prayed to be a better person, but so far, her prayers had gone unanswered.

Willa took a bottled water, moving to stand next to Bliss so no one would overhear. "I brought you some of the peanut butter candy you like. I hid it in the kitchen cabinet by the back door."

Bliss looked at her in surprise. "You brought it for me?"

Willa nodded. "I remembered how much you like it. Did you use the last batch to bribe Rider?"

"Yes. He fixed the garbage disposal and cleaned the gutters." Bliss laughed.

"I made you a double batch. You can keep it for yourself or share."

"No one will take it from me. Everyone's pissed off at me because I said something I shouldn't," she blurted out, surprising Willa with the confidence since the club usually kept all their relationships private.

Willa watched the sensual woman who was staring unhappily at Shade and Lily. "Did you tell them you're sorry?" She didn't have to ask if it was Lily she had offended. Everyone loved the soft-spoken woman and would rally around her if they thought she was hurt. The party surrounding them was proof of their love for her.

Bliss gave a bitter laugh. "It's not the first time I've put my foot in my mouth, and the club is getting tired of me saying I'm sorry. They don't believe I mean it when I keep doing the same stupid shit."

"Then prove them wrong," Willa said gently. "Do you really think Lily and Beth are capable of holding a grudge?"

Bliss stared back at her, startled. "You know what happened?"

Willa smiled wryly. "No, they don't confide in me, but I overheard you at the hospital telling Jewell they'll never forgive you." At Bliss's worried expression, Willa attempted to soothe her fears. Since The Last Riders made it a point to keep their business private, and Bliss was already in trouble with the club, Willa wouldn't want them to think she was gossiping. "I only heard that before I went in to see Lily. I don't make a habit of snooping." Bliss relaxed at her words. "Go talk to Lily. Avoiding her isn't going to make it easier." Willa gave Bliss a small nudge in Lily's direction. "By the way, she loves the peanut butter candy, too. She was constantly asking for it when she was pregnant, but because she was eating so many cupcakes, Shade drew the line at the candy."

"That's why you made a double batch? So I could bribe Lily into forgiving me?"

"I made enough for the whole clubhouse to forgive you." Willa smiled, unconsciously showing her dimples.

Bliss gave her a strange look before heading toward the kitchen where she had stashed the candy for her.

Willa noticed Lily had sat down on one of the large couches next to Beth, who wasn't looking well. She walked toward them so she could talk to them then make her escape from the torture of being in such a large crowd.

As she moved forward, she felt someone staring at her. Always sensitive to being the center of attention, she glanced to the side and caught Lucky's eyes on her.

When she had heard the name the other club members called him, she thought the name suited him much better than Pastor Dean. When she had looked at his tall, muscular body and face that held a ruthlessness he kept carefully concealed behind a façade of affable charm, she had never been fooled. Not once. Not from the first moment she had walked into the church several years ago and seen Pastor Saul's replacement behind the pulpit.

The sun had been shining on his chestnut-colored hair that was slightly longer than most pastors she had ever seen. His hazel eyes had stared at the congregation as if he had known their innermost secrets. Willa had sat, stunned in the pew, feverishly wishing for his sermon to end so she could escape the feelings going through her body that were completely inappropriate to experience during a church service.

Willa hastily dragged her eyes away, concentrating on diverting her thoughts. She had long ago learned not to focus on Lucky, too afraid her expression would reveal her secrets. There was nothing more embarrassing than when a popular man realized the fat chick had a crush on him. She tried to never wish for something she couldn't have, and he was as unattainable for her as being a size six.

Willa waited patiently for Lily and Beth to notice her, not wanting to interrupt the sisters' conversation.

Lily saw her first, giving her the gentle smile that never failed to make Willa or anyone else feel as if she was her best friend, even though she knew it wasn't true.

"Willa, thank you for coming. My cake is amazing. I made Shade take a picture before I let them cut it." Lily's sweet voice enfolded her in genuine warmth.

"You're welcome. I'm glad you're home," Willa returned sincerely. Her eyes went to Beth, who winced slightly when she shifted to a more comfortable position on the couch. "Are you all right?" Willa became concerned at Beth's pallor.

Beth nodded her head. "I'm fine. I must have pulled a muscle," she answered evasively.

Willa caught the surreptitious look that Lily sent Beth at her answer. The sisters weren't very good at lying. In fact, they sucked. This was why Willa really didn't consider herself their friend or anyone else's, for that matter.

She always fell in one of two groups. One was where they took pity on her, drawing her into their group. The other was where they took advantage of her to get what they wanted. Lily, Beth, Rachel, and Winter were in the former group. They felt sorry for her and tried to include her, but they didn't consider her a friend enough to really confide in her. They kept her at arm's length, something someone who didn't belong to their club couldn't breach.

Unlike the rest of the town, Willa didn't want to know their secrets. She simply wanted to be a friend they could trust with their confidences, and know she wouldn't spread the gossip to the entire town. She was too used to being the object of malicious tongue-wagging to ever bring that down on someone else's head.

Willa gave them both a strained smile. "I wanted to say hello before I left. I need to leave to pick the kids up from school." Willa made up the excuse to get herself away from the uncomfortable situation.

"I'm sorry you have to leave so soon. I haven't opened your present yet—"

"That's okay. It's not much. I hope you like it." Willa started backing away, downplaying the hours she had spent knitting the powder blue baby blanket that was lying unopened by Lily's side. "Bye, Beth...Lily." She turned to leave, relieved she could finally escape. The room was becoming more crowded by the moment, filling with even more men.

As she made her way through the crowd, she neared the front door which had been left open from the last bikers entering.

"Why won't you at least say hi to Willa?" Willa slowed, recognizing Evie's voice.

"Because I don't want to give her another reason to feel awkward. She sticks out like a sore thumb in there. Every time I approach her, she runs like hell. I'll be glad when she gets over her crush on me. It's damn uncomfortable."

Willa paled. Rider, who had been coming down the steps, came to a stop when he heard Lucky's words and saw her eavesdropping.

Humiliation flooded through her. Straightening her shoulders, she continued toward the door and went outside. Evie saw her first, her mouth dropping open. King, who was standing next to her, was able to hide his surprised reaction, but not by much. Lucky glanced over his shoulder to see who they were staring at, and their eyes met.

"Willa…"

She hadn't believed anything could embarrass the confident man who had a tinge of red beginning to show on his firm jawline.

"I'm leaving. I wouldn't want you to be uncomfortable." She gave him a fixed stare, determined not to make a bigger fool of herself.

"I didn't mean…" Lucky ran his hand through his hair that had grown even longer since he had stepped down from the pulpit.

"You meant exactly what you said. If you think I'm attracted to you, you're wrong, *Lucky*," she said. "I would never be attracted to a man like you. The man I would be attracted to would share the same faith and beliefs I have, be kind and considerate to others, and never deliberately hurt someone's feelings. That man is the one you pretended to be for years, but I knew it wasn't the real man standing behind the pulpit every Sunday. That's why I switched churches. My pastor has to be a man I believe in. I *never* believed in you, and I was right."

Willa brushed past King with an apologetic glance, leaving the group staring after her in bemusement. She forced herself to go carefully down the long flight of steps to the parking lot when all she wanted to do was run. She felt Lucky's shocked gaze on her as she got inside her car then pulled slowly out onto the road.

She was humiliated yet proud of herself for giving him a piece of her mind. The arrogant man was used to women catering to him, trying to catch his attention. Well, she was one woman in Treepoint who wasn't going to make that mistake.

She was so angry she felt like baking him a cake then smashing it in his face. A giggle escaped her as she drove down the road, leaving the clubhouse behind. The image of Lucky with cake all over him gave her a tiny bit of confidence, as did the fact that he now believed he had been mistaken in his assumptions that she was harboring lovelorn feelings for him. *Which I don't*, she told herself firmly. No, she wasn't in love with him at all. However, she was forced to admit to herself—because she was afraid God was privy to her innermost thoughts—that she might have had a few fantasies about the self-assured man. He did fill her dreams late at night when her defenses were down. The longings she kept at bay during the daylight hours couldn't be suppressed during those long, lonely nights that seemed never-ending until the first streams of daylight would return, and she could bury them once again in hard work, exhausting herself so she could make it through another one.

Her mother had drilled into her mind since infancy to be a virtuous woman. Her mother would not only disapprove of her unwanted attraction to Lucky, whom she'd never met, but if she were still living, she would have heart palpations at the thought of her pure daughter being near the sexually magnetic man. Did people suffer anxiety attacks in Heaven? Willa placed it on her ever-growing mental list of questions she wanted to ask God when they met, hopefully in the far, far future. *Lord willing that I meet him,* Willa corrected herself. Her feelings for Lucky were putting her everlasting soul in jeopardy.

"God, if you're listening, I have something to confess. I lied. I kind of do have a crush on the big jerk," she said out loud, watching for oncoming vehicles in the other lane, afraid she would be punished for telling an even bigger lie. "Okay," she said, starting her confession over. "I like him a lot."

ଚ ଓ

Lucky stood on the front porch, watching until the taillights of Willa's car could no longer be seen. Reluctantly, he turned to confront a glaring Evie and King.

When Evie's mouth snapped open, Lucky raised his hand to stop her angry recriminations. "There's nothing you can say that I'm not saying to myself. I'm aware I came off looking like a dick and hurt Willa's feelings."

"You going to fix it?" Evie's features fueled his regret.

"No. I'm going to leave it alone. I didn't mean to hurt her, but it's for the best." Lucky averted his eyes from King's discerning gaze.

He smothered his guilt, something he was becoming an expert at. Willa's infatuation with him needed to be stopped, and he would rather her feel hurt now than prolong the attraction she felt for him.

"When did you become such an ass?" Evie stormed inside the clubhouse, leaving him and King alone.

King leaned against the porch banister, folding his arms across his chest.

"Go ahead and give me shit. I know you're dying to." Lucky was aware King had taken a liking to Willa.

"Why should I say anything? You wanted Willa to hate you, and you succeeded. You have your reasons. They're probably bullshit, but they're your reasons."

"They aren't bullshit. Willa's a sweet woman, and I refuse to lead her on. I'm not attracted to her, and I never will be," Lucky denied heatedly.

"Who are you trying to convince, me or yourself?" King's mouth twisted with a mocking smile.

"Neither. I'm stating a fact. The sooner she gets over me, the sooner she'll find someone else."

King looked at him in disbelief. "You really believe she has a thing for you?"

"Yeah, Evie told me...and the way she acts around me." At first, he had thought her keeping her distance was because she didn't approve of him as her pastor, but Evie's comments on Willa's attraction to him one night had opened his eyes to the fact that she didn't know how to deal with the one-sided attraction she felt toward him.

King shook his head, making Lucky doubt the validity of Evie's claim. "That woman has a thing for you about as much as I do. Willa is very perceptive; she sees past the pretense you put on in front of everyone, and it scares the hell out of her. She has a thing for one of The Last Riders, but it isn't you."

Lucky stiffened, as if receiving an imaginary punch to the gut. If he didn't know better, he would think it was jealousy. Fuck, he didn't get jealous. There wasn't a woman he wouldn't share or hadn't shared with the brothers, so why would he give a fuck if Evie was wrong about which brother Willa wanted?

"Who?" he demanded, not realizing his voice had deepened into a growl.

"Rider." King gave a sardonic laugh. "That's why she was so embarrassed when she heard your big mouth spouting stupid shit. Rider was behind her when she came outside."

Lucky felt a lessening of his tension. "She doesn't like Rider. She's never been around him," he stated confidently.

"Really? Hmm…I wonder whose ass is sitting in my restaurant every Wednesday afternoon when she's scheduled to make her deliveries. It sure as fuck looks like Rider helping her carry all those pastry boxes inside."

"You're shitting me." Lucky started to brush off King's words then remembered Rider had been disappearing from the factory every Wednesday afternoon.

"Why would I do that when you said you don't care about her and want her to find someone?" King threw his own words back in his face.

"I do. Then why did Evie think Willa liked me?" His brow furrowed in thought. He had even been given the impression that Shade had believed the same thing.

Looking over King's shoulder, through the open doorway, he saw Shade eating a large slice of the cake Willa had made. Could that cold-hearted bastard have his own agenda? Like feeding his sweet tooth? Could Shade have been the one to give Evie the idea?

"I don't know. Evie's not the best judge. She believes I'm helpless around the house." King gave a laconic shrug.

"You are." Lucky remembered King's failed attempts to do even minimal household chores. Hell, one day, Lucky had ridden past his house and seen him trying to mow the lawn. Lucky had pulled over to the curb and finished the job for him instead of leaving Evie to find an uneven lawn when she arrived home.

"Am I? Or maybe I'm smart enough not to have to do that shit. I'd rather get someone else to work on a broken disposal, mow the lawn, or put together a bookshelf. I have the money to pay for it, but Evie insists I at least try. Pretending to be helpless keeps Evie off my back, and I don't have to fix crap on my day off. I also have the advantage of seeing the men my wife used to fuck have to do my shit jobs."

"I'm going to tell her," Lucky threatened, becoming madder by the second. It had been hot as fuck that day he had mowed the lawn.

He didn't know what was pissing him off more: King's attitude or the thought that Willa did actually want Rider.

"Go for it. She won't believe you."

King's smugness had Lucky wanting to punch him as he straightened from the banister.

"I don't know why you're getting so angry. A few minutes ago, getting rid of Willa was more important than making sure she was having a good time. Rider wouldn't hurt her. In fact, I think they would make a great pair. He's obviously more sensitive to a woman's needs."

"You don't know what the fuck you're talking about! Willa needs someone who will lead a quiet life with her. She's very firm in her beliefs. She's shy. Rider would—"

"Rider's very gentle with her," King cut him off. "See for yourself. Come to lunch at the restaurant on Wednesday."

"Why would I do that? It's no concern of mine if she becomes involved with Rider. I'm not her pastor anymore."

"Suit yourself. The only reason I told you was so you would quit making an ass of yourself around her, but I can see that's going to be impossible for you." King went inside, leaving him on the porch alone.

Could he be wrong about Rider chasing after Willa? Lucky didn't think so, but he recalled Rider's face when he had stood in the doorway. When had Rider ever given a fuck about anyone besides himself? The brother forgot about women as soon as he found a new place to stick his dick. He loved breaking in new women...

Lucky cut the thought short.

Maybe he would stop by King's restaurant on Wednesday. He would reassure himself that Willa was safe from Rider's charm. After all, the man didn't deserve a woman like Willa. She deserved a man like he had pretended to be—a decent, God-fearing man, a man like he used to be before he joined the military and left his hometown that was even smaller than Treepoint.

It hadn't taken long for the war to strip away his beliefs in the integrity of the human race and then turn him into a man who had discovered his own weaknesses and failings. She deserved more than a man with blood on his hands and a target on his back. No woman deserved to be made a widow and left alone brokenhearted or to have her children left behind to mourn his passing. He had been forced to deliver too many condolence visits to want his own family to experience that kind of grief. That was why he had long ago decided he would have no children he wouldn't be around to protect. Even if he were to get married, it would be to a woman who lived off the logic that one man was as good as the next. After all, a slut wouldn't grieve for him when the man who was waiting to end his life finally struck, when his luck finally ran out.

# CHAPTER TWO

Lucky ignored King's amused look when he entered the restaurant on Wednesday, seeing Rider already seated at one of the bar tables that faced the door. He walked to the table and slid into the seat across from him.

"What are you doing here?" Rider asked.

"Thought I would try out the lunch special that has you here every Wednesday," Lucky stated, taking the menu from the bleach-blonde bargirl who gave him a flirtatious smile as she waited for his order. Lucky stared at her long legs before meeting her eyes with a blatantly sexual grin of his own.

"Give me a burger, fries, and a beer," he ordered.

"That's all?" Her teasing reply and the huge display of flesh overflowing her top drew his deepening interest.

"For now." Lucky gave her a wink, ignoring Rider's apparent aggravation.

When the waitress moved away, he glanced around the busy restaurant.

"So what has you eating here? I thought the diner was your favorite place."

Rider shrugged. "Obviously, you already know Willa brings her desserts in today. If you don't get them the day she brings them in, they're gone by Friday. Why do you give a fuck where I eat?" He looked across the table at him quizzically.

"I don't," Lucky stated matter-of-factly, gazing at the waitress's cleavage when she bent over to place his beer down in front of him then left with a seductive swish of her hips.

"Doesn't sound like it to me," Rider contradicted.

This time, it was Lucky who shrugged, taking a drink of his beer. "So her desserts are the only reason you're chasing after Willa?"

"Fuck no. Are you blind? Her tits and ass are why I'm sitting here. The desserts are merely a bonus." Rider gave him a cocky grin.

Lucky's hand tightened on the beer bottle, tempted to smash it over Rider's head.

"Willa's not a slut you can fuck and walk away from. She's not that kind of woman."

"How do you know? Maybe she is. Maybe I won't want to walk away from her. Razer settled down," he pointed out.

"You're thinking of settling down with one woman?" Lucky asked in astonishment.

"Are you motherfuckin' crazy? Hell no, I'm not ready to settle down." Rider stared at him as if he had stepped in dog shit. "I'm too young to settle down with one woman. I might when I'm over sixty so I'll have someone to take care of me when I get old, but until then, no."

Lucky's teeth ground together, beginning to understand Shade's exasperation with the brother.

"So, you want Willa to use as your fuck toy and to make desserts for you at the same time?"

"Yeah." Rider grinned in satisfaction. "It's a win-win situation."

Lucky lost it. He was about to reach across the table and wipe the smug grin from his face when the waitress inadvertently saved Rider by placing his food down, Rider took the opportunity to slip out of the booth before she moved away. His earlier flirtation bit him in the ass as she lingered, blocking him from following after Rider.

Lucky's head snapped around to see Rider taking the stack of pink boxes Willa was carrying through the door King was holding open.

"I get off in twenty minutes," the waitress commented, drawing his attention back to her.

Lucky quickly glanced at her name tag. "I'll be outside. Don't keep me waiting, Anna."

Her appreciative gaze slid over his body before returning to meet his eyes. "I won't." She hurried away, her lush ass drawing his own appreciative gaze. It wasn't as perfect as Willa's, but it would do.

Lucky remained seated, eating his burger and fries as he watched Rider charm Willa. The pretty woman was becoming flustered at the brother's attention, nearly dropping the boxes of desserts. Lucky prayed she would drop them and deny Rider the treats he was after.

Then Willa handed Rider the boxes, and he nearly choked on a french fry when the top she was wearing was revealed. She had on a peach top that was over large on her except through the breasts, which were snugly outlined, and the top button had come undone, leaving a generous portion of her breasts bare. Rider's ravenous gaze lighted on the display, and the brother nearly dropped the boxes he was juggling. King hastily snatched them away before they ended up on his polished hardwood floor.

Lucky finished his food as he continued to watch Rider and Willa talk near the doorway while King disappeared into the kitchen. Lucky assumed she was waiting for her money since she appeared to want to bolt from Rider's attention. Rider fucking got off making women uncomfortable, overwhelming them with his attention until they found themselves in his bed, wondering how they got there.

Willa took a step to the side when Rider stepped closer to her, her eyes inadvertently catching his. Blushing, she jerked her gaze back to Rider. Lucky wished he could read her thoughts at that moment. He was willing to bet she saw herself in the crosshairs between two wolves.

When she adjusted her stance so her back was to him, he threw some cash down on the table and stood, making up his mind to rescue her from Rider. He was doing her a favor, not because it bothered him to see her within touching distance of the lecherous biker, but because watching her about to be Rider's next lay was like watching a cute kitten about to be devoured by a pit bull.

As he strolled nearer, he almost rolled his eyes at hearing Rider invite her to lunch, though he had to admit he was stunned Rider knew what a lunch date was. Usually, he crassly asked the women he wanted back to his room at the clubhouse.

Lucky refused to admit to himself his own recent behavior wasn't much better. He was even more shocked by Willa's answer.

"I'm already having lunch with someone," she stated. Rider looked unhappy, but he didn't have time to say anything else when the door opened and Drake Hall entered.

"I'm sorry I'm late. I had an unexpected phone call when I was about to leave the office. Have you been waiting long?"

"No." Willa gave Drake an appealing smile, flashing those damn dimples of hers.

Drake gave Willa an affectionate kiss on her cheek that had Lucky's eyes narrowing on the other man. Willa should know better than to trust a man that good-looking. Lucky was rapidly beginning to wonder if the shy woman was as virginal as he had assumed with the number of men in town pursuing her.

He wished Willa had her gun on her. He wouldn't mind if she placed a bullet hole or two in the town's most lecherous citizens.

Drake's hand took Willa's arm as King approached with his elegant menus in hand.

"I have your table ready, Drake."

"Thanks, King."

Both Lucky and Rider watched as the sophisticated man led Willa away.

19

"What the fuck?" Rider grunted. "Why's she having lunch with him?"

"I don't know. King might."

"You think he'll tell us?" Rider was definitely pissed off with the turn of events. Lucky could practically see the wheels spinning in his mind on how to overcome this new obstacle that was blocking his cock and stomach from what he wanted.

Anna came from the bar area with her purse in hand. "I'm off. I talked the owner into letting me leave early."

Frustrated, Lucky saw King give him an amused smile as he handed Willa and Drake their menus. Lucky wanted to tell Anna he had changed his mind, but he gathered his senses in time.

He had no business being here, certainly not being curious about Willa's relationship with Drake or preventing her from getting hit on by Rider. He needed to remind himself why he had stayed the fuck away from the attractive woman who had an abundance of curves that his hands and lips itched to explore.

"Let's get out of here." Lucky took Anna's hand, opening the door with the other one.

"See you back at the clubhouse," Lucky told Rider, who was staring at Anna with new interest.

"She going to be there?" Rider nodded toward Anna.

When Lucky gave Anna a questioning glance, the excitement in her sultry eyes was the only answer he needed.

"Meet me in my bedroom; it has a bigger bed," Lucky offered graciously to the other brother. "See? I can share."

Lucky congratulated himself for proving he had no desire for a monogamous relationship. Of course, Anna wasn't Willa, and she didn't raise the same feelings of protectiveness, but Lucky wasn't going to analyze the differences between the women even further. There was no way to compare perfection against a cheap copy.

ঙ ও

Willa had to force herself to listen as Drake discussed the properties that were available to rent in Treepoint. Her gaze kept straying to the mirror on the back wall that gave her a perfect view of Lucky and Rider leaving with the pretty waitress. She had blonde hair knotted smoothly on her head in a way that Willa was never able to achieve with her own messy hair, despite several spritzes of hair spray. She had even tried becoming a blonde herself during the time Lucky had been dating Beth.

Lately, Willa had given up trying to turn herself into a woman who would attract the opposite sex—Lucky in particular. It had taken a lot of soul-searching, but she had finally come to the conclusion that *The Ugly Duckling* was a work of fiction, and there was no way her size twenty body was going to miraculously become a size six.

"I think your best investment would be to purchase the small lot of land next to this building. King's customers could get a taste of your desserts here and then stop at your shop to take more home. Several large restaurants are having their bakeries set up next door. It not only builds a customer base, but repeat business. There is also a spot opening in two months that's close to the diner. It wouldn't be as upscale as what you could accomplish if you built next to King's, but I think it would be lucrative all the same."

Willa dragged her eyes away from the window. The waitress had climbed on the back of Lucky's bike, holding tight to his lean waist as they roared out of the parking lot.

"I can't afford to buy the property and build new. How much is the rent for the one beside the diner?"

"Nine hundred a month," Drake answered. "If you're interested in buying the property, I would be willing to invest, Willa, and handle the financing."

Willa shook her head. "I would be too afraid you would lose your money. If I go under, at least it will only be my money lost."

Drake's lips twisted at her words. "You're not going to lose money. If anything, I think you're going to have a hard time managing to keep up with the demand you're going to have."

"There's already one bakery in town. Plus, the grocery store has a good selection. It's going to be hard making a go at a new business, but I can't keep up with the customers I have now in my kitchen. If I open a bakery, at least I can come home and not be surrounded by cakes and candy all the time. I might even manage to lose a few pounds."

Drake tilted his head to the side, his eyes going to her breasts that were pressed against the side of the table. "God, I hope not."

Willa gurgled with laughter. "If I didn't know the women you dated, Drake, I would be worried, but I happen to know who you're after."

Drake's affability disappeared, but his changed attitude didn't deter her.

"Everyone in town knows you want Bliss."

"Everyone but Bliss." Drake's short reply didn't arouse sympathy for him since Drake often dated more than one woman at a time, so it wasn't like he was sitting home, pining for the attractive woman.

They had grown up living next to each other until he had moved out of his parents' home after graduating high school. Drake had married his high school sweetheart but they divorced when Jace was a baby. Willa didn't know the details of his failed marriage, but she had seen a change in Drake soon after his marriage. The laughing boy she had grown up with had gradually disappeared until Willa only saw traces of him the few times she spotted his motorcycle, riding through town.

"I think she does, but from what little Rachel has told me about The Last Riders, the women aren't allowed to see men who don't belong to the club."

"It doesn't stop the men from seeing women who don't belong to the club."

"Since when have women ever been given equal rights?" Willa questioned sarcastically.

"Ouch! I think I'm going to change this subject while I still have a dick." Drake laughed.

"Don't worry, Drake; your dick isn't the one I'd like to neuter."

# CHAPTER THREE

Hearing the commotion from outside, Willa opened her front door hurriedly to find her house in complete disarray. The two older girls were arguing over the laptop needed to do their homework; Charlie was sitting in front of the television, playing a video game; and the two little ones were sitting on the carpet, the contents of her catering bag out onto the floor.

"Leanne and Sissy, I asked you to keep an eye on the children until I could get home." Willa brushed her fine hair away from her face.

The mutinous look from Sissy reminded Willa so much of her mother Georgia. Willa thrust the unkind thought away, not wanting her feelings toward Georgia to affect her feelings toward Sissy. The seventeen-year-old wasn't responsible for her mother terrorizing Willa through high school.

"I did. They're just playing," Sissy snapped.

Willa went to the younger children and began picking up the decorating tips.

Taking one of the tiny, metal tips in her hand, she showed it to Sissy and Leann. "This is small enough for one of them to choke on. I had this bag on the top shelf of the pantry. How did they reach it?"

Charlie took his attention away from the video game long enough to explain. "I climbed up on the stool to get it. I remembered you had markers. I thought the girls could play with them. I gave them paper to color on."

Willa sighed. The edible markers were strewn across the floor with the papers that had been neatly stacked on the kitchen counter when she had left.

Willa stared in dismay at the ruined orders that had been arranged by the date they were expected to be prepared, many now unreadable. It was going to take hours to call her clients and retake the orders, which was going to not only take time she didn't have to spare, but make her look unprofessional right when she was thinking about expanding her business.

Willa turned away, not wanting the children to see her blinking back tears that were not only from frustration but exhaustion.

"Willa?" Leanne's worried voice had her turning back to the children, pasting a composed expression on her face.

"Charlie, help the girls get cleaned up in the bedroom while I straighten up the living room. Leanne, can you pick up the decorating bag and place the items on the counter? They'll have to be washed."

Leanne began picking up the markers. "I'm sorry, Willa. I should have paid more attention to what they were doing."

Sissy made no attempt to help her sister. Her stubbornness, surely a result of the traumatic adjustment she was going through. It had to be hard on the girl losing her mother, then her uncle, and then being forced to live with the woman who had killed him.

"Are you finished with your homework, Sissy?"

"As much as I can do on my own. I'm not good in chemistry." She snapped the computer closed, carelessly tossing it onto the couch.

"After I finish dinner, I could help you…"

Sissy snorted. "How could you help me? You're a stupid, fat cow!"

Willa flinched, but she didn't let her expression betray her hurt.

"A friend of mine is very good in chemistry. I could call her and ask if she would be willing to help," Willa offered.

"Who?" Sissy asked suspiciously.

"Rachel Adams."

"That's Jace's cousin."

Willa saw the first spark of interest in the girl since she had moved in her home. *Leave it to a male to accomplish what I can't,* Willa thought.

"Yes. Would you like me to call her?"

Sissy tried to unsuccessfully appear disinterested. "Whatever."

"I'll call as soon as I finish picking up."

Sissy began to put away Charlie's game controllers then helped Leanne without Willa having to urge her. When the living room was done, and she had settled the little ones in the backyard to play with the cat she had adopted, she placed the call to Rachel.

"Hello."

"Hi, Rachel, this is Willa. I hate to ask, but I have a favor if you're not too busy."

"Not at all. What do you need?"

"I was wondering if you would be able to help Sissy with her chemistry homework tonight. I know it's an imposition at this late notice."

"I'm sitting here, bored to death while Cash is working late at the factory. I can be there in thirty minutes."

"Thanks, Rachel."

"No problem. I'll see you in a few minutes."

Willa hung up and glanced at a waiting Sissy. "She'll be here in thirty minutes."

Sissy nodded then went back inside the house without a thank you, wearing the same expression of dislike that she constantly wore.

Willa played with the children outside for twenty minutes then hustled them inside so she could finish dinner.

She was wiping Caroline's face off when the doorbell rang. She went to answer the door, but Sissy was already opening it.

"Hi, Rachel. I really appreciate you helping Sissy."

Rachel came inside with a bright smile on her face, relieving Willa of the thought that she had possibly put her out.

"I was only watching some television, Willa. I don't mind at all."

Willa left Rachel and Sissy alone as she went to the kitchen, afraid she would draw a sharp comment from Sissy. She let the children play at the table with the Play-Doh she kept on hand for the girls to keep them busy when she was baking so as not to disturb the tutoring session.

She fixed dinner plates for the children, sitting at the table with them while they ate. The younger girls played with their food more than they ate, but Willa didn't force them to finish their food. Charlie finished his plate, even asked for seconds. The children were each so different it kept Willa on her toes to keep them satisfied.

When Charlie finished, she took them upstairs and readied them for bed. The girls were yawning, while Charlie was fighting bedtime. Willa let them all lie on her bed and put on their favorite show as she lay and watched it with them. Chrissy fell asleep, cuddled next to her, while Caroline and Charlie watched the program.

Once it was over, she put the girls in bed before checking on Charlie. She pulled his covers up from the bottom of the bed, covering the boy who was staring up at her.

"Willa, I'm sorry I gave the girls the bag. I wanted to play my game, and they were bugging me."

Willa smiled down reassuringly at the sleepy-eyed boy. "It was Sissy and Leann's responsibility to watch you and the girls. You're a little young to be a babysitter. But I do want you to be more careful with what you give them, Charlie."

"I will. I promise."

"I'll take that promise and give you one in return. I won't leave the girls with you anymore without a responsible adult." Willa made the vow to herself and Charlie, always learning from her mistakes.

"Are you mad at Leanne and Sissy?"

Willa shook her head. "I don't get mad. I just want to take care of you and your cousins."

Charlie's eyes drooped as she turned out his light, closing the door softly as she left.

Willa knocked on Leanne's door, opening it when she heard the girl's reply. The fifteen-year-old was sitting at the desk Willa had purchased for her.

"It's almost bedtime."

"I'm almost finished. I was about to take my shower."

When Willa turned to leave, she saw that Leanne was about to say something, but didn't. The girl knew she had made a mistake, yet like her older sister, she wasn't ready to take responsibility for the house being in chaos when Willa returned.

"Good night, Leanne." Willa left, wishing the girl would learn to trust her. It was going to take time, and Willa realized the adjustment was clearly as difficult for her as for Sissy. Just because she was the least troubled, it didn't mean her emotions weren't in turmoil.

Willa went down the steps as Sissy and Rachel were closing the laptop.

"Thanks, Rachel." The friendly tone in the usually abrasive girl had Willa raising her brow.

"Sissy, I left a plate for you in the kitchen," Willa told her, hoping her better mood would save her from another of Sissy's stinging retorts.

"I'm not hungry." Sissy brushed past her as she went to the steps.

Willa moved to the side of the couch, seeing Rachel's concerned gaze. It was the same expression everyone always gave her. They believed she was weak and helpless. She wasn't, though. She simply didn't like confrontations, preferring to go out of her way to avoid them, but that didn't make her a wimp. It made her cautious.

"Is there anything else I can do to help out?" Rachel offered.

"No, I have everything under control." Willa kept her voice firm.

"All right then. Don't hesitate to call if you do. I imagine it can be overwhelming with five children and a business to run. I don't mind pitching in if you need me."

"I'll keep that in mind."

Willa walked Rachel to the door where Rachel paused with a confused frown directed at her.

"Can I ask why you didn't help Sissy?"

"She didn't think I could." Willa refused to show that her feelings had been hurt by a teenager. After all, everyone knew teenagers were difficult to deal with.

Willa tried to be understanding. If Sissy needed to spill her venom in her direction, then she could tolerate it until her relative could be found.

"You didn't tell her that you won the science award four years in a row?"

"Sissy wanted you. I think she wanted an in with your cousin Jace."

Rachel shuddered. "She asked me several questions about him, which I avoided. Those two together would not be good."

Willa stiffened. "You think Sissy would be a bad influence on Jace?"

Rachel shook her head, laughing, and then placed her hand on her arm. "Relax, mother hen. Jace would be a bad influence on Sissy. Drake is constantly getting him out of trouble."

"In that case, I agree." Willa smiled back. "The last thing I need is to deal with a teenager whose hormones are going crazy over a bad boy."

"Take it from me; some bad boys are worth the trouble," Rachel quipped.

"I'll take your word for it." Willa said tiredly, already thinking of the baking she was going to have to do before she could go to bed.

A strange look crossed Rachel's face. "I have a feeling you're going to find out for yourself." Her hand dropped to her side when Willa took a step back. "Goodnight."

Willa closed the door after Rachel left, shivering at Rachel's words. She didn't need any more trouble in her life. She was almost at her breaking point.

"God, if you're listening, please…please let me get these children settled before anything else can go wrong. If not, then give me the strength to bear whatever you have in store for me because, from that look on Rachel's face, I'm going to need all the help I can get."

◈ ◈

Lucky stared out the window into the darkness of the mountains, seeing a lone figure walking across the backyard. He watched as Lily stood, staring out at the mountains with her head bowed, and he felt a lump rise in his throat. No other parishioner had more faith than the woman who was obviously praying.

As a flicker of movement caught his attention, he turned his gaze to where Shade stood in the shadows of the gazebo, keeping his wife within view. Lucky's mouth quirked. The lucky bastard kept Lily on a tight leash she was unaware of, or if she was, she didn't mind. Lucky hadn't figured out which one it was yet.

"You done?"

Rider's question drew his focus back toward the bed he had just left.

"Not yet."

Indifferently, Lucky stared at the woman lying on the bed, sucking Rider's cock. Her body bore the marks of the rough sex he enjoyed, her ass bright red from his hand.

At his words, her gaze met his with trepidation. The woman hadn't even blinked one of her impossibly long, fake eyelashes when he had asked if she wanted Rider to join them.

Lucky felt his tired cock twitch. The way she looked at him reminded him of Willa—fear and need intermingled. In Anna's eyes, need reigned supreme, while Willa's fear always had the upper hand when he was around.

Lucky let the curtain drop back in place, squelching the internal struggle he fought daily. He went to the bed, staring down at Anna sucking Rider's dick, his own hardening and jutting upward. Leaning down, he moved his hand through her hair, pulling it back and forcing her to release the cock she had been eagerly enjoying.

"Dammit, Lucky, I was about to come!" Rider complained.

"Did I tell her to let you come?"

Rider's head fell back against the headboard. "Brother, you're killin' me."

They had begun the night in his room then made their way to the main floor for a few beers before heading upstairs to Rider's room. Lucky made sure to leave the door open for anyone else who wanted to join in the impromptu orgy.

Viper secluded Winter in his bedroom whenever Lucky wanted to play since he was still uncomfortable to do so in front of her, but not to the extent he was with Lily. Therefore, the night had been a much needed release from the façade he still presented in front of Lily.

Lucky refused to admit to himself that guilt was the reason. He wasn't the man Lily believed he was, and he never would be.

Lucky reached over to the night table beside Rider's bed. Picking up the red candle, he held it over the blonde staring up at him cautiously. Her hand went behind her back to cover one rosy cheek.

"What's your safe word?" Lucky took a step back from the bed, giving her space to make up her mind. "You just want to fuck? 'Cause we don't have to play if you've had enough."

"Fire." She licked her bottom lip. "I want to play, and I never have enough."

*I would bet my last paycheck on that statement being true*, he thought cynically.

Lucky tipped the candle, the hot wax slipping over the edge and dripping onto her stomach in a stream which trickled toward her cunt, stopping a centimeter from the fleshy lips, making the woman moan in ecstasy.

Lucky set the candle back onto the nightstand before reaching for the lethal looking knife he had placed there earlier. Expertly, he leaned over Anna, letting the tip of the knife rest against the base of her throat before sliding it down between her breasts toward her stomach without leaving so much as a scratch on her flesh. When he came to the line of wax, the knife slipped under it, removing it deftly and leaving behind a faint red line.

The hand holding the knife went upward before striking downward, burying the knife in the mattress between her splayed thighs, a hairsbreadth from her glistening pussy.

"Fuck, Lucky, you're going to ruin my mattress."

Lucky rose, lifting a brow at Rider's hand on his cock as he tried to give himself the orgasm Lucky had interrupted.

Anna's eyes narrowed in jealousy as Raci and Jewell strode in barely clothed and jumped on the bed.

Lucky made a couple of tsk sounds at the woman's reaction. "I told you not to put your mouth on him. You were supposed to use your hand. Rider can't resist coming in a woman's mouth."

His hands went to her thighs, tugging her downward until her clit rested against the hilt of the knife.

"Am I playing or watching?" Raci asked, staring enviously at Anna.

"Playing. Rider could use some help." Lucky mocked Rider's frustrated groan.

The brother was putty in a woman's hand when she had her mouth on his dick, and Lucky had wanted to make sure the brother's dick would be too sore from the hand jobs to ride his bike for a week, much less chase after Willa.

Raci immediately crawled toward Rider, hooking a knee over his hip before sliding her pussy down on his cock that he had rolled a condom onto before taking her hips and slamming his dick deep inside of her.

"What about me?" Jewell pouted.

"Have I ever left you out?" Lucky reached beside Anna, dragging Jewell across the bed toward him until she was hanging off the side of the bed. He reached for a condom on the nightstand, expertly sliding it on his thick cock.

If he and Rider fucked anymore tonight, they were going to have to grab more condoms from one of the other brothers.

When he was covered, he parted Jewell's pussy lips with his fingers, seeing she was more than ready for his cock. Her perfect pussy was red and shiny, waiting to be plundered.

As Lucky placed the tip of his cock at her entrance, thrusting inside of her in one stroke, she arched, jutting her breasts upward. Lying next to them, Anna groaned, as if she was the one he had entered. Lucky watched her rub her clit against the hilt of the knife as she watched the two couples fucking.

Jewell writhed under his steady strokes as his hands gripped her hips, raising her ass off the bed so he could fuck her harder. She clawed at the sheets as his cock slid through her tight pussy. It never failed to surprise Lucky how good it felt to fuck her.

She clamped the muscles of her pussy around him, damn near making him come before he was ready. He reached over her, taking a nipple between his fingers and pinching the bud into a point.

"Stop," he commanded, and the muscles around his cock relaxed.

"You take all the fun out of it," Jewell complained.

"You think so?" Lucky murmured, speeding up his strokes so she couldn't catch her own climax, building her frustration until a sheen of sweat glistened on her lithe body. Her breasts shook with her rapid breaths and the ferocity of his driving thrusts.

"Lucky, you've got to let me come," Jewell panted.

Lucky lifted her hips higher until only her shoulders rested on the bed. She tried to twist her hips but Lucky held her steady, forcing her to take only what he was willing to give her.

Raci's moans filled the bedroom as she began to come, and Jewell began to shake with her own orgasm as her head tossed back and forth on the mattress without making a sound. Lucky liked that the woman wasn't excessively noisy.

His own climax built, and he was barely able to maintain the iron control to prevent himself from coming. When Jewell's climax had played out, Lucky removed his dick from her, ripping off the condom and throwing it in the trash can.

Anna was frantically using her fingers to achieve an orgasm on her own. Going to the opposite side of the bed, he took her under the shoulders, tugging her until her head fell over the side of the bed.

"You still want to suck dick?"

Anna's mouth opened, and Lucky drove his cock into it as he leaned over her, sucking her clit into his mouth, ravenously licking at it as if he had never sucked one before. His expert tongue had her convulsing with her orgasm before he could work his cock to the back of her throat.

Without stopping, he continued to play with her clit until he felt her begin to climax again, and then he gave in to the frantic desire that had his cock twitching his own release into her greedy mouth.

When he finished, he raised her head up and turned her until the unconscious woman was lying back on the bed.

"She dead?" Jewell asked, turning her head to look at Anna.

"No, she passed out when she came the last time," Lucky said, unconcerned for the woman he had never seen before today and wouldn't see again.

He picked his jeans up from the floor and slid them on. He was zipping them closed when Anna began coming to, staring dazedly around the room.

Lucky sat down on the side of the bed to tug on his boots. Standing, he grabbed the T-shirt he had thrown on the chair. After putting it on, he turned to Rider, who was sucking on Raci's nipple.

"Make sure she get's home." Lucky stated, checking to make sure his wallet and keys hadn't fallen out of his jeans.

"I'll take good care of her." Rider grinned, content to be the lone man with three naked women.

Lucky nodded, moving away from the bed.

"That's it? You're not even going to tell me good-bye?" Anna rose up on her elbows, glaring angrily at him.

He turned on a booted heel, returning to the bed. Reaching down, he jerked his knife from the bed. Then, picking up her shirt off the floor, he wiped it off before sliding it into his boot.

"The last time you came was my good-bye."

Leaving the room that had become stifling, he went down the steps to where the party was still in full swing. Lucky went out the front door, heading down the large flight of steps to his bike. He rode into town, the cool night air cleansing the scent his carnal night of sex had produced. He had wanted to shower yet hadn't been in the mood for any of the women to join him.

Lucky slowed his bike and pulled into a dark lot. Parking, he went to a side door and inserted his key before walking through the eerily quiet building that had once held him hostage through his desire to stop a dangerous drug ring.

Walking down the long hallway with the gleaming wood floors, his eyes went to the stained glass doors. His hand shook when he reached out to open the door, going inside where he took a deep breath. Why was there always a distinct smell that seemed to belong to all churches?

He sat down in the last pew, staring at the pulpit where he'd stood and preached for so many years. The case had dragged on too long, trapping him in the profession he had walked away from in the military.

Lucky bowed his head, clearing his thoughts before he began.

"Lord God, forgive me, for I have sinned against you."

# CHAPTER FOUR

Willa brushed her hair back from her flushed cheek. Without a doubt, this was the worst idea she had ever had. Bringing all five children to the diner for lunch had been meant to give herself a welcome break from cooking and cleaning for the afternoon. Instead, it had become a visit to Hell.

Caroline was ready for her nap. Chrissy was grumpy, and nothing was making her happy. Then there were Leanne and Sissy who were arguing, and Charlie was still angry that she had made him leave his video game when he had reached a new level.

As if that wasn't enough, The Last Riders came in to take a table not far from hers and were able to easily observe the pandemonium going on at her table.

Chrissy spilled her glass of milk then burst into tears as the cold liquid dripped onto the new dress that Willa had put on her.

She gratefully took the towel from the waitress hovering near The Last Riders' table, cleaning the mess and trying to ignore being the center of everyone's critical gazes.

Opening her purse, she took out the plastic bag of toys she kept for emergencies. She found a toy car and a small stuffed bunny she hoped would occupy the girls then gave each of them one to play with. They instantly began to fight each other for the toys, wanting what the other had, so Willa took the toys away, switching them then giving each girl the toy they wanted. Silence reigned for a short time until they became bored. Thankfully, the waitress was able to drag her attention away from the bikers long enough to serve their food, and Willa was given a few moments of peace as they ate.

Her food grew cold as she concentrated on the younger girls not making a mess. She was wiping Chrissy's ketchup-filled fingers when she heard the sound of a chair scraping back.

Lucky dragged his chair closer, placing it between the girls and her chair, blocking her from them.

"Eat," he ordered.

Willa didn't know if he was commanding her or the girls, but all three of them obeyed. Chrissy and Caroline stared at Lucky while they chewed on an apple slice. She took a bite of her grilled chicken sandwich, trying not to choke on the nervous tension his hardened expression was raising. Even Sissy and Leann stopped arguing, picking up their forks.

He motioned to the waitress to bring his coffee, leaning back as she poured him a fresh cup. Razer, Viper, and Shade all watched from their table as Lucky calmly poured sugar into his black coffee.

Willa forced herself to swallow the bite she had taken before she told him quietly, "I have it under control."

Lucky's hazel eyes met hers directly. "Willa, you've not had control of your life since I've met you." He reached over, taking Caroline's cup away before she could take the lid off. "You need to get them some sippy cups."

Willa raised her brow at his authoritative tone. "They need to learn to drink out of regular cups."

"Doesn't seem to be working." He picked up the towel still lying on the table and cleaned the new mess Caroline had made.

Willa refused to sit still and let Lucky intimidate her. She opened her mouth to snap at him then changed her mind. Taking another bite of food, she instead stewed silently as the children suddenly seemed to remember how to behave appropriately in public.

When the waitress came back with his food, Willa, feeling self-conscious, tried not to stare as he ate his burger and fries while she continued to eat her own food.

She had no idea how to talk to men, much less one she battled her constant attraction to despite telling herself it was only his handsome face that drew her. His muscular body in suits had been a thing of fantasies, but Lucky in jeans and T-shirts with his tattoos showing on his arms was enough to make any woman speechless.

"You must have had a hard time keeping your tattoos covered." Willa blushed, not able to believe she mentioned something personal about his body.

"It was hard during the summertime, but I was used to hotter temperatures overseas, so it wasn't too bad."

"Do you miss being a pastor?" Willa asked curiously. "You had the whole town believing that ministering was your calling in life."

He left her question unanswered. "Everyone, it seems, but you." Lucky tilted his head to the side. "Why?"

Willa took her time answering, trying to come up with exactly why she hadn't believed in the man all the parishioners had taken into their hearts.

"I have an uncle and several cousins who are pastors. I was raised in the church."

"So were Beth and Lily, and they were just as surprised when I left the church." The women's father had been the pastor Lucky had taken over for after his 'death.'

"Saul Cornett wasn't a real pastor. Thank God my parents weren't some of the fanatics who followed him."

Lucky's voice turned grim. "I won't disagree with that assessment."

Willa took a drink of her ice water. From his expression, he was still waiting for her to answer his question.

"You did everything perfect: gave the right sermon, were gentle with the children, even when their crying disturbed your sermons…" Her eyes went to Caroline and Chrissy who were playing contentedly next to him with their toys, chewing on the french fries he had given them. The other three children were sitting, listening quietly to their conversation.

Charlie had lost his angry expression and was awestruck by the large biker sitting at the table. Sissy wasn't awestruck; she was eying the bikers as if they were her dessert. Thankfully, the bikers didn't return her flirtatious smiles.

"You never paid too much attention to the women parishioners, even when they threw themselves at you. I couldn't find fault with anything you did. That was the problem. Nobody's that perfect; we all have weaknesses."

Lucky's mouth twitched in humor. "What's your weakness, Willa?"

Willa gave a wry twist of her lips. "I think that's obvious."

He frowned at her answer. "Enlighten me…because, from what I've observed, you place yourself on a moral high ground."

Willa paled at his harsh assessment of her. "Is that what you truly believe?"

Chrissy began to try to climb out of the highchair Willa had placed her in, but Lucky deftly unsnapped the front tray, lifting the fussy toddler onto his lap and giving her the toy she had dropped onto the floor.

"If you believe your weight is a weakness in God's eyes, then, yes. Believe me, He has much more damning sins to forgive than worrying whether you have a cheeseburger or grilled chicken for lunch."

Willa stared back blankly at Lucky, not knowing how to respond to him. From the time she was Caroline's age, she remembered her mother being critical of her size. As she grew older and began school, it was obvious she was bigger than the other girls her age—another criticism her mother pointed out.

Her mother was small and delicate. Willa would try to emulate her so hard, yet despite her efforts, she was never able to achieve her mother's approval. Then her father and mother would argue over her, making her feel worse for causing contention between the usually loving couple.

As an only child, she had felt like she was an interloper in her own home. The loving couple had planned on not having children, so she had been an accident and stolen her mother's freedom, something her mother had reminded her of frequently. Willa had tried to be a good daughter, striving to please her mother and father. However, each parent resented the time she took away from the other; as a result, Willa had learned early not to make demands on her parents' time.

Had she unknowingly developed the same critical attitude she disliked in her mother? Willa hoped not. She wanted to be liked, not resented.

She stared down at her half-eaten plate of food, placing her fork on the table, unable to eat another bite.

"You don't like me very much, do you?" Willa raised her eyes, unaware they were filled with hurt, to meet Lucky's surprised gaze.

Lucky shook his head. "That isn't what I meant, Willa."

"You practically called me a self-righteous bitch." Her bottom lip trembled.

Lucky's eyes narrowed on her mouth, and Willa shivered in sudden awareness. Jumping up from her chair, she bent over, snatching Caroline from his lap and handing her over to a startled Leanne who had risen when Willa had. Then she unsnapped Chrissy's highchair and picked up the little girl who started crying when she dropped her toy. Lucky reached over, picking it up and giving it to her.

"Thanks for helping with the children."

Willa motioned the rest of the kids to the register where she paid before exiting the diner. As soon as the door closed behind her, she felt a rush of relief, despite the knowledge that she had made a fool of herself in front of Lucky again.

"What's wrong, Willa?" Leanne asked, shifting Caroline to her other hip.

"Nothing," she prevaricated. "Caroline and Chrissy are ready for their naps. Let's get them home."

Charlie and Leanne moved toward her minivan, but Sissy held back. "You like him, don't you?" The observant seventeen-year-old stared at her with pity.

"Of course not," Willa denied.

"Good, because I don't think he likes you back."

Willa's chest filled with hurt. Sissy wasn't being ugly; she was actually trying to be nice to her for the first time.

Willa turned away from her, wishing with all her heart she had reacted differently when he had stared at her. She had acted like the frightened virgin she was. Now Lucky was probably inside, laughing his ass off at her.

She bundled the kids inside her van before driving them home, and all the while, her mind played the last few minutes in the diner over and over. Had it been a figment of her imagination? For a second, she could have sworn she saw a spark of desire in Lucky's eyes. If it was desire, though, what was she going to do about it?

What she always did when she became frightened—run.

೪ ೞ

Lucky returned to the table where Razer, Shade, and Viper were sitting. He motioned for the waitress to reheat his coffee.

"What did you say to her to send her running like a scared rabbit?" Shade asked after the waitress left.

"Nothing," Lucky pretended innocence, which he knew damn well didn't fool any of the experienced men surrounding him.

Shade wasn't about to let him get away with it, though. "She reminds me of Lily whenever I frightened her."

"There's a big difference between Lily and Willa," Lucky said, taking a drink of his hot coffee and nearly burning his tongue off.

Shade arched a brow, waiting for an explanation.

"Lily was afraid of her sexual attraction to you because of her past. Willa doesn't want to be attracted to me because she doesn't like the type of man I am."

Shade gave a bark of laughter. "Lily hated me at one time. She definitely didn't like the man I was when she stumbled into that Friday night party."

"Willa's attracted, all right, both to the good and bad in you. The question is are you going to do anything about it?"

"No." Lucky threw some money down on the table then got to his feet, leaving the restaurant before Shade could ask more questions he didn't want to answer, either to them or himself.

Instead of going to his bike, he crossed the street to the police station. The older woman sitting behind the desk gave him a wink. She had overly-tanned skin that had the appearance of dried leather. She was at least sixty and was wearing a tight dress that showed she weighed maybe ninety pounds. When he had been a pastor, she had attended church regularly, her behavior always respectful. However, since he had re-joined The Last Riders, she stared at him like he was one of Willa's cupcakes.

"The sheriff isn't busy; he's in his office."

Lucky avoided her appraising look, briefly knocking on Knox's door before entering to find Knox sitting behind his desk, staring at a computer screen.

"What's up?" Knox leaned back in his chair.

Lucky didn't beat around the bush. "Have you found out any information on Georgia and Lewis's next of kin?" The only way he could help Willa was to try to get the children off her hands.

Knox folded his hands across his stomach. "Found Lewis's ex-wife, the younger three children's mother. She's in a state mental hospital. She can't take care of herself, much less the kids. From what little her doctor told me, Lewis practically beat her to death when he found out she left him. She took off with the kids, but Lewis found her, took the kids back, and left her for dead."

"Why weren't charges filed against him? The son of a bitch should have been sitting in a jail cell instead of terrorizing Willa."

Knox's face was grim. "No witnesses and she refused to press charges."

"What about Leanne and Sissy?"

"Georgia never told anyone who the fathers of the girls were."

"Fuck. No other relatives are able to take the kids?"

"There aren't any. The only other relative we know about is Georgia and Lewis's half-brother, Clay Meyer, whose mother took him then disappeared years ago. She died twelve years ago in Tennessee. I'm trying to track Clay down, but it's like he's disappeared off the face of the earth. I have a couple of men searching for him, but so far, they aren't making any progress."

"What's Willa supposed to do, keep them indefinitely? It would be hard for any set of parents to keep up with that many children."

"Maybe that's why Lewis was trying so hard to get Willa."

Knox's words struck Lucky's temper, and his foot kicked at the chair Knox was leaning back in, nearly toppling the large man over.

"Son of a bitch! I'll throw your ass in one of the cells!" Knox threatened as he stood.

"You can try." Lucky braced himself as Knox scowled, sitting back down.

"I've talked to Willa. She understands this is going to take some time. Even if I find Clay Meyer, he's never met those kids, so why would he agree to take them? I advised her to let me find foster homes for them."

"I don't have to guess what she said."

"She feels too guilty over killing Lewis," Knox confirmed.

"The bastard would have killed Rachel if she hadn't shot him."

"We both know that, and Willa knows that, but she feels like she's doing the right thing. Maybe she is. They're better off with Willa than in foster care. It's her decision to make; that's for fucking sure."

"Offer the men you have searching more money to find the uncle. I'll pay their fee."

"It's your wallet. I'll give them a call." Knox reached for his phone. "You going to tell me why you want to help Willa out?"

"She used to be a member of my church. I just want to help; that's the only reason."

"Keep telling yourself that, brother, and maybe you'll start to believe it."

Lucky left Knox's office, going to his bike, while Knox was on the phone with his investigators. The other brothers were sitting on their bikes, waiting for him.

"Find out what you wanted to know?" Viper questioned.

"Anyone want to make a bet that it concerned Willa?" Lucky didn't have to see Shade's eyes behind his sunglasses to know they were mocking him.

"Kiss my ass!" Lucky snarled, already pissed off at Knox's laid-back attitude toward helping Willa.

"No, thanks."

Lucky sat down on his bike. "Shade, one day, you're going to push me too far. You've had a problem with me since I was discharged, and I'm getting fucking sick of it. Either tell me what the beef is or get the hell off my back."

Shade's face, as always, was impassive unless he was with his wife. "You're not ready to hear what I have to say. When you are, believe me, brother, I'll let you know."

Lucky's hands tightened on his handlebars as he backed his bike up. "You're a fucking asshole. I don't know what Lily sees in you."

His anger didn't faze Shade. "Probably the same thing Willa sees in you. At least I was smart enough to catch my woman. I thought Rider was the dumb fuck in the club, but you proved me wrong."

Lucky roared out of the parking lot, leaving the three men behind.

*One day*, he promised himself, *I am going to kick Shade's ass.* The bastard would have to be drunk off his ass, and Lucky would have to leave town for a few weeks afterward to give Shade time to cool down, but it would be worth the beating Shade would give him to even the score. Some things in life were priceless, and getting one over on Shade would be one of them.

He eyed the street Willa lived on as he passed. Getting his mind off the curvy woman would be another. He hated to admit it, but he was beginning to believe Shade was right—he was a dumb fuck.

&#8253; ‘’

He was sitting at the kitchen table later that night when Viper called a meeting. The brothers gathered in the room next to the kitchen, filling the two large rooms.

Viper's hand went up, quieting the room. "The brothers from Ohio will be coming in this weekend. We have two new recruits who are ready to be initiated. Also, Moon wants to stay here. He wants to get out of Ohio for a while."

"Why?" Rider asked from the back of the crowded room.

"He's feeling the heat. The mayor's daughter wanted to join the club because of Moon, so now the mayor has the cops constantly watching the place. He's hoping that, if he leaves, the bastard will leave the club alone."

Train groaned. "Don't tell us we have another Brooke on our hands."

"Not hardly. Moon says the woman's not the problem; it's the father. She's moved on, but the mayor's holding a grudge. Guess he doesn't want to be reminded that his daughter was fucked by a biker," Viper reasoned.

"It'll be nice having another member taking a shift at the factory," Rider gloated. Lucky wondered if Rider would use his additional free time to renew his pursuit of Willa.

"I'm due some time off, so I get first dibs." Lucky glared at a crestfallen Rider.

"That's up to me," Jewell spoke up, quelling the budding argument between the two members.

Jewell had taken over managing the factory from Shade and had been doing a good job. Lucky promised himself he would fuck her senseless tonight. When he was finished with her, Rider would be working the next two weeks without a day off. Of course, Lucky saw the same determined expression on Rider's face.

Jewell sat on her chair with a grin on her lips.

As soon as Viper concluded the meeting, Lucky moved to Jewell, taking her hand and tugging her closer to his body until her breasts were pressed to his chest.

"Let's go to my room," he murmured seductively.

Rider came up behind her, pressing his cock against her ass. "Mind if I join you?" His mouth went to Jewell's neck.

"Yes, I do. I'm not in the mood to share tonight. Pick another woman."

"Don't want another woman tonight. You pick someone else," Rider countered.

Lucky pulled Jewell closer, notching her pussy against his cock.

"Before you two use your dicks to pull strings for days off, I'll be doing the schedules." Viper gave each of them evil grins.

Jewell's face dropped. Seeing it, Lucky felt like an asshole for his plans to manipulate her.

"In that case, Rider, you can pick the bedroom," Lucky offered to make amends.

"Why not here?"

Jewell's eyes filled with lust.

Lucky checked out the occupants of the room, seeing Lily and Winter weren't around.

His hands tugged off Jewell's top, baring her breasts. "Good choice."

# Chapter Five

Willa stared at the empty space she was contemplating renting. Was she making the right decision? She had asked Drake for the key to take another look at the space. It used to be a small clothing store that had gone out of business and had sat empty for over a year. Drake had advised on renovating the building, but it would take a large amount of cash to convert the store to a bakery, and she was too afraid to sink all her money into a new business.

She was walking toward the back of the store, mentally debating if she was making the right decision, when a sound from the doorway had her spinning, her breathing accelerating in fear. Seeing a grim Lucky leaning against the doorway didn't lessen her fear, either.

"What in the fuck are you doing here so late?"

His harsh question had her finding her backbone, resenting the tone he was using with her.

"It's only eight o'clock," Willa snapped.

"The diner closes early on Sunday. You shouldn't be in a deserted building so late."

She refused to feel guilty for her snapped response. "It's right across the street from the sheriff's office. If I needed help, all I would have to do is yell. I'm hardly in any danger."

Her words didn't lessen his anger; instead, his face became even grimmer as Lucky straightened from the doorway, walking toward her. Unconsciously, she backed away, coming to a stop when she felt the wall at her back. Lucky didn't stop until he was practically touching her.

"You think someone who is going to rob or rape you will give you the time to make any noise?"

Willa tried to keep her breathing calm, afraid if she breathed too deeply, her breasts would brush his chest. She pressed back harder against the wall.

"There hasn't been a robbery in Treepoint in ten years, and no one is going to rape me."

"That's the most asinine thing I've ever heard. Why are you in here, anyway?"

"I'm thinking of renting it to set up a bakery." Willa was angry at herself for explaining anything to him after his cutting remark.

"This dump?" Lucky snorted. "Don't waste your money."

"You don't have to be so negative. It's in a good location—"

"It's going to take a shit load of money to convert this to a bakery. You have that kind of cash?"

Willa turned her head to the side, tearing her gaze away from his intense focus. "Why do you have to be so mean to me? I'm never rude to you unless you provoke me."

Lucky's hand reached out, turning her face back to him. His voice dropped. "You really want to know?"

Willa shivered as her body reacted to the attraction she was helpless against.

"Because I'm a bastard. There's nothing redeeming about me." When he stepped closer until his chest was pressed against her breasts, her legs trembled, barely supporting her.

"Don't say that." Willa refused to believe anyone was unredeemable.

"Why? It's the truth," he stated.

Lucky lowered his head, and Willa felt the faintest touch of his mouth against the pulse beating at the base of her throat. Before she could tell him to stop, however, he was stepping away.

"Don't waste your money." Turning, he left her gawking after him as if she was an immature sixteen-year-old.

She looked around the store again, reluctantly agreeing with him. It would take more money than she wanted to spend on her initial investment. That left her with two options: either she built new on the property that Drake had suggested next to King's restaurant, or she kept searching for another spot.

Sighing, she went to the light switch, flicking the lights out before going outside and locking the door behind her.

Willa saw Lucky across the street, sitting on his motorcycle as he talked to Knox. The sheriff had his back to her, but Lucky's gaze was pinned on her as she got inside her van.

Driving home, her hand went to her throat, touching the spot Lucky's lips had brushed. Why had he touched her? He had made no attempt to touch her before. The coward in her wanted to shy away from him, run when he was near. However, the bolder side of her, which she had never given reign to, had wanted more than the brief touch he had given her, even if the attraction she felt was one-sided.

She stopped in her driveway, and for a split second, she wanted to escape the responsibilities waiting for her inside. She was so tired of doing everything herself. Just once, she wished she had someone to lean on, to share her problems with instead of constantly worrying about the decisions she was making. Gathering her purse, she locked her car.

As she was unlocking her front door, she heard a motorcycle roar past. Willa paused, seeing Lucky ride by on the main street. Envying him his freedom, she went inside.

"All done?" Willa asked Rachel, who was sitting at the table with Sissy.

"Just finished." Rachel closed the laptop before rising to her feet.

"I appreciate you keeping an eye on the children while I went out."

"I'm happy to help." Rachel grinned at her. "Sissy is almost caught up with her work. A couple more sessions and she should be good for the rest of the school year."

"Let me know how much I owe you—" Willa began.

"Don't be ridiculous." Rachel shook her head. "I enjoy working with Sissy. Since Cash built me a lab at the factory, I spend too much time buried in my work."

"Cash is like a different man since he's married you."

Rachel's face glowed with happiness. "I never thought that he'd settle down and make such a wonderful husband."

Willa reached out without thought, giving Rachel a hug. Rachel gave her a strange look when she released her.

"I think that's the first time I've ever seen you voluntarily touch someone."

Willa blushed.

"I better be going." Rachel picked up her laptop. "Sissy, I'll see you tomorrow night."

All Rachel received in response was a curt nod.

As soon as the door closed behind her, Willa began straightening the living room, expecting Sissy to give her the silent treatment as she went to her room.

"Why did you wait for Rachel to get here before you left?" Her tone alerted Willa to the fact that Sissy was angry.

"I didn't want to leave Chrissy, Charlie, and Caroline unsupervised," she explained.

"I could have watched my cousins," she snapped.

"I won't leave them alone with you again until I'm sure you will watch them closer than you did the last time," Willa explained.

Sissy stood, her hands clenching into fists. "You fat bitch, they're my family, not yours. As soon as I turn eighteen, I'll get custody of them and take care of them myself."

Willa wished she could become immune to the insults Sissy was constantly giving her, but the fact was each hurt as much as the first one she had given the night she had brought the children home.

"Do you seriously believe that Child Services will give you the children? You don't even have a job to support them." Willa tried to make the girl see reason.

"I'll find one when I graduate."

"Really? Because I haven't seen you lift a hand to so much as load the dishwasher. You think you will be able to find a job that will give you the finances to support the five of you in a town filled with unemployed workers?"

"If you can do it, I can." Her arrogance was dooming Sissy to failure.

"Sissy, I'm working before you get up in the morning and long after you go to sleep. If you have the motivation, then you can accomplish your goal, but you're going to have to have a bigger motivation than trying to hurt me."

"Sorry I'm not going to kill someone so that I won't be a lonely, old hag. Do you think giving them a home to live in is going to make up for murdering their father?"

Despite herself, Willa couldn't hide her wince. "I think you should go to bed."

"I'm going." Sissy stomped to the stairway in a teenage snit that had her believing she was right and everyone else was screwed up. "Willa, the next time you go out, I'll watch the kids." Her hands were clenched by her sides when she made her demand.

"No, Sissy, you won't. It's not about proving you're capable of watching them or that you can make me give in to you; it's about their safety."

"Are you saying they aren't safe with me?" she spat at her hatefully.

"I'm saying I won't take the chance with their safety," she countered.

"I'm going to prove you wrong. I'll make sure we're here only long enough for me to turn eighteen."

"Go for it, Sissy. Prove me wrong. No one will be on your side, cheering you on as much as me."

Sissy's mouth tightened into a sneer. "I hate you!"

"I love you," Willa replied, listening to the girl run up the steps and slamming her bedroom door.

"Lord, give me the strength to deal with her pain. Can my life become any more difficult?" she mumbled the question out loud to herself as she straightened the couch cushions.

Loud music blared down the steps.

"I'll take that as a yes."

# CHAPTER SIX

A knock sounded at the door as Willa was placing a cake in the oven. Using a dish towel, she wiped the powdered sugar from her fingertips as she went to answer it.

"I've got it."

Willa watched as Sissy came down the steps, dressed in a short skirt and cream tank top. Sissy opened the door, revealing a young man Willa wished she didn't recognize.

"Hey, Sissy, you ready?" Jace asked, his eyes going over Sissy's trim body appreciatively.

Before she could answer, Willa broke in. "Where are you going?"

Sissy rolled her eyes at Jace before she answered. "We're going to a movie. I'll be back later."

"I'll expect you by ten," Willa stated firmly.

Sissy brushed past Jace, leaving without either confirming or denying she would keep her curfew.

"I'll have her back by ten," Jace promised before following after the headstrong girl.

"Thanks," Willa said, closing the door after them.

Returning to the kitchen, she continued with her baking. She had several orders to complete tonight so they could be delivered in the morning.

She worked steadily until she had frosted the last order of two dozen cupcakes for a birthday party. Closing the pretty pink box, she glanced at the clock, frowning when she saw the time—ten forty-five.

"So much for Jace's promises." Biting her lip, she went to her living room window, looking outside at the empty street.

Taking her cell phone out of her pocket, she called Sissy's phone. When she didn't answer, she called Drake, Jace's father.

"Hello."

"I'm sorry to disturb you, Drake, but are Jace and Sissy there?"

"No, Jace isn't here. Why would Sissy be here?" he said sharply.

"They went out earlier tonight. I asked Sissy to be home by ten, and she's not home yet."

"He's out with Sissy?"

"Yes. Do you have a problem with him dating Sissy?" Willa began to feel outrage on behalf of Sissy.

"I don't"—his voice was filled with amusement—"but his girl-friend Nicole might."

"Oh. Do you have any idea where they could be?"

"No, Jace doesn't confide in me where he takes his women."

"Sissy is just seventeen. She's a child," Willa snapped.

"Maybe to you and me, but not to Jace." Willa sensed that Drake thought she was overreacting. "Hang on, Willa. I have another call." The other end of the phone went silent.

She was about to hang up in frustration when he came back on the line.

"I know where they are. I'll be there in five minutes to pick you up."

"Wait, I have the other children…I can't just leave."

"They're at the sheriff's office." His statement had Willa's pro-tests dying on her lips.

"I'll be ready." Willa disconnected the call before hastily punch-ing in another number. Thankfully, her neighbor from across the street agreed to come over.

Willa was stepping out her front door when Drake pulled up in her driveway.

"What did they do?" Willa asked as soon as she closed his car door.

"You know as much as I do. Knox told me he would talk to both of us when we reached his office."

"Do you think it's really bad?" Willa asked worriedly, never having dealt with a problem like this before.

Drake took his eyes off the road for a second. "Yes, Willa, I think it's bad."

His grim response had her apprehension increasing until her nerves were wrung tightly. When they arrived at the sheriff's office, she followed Drake, who seemed much more familiar with the situation than she was.

They took a seat until Knox called them into his office. Then Drake demanded answers as soon as Knox closed his door, confirming her suspicions that Drake had been in this position before.

"What did Jace do this time?"

Knox motioned for them to take a seat. When they were both seated, the sheriff took the chair behind his desk.

"Jace, Cal, and Sissy were caught breaking into the factory of The Last Riders."

Willa's heart sank in dismay.

"Why in the fuck did they want to break into the factory?" Drake was angrily unfazed.

"Jace said he had heard that one of the buildings held a motorcycle collection, and he and Cal wanted to see it. Sissy went along with them."

"Who caught them?" Drake's hands clenched on the arms of his chair.

"Shade. Their security system alerted them to the break-in."

Willa was unable to raise her voice past a hoarse whisper. "How much trouble are they in?"

"Viper's not pressing charges this time, but if he catches them trespassing again, he will. They busted the lock on the front door, and he wants it replaced."

"I'll take care of it. I'll call Viper and thank him for not pressing charges." Drake stood.

Willa, still following Drake's lead, stood also, drawing Knox's gaze.

"Unfortunately, Ms. Tackett was in the office, dropping off paperwork, when Shade brought them in."

Willa paled. Flora Tackett was the worker supervising the case involving Georgia and Lewis's children.

"I was able to keep the bitch from taking Sissy into state custody, but if she gets in trouble again, that's where Sissy and the rest of the children will be placed." Knox's words stopped Willa in her tracks.

"I'll keep a better eye on her," Willa promised. "Thank you, Knox."

"That girl has more problems than you can handle." Knox's stern voice sent warning signals through her brain. If he could see it, then everyone else did, too. It was only a matter of time before she lost all the children due to her inability to control them.

"I'll talk to her and make her understand what's at stake."

A flicker of sympathy shone in his eyes. "Would you like me to talk to her?"

Willa shook her head. "I'll handle it."

Both men didn't hide their skepticism. However, Rachel had already tried and had been met with resentment, and Knox didn't seem the type to tolerate Sissy's disrespect for authority.

Knox picked up a set of keys from his desk. Opening the door, he motioned them forward as he walked down a hallway, leaving them in a small room alone as he went to get Jace, Cal, and Sissy.

"I think's it's best if Sissy doesn't see Jace again," Willa broached the sensitive subject.

"You think you're going to be able to keep two randy teenagers from seeing each other? It will make the situation worse," Drake warned.

"I think it's for the best," Willa repeated firmly.

Drake shrugged. "It's your call. I'll have a talk with Jace."

The metal door opened, and the three teenagers were led into the room with varying expressions. The boys were apprehensive, while Sissy was openly defiant.

"Let's go home, Sissy." Willa started to touch her arm, but she jerked away.

"I don't have a home."

Willa didn't become angry at her reaction since it was her fault the girl's world had been turned upside-down.

Sissy was smart enough to recognize the others weren't as sympathetic to her treatment of Willa.

"I'll drive you and Sissy home," Drake offered.

As they left the office, Willa and the others were the center of attention. Lucky, Rider, and another biker Willa didn't recognize were standing in the waiting area. The teenagers lost what bravado they had when they saw the bikers waiting for them.

Rider was the one who took a step forward, blocking Jace and Cal.

"All you had to do was ask me to see my bikes. You didn't have to resort to breaking and entering." Rider's reaction wasn't what Willa was expecting. The biker was almost affable to the teenagers.

Jace and Cal both looked shamefaced, while Sissy was too busy ogling the bikers.

"We're sorry, Rider," Jace apologized when his father gave him a nudge forward.

"Make it up to me. How did you find out about the bikes?" Rider's voice was friendly, as if they were all good ol' boys. Regardless, sudden comprehension filled Willa as she realized his true motive for coming across laid-back. He wanted to know who was talking about their club's business. Willa had a horrible feeling she knew who had inadvertently supplied the information.

"I told them," Willa spoke up, turning bright red.

With all the attention now focused on her, she felt the flood of red run up from her chest to her face.

"How did you find out about the bikes?" Rider asked quizzically.

She became nervous under his scrutiny. Unconsciously, she licked her bottom lip before tugging on it with her teeth. "I-I... must have heard it from somewhere. Drake was telling me he was going to buy Jace a motorcycle, and I told him maybe Rider would sell him one."

"Is that so?" Rider turned to Drake.

Willa's eyes wildly flew to Drake who was staring at her in bemusement at her flustered behavior.

"Uh...That's right." Jace and Cal's faces had lit up with excitement before Drake crushed their burgeoning hopes. "Of course, now after this lame-ass stunt, I wouldn't buy him a secondhand tricycle to ride."

Their disappointment provided Drake with the opportunity to punish them more effectively than she would be able to Sissy. She never asked Willa for anything. The only thing Sissy would let Willa provide her with was food and a bed. Anything extra she needed was provided by an allowance from her mother's insurance money, and Sissy kept track of every penny in the account.

From the men's expressions, they knew she was lying. She had deliberately made a fool of herself to protect someone else, which

Willa didn't regret. Everyone thought she was useless unless she was baking, anyway. She was just proving them right.

Lucky's eyes narrowed on her as she wiped her clammy hands on the side of her jeans. His gaze lowered to the tight jeans she had thrown on when Drake had told her about Sissy. The top she had on was an older, pink one that had faded from numerous washings. She always wore it when she was baking. The buttons were strained at the breasts, threatening to pop at any second.

Becoming even more embarrassed at her appearance, she focused on the stranger with them and almost lost what little composure she had left. The biker was tall and muscular through his chest, tapering down to a lean waist that Willa was sure had a six-pack of abs hidden behind his T-shirt. His wavy, brown hair and finely chiseled features would have made him too pretty if not for the square jaw and the dangerous aura that clung to him.

Willa wasn't the only one having a hard time keeping her eyes off him. Sissy's gaze was glued to him, too.

"Ready, Drake? I need to get home." She needed to get the hormone-riddled teenage girl away from the bikers. They were even affecting Willa, and she was older.

Wishing she had the courage to act like one of The Last Rider women, Willa did what any sane Christian woman would do—she fled.

"I'm ready." Drake moved to the side, motioning for her to go in front of him.

Willa started for the door, somehow bumping into Lucky, though she could have sworn she had left more distance between them. Her nipples hardened behind the thin shirt.

When Rider nearly tripped over a chair rushing to open the door for her, she gave him a smile yet didn't stop until she reached Drake's car. The teenagers followed reluctantly, not wanting to leave the presence of the bikers.

Cal and Jace both admired the motorcycles sitting in the parking lot, while Sissy was in la-la-land. Willa could imagine the teenage fantasies going through her mind, picturing herself on the back of one of the motorcycles with her arms wrapped around one of the good-looking men. Willa knew because she'd had a few of those fantasies herself. For Sissy, though, those fantasies had a possibility of becoming a reality in the future. For Willa, not so much.

The most hurtful insult she had ever been given to her had been from Sissy's mother when she had said her fat ass was too big for a motorcycle. She had wanted to burst into tears from the remark; instead, Willa had never allowed herself to fantasize again. She kept her feet and mind planted in reality. Fantasies were for women who didn't wear a size eighteen on a good day and a twenty when it wasn't.

The car ride was silent to her house, each lost in their own thoughts. Willa tried to determine the best way to deal with Sissy and came up blank. When Drake pulled the car to a stop in the driveway, Sissy jumped out.

Drake's "good luck" sounded in her ears as she rushed after her.

Mrs. Stevens opened the door, and Sissy barged past her. Willa took the time to thank her then waited for her to leave before going upstairs to knock on Sissy's door.

"Go away!"

Willa didn't want to wake the rest of the children. Leaning her forehead against the door, she admitted defeat for now.

"Go to sleep. We'll talk in the morning." She kept her voice low.

Hearing no response, Willa went into her room, sinking down on the side of her bed. Then she buried her face in her hands and let the tears of frustration, hurt, and anger escape. When the last of her tears were spent, she lay back on her comforter.

"God, I thought I could do this without any help, but I was wrong. Anything you could do to help, I would appreciate." Her swollen eyes closed in exhaustion then opened quickly. "And if there was any way to make Sissy like me, I'll never miss church again."

∞ ∞

"That sweet piece of ass live in town?" Moon asked, still staring at the door Rider was watching Willa through.

Lucky's teeth ground together, leaving Rider to answer his question.

"Yeah."

"And you fuck-wads haven't brought her into the club?"

"No," Lucky managed to answer this time. "She's not the type."

Moon burst into laughter. "Are you fucking kidding me? Did you see those tits when you tried to cop a feel? The least you motherfuckers could have done was to introduce me to her. The next time I see her, I'll introduce myself."

"Stay away from her." Lucky's body went taut. "You're in enough hot water in Ohio from fucking the wrong woman."

"Sweet tits daddy the mayor?"

"No."

"Then who's going to give me shit? You should be kissing my ass for trying to accomplish what you haven't had the balls to do. By the time I head back to Ohio, she'll be our newest member."

If any other brother was doing the bragging, Lucky would doubt they would be successful with Willa. However, Moon was notorious for his skills with women. He had been given his nickname because the brothers all joked, when the moon came up, the women's panties dropped. They were attracted to him like flies to a corpse.

"I am." Lucky's voice dripped ice.

"Since when do you care who I fuck?"

"Since you think you're going to fuck Willa."

"The Last Riders share, and you've never had a problem with it before."

"I'll share any woman you want, just not Willa. She's not ours to share," he reasoned.

"Yet," Rider broke in. "I agree with Moon. He may be able to convince her to join. He's new to town, so she may lower her guard with him."

Lucky glared at Rider's anticipatory grin.

"Never." Lucky blasted both men with a heated glare. "Besides, she's seeing someone," Lucky threw out another attempt to dissuade the two men.

Knox was standing by, watching the men impassively.

"Who?" Rider grumbled.

"Drake."

"You sure? I know they had lunch together, but I don't think they're together."

Rider's perception of the relationship between Drake and Willa loosened a knot in his stomach he had been unaware of.

Lucky shrugged. "How do I know? It's not like we're best friends."

"Good. Then it's settled." Moon slapped Rider on the back. "Sit back and watch the master at work."

Lucky frowned. "It's not going to be as easy as you think."

"Why not?"

Moon's attitude toward Willa had gradually been getting on his frayed nerves, but his cocky arrogance was the last straw. Lucky turned on his heel, he had to blink several times to clear the red mist of fury nearly blinding him. He stood in the doorway as Drake's car pulled onto the road.

"Don't worry, brother; I'll make sure you get a taste."

Moon's voice behind him released the fury that Lucky had been holding back. Without thinking, Lucky swung around.

"Willa wouldn't look at you on a good day."

"Brother, it must be my day then 'cause she was looking," Moon retorted.

"Only because I was standing in front of you. Everyone in town knows it's me she wants," Lucky ground out, trying to convince himself that Willa wouldn't be swayed by Moon.

Rider shook his head. "I don't know about that."

"Shut up." Lucky's scowl had Rider taking a step closer to Knox.

"Is that a challenge? Let's make a bet, brother. The first one who manages to get sweet tits in bed gets the pick of Rider's bikes."

"Fuck no!" Rider shouted. "Why should I give up one of my bikes?"

"You getting anywhere with her?" Moon surveyed him critically.

"No," Rider admitted.

"That's why. Isn't getting that bitch to become a member worth giving up a bike?"

Rider's face reflected his dilemma. "Shit, if she wasn't such a good cook, I would say no. I wouldn't give one of my bikes for a hundred women, but Willa's peanut butter candy anytime I want it is worth a bike," he reluctantly agreed.

The chance to get one of Rider's cherished motorcycles didn't tempt Lucky, but he had no intention of standing back and watching Moon initiate Willa into the club when he had stayed away from her for her own good. There was no way he could prevent Moon from trying to go after Willa, but he could place a road block in his path.

"Fine, I'll take the bet. To make sure it's fair, none of the other brothers can get in on the bet, just you and me," Lucky stated his terms.

If the other brothers who didn't have an old lady heard that one of Rider's bikes was the prize, all the single men would be trying to get in on the bet.

"Works for me," Moon agreed with a calculating expression.

Lucky's fist connected with his cheekbone, knocking him backward and pushing several chairs over in the waiting area. Lucky then reached down and took a handful of his T-shirt, lifting him out of the chairs enough to punch him again. Knox and Rider both pulled him off the dazed man before his fist could connect a third time.

"Stop it, Lucky!" Knox yelled. "What in the fuck is wrong with you?"

Lucky shook him off. "Leveling the playing field."

After Moon was helped to his feet by Rider, spitting out blood onto the floor, Rider stared back and forth between Moon and Lucky, his body taut, waiting for the two men to go at each other. Moon sat on the chair that Knox had placed near him until the brother could regain what sense he had left.

Lucky wanted to punch Rider for agreeing to put up a motorcycle because it would only incite Moon further. Moon's bet would provide him with the woman he wanted with none of the work to actually get to know Willa.

Lying in wait for Willa at King's was the most effort Rider had put out on a woman. Usually, he sat back and let someone else lead his prey to him. As a result, Lucky wasn't worried that Rider would get near enough to Willa to seduce the woman, because he lacked the one thing that would lure Willa to his bed.

Lucky stormed from the police station before he changed his mind and taught Rider his own lesson. Reaching his bike, Lucky managed to calm his raging fury. With his hands on his handlebars, he sat facing the church that was completely dark.

"I won't be led back to you." Unconsciously, Lucky lowered his head. "For years, I've watched and waited as others lived the life I wanted. I can't live the life I would have to in order to serve You. *Let me go.*"

Lucky raised his head, and the invisible thread that always seemed wound around him felt like it was suddenly released. Blood rushed through his veins, his heart pounding as Lucky felt the last tie holding him back evaporate. He breathed in as if his lungs were no longer constricted for the first time in years. Lucky breathed in deeply again then released it, tasting freedom on the tip of his tongue.

Starting his bike, he pulled out of the parking lot, riding away from the church without glancing back.

# CHAPTER SEVEN

Lucky glanced to his side, grinning at Viper as they rode their bikes through the countryside. Decreasing his speed as they neared Treepoint, which was busy with traffic, he heard Bliss make a sound at his back. The woman loved speed.

As he brought his bike to a stop at the red light, a car pulled to a stop behind him. Looking in his mirror, he saw Willa sitting behind the wheel, her ugly minivan filled with the children she had taken in. His hands clenched his handlebars when he saw where her gaze was focused. He knew exactly because it was the same sight he had been treated to when they had first departed from the clubhouse.

Bliss was wearing a black leather halter top with a pair of low, hip-hugger blue jeans that showed the top of her ass when she leaned forward to hug the rider. She had begun the trip on the back of Train's bike, but when they had stopped for lunch and returned to the bikes, she had climbed on behind him. He had almost told her to get off, but the other brothers had already peeled out.

He could imagine the thoughts going through Willa's mind, remembering Georgia's cruel comment to her about being too large to ride a bike.

The sound of Viper's accelerating engine when the light turned green had Lucky riding forward, following the president's lead, but the hurt expression on Willa's face tore at him the entire ride back to the clubhouse.

When he came to a stop, Bliss jumped off, joining the rest of the members as they went up the steep flight of steps.

"Coming?" Shade asked with his arm around Lily's shoulder, keeping her close to his side.

"No, going out for a while." Lucky backed his bike out, turning once again to the road.

He wasn't ready to go inside yet. Shade would disappear inside his home with Lily, and the rest of the crew would be ready to party. However, with Willa's reaction to Bliss heavy on his mind, he wasn't in the mood to fuck or drink.

The feelings the timid woman roused in him were harder to escape than leaving the church. The more he fought against them, the harder he was being wrenched back.

After two hours of riding, Lucky came to a stop behind a stand of trees that hid him from the sight of a solitary small house where a light shone in one of the windows. He leaned against one of the trees, watching as the sun set and darkness fell.

He was still as a statue when the front door opened before a heavily built man left the house and went down the front steps into the yard, moving to the side to pick up a bucket. Lucky watched as he went to a kennel containing the two dogs inside, his lips thinning as the dogs were fed and watered. He had observed the same scene several times, enough to know what was coming next.

After they were fed, they were released to roam the land. Bridge used the dogs to guard his property from the predators that roamed the night.

Bridge went back inside the house as the dogs took off, running in Lucky's direction. Lucky straightened as the dogs skirted between the trees, searching for his scent.

They stopped in front of him and Lucky reached into his pocket, pulling out the two treats he had taken out of his saddle bags and tossing them to the two dogs. Bridge didn't spoil the dogs, so Lucky took advantage, training the dogs to his scent to reward them.

Once they raced off with the treats in their large jaws, Lucky remained until his legs began to cramp then went to his bike. Starting the motor, he revved the engine, wanting Bridge to hear from inside before Lucky headed back to Treepoint.

He had made the same trek over a dozen times since he had left the church, each time hoping to incite the man into making his move or to force a confrontation that Lucky was tired of waiting for. And, each time, he battled the temptation to leave the stand of trees and end the waiting game. Only the fact that the former Seal was justified in his need for revenge held Lucky back from provoking a confrontation that would leave one of them dead. As a result, he always left without coming face to face with Bridge.

His soul couldn't live with another death on his conscience, one that would either damn his soul or give him solace, although Lucky wasn't sure there was a soul to save anymore. What was left had been damned the night he had accepted Moon's bet. The devil's wager had been the knife that severed his last tie to the church.

Murder or forgiveness—the first would send him to Hell, and the second, Bridge wouldn't give.

Lucky sped through the dark night with his demons hounding his trail as he rode back to the clubhouse.

ಇ ಅ

The front room was packed as Lucky came in. The brothers were drinking. Train was fucking Raci on the couch, and Jewell was naked, dancing on the bar. Lucky strode forward and, reaching up, he grabbed Jewell, tossing her over his shoulder. He felt her laughter as he carried her upstairs to his bedroom, placing her on her feet beside his bed.

Lucky unbuckled his jeans as he toed off his boots.

"You're in a hurry." Jewell licked her bottom lip as he pulled out his dick.

Kicking his jeans and boots away, he lifted his arms in the air. Jewell took a step forward, lifting his T-shirt off and throwing it on the floor. Then she licked his chest as her hands went to his dick.

"The only thing I want on my dick right now is your mouth," Lucky groaned.

Jewell lifted her head, giving him a seductive smile. Her tongue traced down his flat stomach until she reached his cock, finding the drop of pre-cum on the tip.

She dropped to her knees in front of him. "What has you so worked up tonight? Usually, you like it slow, not that I'm complaining." Her hands cupped his balls, giving them a gentle squeeze.

"I don't want slow tonight. I want fast and hard. I can do slow after I come down your throat." Lucky buried his hand in Jewell's hair, keeping her mouth where he wanted it as he began fucking her experienced mouth.

This was what he needed to drive Willa from his mind, to keep him from the virgin who would trap him in a heartbeat if he gave in to the desire tormenting his body and soul. He needed a woman like Jewell to remind him what he was searching for—a woman who would never grow too attached to him, could never touch the good side of him and tempt him back to a life he had forsaken.

Jewell took him to the back of her throat, sucking on him greedily, and his balls tightened when her teeth nipped at him. She then leaned her head back despite his harsh grip, and his cock popped out of her mouth.

"Don't you want to punish me?" she teased.

Lucky gave her a feral grin before reaching for his jeans. Taking out his knife, he opened the blade before grabbing Jewell and throwing her onto the bed.

Jewell immediately got on her hands and knees, giving him access to her ass.

He climbed on the bed behind her. "You're getting as bad as Bliss, wanting to be spanked all the time."

Lucky expertly turned the knife in his hand. If he was actually going to use his knives on her, he would have her shower first, but that wasn't necessary for the use he intended tonight.

He reached to his nightstand then grabbed an alcohol pad and a condom. Ripping the condom open, he rolled it onto his cock before opening the alcohol pad to carefully wipe his knife. He loved this particular one with a pearl handle that he used against their clits and the wide blade that he could use as a paddle.

He brought the flat side of the blade down on her ass, and Jewell moaned as her perfect, red clit grew damp. Lucky gave her one finger as the knife repeatedly struck her ass, turning it a rosy red.

"You ready to finish sucking my dick?"

When Jewell shook her head, clutching the sheets, Lucky brought the knife down on the other ass cheek, his cock nearly bursting. Replacing the finger that had been pumping inside her with his dick, he rammed his cock in her to the hilt, and a scream filled the room.

"Fuck me!" Jewell chanted over and over while he thrust his cock inside of her as he kept spanking her with his knife. Once her ass glowed red, he threw the knife at the headboard, burying the tip into the dark wood while he buried his cock in Jewell's clenching pussy as she came.

Feeling her climax, he let himself come, ramming his cock into her over and over until his own orgasm was played out.

Jewell dropped to the mattress, shuddering, and Lucky got off the bed.

"Where you going?" Jewell mumbled.

"To take a shower." Lucky reached for her ankle, dragging her across the bed.

Her eyes went to his still-hard cock. "You're not done?"

Lucky opened his nightstand, taking out the leather pouch. Slowly, he opened it, showing the glinting blades.

"Go get in the shower and get the water warm for me while I get the bed ready."

Jewell practically ran into the bathroom as Lucky went to the cabinet to get what else he would need, taking out rope and a blindfold. The knives in the pouch had already been cleaned and readied for when he wanted to use them.

When he had everything just as he wanted, he opened the bedroom door before walking toward the bathroom, hearing the water running and wishing it was another woman waiting for him impatiently.

His hand went to the doorknob, pressing his forehead on the closed door.

"Willa." Lucky let her name slip from his mouth, his cock swelling in reaction. He wanted to hit his fist against the door in frustration at the inability to exorcise her from his mind. Instead, he straightened, opening the door and going inside.

"What took you so long?" Jewell asked when he stepped into the shower.

Out of the corner of his eye, he saw a male figure enter the bathroom. As Jewell's eyes went over his shoulder, seeing Moon, she started shaking under the warm water.

Lucky gave her a menacing smile. "Ready to play?"

# CHAPTER EIGHT

Willa held Chrissy and Caroline's hands tightly as she walked across the gym floor, showing them the booths that had been set up for October Fest. Winter had done a fantastic job of transforming the large space in her fundraising efforts for the alternative school.

"Can I go with my friends?" Charlie asked from where he had been trailing behind them.

She let go of Caroline's hand long enough to reach into her purse and hand Charlie some money.

"Don't leave the gym," she cautioned.

"I won't," Charlie said before running off to join the two boys waiting at the next booth.

Willa reached down to take Caroline's hand again, only to find the little girl had disappeared.

"Oh, God..." Frantically, she looked around, searching for a small figure wearing the bright orange shirt she had helped her put on before leaving the house.

"Caroline!" Willa yelled, her voice smothered in the noise from the crowded gym.

She moved forward, panicking when she didn't immediately find her. Chrissy started whimpering at being tugged along, so Willa stopped and picked her up.

"It's okay. We're going to find her."

Chrissy nodded her head, placing her hand on Willa's shoulder.

"Caroline!" Chrissy pointed in a direction that was blocked by a large group of people.

Trusting that Chrissy had seen her sister, Willa went in the direction she was pointing. She was jostled several times as she tried to squeeze past and accidently knocked a plastic cup out of a man's hand as he was served at one of the booths.

"Excuse me."

Curt Dawkins lowered his angry eyes to his wet pants then shuttered them before lifting them. Willa noticed how quickly he was able to hide his irritated reaction.

"That's all right. Next time, try to be more careful, or you could hurt someone. It's a shame you never played football. You could have taken out half the opposing team." Willa listened to his snide comment as he placed a charming expression on his face. No one looking on would know how cruelly he had just insulted her.

Willa held Chrissy tighter to her as his eyes roved sleazily over her body.

"Send me the cleaning bill, and I'll take care of it." Willa attempted to move away, desperate to escape his venomous presence, only to bump into someone passing behind her.

Curt grabbed her arm, pulling her nearer to him. "Watch out."

Willa's eyes widened when she saw it was Lucky and Rider she had nearly bumped into. As both men came to a stop, Willa tried to hide her fear of the man who hadn't released her arm and was now pressed like a leech to her backside. She wanted to heave when she felt his penis hardening against her butt.

"Hi, Willa."

"Hi, Rider," she greeted before she reluctantly acknowledged the man standing quietly. "Lucky." Jerking her arm away from Curt's tight grip that she was sure would leave a bruise, she tried to step around Lucky and Rider. "I need to find Caroline. I'm afraid she managed to escape from me."

Willa didn't slow down, trying to put as much distance between her and Curt as possible. Why was it every overbearing person in Treepoint tried to overpower her? Did she have a freaking sign on her back that told them she was a coward?

"Let us help you find her," Rider offered.

"That's not necessary. I have it under control," Willa said without turning around.

"That's not what it seems like to me."

She ignore Lucky's snide comment, blinking away frustrated tears. Why did she have to always make a fool of herself in front of him?

Willa released a sigh of relief when she saw Winter with Caroline as they walked in a circle while music played. As the melody came to a stop, the two stood on the last available circle, winning the cake walk.

Winter laughed, picking Caroline up and tossing her into the air. "You're my good luck charm."

The girl squealed in laughter when Winter caught her.

"Thank God you found her. I was worried sick."

Winter took the cake she had won. "Caroline's been helping me win one of your cakes."

"Thank you, Winter."

"I'm going to share my winnings with my partner." Winter gave Caroline a wink.

"I don't think she deserves it for leaving my side." Seeing that Winter was about to protest, she relented. "I have several cupcakes at home. I'll give her one of those. You keep the cake for yourself and Viper."

"I'll take you up on that. I'll be lucky to save Viper a slice when the other members find out I won it. All the men tried to win it as soon as they saw it was chocolate on chocolate."

"Would you like me to hold it for you?" Rider asked, greedily eyeing the cake.

"Over my dead body." Winter pulled the cake closer to her. "I'm going to lock this beauty away in my office until I'm ready to go home. Want to help me, Caroline?" Winter held her hand out, and the girl took it. "I'll keep her with me and let her play a few games if that's all right, Willa?"

"Are you sure? She can be a handful," Willa warned.

"I deal with The Last Riders every day. Caroline will be a breeze compared to them." Winter moved away with Caroline obediently walking beside her. Willa wished she handled her as easily.

Winter bent to place Chrissy on her feet. Straightening, she saw both Lucky and Rider gaping at her. Glancing down, she turned bright red at seeing her top button had come loose when she had been carrying the child. When she had leaned over, she had flashed the men a generous view of her breasts.

Clutching Chrissy's hand in one of hers, she tried to button her top with her other hand.

"Where are the other three tonight?" Lucky's hoarse voice had her taking an involuntary step backward.

"Charlie is with his friends at one of the booths, and Leanne and Sissy are both at home. They said they were too old for school carnivals."

"Neither volunteered to help you with their cousins?"

"You know teenagers…" Willa began to defend the two older girls.

"Yes, I do, and they'll take advantage if you let them." Lucky's eyes were still pinned to her trembling fingers trying to button her blouse.

"I wanted to give them some free time." His nerve-wracking observation of her fumbling attempts made her even clumsier.

"Exactly when was the last time *you* had any?" He took a step forward, brushing her hand away then fastening the button for her.

Her mind went blank as she stared into his hazel eyes. "Wh-What?"

"Free time?" This time, a small smile played on his sensuous lips.

"Oh." Reason gradually returned when Lucky reached down, picking up Chrissy and placing her in Rider's surprised arms.

"Keep her occupied. We'll be back in an hour," Lucky told Rider before taking Willa's arm.

"Wait. I can't just leave her with him."

"Why not? He'll take good care of her." Lucky hustled her through the crowd toward one of the booths.

Willa stared down at the rubber ducks going in a circle of water, dumbfounded at Lucky planning to spend an hour with her. She had never managed to be in his presence for five minutes without feeling awkward. An hour would be torture.

Lucky handed the girl behind the table a dollar. "Pick one." He motioned at the innocuous yellow ducks.

"Why?" Willa asked in confusion.

"For fun. Do you even know what fun is?"

"Yes, I do." Willa pretended to be fascinated by the ducks going in a slow circle, hurt by his comment. "For your information, you being rude to me is not fun."

She reached out, picking up one of the ducks and handing it to the girl who reached into a box and pulled out a string of brightly colored beads. Before she could take them, Lucky did then lifted them over her head, and they nestled in the cleft between her breasts. He reached out, taking the beads in his hand, his knuckles resting against the flesh of her breasts. Her breathing escalated at his intimate touch, so she tried to move away yet was held in place by the necklace until she felt it biting into the back of her neck.

Her nipples hardened as she tried to calm her breathing and pretend to be unaffected. His eyes moved to her side before returning to hers. Willa turned to see what had caught his attention and saw the biker who had been with Lucky and Rider the night she had picked Sissy up at the sheriff's office. The stranger had two black eyes and looked frightening with the determined expression on his face. Before she could try to move away from Lucky again, he released the necklace then steered her toward a photo booth tucked against the wall.

He raised the curtain, propelling her forward before stepping inside with her.

"I don't want my picture taken," Willa protested.

A hand on her shoulder had her taking a seat as Lucky put a dollar into the slot. As soon as the whirling motor sucked the dollar inside, Lucky sat down next to her on the small seat. Embarrassed, she tried ineffectively to scoot over, only to find herself pinned between the wall and Lucky's imposing body. She noticed his T-shirt was short-sleeved, and his large biceps were highlighted by the tattoos covering his arms.

When his hand covered her throat, turning her to face him, Willa froze for a split-second before her survival instincts screamed at her that he was about to kiss her. Putting her hands on his chest, she tried to place some space between them. A kiss from Lucky was something she had never expected to experience, and she was pretty darn sure it would be more than she could handle.

"Have you been kissed before?" His low voice had her trying to wiggle away from him, but his body merely leaned closer until her breasts were flattened against his chest with her hands caught between them.

"Of course." She tried to turn her face away but Lucky gripped her chin, denying her a chance to avoid the deepening intimacy that he was weaving between them.

His mouth moved closer until she felt his lips brush hers when he talked. "Who?"

"None of your damn business," Willa said defiantly. There was no way she was going to tell him it was Lewis who had managed to kiss her in high school. It had been a terrifying moment which she'd had nightmares about for several months afterward.

The tip of his tongue traced her bottom lip.

"Don't, Lucky," Willa pleaded, seeing the flash of the camera.

"Why not? Don't you want a taste? I want to taste yours," he groaned. "I want to see if it's as sweet as your frosting." His mouth pressed harder against hers, parting her lips that she tried to keep closed, and her nails pressed into his flesh.

"You taste like vanilla," he murmured.

"Please, Lucky..."

"What do you want, Willa? Do you want me to stop?"

Willa saw the flash go off again, and her head fell back against the wall of the booth. She'd had every intention of stopping him; instead, she had lost all control when Lucky deepened the kiss, driving all caution from her mind.

"Please...don't," she breathed into his mouth.

"Didn't I tell you there isn't anything redeemable about me?" He caught her lips again, exploring her mouth with his tongue as she went limp against him, letting him take what he wanted from her, guiltily aware she wanted it also. However, she wasn't brave enough to give in to the desire he was wringing from her tense body.

Willa saw another flash across her closed eyes before Lucky tore his lips from hers and pressed his thumb down on the pounding pulse at the base of her throat. Then he gave her a hard look before standing abruptly, leaving her alone in the photo booth.

Willa gathered her composure, straightening her blouse before pushing back the curtain and stepping outside. Although Lucky was thankfully nowhere to be seen, Rachel and Cash both gave her curious looks as they approached the photo booth.

Willa wanted to press her palms against her flushed cheeks, but she forced herself to keep her hands to her side.

"Having fun?" she asked the couple.

"Yes, Cash is still bummed out about losing the cake walk, but I promised him a few of your cupcakes the next time I tutor Sissy." Rachel gave her a mischievous grin.

"That works for me." Willa spoke to the couple for several minutes before excusing herself, going in search of Rider.

She found him sitting on the bleachers, watching the little girl eat a candy apple warily. He couldn't hide his relief when he saw her.

"Thanks, Rider. I appreciate you watching her for me."

"It's cool. I babysit for Beth and Lily occasionally. Not often," he hastened to add, "but enough to take care of them for about an hour. I always shove food in their faces."

"That always worked on me," Willa joked.

Rider's eyes turned frosty. "Why do you always put yourself down?"

Willa shrugged. "Rider, it's pretty obvious I like food."

"I like it, too, but I don't put myself down because I do."

Willa surveyed his muscular body. "There's a big difference between your body and mine." Willa couldn't keep the amusement out of her voice. She liked Rider. He was sweet and uncomplicated.

"Yes, there is." His eyes went to her breasts.

She burst out laughing, unable to help her reaction to his sense of humor.

"If I had a brother, he would be just like you," Willa complimented, guessing from the thunderstruck expression on his face that it was the first time he had been placed in that category.

Rider stood up, brushing down his jeans before straightening. "I'm going to go mend my broken heart with those two women about to go into the haunted house."

"You do that. I'm sure they'll appreciate your help through the maze. Winter told me it goes through eight classrooms."

"You're not jealous at all?"

"Nope." Willa couldn't miss the amused twinkle in Rider's own eyes.

"It's a sad day when a woman refers to me as brotherly."

"I'm sure you'll recover," Willa mocked.

"I might be heartbroken...You just don't know." Rider's mouth twisted mischievously. Before she could react, he brushed his mouth over hers in a brief kiss. Raising his head, he stared down intently at her. "Nothing?"

"Sorry, but no."

"Woman, you're heartless," Rider groaned. "I guess it's the haunted house after all."

"Don't get lost," Willa teased to his retreating back, not missing the one finger salute he turned and flipped her.

"Ready?" Willa took Chrissy's hand, helping her down the bleachers before going in search of the other two children.

She found Charlie coming out of the haunted house and Caroline helping Winter at the fish pond.

"Leaving?" Winter asked.

"Yes, I need to go home and get started on tomorrow's orders."

"I would tell you to take a vacation, but I think the town would lynch me."

Willa always felt a spurt of pride about her baking skills. It was the one thing she did well.

"I see you went to the duck pond."

Willa's hand went to the blue beaded necklace around her throat. "Yes, and the photo booth."

"I'm glad you had fun. Where are the pictures?"

"Pictures?" Willa stared at her blankly.

"That is what the photo booth is for. I should check and make sure it's working if you didn't get photos." Winter frowned. "No one has complained…"

"I forgot to look. I'm sure it's fine. I'll go check, and if anything's wrong with the booth, I'll text you."

"I would appreciate it. I can't leave the table right now."

"I'm happy to help."

Willa hustled the children away, dismayed she had left the pictures for anyone to see. She would die of embarrassment if anyone saw her and Lucky kissing, and she didn't imagine he would be any happier.

When Willa found the slot where the pictures came out empty, she even looked around the floor to make sure they hadn't fallen out.

"Can we take a picture?" Charlie asked.

"All right." Willa lifted the curtain, hoping against hope that it wouldn't work.

She smiled as the camera flashed, the children all making silly faces.

When it was over, Charlie jumped up. "Let's get the pictures."

Willa lifted Caroline and Chrissy off her lap, praying the slot would be empty. The children eagerly waited for the thin strip of pictures to emerge, and she swallowed hard when it did. Charlie picked them up, showing them to his sister.

"I guess it's working fine. Let's go home."

As they left, Willa felt as if everyone's eyes were on them yet knew it was a figment of her imagination. Her last hope was that someone had seen the pictures were left behind and thrown them away. She was tempted to search the trash can closest to the photo booth, but she knew it would look ridiculous.

"God, could you please, please destroy those pictures? Maybe make sure that one strip didn't develop? Or a tiny, little fire?" she mumbled.

"What did you say, Willa?"

"Nothing, Charlie. I was praying to find something I lost." That tiny strip of photos in someone's hand would be humiliating if they surfaced.

"I'll pray, too." Charlie climbed into the backseat when Willa opened the car door.

"Me, too," both girls chimed in as she buckled them into their car seats.

Willa shut the sliding van door before getting in behind the steering wheel.

"How about we all pray?" Willa said fervently.

She was so upset over the pictures that the actual kiss didn't register until she was about to go to bed. Could it be that Lucky was as attracted to her as she was to him? A spark of hope was lit deep inside.

Willa sat down on the side of her bed, stunned at the thought. Maybe her life was going to make a change for the better.

"It certainly couldn't get any worse." Willa wanted to take the sentence back as soon as she uttered it. She had learned long ago never to tempt fate. Even the Devil would laugh at her believing Lucky was attracted to her.

"Miracles happen." Willa fell back against her bed, staring up at the ceiling as a fragile hope began to grow. Maybe, just maybe... all her prayers were about to be answered.

# CHAPTER NINE

Lucky found Viper in the kitchen, sharing a bottle of whiskey with Shade.

"I need to talk to you."

Viper used his foot to push a chair away from the table. "Take a seat."

Lucky sat down at the table.

"You need me to leave?" Shade asked, lifting the bottle as he began to stand.

"Stay." Lucky reached for an empty glass, raising it for Shade to fill, and the enforcer lifted a brow as he filled it.

"What's up?" Viper asked, motioning for Shade to refill his glass, too.

"I want to go to Ohio for a while."

"Why?"

"With Moon here, there really isn't anyone to keep the brothers in Ohio in check. I can stay there until Moon comes back. Besides, I'm ready to leave Treepoint, been here too long as it is."

"You're needed here. It's been nice to have all the club business off my shoulders."

"Moon is just as good. If any trouble comes down, I'm only a few hours' ride away."

"You've made your mind up?"

"Yeah."

"Then I won't stop you. I was going to send Train, but he doesn't want to leave."

"This solves both of our problems, then."

"What problem of yours does it solve?" Shade butted in.

Shade wasn't going to trick him into revealing more than he intended, though.

"Me wanting to dust off Treepoint."

"Lily's going to miss you." Shade lifted his half-filled glass, drinking it in one swallow before placing it back on the table.

"I'm not Lily's pastor anymore. She needs to find someone else to get spiritual guidance from. I'm certainly not the one to give it to her anymore. I never was." Lucky stood, the chair scraping against the floor.

Stori and Bliss came into the kitchen.

"Going to Ohio in the morning," he told them. "You girls want to be the ones to give me a send-off?"

"Hell yes." Stori eagerly twined her arms around his neck.

"You're leaving?" Bliss's quiet sentence had Lucky putting an arm around her, drawing her close to his side.

"For a few months."

Bliss shrugged his arm off. "Train's waiting for me in the other room. I'll ask Raci if she wants to join your party."

Surprised, Lucky watched as Bliss went back into the other room.

"What has her so pissed?" Lucky asked the others in the room. "Since when has she ever cared about anyone but Shade?"

"Don't know, but I'll ask her later. We still partying?" Stori's hand went playfully to his belt buckle.

"What do you think?" Lucky started toward the basement door with Stori still attached to his side.

"Send Raci downstairs," Lucky told Viper and Shade.

"Will do." Viper lifted his glass toward him. "Have fun."

A knife went through his heart at hearing the same words he had given Willa earlier in the night, and Shade's perceptive gaze didn't miss the flinch.

"I always do." His hand lowered to Stori's ass. "Always, brother."

Lucky stood up, covered in a fine sheen of sweat as he stared down at the bed where Stori was naked, still tied to the headboard. Gripping his knife, he cut the ropes binding her wrists. She lowered her arms, curling onto her side, too exhausted to move. Raci was already asleep, having passed out before he was finished with Stori.

Ember rolled over, pulling the sheet from the bottom of the bed to cover her trembling body before going back to sleep. All the women were too tired to be made to leave his bed so he could grab a few hours' sleep before he left town, but he wouldn't allow himself to sleep deeply if they were in the bed next to him.

He raked his long hair back from his face. He hadn't cut it since he had stepped off the podium for the last time.

He tugged on the jeans lying on the floor then quietly left the bedroom, going through the basement and upstairs to the kitchen. Then his bare feet carried him outside into the backyard. He paused long enough to fill his lungs with fresh air, driving out the scent of sex that clung to his damp skin before he walked forward until he came to the view that Lily often stared at.

The majestic mountains of Kentucky were one of three things he was going to miss about Treepoint. The club was another. His mind shied away from the third, however, not wanting to sully her image after his night of sexual gluttony.

Lucky raised his head, staring at the moon as it began to sink behind the mountains. He pressed the heels of his hands against his eyes. He was unable to bring himself to pray. He had gone against the very essence of everything he believed in, committing untold sins then repeatedly asking forgiveness. It was a vicious cycle that had held him prisoner until the only hope he had left was to cut the tie to Treepoint as he had the church. The door was now closed to that source of solace, and he was on the outside where he wanted to be.

That was what he had been telling himself over and over, trying to make himself believe he was ready to move on to a different way of life. He had to give himself time to adjust, and leaving would give him that, another lie he repeatedly told himself.

Sinking to his knees, he shivered, not from the chilly morning air, but from having his soul ripped apart.

He jerked when a hand gently touched his shoulder.

"Dean, are you okay?"

Lucky dropped his hands but he didn't turn to face Rachel, unable to look at the woman who had sat in his church since high school.

"I'm fine." Lucky cleared his throat. "What are you doing out here? It's freezing."

"I don't know. I woke up, and something told me to come outside. Then I saw you..." Her voice trailed off into silence.

"Go back inside. I'm fine." He didn't want to talk to her. The one he wanted to talk to wasn't listening to him anymore.

Her hand flattened against his shoulder and a warmth began to seep into his damp flesh from her touch, spreading down his arm and coursing through the rest of his body.

"I don't think you've been fine for a while, Dean. For years, you've given everyone else your strength until you have nothing left for yourself when you need it the most."

Lucky shook his head. "I turned my back on what gave me strength."

"My gift left me for a while before it returned even stronger. He doesn't leave us. My ancestors came across the Appalachian Mountains during the Trail of Tears. It would have been easy for them to give up, but they didn't. Instead, their beliefs were handed down for generations. They weren't given an easy path. My grandmother told me stories about how they would look for the moon to rise every night to rest and give thanks for surviving another day. Then they looked for the sun to rise so they could see their way."

Rachel's hand tightened on his shoulder as her voice dropped reverently. "Look, Dean, the sun is rising. You can find your way if you just open your eyes."

Lucky raised his head, seeing the sun's rays just beginning to break the dark sky. "I don't deserve to be found."

"Dean, I would quote several passages to you that show you how wrong you are, but I'm sure you know the passages better than me. God rejoices when His sheep return home. You were the one lost, not God. He's been waiting for your return all along."

The warmth from Rachel's touch began to burn, as if his soul which had been ripped apart was being welded back together. The sun's golden rays surrounded him in an abundance of colors.

Rachel gasped behind his back, dropping her hand, while Lucky shakily stood, his turmoil for now quieted.

She crossed her arms over her chest, shivering.

"Go inside. If you get sick, Cash will kick my ass."

She nodded yet didn't move. "Cash said you're leaving for Ohio?"

"Yes."

"Why?"

"I told Viper I would. Train doesn't want to go." Lucky reached out, cupping Rachel's cheek. "Thank you, Rachel."

"Goodbye, Dean."

He shivered as a chill of foreboding swept through him.

They walked back together, each lost in their own silence as they neared the house until several lights in the windows came on.

"Everyone is getting up early for a Saturday," Rachel remarked.

Lucky began to walk faster. The brothers were usually going to bed at this time, not getting up. Opening the back door, he ushered Rachel inside, finding the members gathered in the kitchen.

"What's going on?" Lucky asked Rider who was sitting at the table, looking hungover as he put on his boots.

"Willa called Winter, asking for Viper's help. Sissy ran away last night. She found her missing when she got home from the school festival."

"Shit."

"Willa's been out all night, searching for her. She thought at first that she was with friends, but they all say they haven't seen her."

"Cal and Jace?"

"Drake says both boys are home and have been all night."

"Fuck! Willa's probably terrified." Lucky wanted to shake some sense in the teenager, but to do that, he was going to have to find her first.

Viper strode into the room, immediately breaking the town into sections to search among the brothers.

"Lucky, you take Jamestown. If she's been missing since last night, it's going to be a crap shoot to figure out how far she's gotten."

"I'll get dressed and head that way. I'll call Stud and ask if the Destructors can start searching."

Viper nodded grimly. "Be quick. Knox had to alert Child Services when Willa reported Sissy missing. If the girl wanted away from Willa, she's got her wish now."

Lucky went downstairs to his room, taking a quick shower after calling Stud who said he would begin the search in Jamestown and offered to have the Blue Horsemen begin searching over the West Virginia line in case she had gone in the opposite direction.

He was tugging on his shirt when a thought occurred to him. Picking up his cell phone, he called Knox.

"Lucky?"

"Yeah. Have a quick question."

"Go ahead."

"Willa there or at home?"

"Willa's here with the rest of the kids. Flora Tackett's sitting here, ready to take custody of them. Willa notified her Sissy was missing."

"Fucking bitch couldn't wait until Sissy was found?"

"You know Flora." Unfortunately, Lucky did. The self-righteous bitch wouldn't think of taking in foster children, but she had no problem giving a hard time to anyone who did.

"Have you talked to Leanne?"

"I did. She swears she doesn't know where her sister is."

"She's lying. Get her away from everyone and she'll break."

Knox's voice lowered. "I can't threaten a kid." Lucky heard the door close in the background, and then Knox's voice returned to normal. "Besides, Flora won't leave me alone with her."

"Send them all to the diner for breakfast and ask them to bring back something for Leanne. Tell them you need Leanne to go over a list of Sissy's friends."

"I already did that."

"Do it again. Tell them she may have missed one. I don't give a fuck what you tell them, just get them away from Leanne."

"Then what? I can't lay a hand on her."

"Threaten her with arrest. Lock her up in a cell."

Knox started laughing. "She'll piss herself. I have Lyle back there."

"If she knows where Sissy is, she'll talk," Lucky insisted.

"All right. What's the worst that can happen? Diamond can sue the city and get my job back if I get my ass fired."

"Those girls have been running circles around Willa for months. If Leanne breaks, give me a call. I'm going to Jamestown to check if she managed to get that far."

"Wait fifteen minutes before you head out. No reason to backtrack if Leanne decides to talk."

"All right. I have a few minutes to spare since Stud has the Destructors out searching."

"I'll call you back." Knox disconnected the call.

Lucky stared at the women who were still lying on his bed, sleeping, and self-disgust filled him. While he had spent a night here in debauchery, Willa had endured a terrified one, worried about the girl she had tried to help.

Raci's eyes flickered open. "Where are you going?"

"I need to take care of something. Can you clean the room for me?"

"Sure thing. It's the least I can do after the night you gave me." She sat up in bed, stretching.

"What do you want me to do with your knives?"

Lucky's cell phone began to ring, but he didn't immediately answer. He needed to get away from the memories of last night before he could deal with anything concerning Willa.

"Lay them on the nightstand. I'll clean them and put them away myself." He never trusted anyone other than himself to clean his knives. They would be left untouched until he had the time to sterilize them. Everyone in the club knew to never touch his knives, or there would be hell to pay.

Lucky left the bedroom, closing the door behind him before answering the insistent ringing, seeing it was Knox calling him back.

"What did you find out?"

"Brother, we have a big problem."

# CHAPTER TEN

Willa's hands twisted in her lap. She prayed good news about Sissy would be waiting for them when she returned from the uneaten breakfast she had tried to choke down. With fear for Sissy on her mind, the food hadn't tempted her, and Flora Tackett's stony silence hadn't helped. However, disappointment filled her when she stepped inside the sheriff's office and found there wasn't any new information.

Willa looked up when the door opened, swallowing convulsively as she saw a couple she recognized from church approach Flora. She didn't have to ask why they were there. Her arm tightened around Caroline's waist, her other arm pulling Chrissy closer to her side. Charlie sat on the chair next to her, his feet swinging back and forth.

Flora and the couple walked toward her.

"Willa, you know the Wests?"

She nodded. Dalton West and his wife Lisa were both deeply involved in the church, considering it their sacred duty to live their lives in service to God. Willa couldn't explain the feeling of distrust she felt whenever they were near, although she had marked it down to Lisa's flirtatious behavior with Lucky when he had been pastor. The husband had witnessed the behavior and had even seemed to encourage the inappropriate conduct.

They had taken in several children from the community. The younger sister of Cal, Jace's friend, was one, whose mother had died from cancer. There was also an older girl who had been raised in the home and had moved out on her own. She still attended church yet refused to have anything to do with the couple. Willa took that as a sign that no close relationship had formed between them in the time she had been in their home. Ginny had spent six years living with the couple; therefore, some kind of attachment should have been formed. Instead, the girl wouldn't speak to the couple when they approached her at church gatherings.

Willa couldn't place her finger on exactly why she didn't like them. They were always polite and constantly volunteered at the church and school. They were just too perfect. Not to mention, there was something about the way they would look at The Last Riders' women when they attended church that made her think of her own mother when she would lecture her on being a good Christian girl.

"Yes." Willa didn't stand, not wanting to wake Caroline who was asleep on her chest.

"They will be taking charge of Caroline, Chrissy, and Charlie." Flora's brusque voice was matter-of-fact as she ripped the children's world apart.

"Please, can't we wait—?"

"You are clearly unable to handle these children and keep them safe."

Leanne, who had been sitting quietly, sprung to her feet. "I won't go!"

Flora ignored the girl's outburst, continuing to talk to Willa. "Don't make this hard on the children. The Wests are able to take all the children except for Leanne. I'm still searching for a foster home for her. If I don't find one by the end of the day, I'll place her in one of the group homes where I have a bed available until I can find someone willing to take her."

Leanne started crying, retaking her seat.

"You're frightening her, Flora. Can't she stay with me until you at least find a home for her?"

Her brusque refusal was stopped short when Viper and Shade entered the office, followed by a mutinous Sissy who was being trailed by Lucky.

Willa jumped to her feet, jostling Caroline and Chrissy awake. "Sissy! Thank God you're all right." Willa was so relieved she wanted to burst into tears; only the grim faces of the men prevented her.

"Where did you find her?" Flora asked before Willa could get the question past her trembling lips.

"We found her just outside of town." Viper spoke when Sissy remained quiet. "She had managed to make it to Rosey's."

Willa's horrified gasp was drowned out by the ones from the Wests and Flora.

"Mick didn't see her. She stayed out in the parking lot, trying to catch rides," Viper explained.

"Sissy!" Willa cried out at the danger the girl had placed herself in.

"I'm fine," Sissy snapped. "None of the losers would give me a ride."

"Thank God." Willa soothed Caroline, who began crying.

"She fell asleep in the back of Mick's car. He found her when Lucky called him and asked him to search for her."

"How did you know she was there?" Willa asked the man standing silently by the door.

Lucky's eyes flickered to Leanne. "Call it a hunch." He shrugged.

Willa buried her face in Caroline's hair. Understanding now why Knox had wanted Leanne to remain behind when they had gone to the diner, Willa realized she was a complete and utter failure at taking care of the children.

"I'll call off the search," Knox said, going to the phone behind the counter.

Flora immediately took charge of the situation. "Leanne and Sissy, you come with me. Dalton and Lisa, you take the other three.

I'll check in with you tomorrow. Willa, if you pack their things, I'll stop by this afternoon to pick them up."

Dalton reached for Caroline as Lisa reached for Chrissy, both girls beginning to cry.

"Please, Flora…" Willa pleaded.

"We're not going back to Willa's?" Sissy frowned, asking her sister who had also begun to cry.

Leanne shook her head. "They're placing us into a group home."

"You fat bitch…." Sissy lunged for Willa but Lucky snatched her by the waist, pulling her back.

"Don't touch her. Ever." Lucky's voice froze everyone in place, and fear entered Sissy's face.

"It has nothing to do with what Willa wants." Knox slammed down the phone. "If you want someone to blame, look in a mirror! Why are you so mad, anyways? You didn't want to stay with Willa, so your ass just got what it wanted."

"Knox, it's all right. She's upset." Willa reluctantly released Caroline. She didn't want to further upset the children by struggling with the inevitable. She would end up in one of the jail cells, and the children would still be gone.

Caroline and Chrissy began screaming and fighting against the people holding them, and Charlie ran forward, grabbing Willa around the waist. "Please don't make me leave. I'll be good."

Tears fell from Willa's eyes as she lowered herself to her knees, holding Charlie in her arms.

"The children aren't going anywhere. They're staying with Willa." Lucky's statement caught everyone's attention.

"No, they are not." Flora's hands went to her hips. "They will be placed in their new foster home. Leanne and Sissy will go to a group home until I can find a placement for Leanne. Sissy, unfortunately, will not be placed due to her running away. She'll stay there until she turns eighteen."

"The children and Leanne will remain with my fiancée until we're married. Then they will all move into my home after we're married in two weeks. Sissy can stay with Knox and his wife until our marriage. Then she can move in with us, also."

"You and Willa are engaged?" Flora asked, staring back and forth between them.

"Yes, we became engaged last night."

Willa couldn't believe the lies coming from Lucky, but she didn't try to deny their fictitious relationship, because the children had stopped crying. She reached for the girls who were frantically trying to throw themselves out of the adults' arms. Barely managing to hold both girls, she felt Lucky take Chrissy from her, placing a supportive arm around her shoulders.

Flora stood with indecision on her face. "Where do you plan to live after you're married?"

"The church, of course. I'll be taking over the role of pastor again next weekend."

"Why haven't I heard of this before?" Flora asked suspiciously.

"The deacons of the church gave me time to make up my mind. I was going to inform them after church tomorrow morning."

Dalton reached out, shaking Lucky's hand. "We'll be glad to have you back."

"I knew you would come back." Lisa and her husband shared a glance that Willa didn't understand. "The whole congregation has missed you."

"As I have them," Lucky replied, his arm tightening across Willa's shoulders.

Flora frowned. "I don't know..."

"I will be around the children constantly during Willa's and my engagement. They will be perfectly safe in our hands. I can supply as many references as you need. The governor will be one of them."

"I'll bring the paperwork to Willa's this afternoon. The state always wants what is best for the children." Flora's overbearing attitude went through an abrupt change. She was almost nice when she asked Knox. "You and your wife are willing to take in Sissy?"

Knox remained silent for a brief second, his lips tightening. "Diamond and I will be happy to take her until Willa and Lucky are married."

Willa didn't think he sounded very happy, but she was grateful he had agreed with the social worker.

"That's settled, then. I'll see you this afternoon, Willa."

Willa could only nod as Flora and the Wests left the sheriff's office.

"I better call Diamond and tell her we're having company for a couple of weeks." Knox went into his office, closing the door.

Lucky's arm dropped from her shoulder. "You go ahead and take the kids home. I'll be there in a few." He handed Chrissy to Leanne.

Sissy stood as if she was shell-shocked. Willa started to go to her, but Lucky blocked her by opening the front door for her.

"Lucky"—Willa paused beside him—"I appreciate you keeping them from taking the children, but it's going to be a mess to explain when we don't—"

"Go home, Willa. We'll talk when I get there."

Willa nodded weakly, too tired to argue. "Okay." Shifting Caroline's weight, she left, relieved the children were docile and silent as she placed them in the car.

She was backing out of the parking space when her eyes were caught by Leanne's.

"I'm sorry, Willa. Sissy made me promise not to tell anyone where she was going."

"Promises are meant to be pledges of trust between two people. When those promises can hurt someone, it's you who must decide if honoring it is worth the consequences."

Leanne lowered her head. "I really didn't think she would go through with it. She was trying to find that good-looking biker she's seen around town."

Willa didn't have to ask. She remembered the girl being fascinated with the biker the night of her escapade with Jace and Cal.

"Thank God she didn't find him."

Viper picked the stapler up from the reception desk, throwing it at the wall.

"Dammit!" Viper snarled at Sissy.

"I kept my mouth shut. I told you I wouldn't tell, and I didn't." Sissy backed away from the furious president.

Knox came out of his office. "They leave?"

"For now," Lucky grimly answered.

"You find her hiding inside Rosey's?"

Viper grimly nodded his head. "Jenna sneaked her in the back door."

"Fuck." Knox looked like he was going to follow his leader's example and throw something.

"She's been pissed at the club since Lucky stopped seeing her and told the brothers not to touch her." Viper continued, "It didn't help that King fired her when he heard she hit Willa. Nothing's worse than a slut with a grudge."

Sissy backed a step away at Viper's anger. The girl certainly didn't look her age, dressed in the short, black skirt and the tight, green top she was wearing.

"None of the other brothers recognized her?"

"The bar was too crowded with all the brothers from Ohio wanting to stop by and see Mick."

"Shit." Knox's expletive was what the rest of them were all thinking. "Did any of the brothers touch her?"

"No, thank fuck. We found her hiding in the back room."

"Jenna?"

"Lied about it at first then finally owned up to giving her a couple of beers."

"Mick could lose his license if it gets around town." Knox scraped his fingers along his shaved head.

"That's not all," Viper seethed. "Jenna decided to tell her about the clubhouse when Moon and Rider were talking about Lucky's night."

Lucky kept his face composed. His anger at Jenna had seethed when Sissy had confirmed she had heard about Raci, Stori, and Ember. Jenna had even told Sissy he used knives. The slut hadn't cared that she was talking to a seventeen-year-old child.

Knox leaned against the tall counter. "Mick fire her?"

"Told her to get the fuck out of his bar and not come back. Mick trusted Jenna; she had worked for him for a long time. He even rehired her when she came begging for her old job back."

"We're fucked. There won't be a person in town who doesn't know about the club by the time Jenna and Sissy get done running their mouths." Knox shot a dirty look at Sissy, a warning to keep her trap shut.

"No, we're not," Lucky finally spoke up. "None of us touched her, and Mick didn't intentionally serve her liquor. I don't really give a fuck about anyone finding out about me using knives. I'm not a pastor anymore. The problem is Jenna told her names of women she had seen at the club."

Marriages could be destroyed if a few of the names were dropped. Not only that, but Winter, Lily, Diamond, Beth, and Rachel would be embarrassed publicly, and the brothers didn't want their women hurt.

Lucky wouldn't mince words in front of the girl. They were fortunate Knox had called with the information to find her when he did. Sissy would have sneaked out and exposed several people there who sure as fuck wouldn't want their presence made public.

"She's going to keep her mouth shut," Lucky promised.

"Remember, Moon promised I could join your club when I get older," Sissy reminded the men.

Viper stiffened. No one lived after they tried to intimidate the club, but it went against club rules to harm an innocent. Despite the girl showing she was already a hardened bitch, her age held their hands.

Knox threw Viper a surprised look. "But Moon——"

Lucky imperceptibly shook his head at the brother. He knew Viper had no intention of letting Sissy join. She would be quickly disillusioned about the fun in the club. By the time the women members were done with her, she would be too frightened to look at a man wearing leather.

"What about Jenna?" Knox asked instead of finishing what he had been about to say.

"She's decided it's in her best interest to leave town. I gave her a week." Lucky had been furious with Jenna, and the woman had known him well enough to agree to leave Treepoint.

"You know what you're doing?"

Viper's direct question had Lucky wondering the same thing. He had reacted without thinking when he had seen the Wests take the younger girls from Willa's arms.

"When has he ever had a fucking clue?" Shade gibed.

Lucky ignored Shade. "Go inside Knox's office and wait for him," Lucky directed Sissy. Her resentful behavior was the last straw. "Knock it off! Change the attitude, or the closest you'll ever get to The Last Riders' clubhouse is the parking lot!"

"That isn't fair," she protested.

"Do you want fair, or do you want to join The Last Riders? Moon promised you could try to join, but Jenna told you how the club works, that you have to get the votes to be a member. You think you'll get any of the brothers to lay a hand on you with that attitude? Why do you think Jenna never became a member?"

Her silence spoke for itself.

"Every time you piss me off, I'll add another year to your wait. Moon told you that you could join when you're nineteen, but if you mess up, you'll be old and grey before you get your ass through the door."

Sissy's hands clenched, but her mouth snapped shut. Turning around, she went into Knox's office and slammed the door.

"Someone please remind me she's a kid." Shade's sarcasm had the brothers eyeing him cautiously.

"We're responsible for her behavior. It's because of us that her mother is dead." Lucky hated to believe the girl who had just left the room was as nasty-tempered as her deceased relatives.

"You mean me, not us. *I* was the one who pulled the trigger that killed her mother." Remorse had never been Shade's strongest personality trait.

"I was the one who gave the okay. We would have all died if that fire alarm hadn't gone off. Another five minutes and Shade and Lily would have been burned alive. When I okayed the hit, Georgia's brother already had custody of her children. I didn't plan on Lewis getting himself killed, too."

"Sissy's behavior isn't a result of her circumstances; it's born and bred. Georgia and Lewis were both bullies and sick fuckers.

Sissy attacks Willa the same way her mother did." Shade's reasoning angered Lucky.

"I don't believe that. *You're* not a result of your upbringing."

"I'm an aberration."

"I have to agree with that," Lucky mocked.

"Will someone tell me when Moon got the right to decide who joins the club?" Knox stared at the brothers around him, breaking up the budding argument.

"Club doesn't have to keep any promises an original member doesn't make. Moon didn't have a problem deceiving the girl. After what's she's put Willa through, none of us do."

"If Willa couldn't control Sissy, what makes you think Diamond will handle her any better?" Knox questioned.

"Because Diamond isn't responsible for her uncle's death, and you'll be around. Right now, her goal is to become a member. As long as she wants that, she'll somewhat behave."

Knox shook his head. "Teenagers expect immediate gratification. She'll get tired of waiting."

Lucky couldn't blame him for his concern. The brother didn't want his wife exposed to the same treatment from Sissy that Willa had tolerated.

"Diamond is also related to Sex Piston," Lucky clued him in. "Her sister isn't going to let Diamond be mistreated."

"Sex Piston will sic Killyama on her ass." Knox chuckled.

"That's what Lucky's counting on. We can't touch the girl; however, Killyama will have no hesitation about knocking some respect into her." Shade's usually impassive face broke into an evil grin.

"That bitch will wring her fucking neck if she pisses her off." Viper joined in on the laughter.

Lucky barely held back his own amusement. The Last Riders hated to deal with the biker bitches. If Sissy made the mistake of getting in their faces like she had with everyone else, the girl would be confronted by a group of women who wouldn't let her age and circumstances affect them. They would beat the shit out of her, which is what he hated to admit he had wanted to do when Sissy had lunged for Willa. He had wanted to drop her on her ass. The only thing that held him back was the presence of the Wests and the social worker.

"Knox, can I borrow your office? I need to make a few calls." Lucky's mind was turning to the numerous phone calls he needed to make to resume becoming a pastor and collect the references that would keep Flora at bay until he could marry Willa.

"Help yourself." Knox waved his hand toward his private office.

"You really going to go through with it?"

Lucky had thought Shade would be pleased with his decision; instead, he was looking grimmer by the second.

"Yeah."

"How are you going to convince those straight-assed deacons to give you the church back?"

"That's the easy part. They won't turn me down, because I found out their secrets when I was their pastor. I just have to remind them that, as long as I'm no longer their pastor, I feel no obligation to keep them. If I have my job back, I would feel bound by my position to make sure their transgressions remain private."

"The golden rule: scratch my balls, or I'll cut off your dick."

"Exactly. I'll see you later at the clubhouse."

Lucky went into Knox's office, motioning for Sissy to go back out front then shutting the door behind her. He expected a bigger challenge at regaining his job as pastor, but none of the deacons gave him any trouble, relieved they wouldn't have to listen to another on-call pastor. Only one broached the subject of The Last Riders.

"Your association with them may make regaining your position difficult," Angus Berry brought forth the fears of the other deacons.

"I understand and will be moving back into the church. My future wife and I are looking forward to serving the community."

"You're getting married?" Lucky could imagine Angus's furry grey brows lifted in surprise.

"Willa and I plan to be married in two weeks."

"You're marrying Willa?" Angus didn't give him time to answer. "She's a sweet girl. She made my seventy-fifth birthday cake and didn't even charge my wife. You couldn't have made a better choice. Damn...Excuse me, Pastor. I'll finally be able to look forward to a service again. The pastors who have been visiting and Merrick have been giving me a sour stomach. My ass couldn't take another long-winded sermon."

Lucky laughed. "I'll keep that in mind when I'm writing mine out."

"Do that and I'll put an extra five in the collection plate."

Lucky disconnected the call with a smile on his face. It didn't take long for his smile to disappear as he punched in the next number.

The voice answering the phone was brisk and short. "What do you want?"

"Colt, I need a favor."

"Why is it that you and the rest of The Last Riders only call when you want something?"

"Because we can't stand you," Lucky said truthfully.

Dead silence was on the other end.

"I can't stand you fuckers, either. What do you want?"

"I'm getting married."

"Bridge know?"

"Not yet."

Lucky knew he had won when he heard a deep sigh.

"What do you want?"

# Chapter Eleven

Willa fed the kids then laid the younger girls down for a nap. Both Leanne and Charlie looked exhausted and took her advice to rest for a while, seeking their own beds. She was just as tired, but instead of lying down, she rushed around her home, picking up the clutter.

Pushing back her hair from her face, she straightened and froze in place when the doorbell rang. Maybe, if she didn't answer, they would go away. She didn't want to see Lucky or Flora. She wanted to go to bed and pull the covers over her head.

"Open the door, Willa," Lucky's voice demanded.

Willa stiffened her spine, telling herself she could do this.

Her mouth almost dropped open when she opened the door. Lucky was standing in the doorway in a suit she recognized from when he was a pastor. She was familiar with all his expensive suits since she had stared at him enough on Sundays that every detail of his appearance had become ingrained in her memory.

She took a step back to let him enter, making sure there was enough room between them to avoid having him brush against her.

"Where are the kids?"

"They're taking a nap." She closed the door behind him as he walked into the living room.

"Let's pray they don't wake up until Flora leaves."

Willa frowned. "That wasn't nice."

"The less Flora sees them, the better." Lucky took a seat on her couch, making the flowery furniture seem silly against his muscular body. "Are you ready for her?"

"As much as possible."

When Lucky stared at her doubtfully, Willa smoothed her blouse down over her jeans.

"We have a few minutes, so why don't you take a shower and get changed into that blue dress with the black belt?"

"I haven't worn it for a while. It's a little tight," Willa was ashamed to admit. She had worn the dress to church only one time.

"Perfect. Usually, your clothes are so loose you can't tell that you have breasts."

Willa's face flamed at his comment. Her mouth opened and closed while his mouth twitched at her reaction.

He was right; her clothes had been so loose it had made her appear even heavier. She had bought the dress when she had been at her smallest weight since high school. Lucky had been dating Beth Cornett at the time, and they had seemed serious about each other.

The last time she had tried it on, it had been tight through the breasts. Her dieting had gone through a snag when Lucky had stepped down from being a pastor. The diet had gone out the window entirely and the ice cream had come out of the freezer when she had noticed his visits to Jenna's home.

She had stopped attending his church before he had left, but it had still been shocking to see him enter the woman's house in jeans and a leather jacket. She had despised herself as she kept track of the time he spent at her neighbor's house, eating a pint of chocolate cookie dough ice cream while she watched Jenna wave goodbye to him from her front door. The look on both of their faces had been self-explanatory.

That moment was even worse than when she had found out he was dating Beth years ago. They had only dated a few months, but Willa had tried everything she could to emulate Beth during that time. She had dyed her hair blond, lost weight, and even bought similar dresses.

Lucky had never noticed her. No man would when Beth was the epitome of femininity, with males always eyeing her appreciatively. With Willa, unless they needed her skills as a baker, she was avoided. She would never forget when she was in the grocery store and had passed a man she had made several cakes for. She had smiled at him and had been about to greet him when he had turned around in the aisle and pushed his buggy away as fast as possible.

"I'll get changed. I'll be right back." Willa excused herself, actually glad to get away from him long enough to gather her thoughts.

As she changed, she worded her thoughts carefully. She had the tendency to lose track when he gave her attention, and she hoped her mental practice would make her seem more composed.

She turned white when she saw herself in her mirror. Lucky must have been horrified when she had opened the door. Her brown hair was in a tangled ponytail, her blue blouse had splashes of spaghetti sauce that she had fixed for lunch, and she also noticed the faint odor of garlic clinging to her.

No one in their right mind would believe the sophisticated man sitting downstairs was engaged to her. She showered as fast as she could, nearly slipping when she stepped out of the shower and then almost electrocuting herself when she blow-dried her hair at the same time as brushing her teeth.

She brushed on some mascara before pulling on the blue dress Lucky had mentioned, sliding on the matching shoes before bracing herself to face the mirror again. She sat down on the edge of the bed, nearly in tears. Just once, she wanted to see herself in the mirror and like what she saw.

She would have to change; the dress was even tighter than she remembered. It was her own damn fault. Had she really needed spaghetti for lunch? She had intended to stick to her salad, but the mouthwatering aromas had broken her determination. She had the determination of a rabbit needing to use birth control.

As she reached to take the dress off, she heard the doorbell, heralding that she was out of time. Putting on an unconcerned look, she left her bedroom.

Lucky had let Flora in, and they were sitting next to each other on the couch. He was handing her a thick envelope.

"This should provide you with enough adequate references," Lucky was stating.

Flora, who usually had a perpetually sour expression when dealing with her, was giving Lucky a gracious smile and fluttering her mascara-caked eyelashes at him.

Willa walked by the couch, intending to take the lone armchair, but Lucky reached out, tugging her down beside him. She jumped when he placed his hand familiarly on her thigh, his fingers tightening in silent warning.

"How long have you been seeing each other?"

Willa stared at Lucky out of the corner of her eye, not knowing how to answer Flora's question.

"We've been seeing each other off and on again." Technically, he didn't lie.

It went against everything she believed in to deceive the woman, but the mental picture of the girls being taken by the Wests soothed her guilty conscience.

"I see." Flora tore open the envelope, pulling out a sheath of papers. "You must be very understanding, Willa. I've seen you"— she pointed to Lucky—"around town with several women."

Willa had known deep down that there was no way anyone would believe there was a relationship between her and Lucky.

"I don't deny it wasn't love at first sight. I'm afraid I have a lot of work ahead of me to convince Willa that I'm going to make her a good husband. She's a special woman, that I will have to prove to both Willa and God that I am worthy of being her partner."

Willa kept a smile pasted to her lips despite the astonishment she was feeling at Lucky placing himself as the one who wasn't good enough for her.

Flora read through the papers, her face paling before she refolded them and placed them back in the envelope. "I'll give these to my supervisor, but I don't anticipate any problem with the outstanding personal references you've given. I apologize if I offended you, Willa. Congratulations on your engagement. I hope I'll be invited to the wedding?"

This time, Willa wasn't able to keep her jaw from dropping at Flora's about-face.

"I haven't thought that far ahead—" Willa began.

"It's going to be a private ceremony, but we'd be very happy if you attended the reception we'll be having at the church," Lucky cut her off. Standing up, he gave Flora one of his handsome smiles that had Flora blushing as she gained her feet. "I'll make sure you receive an invitation."

"Now I have two things to look forward to: you returning to the church and a wedding."

Willa went to the door, practically wanting to beg the woman to stay. She didn't want to be left alone with Lucky. She knew they needed to discuss how to get out of this mess, but she could offer to meet him at the diner or King's where other people were around to buffer his affect on her.

Willa stood, staring at the closed door, listening to Lucky walk back into the living room.

"I believe she's gone."

Lucky's amused voice gave Willa the courage to turn around.

"How are we going to get out of this? We're both going to go to jail for fraud."

"We're not going to jail," Lucky reassured her.

"People go to jail for committing fraud."

Lucky shook his head. "What fraud? Couples get engaged all the time."

"But we're not really engaged. When we don't get married, they'll know we're lying. I need to hire a private detective to find the children's uncle. Maybe I can find him in time, and no one will find out the truth. We can tell everyone you changed your mind."

"Calm down. I already have several people searching for their relative." He cocked his head to the side. "Why not tell them you broke up with me?"

Willa rolled her eyes. "No one will believe that."

"I'm getting tired of you putting yourself down. Don't do it again."

Willa felt the chill of his displeasure and unconsciously shivered. Desperate, she changed the subject.

"Thank you for helping me keep the children and finding a place for Sissy. I know she regrets her actions."

"No, she doesn't. I didn't do this for the children and for damn sure not Sissy. I did it for you."

"Why?" She was confused. Why would Lucky help her?

"You've worked hard to keep that family together. They owe you a debt, not the other way around. Lewis attacked you. No one blames you for killing him."

"I blame myself. I should have hit him with the gun, tried to knock him out." She had bought the gun to protect herself. Lewis had been more and more demanding, frightening her into the rash purchase, a decision she would regret to her dying day.

"What if you hadn't? What if he took it away and killed you?"

"I wish I had never bought that gun."

"Why? It served its purpose. It protected you and Rachel. What if you didn't have it that day?"

111

Rachel would be dead, and she would be, too. There had been a mad glaze in Lewis's eyes that day. Willa saw it every night in her nightmares.

"You can't bring the bullet back, Willa. Unfortunately, there aren't any do-overs where a life is concerned."

"No, there aren't," Willa agreed.

"Since you're dressed, I suggest we wake the children and go out to dinner. We need to let people see us around town together. Go wake the girls. I'll get Charlie."

"But I have orders I need to get done for tomorrow."

"I'll help you when we get back."

"You'll help?"

"I can keep the kids occupied and put them to bed. It will get them used to me."

"Why do they need to get used to you? We'll have to pretend to break up before the two weeks are up." Willa tried to think about how hard it was going to be to get out of the lies they had told.

"We'll worry about that when the time comes. Right now, our priority is to make Child Services believe us."

Willa nodded. The threat of the Wests taking the girls was the only incentive she needed to keep the pretense of being engaged.

She woke the still-sleeping girls.

"We're really going out to dinner with Lucky?" Leanne asked, rising up in her bed when Willa told her where they were going.

"Yes," she answered, dressing Chrissy and Caroline in warm clothes.

"Why does he want to take us out to dinner?" Leanne asked, jumping out of her bed.

"He wants to get to know all of you better."

"Sissy got us into a lot of trouble, didn't she?"

"Yes, and Lucky wants to help." Willa studied the girl seriously. "Leanne, if you want to stay with the girls and Charlie, we have to show that I can care for you and your cousins. Can you please help me with that?"

Leanne lowered her head, unable to meet her gaze. "I'm really sorry, Willa. I didn't think they would take us away. I shouldn't have let Sissy talk me into not telling you she was sneaking out."

"She could have really gotten into a bad situation and been hurt."

"I realize that. I was stupid."

"Not stupid, you were just trying to make your big sister happy." Willa handed her the hairbrush after she brushed out the two little girls' hair.

"Ready?" Willa asked the apprehensive girl when she was done with the brush.

Without her sister, a different girl was emerging, although she didn't like to think unkindly that Sissy wasn't a good influence on Leanne.

Downstairs, Lucky was waiting with Charlie, who couldn't hide his excitement about going out with the large man standing patiently by the doorway.

Willa grabbed her purse, holding the girls each by their hands. Lucky reached down, taking Chrissy's.

"Leanne, take Caroline." Leanne took Caroline's hand as she went through the door.

"I had her," Willa protested.

"Leanne is able to place her in the car." Lucky closed the door behind them.

Willa was walking toward her car when Lucky stopped her.

"We'll take my car."

Willa stopped in her tracks, used to him on a motorcycle. She looked at the curb, seeing a large, black Yukon sitting there.

"Caroline and Sissy need car seats."

"Knox put them in the back seat," Lucky stated, opening the back door.

Willa stood aside, watching him first buckle Chrissy then Caroline into their seats. Leanne climbed in then Charlie.

"Wow, we each have our own seat."

"You had your own seat in my van, too," Willa reminded them as she got into the SUV after Lucky opened the side door for her. They had been cramped, but they had fit.

Charlie remained silent, fidgeting in his seat.

"Where would you like to eat?" Lucky asked, getting in behind the wheel.

"Anywhere is fine."

"The diner," both Leanne and Charlie spoke from the backseats.

Lucky raised his brow at her, waiting for her response.

"The diner is fine." Willa smiled, wanting to make the children happy and get the night before them over with.

It wasn't far to the diner. When they parked, Willa was the last to exit the car. Lucky opened her door, holding Chrissy comfortably in his arms.

"You coming?" His questioning gaze didn't ease her nervousness.

"Do I have to?"

Lucky gave her a devastating smile. "I think that's the first time you ever said a joke in front of me."

Willa slid out of the SUV, closing the door. "I wasn't joking," she mumbled.

"Did you say something?"

"I said, they're busy tonight."

"They usually are on a Saturday night."

They stopped inside the door, searching for a free table, but it took a few minutes for one to become free. Willa felt the curious gazes directed toward them as they waited, so she was relieved when the waitress escorted them to a large table at the back.

The younger girls were settled at the table before Willa took a seat. Lucky sat down next to her with Leanne and Charlie sitting across from them. She tried to relax as if it was a normal thing to sit at the table with Lucky.

"Do you know what you want, or do you need me to come back?" The waitress paused.

"We can order and save you a trip."

Willa caught the grateful smile from Ginny. She was unaware the former foster child of the Wests had begun working here.

Willa ordered meals for Chrissy and Caroline and let Charlie and Leanne order for themselves. Lucky ordered a steak and fries.

"How about you, Willa?" Ginny gazed at her expectantly.

"I'll just take a coffee."

"Bring her the same as I'm having." Lucky closed the menu, handing them to Ginny who took off in a rush before Willa could change the order.

"I'm not hungry. I had a big lunch," Willa snapped.

"This is dinner. If you can't eat it all, I can finish it. I'm starved. It's been a long day."

Willa felt terrible. If not for his help, she would have been sitting home alone tonight, crying her eyes out over the children who were sitting happily at the table next to her. Not to mention, he did look exhausted.

"I'm sorry. I didn't mean to sound like a witch."

"It's cool. I imagine you had a terrible night. Attitude in a woman never bothers me. I can hold my own ground."

Willa nodded. She didn't doubt that for a second.

It didn't take long for their meals to arrive. The younger girls played with their food more than they ate, but the atmosphere at the table wasn't as uncomfortable as Willa had thought it would be.

The other restaurant-goers eventually stopped staring at them, and she was able to relax and finish most of her meal. Lucky ate his own then sat back, enjoying his coffee.

"That won't keep you awake tonight?"

"Six cups of coffee couldn't manage that tonight."

"You didn't sleep well?"

Lucky's face became closed-off as he motioned for Ginny to bring their check. Willa didn't miss the strain on the woman's features when she laid the check on the table.

"I didn't realize you were working here," Willa probed delicately.

Ginny paused in her frantic pace to wait on her customers. "I was fired from my last job."

"I was wondering where you were the last time I stopped in at the insurance office."

Ginny didn't explain why she was fired, and Willa didn't probe further, only nodded sympathetically. It was hard to have your income depend on another.

"I have to work two jobs to make up for losing that one. I'm also working at the theatre."

"I imagine working two jobs can't be easy."

"I'd rather work four jobs than put up with old man Dawkins."

Willa didn't blame her. Carter Dawkins was as unlikable as his son.

"I didn't mean to upset you. If there's anything I can do, let me know. If I open the bakery I'm planning, maybe I can offer you a job. But it's going to be a while," Willa added hastily.

The woman's face brightened. "Let me know. I don't mind this one, but the theatre is third shift."

"I'd be glad to hire you."

"Thanks, Willa. I heard you're engaged. Congratulations," she said.

"Thanks." Treepoint's grapevine had already been hard at work. "I'll see you tomorrow in church."

Ginny moved away to wait on another table.

"You always try to help everyone, yet you hate to take it yourself." Lucky leaned down, picking up Chrissy.

"She needs help. She looked exhausted," Willa stated simply.

"Who's going to help you?" Lucky's expression tightened.

"I can handle it. I have a secret weapon."

"You do?"

"Yes, it brings the girls to a stop for at least a good hour a day."

His mouth twitched. "What's that?"

"*Peppa Pig*. I've recorded every episode," Willa said fervently.

He burst out laughing as he stopped long enough to pay the check.

Feeling the center of attention again, Willa fled outside to wait, practically running into the man and woman about to enter the diner.

"Watch where you're going!"

Willa came to a sudden stop at Jenna's harsh command.

"I'm sorry. I didn't see you." She tugged Caroline closer to her to give Jenna and Curt Dawkins enough room to pass.

Curt held the door open for Jenna as she walked past her, deliberately knocking Willa back a step.

Willa gasped as Caroline fell down.

Jenna didn't pause, throwing a gloating look over her shoulder, and a flash of fury struck Willa.

"Leanne, take Caroline and Charlie to the car."

Before the girl could say anything, Willa went through the door after Jenna and Curt.

Lucky was turning away from the cash register, giving her a questioning look as Willa moved in front of Jenna, blocking her.

"If you don't like me, that's fine, but don't you dare touch one of those children again."

Jenna cast a wary glance toward Lucky. "It was an accident."

"Usually, when you have an accident, you apologize."

No apology was forthcoming from her, and Willa could tell she wasn't about to get one.

"If you have a problem with me, take it out on me, but don't *ever* think I'll stand by and watch you hurt someone I care about to get back at me."

"I don't have a problem with you, Willa. You're not that important to me," Jenna said cuttingly.

"The feeling's mutual." Willa brushed rudely past her, for once happy that her weight came in handy. She knocked Jenna against an empty table, and Jenna would have fallen if Curt hadn't grabbed her arm. Willa waited for Jenna's reaction, stubbornly refusing to leave before Jenna could.

The woman regained her footing, giving her a hateful glance.

"Let's go eat, Curt." With that, the pair moved away.

"You want to go after her and beat the shit out of her, don't you?"

Willa took a shuddering breath at Lucky's amused question.

"Don't cuss in front of Chrissy," she reprimanded.

"Yes, ma'am."

She gave him a frustrated glance before going out the door. It was his fault the woman hated her guts. Jenna had been a cordial, if not friendly, neighbor before the day his motorcycle had been spray-painted. Willa believed Jenna blamed one of the children for the damage. For all she knew, Jenna might think she had done it.

"What did she do to make you so mad?"

"She knocked Caroline down," Willa answered, her concern for the little girl alleviated when she saw her standing next to Leanne.

"Why would she want to hurt Caroline?"

"She didn't. She wanted to hurt me." Willa picked up Caroline, brushing her hair away from her damp cheeks. "You okay, sweetie?"

Caroline nodded, placing her thumb into her mouth. "I want my blankie."

"As soon as we get home," she promised.

Lucky buckled the girls in while Willa climbed into the front seat. When Lucky settled into his seat, he paused before starting the SUV.

"I'll talk to Jenna and make sure she doesn't bother you anymore. You don't have to put up with her much longer. She's decided to move away."

"Don't bother. It will just make the situation worse. She already thinks I'm the neighbor from Hell. That's probably why she decided to move."

"I doubt that's the reason, but if she tries to touch you again, she'll find out exactly what Hell is." Lucky's vehemence brought a fleeting moment of concern for Jenna until she realized she was being ridiculous.

Lucky may have been hanging around The Last Riders lately, but the pastor constantly preached about violence during his sermons. She seriously doubted he could harm a fly. She tried to ignore the voice at the back of her mind that reminded her he had also preached against promiscuity.

# Chapter Twelve

Lucky walked to the front of the crowded church. With every pew filled, he felt conscience-stricken at the welcome the parishioners were giving him.

He stopped behind the pulpit and turned to face the expectant crowd, each waiting to hear his sermon. His hands gripped the sides of the wooden pulpit, sliding against the smooth wood that had been rubbed every Sunday by him during his tenure as their pastor. Then his eyes roved over the ones seated in the audience: Winter, Beth, Evie, Lily who was holding her child in her arms. Lucky swallowed hard at her bright smile. He felt his weakest whenever he looked into her violet eyes.

He would never be the man she thought he was, and he felt like a failure each and every time. Not only because of her, but everyone there who wanted him to provide them with the guidance and ministering they needed. How could he help them find their way when he was more lost than them?

His eyes came to rest on Willa who had Caroline and Chrissy on each side of her in the front row where he had asked her to sit. Charlie and Leanne completed the picture of a family, one he would never allow himself to have.

Lucky bowed his head and heard the parishioners mimicking his action. He repeated the same prayer he opened each of his services with then raised his head.

"I had planned a sermon for today, thanking you for allowing me back into the church. I planned to explain my actions of the past months and ask forgiveness from the Lord and you." His knuckles whitened from the grip he had on the pulpit.

"I love being a pastor. I always have. It's something that I feel driven to do, but at the same time, I'm at war with myself. I want to stay your pastor, but for me to do this, I do not want to be judged by how you believe I should live as a servant of the Lord. Our belief in God is what has brought us here today. If you want to judge me, then do so on my work as your pastor in the past and in the future. If you're not happy with that, I am useless to this church as the leader it needs."

Lucky opened his Bible and began reciting it as he gazed at Willa. She gave him the same timid smile she always gave him then glanced away, as though afraid he would read too much.

He had spent the night before at her house, playing with the children then getting them ready for bed while she had baked. The smell had filled the house as the children had laughed. It had brought back memories of his own childhood, and he hadn't been able to bring himself to regret stepping forward so he could keep them safe.

The Wests sat in the middle of the church, piousness practically oozing out of them, while inside, the ugliness of their souls made him want to have them expelled from the church. He had made a promise never to divulge their secrets, and he wouldn't, but he had every faith that God's justice would be waiting for them, just as it was for him.

He had pretended to be unaffected by Willa, leaving her with a brief goodbye. However, all the while, he had wanted to take her with him to the clubhouse and barricade them in his bedroom until he had found out everything he wanted to know about her.

How soft were her breasts? Did her mouth really taste as good as he remembered? Would her pussy open to him in need or be tight with trepidation at the pounding he wanted to give her?

Lucky dragged his mind away from the lust-filled images trying to overtake the holier images that he was trying to convey to the parishioners. He was willing to bet the bike he loved he would gain a more rapt audience if he were to describe the impure desires for Willa he constantly had to fight. Then he concluded the service, motioning for the organ to begin playing. Leaving the podium, he went to Willa, reaching out to take her hand. She shook her head yet rose from her seat.

"Come stand with me. Leanne, you bring Chrissy, and Charlie, you hold onto Caroline." The small group went to the doorway and stopped.

"I can't do this," Willa murmured under her breath.

"Yes, you can. Just smile and I'll do the rest," he reassured her.

The congregation began lining up to speak to Lucky, and out of the corner of his eye, he saw Willa give each parishioner a hesitant smile.

Drake Hall with his son Jace and Jace's friend Cal were the first ones in line. Drake bent down, giving Willa a kiss on her cheek. "I heard the good news. Congratulations to you both." Drake reached out, shaking Lucky's hand. Then the two younger men followed his example. "Willa, why didn't you tell me you two were seeing each other?"

"She wanted to make up her mind about continuing to see me. Willa was a hard woman to convince, but I finally managed to get her to admit I would make a good husband." Lucky winked at Drake, giving the impression that Willa had kept him dangling like a fish on a hook.

"She's worth the trouble; that's for sure." Drake's hand tightened on Willa's, pulling her closer for a hug.

Lucky's mouth tightened into a grim line, his arm going around her waist and tugging her away from Drake to his side. "Yes, she is."

Drake took the silent hint, moving away with Jace and Cal.

The women of the congregation moved in next, swarming Willa in a rush of hugs and well wishes.

"Have you set the date yet?" Winter's voice could be heard over the rest.

"No—" Willa began.

"Yes. November sixteenth. We want to celebrate Thanksgiving Day as a family."

The women stared at him in dismay at the close date.

"That doesn't give us much time to do any planning." Beth bit her lip then gave Willa a determined look. "We'll get it all done. If we can arrange Lily's wedding on forty-eight hours' notice, we can make a wedding that you'll always remember with two weeks to work on it."

Lucky frowned. "We don't want anything too fancy. We were thinking of going to the courthouse then having a reception at the church."

The women stared at him as if he had grown two heads. He expected Willa to have the same expression; instead, she was nodding her head in agreement.

"Neither of us want a big church wedding," Willa said, breaking the uncomfortable silence.

"Are you sure? You cried your eyes out during Lily's wedding." Beth's reminder had the women rallying around her, trying to convince her to have a more formal wedding.

Finally, Willa raised her hand so the group would listen.

"I cried because Lily's wedding was absolutely beautiful, not because I wanted one like it for myself. I would actually prefer a spring wedding, but Lucky and I want to spend the holidays together with the children." It was the most Willa had spoken at one time and she had inserted a firmness in her voice so it would be more believable.

"I can understand her feelings. King and I didn't have a big wedding, either." Evie pushed herself to the front of the line. "We're holding the whole line up. Since we're having a wedding, we need to at least give her a bachelorette party."

Willa shot that idea down. "My business is so busy right now. I wouldn't be much fun."

Evie went on as if Willa hadn't spoken. "We can do it next Saturday at King's restaurant. That way, all you have to do is show up. I'll handle the food and the booze."

"The children—"

"I'd be glad to spend the night at your house so you won't have to worry what time you get home," Mrs. Stevens, her neighbor from across the street, offered.

Unable to think of another excuse, Willa agreed.

"That wasn't so bad, was it? Don't worry, Willa; I won't make it too wild," Evie promised.

Willa had attended a couple of parties with the women that Lily and Beth had invited her to, and all of them had been fun, despite her feeling like the outsider.

"I'll look forward to it," Willa said and meant it.

When the women moved on, leaving the rest of the congregation to file past, she breathed a sigh of relief.

"That didn't hurt, did it?"

"No." Willa didn't admit that his presence had kept her nerves steady.

"Ready, kids?" Now that church was over, Willa wanted to escape back to her home.

"Where are you going?" Lucky stopped her when she would have reached for Chrissy and Caroline.

"I'm going home to relax. It's my day off."

"You have to attend the fellowship meeting with me. Then we have to take care of getting a ring for you."

"I don't need a ring," Willa protested.

"No one is going to believe we're engaged if you don't have a ring," Lucky stated resolutely.

Willa followed Lucky into the fellowship hall. She had attended many times before, fading into the background. Today, they were the center of attention since everyone wanted to gather gossip for the rumor mill.

Willa was relieved when the room finally cleared.

She and the kids were hustled into Lucky's SUV. Thankfully, the reception welcoming Lucky back to church and then sitting through the sermon had made the younger children sleepy. As a result, they fell asleep in the backseat as Lucky drove out of town.

Willa turned in her seat. "Where are we going?"

"I thought we would drive to Jamestown to look. The jewelry store is open there on Sunday."

"Oh." At least the children wouldn't be grumpy from being tired.

Charlie turned on the DVD player in the backseat, and both he and Leanne began watching a movie.

"I didn't know you had another vehicle."

"It's two days old," Lucky quipped.

Willa lowered her voice so the kids couldn't hear her in the backseat. "You bought it after you told Flora we were engaged?"

"Yes."

"Have you lost your mind?"

"Fortunately, Willa, money isn't something I need to worry about. When our engagement is over, I'll sell it or keep it for the club to use."

Willa stared out the window at the passing scenery. How did he not have to worry about money on a pastor's salary? Then again, she didn't feel it was any of her business since their engagement was a pretense for the children's benefit, not an opportunity to stick her nose into his private affairs.

"Were you able to finish the cakes you were working on last night?"

"Yes." Willa yawned. "I was able to finish decorating them this morning before the girls woke. I don't get much accomplished when they're in the kitchen. They like playing with the frosting."

"I do, too," Lucky muttered.

"What did you say?"

"Nothing. I was saying your cakes are very good. You've worked hard on your business. Have you found a place to open a store yet?"

"No. You're right; the building next to the diner is going to need too much work, but the other property I was looking at is too expensive. I'll keep looking. The right one will come along," she said. "I may not need more space, anyway. If the children's relative is found, I won't need the additional room"

Lucky gave her a brief glance before looking back to the road. "Willa, we may need to be realistic. He may not be found in time."

Willa's stomach sank as her greatest fear was realized.

"I've already thought of that. I really don't want the girls to go to the Wests. I know they attend your church, but..." Willa shrugged, unable to say just what her objections were and not wanting to come off as silly.

"I agree. I don't think the Wests would be the best placement for them, nor do I want Leanne to be forced into a group home," Lucky said grimly.

"I don't, either. I've asked a few couples in town whom I think would make excellent foster homes, but the idea of taking in five children is too much for them to handle."

"It wasn't for you."

"Believe me, it's been hard. I've almost thrown in the towel several times."

"Why haven't you?"

"Because I know how hard it is to live in a home you're unhappy in, and I can't do that to a child when I can make a difference. I'll do what I have to in order to make them happy."

"Enough to marry me?"

Shocked, Willa stared speechlessly.

"Because it may come down to it despite Knox's efforts, and the investigators searching for their next of kin may not find them in time."

"Maybe we can say we decided to have a longer engagement…"

"Child Services only agreed to let you keep the children because our marriage is soon. If we try to delay it, they could possibly place the children until we are."

"What am I going to do?" She began trying to think of other ways to circumvent the children being taken; however, she was coming up blank.

"We could get married then get an annulment after we find them a suitable home."

Lucky's suggestion was the last one she had expected.

"Why would you do that?"

"You're not the only one who wants to help. Several people in the community would have helped the last few months if you had let them, but you don't have a choice now. Either you accept my help or lose the kids."

Willa stared down at her hands. "I'm used to relying on myself, but I was wrong. If I had taken help, I might not be in this position now. It doesn't come easy to me, accepting help."

Lucky's hand left the steering wheel. "How about you lean on me for a while? If I can handle a church full of parishioners, I think I can deal what comes your way."

His confidence irritated Willa, so she decided to see how well the cocky biker would cope with the pressure she was under. Asking

God if all men were jerks or just the ones she came in contact with was another question to add to her ever-expanding list.

"Jerk."

"What did you say?"

"I said, fine."

ဆ ന

"How about that one?" Willa pointed at a ring with a small diamond that was in the clearance section of the jewelry case.

Lucky stared at the ring. "It's not very big."

"I don't want a big stone. It will make it harder to sell."

She and Lucky each held one of the young girls, while Leanne and Charlie were staring in fascination into the glass cases.

"I like that one." Chrissy took her thumb out of her mouth long enough to point at a large, garish ruby ring.

"That's not an engagement ring, but I like the red, too." Willa hugged the little girl closer.

She felt Lucky's gaze on her as she walked up and down the aisles, looking into the various cases. The middle-aged saleswoman focused her attention on Lucky. If Willa was really engaged to Lucky, she would be jealous as heck at the attention he was getting from her. Instead, Willa skirted the section they were at, going to the end. It was obviously full of the more expensive items in the store. Willa was about to turn away when her eyes were caught by a ring that had her unintentionally gasping.

It was rose gold with a pink diamond in the center, surrounded by smaller diamonds. It wasn't like the other engagement rings. It was more frivolous and feminine looking and completely unlike anything she owned, but she fell in love with it immediately.

"You like that one?" Lucky asked.

Willa jumped. "I was just shocked at the price."

The saleswoman reached in the case, pulling the ring out. "It's one of the most expensive rings we have in the store." Her condescending attitude struck Willa like a slap in the face. When they had arrived at the store, the woman hadn't tried to hide her reaction when Lucky had introduced her as his fiancée.

Then she quoted a price that had Willa taking a hasty step back.

"I like the other ring much better. It won't get in my way when I'm cooking. I don't wear much jewelry."

The cheaper pieces always broke or tarnished, and the more expensive pieces she would have treated herself to occasionally were invariably budgeted out when her bills came.

"We'll take the other one, then."

The saleswoman placed the ring back in the case, walking back to the clearance section to pull out the smaller ring, and Lucky pulled out his wallet.

"Which one are you getting?" Leanne asked, coming to her side.

She looked at the counter, seeing the ring that was sitting waiting to be bagged.

"It's very pretty."

Leanne's reaction didn't bother Willa. She was determined to give Lucky the money back for the ring, and it cost exactly the amount in her savings account. The down payment on her store would simply have to wait until she could sell the ring after their fake engagement ended.

Willa hadn't expected to be able to wear it out of the store, but the ring fit surprisingly well and didn't need to be sized. It felt strange on her finger after she slid it on.

The children were becoming restless. Willa was grateful Lucky was driving since she was able to deal with Caroline's temper tantrum by digging out her blanket from her large purse. Content, the little girl quieted.

Lucky gave her a lighthearted grin. "You okay?"

"The screaming doesn't bother you? Most men would be freaking out."

"Doesn't bother me. Rider throws worse tantrums when he has to work overtime," Lucky joked.

"I can't imagine Rider throwing a tantrum. He seems very laid-back."

Lucky snorted. "Wait until you see him pissed off."

"I'll pass, even though I still think you're exaggerating."

Lucky helped her inside with the children when they arrived back at her house.

"I need to get back to the church to get ready for tonight's service. I'm sorry, but because we're engaged, everyone will expect you to be there."

"I don't mind," Willa assured him.

Lucky gave her a brief nod as he passed by her to leave.

She hesitantly reached out to stop him. "Thank you for all of your help."

Lucky's expression hardened. "Don't thank me, Willa. I don't want to see you get hurt…"

Her hand dropped to her side. "Don't worry, Lucky. I won't forget you're pretending to be engaged to me. I won't make the mistake of believing you care about me for a second." With that, Willa opened the front door.

"Good, I'm glad we understand each other."

ജ ങ

Lucky wanted to slam his fist against the door that was shut at his back. As an alternative, he walked to the new SUV, wishing he had kept his mouth shut. He hadn't meant his words the way Willa had taken them. He had started to tell her what he had meant then realized it was better to leave it alone. After all, they had no future together.

He sure as fuck didn't want to be her friend, and she would run from a sexual relationship with him. He could imagine the shock and disgust on her face if she found out he liked to use his knives on women. The timid woman would be horrified if he ever pulled out his leather case containing the lethal blades of various sizes and shapes that he used during sex.

Lucky drove to the church, going inside to his office and taking off his suit jacket. He was about to toss it onto the leather chair behind his desk when he realized the office wasn't empty.

Slowly, he turned to the window, seeing a large shadow standing in the dimness of the room. Turning on the light on his desk, he wasn't surprised at the man staring at him.

"I was wondering when you would show up," Lucky stated.

Bridge's mouth gave a menacing twist. "I wanted to congratulate you on your engagement."

Lucky kept his expression neutral. "Stay away from her."

"Why the fuck would I do that?"

"Because I'm telling you to. Go near her and I'll kill you."

"Don't make me laugh. If you were going to kill me, you would have already done it or had Shade do it for you. The worst thing you're going to do to me is make my dogs fat." Bridge casually walked across the room and sat down on the chair in front of his desk.

"I made him promise to stay out of our shit."

"I bet that put his balls in a twist."

"He wasn't happy," Lucky agreed. It had placed a wedge between them, but because his and Bridge's vendetta didn't involve the club, Shade wouldn't break his promise.

"That motherfucker doesn't know what being happy feels like."

"Yes, he does," Lucky replied.

"I heard he was married with a kid. So, he's happy?"

"Yeah, he loves Lily."

"Fuck me. Miracles do happen." Bridge snorted in disbelief.

"Yes, they do," Lucky affirmed.

Bridge's expression filled with agony before he concealed his reaction. "Not when it matters and not for the ones who deserve it."

Lucky winced at his jibe. "What do you want me to say that I haven't said a thousand times before? I'm sorry about Kale. If I could go back to that day and make a different choice, I would, but I can't."

"I wish I could go back, too, and ask someone else to watch out for him, someone who would have saved his life, not left him behind."

Lucky's body tautened. "I tried."

"Not good enough. The Last Riders didn't stop until they found Gavin's body, but I'll never have my brother's body to bury."

"I regret it every day of my life; what more do you want?"

"I want more than that. I want you to feel the pain of losing someone you love, to not be able to say goodbye to them, not have their body to grieve over. I want your life to become a living Hell like mine."

"My life has been a living Hell since the day Kale was killed."

"It doesn't seem that way to me. From where I'm sitting, your life seems pretty sweet. You have the church, The Last Riders, and enough pussy to keep ten men satisfied. Is there anything you don't get that you want?"

"Yeah, not to worry about you killing someone innocent because you hate me."

Bridge casually stood, staring at him mockingly. "I guess you can't have everything."

"I'm engaged to Willa because she's about to lose custody of the children she's caring for, not because I care about her. Besides, she'll make a decent pastor's wife and keep the parishioners off my back about marriage." Lucky threw out every excuse he could think of to place doubt in Bridge's mind. "I'm never going to let myself care about a woman and put her in danger from you. If I cared about Willa, there would be no way I would marry her."

"You trying to do some reverse psychology bullshit on me?"

"I'm telling you the truth," Lucky stated, looking Bridge dead in the eyes.

"When have you ever told the truth about anything? You lied to me about keeping Kale safe. You lie to your parishioners about being a just man. You lied to everyone to make those drug busts. I don't believe a word you're telling me, but I will find out the truth before I kill her."

"I'm not going to let you hurt Willa. The only one who is going to get killed is you. I'm done giving you a chance to make your move. I loved Kale like a brother, and out of respect to him, I've put up with your shit, but it's over. I won't warn you again, Bridge."

"Your luck and time have run out." Bridge left his office with those words hanging heavily in the air.

His worst fear had come true—Bridge had taken the target off his back and placed it on Willa's. God help him if his lucky streak failed him a second time.

# Chapter Thirteen

"Having fun?"

Willa took a drink of her pink lemonade, nearly choking on the taste, and was unable to answer Lily's question until she got her breath back.

"Are you okay?" Concerned, Lily hit her on the back.

"I'm fine," Willa assured her, placing her glass back on the table.

Lily smiled, not touching her own glass. "I'll be back in a minute. I need to use the restroom," she excused herself.

"Too strong?" Evie asked Willa sympathetically. "I screwed up and let Penni make the drinks."

Shade's sister had tagged along with Lily and Beth to her bachelorette party. Penni was visiting for a couple of days before leaving to set up for a concert the rock group she managed was having in a city a couple of hours away.

"I didn't," she protested. Then, seeing Willa wipe the tears away from her eyes with a napkin, she corrected herself. "Well, maybe I added a little too much. The recipe is a work in progress."

"Don't touch anything that bitch makes," Killyama yelled from the end of the table.

Penni stiffened. "Everyone begs for my recipes."

"Yeah, they beg you not to make them anymore." Killyama sniffed the brownie she had in her hand.

"Why is Killyama smelling the brownies? Didn't the recipe I give you turn out?"

"I didn't make those." Penni glared at the woman who belonged to the neighboring biker club from Jamestown.

Beth had become friends with them, and they were always included when she planned a party, just like Willa was. Beth and Lily didn't want anyone to feel left out.

"Your recipe was fine after I tweaked it a little," Penni continued.

"How did you tweak it?" Willa asked curiously. Her brownies were one of her most requested items.

"She turned them into pot brownies. Damn near killed me the next day, vomiting them up." Killyama glared.

"I didn't tell you to eat half of the pan."

"Who makes pot brownies in Kentucky? And for a baby shower?"

Penni didn't look bothered by Killyama's sarcastic question. "I didn't make them for the shower. I told you that I was experimenting with the recipe, and Rider accidently put them on the table with the desserts."

Willa broke into the argument between the two women. "How did they turn out?"

"They rocked, but I had to quit making them."

"Why?" Willa asked.

"Because they made me a little cray-cray. It took me a while, but I realized they had a weird effect on me." Penni drank her glass of pink lemonade in one swallow as a look crossed her face that Willa recognized as one she used when trying to perfect a recipe.

"What kind of effect?" Winter asked, passing the brownies to Penni.

"They made me hornier than hell."

The women at the table burst into laughter.

"Beer does that for me," Winter said when she managed to catch her breath.

Diamond grinned next to her. "Knox's tongue ring."

Rachel muttered, "Cash kissing my neck."

Beth was next in line. She turned red yet admitted her weakness. "Razer's tattoo."

"Stud racing his bike. I fuck him as soon as we get home."

Willa's face felt like it was on fire from the women's intimate admissions.

"Rider makes me horny when he works out. I just want to lick his abs."

"Me, too," Jewell wisecracked. "And I have."

Lily came back to the table, sitting down next to her. "What is everyone laughing about?"

Willa would die before she repeated the conversation they had been having while she was gone.

"Everyone is telling each other what makes them horny. What puts you in overdrive?" Crazy Bitch shouted out loud enough to be heard from the outside.

Lily stood back up. "I'll get us some regular lemonade from the kitchen." She paused before leaving. "With Shade, all I have to do is look at him," she admitted before fleeing.

"Me, too." Crazy Bitch slammed her glass down on the table. "I want to count his tats. She ever tell you how many he has?" she asked Beth.

Beth looked aghast at the thought. "No, she hasn't confided that detail to me."

"Why not?"

"I don't know...Maybe because she doesn't want to share, and I don't want to know."

"Liar."

Willa seriously became worried how some of the women were going to get home. Several were already drunk, and the others were well on their way.

Rachel rose from her seat taking Lily's empty one.

"I wanted to thank you for covering for me. Jace told me what you said at the sheriff's office. You took the blame for telling Jace about the motorcycles when it was me. I didn't think when I told him that he would actually try to break into the factory. I was going to ask Cash if he thought it would be okay for Rider to show him." Rachel had leaned sideways to whisper in her ear. Willa smelled the strong smell of alcohol on her breath.

Willa leaned back trying to escape the fumes. "Let's just say we're even for the tutoring."

Rachel gave her a quick hug. "That works for me." Willa was relieved when she returned to her own seat.

Once Lily returned with a fresh pitcher of lemonade, Willa was going to ask for a clean glass yet saw Penni's look of reproach. Taking a deep breath, she sipped the one she had made.

Willa tried not to feel guilty as she ate a piece of pizza after she drank several more sips of her lemonade. Then she decided she didn't care about her waistline and reached for another slice.

"Willa, you never did tell what creams your coffee."

She was about to swallow the cheesy goodness when Killyama's question sent it down her windpipe. She thought she was going to choke to death before she could clear it.

"I don't know," Willa confessed hoarsely. "I've never had sex."

The women quit talking to stare at her in bemusement.

"Why are you staring at me like that? I'm not the only one here who remained chaste until they were married, right, Rachel?" Willa wanted to kick herself, remembering belatedly the humiliation Rachel had suffered at Mrs. Langley's birthday party when Cash had told everyone that he had slept with Rachel.

"It's all right, Willa. I'm not ashamed to admit I had no will power where Cash is concerned."

"Beth was—"

Beth cut her off, looking embarrassed. "Sorry, but...no."

Willa looked toward Diamond.

"Nope, I lost mine in college."

Willa's eyes went to Sex Piston.

"Are you crazy? I lost mine in high school." Something told Willa she wasn't telling the truth.

Deciding to go for a sure thing this time, Willa turned to Lily.

"I think I'll go get some—something..." She trailed off, standing up and fleeing again.

Willa's shoulders slumped. She was the only virgin left in Treepoint over the age of eighteen, and she had a feeling she was going to die a virgin.

She put the pizza in her hand back on her plate.

"I'm a virgin."

Startled, Willa glanced at Penni.

"You're lying," Killyama scoffed.

"I am not. I may have fooled around some, but I've never been with a man. I've wanted to, but I always change my mind."

"How did the men take it?" Willa asked.

"Half understood, some were kind of nasty, and for the rest, I used the self-defense moves Shade taught me." Penni shrugged. "I want to find my soul mate the way Shade found his. I meet a guy and think this could be the one. Then I get to know him, and I simply want to be friends. The men I date tell me I'm playing hard to get."

"Like a stick of fucking dynamite. If you ain't giving it up, then they're doing something wrong. So why haven't you fucked anyone yet?" Killyama asked, turning everyone's attention back to Willa.

"It's not like I've had a lot to choose from."

"So you and Lucky haven't?"

Willa shook her head, wondering at the woman's heavy frown.

Willa heard Lily sit back down at the table.

"Are they still talking about sex?" Lily asked.

"Yes." Willa poured herself some more lemonade, not sure which was the non-alcoholic one.

Taking a sip, she wanted to pour it back in the pitcher; however, she took another sip when Penni smiled at her with pride. Willa couldn't bring herself to dampen her belief that it was good and took yet another drink.

"I have some books Killyama lent me," Lily offered.

"Those aren't going to help her." Willa began to get nervous when the woman became lost in thought then snapped her fingers. "I know. Have you seen *Saw*?"

Willa and the other women at the table stared at her blankly.

"Uh...no."

"You should." Killyama poured herself another glass of lemonade from the spiked pitcher.

"Are we still talking about sex?" Willa asked Lily in confusion.

"I hope not."

"Me, too." Willa started to take another bite of pizza then realized she had lost her appetite. Instead, she sipped her lemonade which was getting better and better.

৪৩ ৫৪

Lucky stared down at his watch. "How much longer do you think they're going to be?"

Shade crossed his arms over his chest. "You never know. When they have their parties, it can last an hour or four. It pretty much only ends when the liquor and food are gone."

"They're in a restaurant with a bar," Lucky reminded him.

"Then we're going to be here for a while. Don't expect any of them to be sitting in church in the morning, either. Lily will be the only one there, and you'll be lucky if the rest show up for the evening service."

"Willa will be in church. She doesn't drink," Lucky bragged.

"Right…We'll see. Penni's in there."

"What does Penni have to do with it?"

"It means Willa's going to come out either drunk or high," Shade advised.

"Not Willa. I know her like the back of my hand."

"Brother, you don't know shit about Willa, but I know my sister, and I'm telling you, there's no way Willa's coming out sober."

"Wanna bet?" Lucky goaded.

"Hell yes. You going to win the way you won the bet with Moon?"

Lucky didn't feel guilty about picking the motorcycle he had tried to buy off Rider for the last six months.

"I didn't cheat."

"You didn't cheat, but getting engaged to her made Moon believe you fucked her, and you didn't tell him any different. It also keeps him from trying to get her in his bed until you're willing to share…if you do."

"Willa would have an anxiety attack if I touched her, much less have her take part in one of the club's parties."

"Like I said, you don't know shit about Willa, and you're too chicken shit to find out."

"I'm not chicken shit. Willa and I aren't a couple. You know we're only engaged to get Flora to leave the kids alone."

"I keep going back and forth, trying to make up my mind on who's the dumber fuck: you or Rider."

"Neither of us. Moon is." Lucky grinned, unrepentant. The brother deserved to lose the bet for thinking Willa would be an easy conquest.

"So what does the winner get?"

"You have to bring Train back from Ohio. He's calling me every hour to come back because I told him I would go."

"Who would go instead?"

"Send Moon back. He's the one who made the mess in the first place."

"All right, and if I win, you have to let me out of my promise to you."

Lucky's face turned serious. "Pick something else. I'm dealing with Bridge."

"You're doing a crap job. He's watching every move you make."

"How do you know that?"

"Because I'm watching him."

"You can watch, just keep your promise."

"If I win, I want you to tell Willa the truth about the club. It's only a matter of time before Sissy or someone else tells her, and it will hurt less coming from you."

Lucky nodded. He had already decided to tell her when she wasn't surrounded by the children.

"Then we have a bet?"

"It's a bet." Lucky repeated, knowing either way, he lost.

The door to King's restaurant opened, and the women came stumbling outside.

Shade took his cell phone out of his pocket.

"Who are you calling?"

Shade looked up. "Knox. We're going to need more cars."

# CHAPTER FOURTEEN

"Why are we at the church? I don't feel like asking for forgiveness right now."

"You will in the morning," Lucky muttered, unlocking the side entrance that led to the part of the church he had moved back into when he had become pastor again.

When the church had been built, the back portion had been designed for the pastor and his family to live. If you came inside the side entrance, you wouldn't assume it was attached to the church, but it was a large home.

Willa stumbled in the darkness before he could flip the light switch on. Lucky closed the door with his foot before sweeping Willa into his arms.

She giggled, wrapping her arms around his neck. "It's too soon to carry me over the threshold. Be careful or you'll throw your back out."

"Stop."

Willa pouted up at him, seeing his stern expression. "Are you mad at me for getting drunk?"

"For getting drunk, no. I get mad when you put yourself down. I've told you not to do it in front of me."

"I'm sorry. Don't be mad at me." She laid her head on his shoulder, patting his chest.

The woman was irresistible when she was drunk because her guard was lowered, showing the real Willa. She had cracked jokes and sang as he had driven the bitches back to Jamestown. Stud had met him halfway and Willa had hung out the door, waving good-bye to them and asking Stud if Sex Piston had been a virgin when they were married. Sex Piston had put her own window down, yelling at Willa to shut the fuck up before she got out and whipped her ass. Then Willa had thrown the woman air kisses, reminding her she had promised to cut her hair.

Lucky had driven off while the women were still yelling back and forth to each other. There was no way he was going to make the same mistake Razer and Shade had made and allow Willa to become friends with the biker bitches. He was going to nip that one in the bud.

"Where are we going? I need to get home to the kids."

"You would wake them up, and I didn't think you'd want your neighbor to see you in this condition." Lucky walked down the hallway, easily carrying her weight.

He opened one of the spare bedrooms, placing Willa down on the bed. As she stared up at him in bemusement, Lucky felt his dick getting hard. The woman was cute as hell when she was sober; drunk, she had a seductive look he had never seen on her before. Apparently, being drunk gave Willa a lethal amount of confidence that Lucky was smart enough to know would be hard to resist if he stayed much longer.

"Go to sleep." Lucky gritted his teeth, heading for the door. He was getting sick and tired of protecting her from himself. Hell, he had never pretended to be a saint.

"Night."

He made the mistake of turning around at her slurred parting and saw that she was still lying in the same position he had laid her down in. Her legs were half off the bed, and she was lying sideways.

"Dammit!" Lucky turned back, bending down next to the bed. He took off her shoes then lifted her again and laid her back down until her head lay on a pillow.

"Thank you."

Lucky straightened, his aching balls killing him. "Do you have to be so polite all the time?"

Willa's drunken stare became angry. "You're a mean asshole; do you know that?"

Lucky burst out laughing, which made Willa even angrier. She rose up into a sitting position and threw her pillow at him.

"It's the truth!"

Lucky didn't try to dodge the pillow, letting it fall to the floor. "Is that so?"

"Hell yes! You're as mean as Curt Dawkins, and I hate him. He's always trying to touch me when no one is around."

Lucky didn't know what made him more pissed: that Curt was touching Willa or being compared to the man Jo had accused of raping her in high school.

"Rider's much nicer to me. He makes me feel pretty. Even that new biker at your club is nice to me. He bought me a cup of coffee the other day when I dropped my delivery off at the diner."

"Did he?"

Willa nodded. "He's very nice."

The backstabbing brother was going to get his boot up his ass the next time he saw him.

"And you know what? He's better-looking than you. You know why?"

"Why don't you tell me," Lucky answered, his voice going lethally quiet. However, Willa was too drunk to notice the warning signs that would have sent the other brothers running.

Lucky almost never lost control of his temper, but when he did, no one ever forgot. He had only really lost his temper twice in his life, and both men were dead.

Willa unwisely nodded her head vehemently. "His grey eyes make you think he's undressing you." Willa sighed.

"He's a horn-dog."

"Really?" The interest in Willa's eyes deepened.

"You need to lie down and go to sleep. Now."

"Quit ordering me around."

Before Lucky could move, Willa's feet came off the bed, kicking him in the stomach. Lucky took the unexpected punch in his gut, releasing his breath in a whoosh of air.

Willa began laughing, and Lucky lost what restraint he had been holding onto. Before Willa could understand what was happening, Lucky lifted her up, flipping her over his knees. Then his hand came down on her jean-covered ass.

"You can't spank me!" Willa screeched.

"Watch me!" Lucky said, his hand swatting her ass again.

Despite himself, he couldn't help letting his hand linger on her luscious ass, but a sudden pain in his thigh had him nearly dropping her on the floor.

"Stop biting me, you little hellcat." Lucky hastily tossed her back onto the bed before she could bite him again.

"Moon would never spank me!"

"Here's something else that son of a bitch isn't going to do."

Before she could open her mouth and make him even madder, Lucky trapped her mouth under his, his tongue taking advantage and slipping inside her warm mouth before she could react.

Being smarter this time, his hand held her face, making sure she wouldn't use those vicious teeth on him again. He didn't need to be worried, though. Willa melted underneath him, opening her mouth wider as her arms slipped around his waist.

Lucky broke the kiss.

"Damn, woman, what did you drink?"

"I just had some lemonade."

"You don't taste like lemonade."

"What do I taste like?"

"Fire. You taste like fire." Lucky groaned, lowering his mouth to catch hers again.

Every promise he had made himself dissolved with his will power. Willa's kiss drove all the other kisses he had ever experienced out of his mind, replacing them with only hers. The soft lips under his trembled as they returned the pressure of his shyly until he took control, showing her what he wanted.

"Like this, siren." Lucky's tongue traced her bottom lip.

Tentatively, Willa licked his before entering his mouth to search his. Her timid efforts had his hand going behind her knee, lifting her thigh so he could notch his dick against her pussy. The jeans separating them were the only thing that kept him from sinking his cock into her.

He groaned when she lifted her hips, grinding her pussy on him.

"Did I hurt you?" Willa whispered.

"Every time I look at you," Lucky confessed as his trembling hand turned her face so her mouth came back to his.

All the desire he had hidden from Willa escaped him in a moment of weakness. In the photo booth, he had stormed her defenses, not giving her a chance to respond. Now, he took his time, teaching her how to kiss.

Her hands glided underneath his T-shirt, exploring the skin of his back in small, fluttering touches as if it was the first time she had touched a man, and his defenses against her crumbled even more. He unbuttoned the blue blouse, letting it fall to her sides. Then his hands unclasped the blue, lacy bra, and it sprung open, displaying her breasts. Lucky would never forget the first time he saw her body. It was golden in the lamplight, her large breasts the size men fantasized about and women had breast implants to achieve.

His hand squeezed the soft flesh, lifting the rosy nipple to his lips. Tenderly, he brushed his mouth over the nipple.

"I've died and gone to Heaven." Willa's pussy ground harder against him.

Lucky pressed down harder, rocking his cock against the seam of her jeans. His mouth then lazily wandered to her other breast, sucking the nipple into his mouth and twirling his tongue across the hardening tip.

Willa clutched his back harder, her nails digging in like small daggers. He shuddered, barely able to hold back from coming, and Willa tautened under him. Less experienced than him, she wasn't able to hold back the climax he had barely managed to avoid.

"Dean!"

Lucky stiffened over her, his name returning him to reason. Tearing himself away from her, he stood next to the bed, trying to catch his breath.

"Lucky? What's wrong?" Willa's eyes were filled with confusion, making Lucky feel even worse for starting what he knew would lead them both down a path there would be no returning from.

"I need to get the hell out of here." Unfilled desire made his voice unintentionally harsh.

"Did I do something wrong?"

Lucky stopped with his back to her. "I can't do this, Willa." He couldn't place her in anymore danger than she was already in with their fake engagement.

"Okay. I understand." The unshed tears in her voice had him rushing from the bedroom, slamming the door behind him as he went into his room.

Pacing his floor, he ran his hands through his shortened hair, trying to get control of his rampaging desire. He knew he could call one of the numerous women he had fucked the last few months and have one underneath him in less than five minutes. Instead, he threw his cell phone against the wall, shattering it into as many pieces as he had Willa's heart.

No matter how much she hurt, he had to keep his distance from now on. Bridge wasn't bluffing. Before he had left the Navy Seals, Bridge had been considered one of the best. Deadly and relentless when he hunted for his prey, his job had been reconnaissance, hunting for the target that had been given to him. Once found, they would send in Shade. Bridge was the hunter, Shade the assassin.

Only two men were living who had the skill to kill Bridge. Shade was held back because of the promise he had given, and the other was held back because his honor refused to let him kill a man who deserved his vengeance.

Lucky went to the window, parting the curtain to stare out at the town. If he wasn't tied to the church again, he would be on his bike, roaring down the street and enjoying his freedom. He had lost count of the times he had stood here when he had been a pastor before.

He expected the same feelings of being caged and bound he had felt in the past. However, those weren't the emotions assailing him tonight. He felt as if he were home. It wasn't because he was back in the church, though. It was because of…Willa.

# CHAPTER FIFTEEN

Willa rolled over in the bed, trying to escape the bright sunlight. She wanted to go to the bathroom, but she was too scared to move for fear of throwing up. She was afraid to even open her eyes since they hurt so badly.

She whimpered, her hands holding the side of the bed as she scooted her butt to the edge of the mattress. She cautiously opened her eyes, feeling her stomach roll.

"I'm never going to eat or drink anything Penni makes again." Willa whimpered in pain as she tried to stand. She was halfway across the bedroom before she realized it wasn't her bedroom.

"What?" She stared around the room for a second, trying to remember the night before. The last thing she remembered was seeing Lucky's shocked expression when she had left King's restaurant.

As images from the night finally penetrated her foggy mind, her hands flew to her cheeks.

"Just let me die," Willa mumbled, praying the door she was headed for was a bathroom. Opening it slowly, she found a small bathroom with an old-fashioned tub.

"This one you give me?" Willa said out loud, thinking of the thousands of things she had prayed for since she was a little girl.

She gently washed her face with a soft washcloth, feeling as if it were a Brillo pad. Then she stared at her reflection. Her eyes were so bloodshot she looked like a vampire, and her blouse had been buttoned wrong. She fixed her appearance as best she could before she went back into the bedroom, nearly tripping over her tennis shoes and barely managing to keep herself from falling onto the bed.

Carefully picking up her shoes, she sat down on the bed to put them on. When she finished, she went to the bedroom door.

"Please, please let me get out of here without Lucky seeing me." She was beginning to feel like she was on a roll when she managed to slip out of the unfamiliar home.

It was still early enough that hardly any traffic was around except a few early risers going into the diner for breakfast. She didn't look in their direction, walking toward her house. It was only a couple of blocks away.

Willa had no choice other than to knock on her front door. She couldn't remember where her purse was. It was a sad day when she hoped a thief had it instead of having to face Lucky to get it back.

After Mrs. Stevens opened the door, letting her inside, Willa thanked her then explained she had to get ready for church. Mrs. Stevens departed, leaving Willa feeling guilty for rushing her off. Then the clock on her wall had her running upstairs to get the kids up for the service.

As Leanne and Charlie both grumbled, wanting to sleep in, she sympathized, wanting to climb into her own bed and pull the covers over her head. She darn sure didn't want to have to face Lucky. However, no catastrophe made attending church impossible, so Willa ushered the children to her van and into the front pew with a few seconds to spare. She had barely leaned back when the side door opened and Lucky entered.

Willa determinedly stared down at the Bible in her hands. Listening to his sermon without lifting her head, she wished there was some way to get out of standing with him at the end of the service.

The service ended much too soon. Hearing Lucky step down from the podium, she began to stand with Caroline in her arms. Lucky stopped next to her, taking the girl from her, then held out his free hand. Willa took it, her fingers trembling within his grip as they walked down the aisle to the doorway.

The line of parishioners seemed never-ending, and Willa simply wanted to escape and go home.

"Willa, Lucky." Curt Dawkins stopped in front of them.

Lucky was slow to take the hand held out to him, shaking it briefly before placing his arm around Willa.

"I heard you were engaged. Congratulations."

"Thank you." Lucky started to greet the parishioner behind Curt, but he didn't take the hint, not moving forward.

"I saw you sneaking out of the back of the church this morning, Willa. Guess you and the pastor decided not to wait for a wedding night, but then, not many do anymore. Isn't that right, Pastor? I was having breakfast with Jenna before she leaves town. I'm thinking of buying her house. We could be neighbors soon, Willa." Willa didn't miss the subtle threat that Curt gave her nor the insulting tone in his voice when he talked to Lucky.

"Jenna found her employment opportunities in Treepoint dried up. It would be a shame if the funding for the new football field dried up, too. The school board wouldn't be happy if they found out the football coach insulted one of the donors."

Curt paled, leaving without another word.

"What was that about?"

"The Last Riders make regular donations to the school and community, and since I'm the vice president, Viper lets me make the decisions on who to donate the money to. That football field is going to cost thousands of dollars. If they don't get a new field, they're going to have to lay out a season until it can be repaired."

"Oh."

Treepoint was fanatical over its football. Curt making one of the donors angry would not only get him fired, but probably lynched by the townspeople. Not even his popularity as a high school football star would save him.

Lily was farther down the line, holding her small son whom Willa managed to snag away from her for a few moments.

"I see you made it to church," Lily teased.

Willa nuzzled the baby's sweet smelling neck, hiding her face.

"None of the other women answered the door when I tried to wake them. I called Stud to check on Sex Piston and the rest of her crew, and they were at the hospital. Killyama was getting her stomach pumped."

"Is she all right?" Willa had come to like the abrasive woman.

"She's fine, but the hospital had to call Penni to find out what she put in the lemonade."

"What was it?" Willa was afraid to hear her answer.

"Moonshine she bought from the Porter brothers."

"Sweet Jesus." Willa used her elbow to poke Lucky in the stomach. "It's not funny."

"Yes, it is." Lucky wiped his tears of mirth away.

"She had drunk half a pitcher. She had alcohol poisoning."

"How much did you have?" Lucky asked, moving away from her elbow.

"Two glasses. I think." Willa found everything after the first glass hazy.

"Penni was going to visit her at the hospital when I was leaving for church."

"She wasn't sick like the rest of us?"

"No, Penni has a cast-iron stomach. I found that out in college. She used to drink men three times her size under the table." Lily took John back into her arms. "I'll see you at tonight's service. I'm going to go home to make Killyama some soup. The hospital is going to release her this afternoon."

"Tell her I hope she feels better soon."

"I will."

"I'll have to make sure I save some time today to prepare," Lucky stated.

"What for?" Willa smiled as Angus approached, his eyebrows looking like two caterpillars attacking each other.

"Penni's eulogy. If she gets anywhere near Killyama, she's gonna die."

Willa laughed so hard her head spun, and she had to lean against Lucky for support. Maybe she should stop by her doctor's office tomorrow to make sure she didn't have any ill effects from Penni's lemonade concoction.

Angus grabbed her in a bear hug, lifting her off her feet. After placing her back down, he slapped Lucky on the back.

"Makes me feel good to see a young couple in love as much as Myrtle and I are. Hope you have as many years together as we've had. Our fifty-third anniversary is next Thursday."

Angus's wife rolled her eyes at her husband. "He's tactfully trying to remind you about our cake."

"I haven't forgotten," Willa said, noticing Lucky had become remote, standing silently until the older couple left.

"I need to leave. I'm having lunch at the diner. The Last Riders are waiting for me."

Willa took Caroline from him. "I'll see you tonight."

He had placed an invisible barrier between them, telling her without words the only relationship they shared was an act to deceive others. The Last Riders were the ones he wanted to spend his time with.

Lucky nodded, locking the church door then leaving her and the children to walk to the parking lot alone. She put the children in the van and drove home, refusing to acknowledge the hurt she was feeling throughout the entire drive.

He had left her last night without making love to her, which told her he wasn't attracted enough to her to actually have sex with her. Today, he wanted to make sure she wasn't building any misconceptions about his feelings toward her.

◌ ◌

Willa stood at the sink, washing the dishes after lunch.

"Why aren't you using the dishwasher?" Leanne asked, placing a glass into the sudsy water.

Willa shrugged. "Sometimes I like to do them by hand."

"Why are you crying?"

Willa sniffed. "I'm not crying."

"I can do the dishes." Leanne took the plate out of her hand, moving in front of the sink. It was the first real overture the teenager had made toward her.

"I'll take the kids out to play." Willa dried her hands on a dishtowel.

All she had to do was open the backdoor and the little girls ran outside. Willa followed them, yelling at Charlie to come out and play with the girls. The sisters loved their brother to chase them around the yard.

Willa came to a stop when she stepped outside and saw what the girls were doing. A solid black German Shepherd was sitting on his haunches while the girls wrapped their arms around his neck. Terror filled Willa at the sight.

"Caroline, Chrissy, come here. Right now. Move slowly toward me," Willa urged, trying to keep the panic out of her voice.

"We don't want to. Isn't she pretty?"

Her eyes traveled down the body of the large dog. "Yes, she is."

"Can we keep her?" Caroline lisped.

154

"No!" Willa lowered her shrill voice. "She must have gotten away from her owner. I'll call Animal Control." As soon as the words out of her mouth, she realized it was Sunday, and the town didn't have the funds to employ someone to pick up strays on the weekend. Thinking quickly, she took out her cell phone and called the sheriff's office, and the dispatcher promised to send someone immediately.

Willa carefully walked closer to the children and dog until she was within touching distance. Then she took each girl's hand, tugging them away from the dangerous-looking dog. The dog whined when she stepped back, placing the girls behind her back.

She was at her back door when Charlie and Leanne came outside. The little boy stopped then ran forward before she could stop him. Leanne went slower, not wanting to appear as excited.

"Where did she come from?" Charlie asked in awe.

"I don't know. Come back here."

Charlie reached out to pat the dog, ruffling his fur.

"I wouldn't do that," Willa warned.

"Why not? He's friendly."

Willa was about to push the girls inside when Knox opened her side gate.

"Thank God you're here," Willa said in relief. She hadn't known who to protect first.

"What's up?"

Willa waved her hand at the massive dog. "I don't know how he got in my backyard, and Animal Control is closed today."

Knox went to the dog, sticking out his hand to be sniffed, and the dog licked his hand after a few moments.

"How is Sissy adjusting?" Willa took advantage of the opportunity to ask about her former foster child as he petted the dog. She had an appointment with Diamond later this week, and she was going to use the opportunity to ask for information since Flora refused to give her any news on the girl, citing privacy guidelines. However, this gave her a chance to keep her appointment strictly business.

"Good. She's spending time with Sex Piston and her crew."

"That must be fun for her."

"I don't know about that," Knox said. "She thought making fun of Diamond's doomsday prepping was hilarious until Sex Piston heard her. Now she's trying to survive working in Sex Piston's beauty shop part-time."

Willa could imagine the biker women making toast of Sissy if she showed them her teenage angst.

"She seems pretty friendly." Knox said, drawing her attention back to the dog. His hand went to the collar Willa hadn't noticed. "Her name is Ria."

"Does it say who to call?"

"No, but if she belongs to someone, they usually call the dog shelter. It will be tomorrow before we can find her owner if she belongs to someone."

"Of course she belongs to someone, or she wouldn't have a collar," Willa reasoned.

"Not if the owner couldn't take care of her anymore. Sometimes, they let them loose, hoping they'll find a new home. What do you want me to do?"

"I want you to get rid of her."

"I don't have any place to keep her. I guess I could chain her up at the dog shelter. They'll find her when they open in the morning."

"Let her stay tonight," Charlie begged.

Willa didn't even think twice. "She may be dangerous. I can't take the chance with the children."

"I can test her and see if you want. I've had several dogs, and we have a K-9 on the force."

Willa didn't want to keep the dog, regardless, but the children made it hard to say no.

They stood around as Knox gave the dog a series of commands that she followed. Even Willa could see the dog was well trained.

"I'll be right back," Knox said before disappearing to the front of her house then coming back with a bag of dog food.

"I keep an extra bag in my car for Bane when his handler works double shifts."

Willa watched as Knox fed the dog out of his hand.

"You have a bowl?"

Leanne ran inside the house, returning with one of her fine china bowls that had been from when her mother was married. Willa didn't chastise her, watching closely as Knox filled the bowl with dog food then sat it down in front of the dog. He took the bowl away after the dog ate a few bites, and the dog sat down on it haunches, wagging its tail.

"I'm no expert, but I think she'll be fine around the kids." Knox's hand smoothed over the dog's head. "You can drop her off at the shelter in the morning," Knox reminded her.

"Please, can we keep Ria tonight?" Charlie moved closer to the dog as if Willa would snatch her away.

"I suppose one day won't make a difference," Willa relented.

"Yay!" the children all yelled.

"We are not keeping her, though," Willa said firmly.

"I'd say she's housebroken. She won't be too much trouble. The shelter's pretty full right now. I had to call them Friday on a hoarder. She'll have to be put down if they don't find her a home." Knox wasn't helping.

Willa shot him a glance as the children began crying, begging her to let the dog stay. Charlie and Leanne glared at her like she was a monster.

"She can stay for a few days until I can find her a new home." Willa caved in to the children's cries.

"I'm glad that's settled. Anything else I can do for you, Willa?"

"No, I think you've done enough," Willa said reproachfully.

Knox gave her a grin, and Willa thought she caught sight of a tongue ring before he caught her staring. He gave her a wink before leaving. Willa blushed when she remembered Diamond's words from the night before.

"Wait, what about my cat? Is she going to eat it?"

Knox's lips twitched. "The cat give you those scratches on your arms?"

"Yes, she doesn't like me, but she likes the kids. Will the dog eat her?"

"If you're lucky."

Willa looked at him aghast, not finding the imminent death of her cat funny.

"The dog won't bother the cat."

"You're sure?"

The cat under discussion wandered languidly across the yard as they talked. When the dog bounded over to the feline, Willa waited for the cat to run or Ria to use the cat as a toothpick. Then the dog lowered his head to sniff the cat, and the feline retaliated by viciously swatting the dog on the nose. The dog took a step backward, whining.

"Yeah, I'm sure. Give me a call if you want me to take the cat to the shelter."

Willa waited until he was a few feet away before muttering, "Jerk face."

Knox came to a stop, turning back to face her. "Did you say anything?"

"I said have a nice day."

ᏸᎧ ᏣᎧ

Lucky was waiting for Knox when he arrived back at his office.

"She keep Ria?"

"What the fuck do you think? After I told her what you told me to say about putting the dog to sleep, the kids bawled. Made me feel like shit."

Lucky grinned. The massive brother hid that he had a weakness for kids and squirrels, but Lucky was more than aware of it.

"How did you talk Colt out of Ria?"

"I gave him twenty thousand for her. According to him, the dog has the most protective instincts of any dog he's trained."

"You buy Willa a cheap engagement ring that all the women are bitching about and then buy her a twenty-thousand-dollar dog trained to be a K-9, and she doesn't even know you bought it for her protection?"

"Yeah."

"Shade's right; you are a dumbass."

# CHAPTER SIXTEEN

Willa stared down at the engagement ring on her finger, twisting it around and around. She felt like the smile pasted on her face would break, and her friends would know she was a big, fat fake.

"How about this one?" The elegant saleswoman held up a beautiful white gown with elaborate beading.

"I wanted something plainer, and it's too puffy." Willa regretted letting Beth and Lily talk her into this fiasco. "We're getting married at the courthouse. Do you have a dress that isn't so formal?"

The woman nodded, lowering the dress. "I'll be right back."

"Willa, even if you're getting married at the courthouse, you still want to feel like a bride." Lily placed a hand on her arm. "Do you see the one on the mannequin? It's beautiful."

"It's too small." She had seen the dress the moment she had entered the store. If she was really getting married, she would have tried to shove her body into the small size, but her engagement wasn't real.

"They may have it in your size. We could at least ask," Beth prodded.

The saleslady returned, carrying a plain white dress that was exactly what she had asked for.

Willa stood. There was no way to fight the inevitable; she was going to have to try it on.

"I'll put it in the dressing room for you."

"Thank you." Willa began to follow her.

"Wait, she wants to try this dress on, too." Lily had gone to the mannequin and was touching the filmy material.

"We have another out back. I'll just grab it and put it in the dressing room also."

"Don't bother; it won't fit." Willa tried to stop the women from taking over, but it was useless.

"Don't worry; we have it in a larger size."

Willa couldn't come up with another excuse, finding herself in the dressing room with the door closed and the two dresses hanging from the hook.

She tried on the short one first. It was exactly what she had been searching for. It wasn't expensive, and she planned to give it to the church store after her engagement to Lucky ended.

When she walked outside, coming to a stop in front of Lily and Beth's chairs, both women gave her encouraging smiles.

"It's very pretty."

Beth nodded at her sister's comment. "It's perfect for a courthouse wedding."

"Yes, it is," Lily agreed unhappily. "Will you at least try on the other dress?"

"I shouldn't." Willa hesitated, seeing the disappointment in their expressions. Sighing, Willa gave in to them. "I'll try it on."

Their faces became expectant as Willa went back into the dressing room.

"This is a really, really bad idea."

"Did you say something?" the saleswoman asked from outside the door.

"I said I'll be out in a moment."

"Take your time. If you need any help, let me know."

"Can you get me out of here?" Willa prayed silently, taking the dress off the hanger and carefully sliding it over her head.

It went on much easier than she expected. Willa turned to face the mirror, her breath catching in her throat.

"This isn't fair."

The dressing room door opened, and the saleswoman zipped her up.

"Let's show your friends." She gave Willa's hand a tight squeeze, leading her into the other room.

Lily and Beth both blinked back emotional tears.

"That's it!" Beth jumped up, hugging her.

Willa stared at herself in the mirror as a veil was placed on her head.

"How much is it?" Willa croaked.

"Fifteen hundred."

"It's too expensive. I'm sorry I wasted your time."

Lily stood, stopping her from leaving. "It's Beth's and my gift to you. Willa, the dress was made for you." Lily kissed her on the cheek, hugging her close.

"I can't accept—"

"Oh, yes, you can," Lily stopped her. "You've given us and the clubhouse enough cakes and candy to pay for the dress. Please, Willa, we both want you to have something special. You deserve a beautiful day."

"It's too much." Willa shook her head.

"I have an idea. If you don't feel comfortable wearing this one to the courthouse, you buy the other white dress to wear. Then wear this one to the reception at the church," Lily reasoned.

"We're not taking no for an answer. We're buying the dress, and you can wear which one you want Saturday." Beth motioned for the saleswoman who was exuberant at selling two dresses.

Willa stood as she was fitted then went back to the dressing room to put her clothes back on. She should go back outside and tell the women no then go home.

Willa returned to the front of the store with every intention of following through with her decision, but found Lily and Beth both waiting by the front door.

"We have to hurry, or you're going to miss your appointment with Sex Piston."

Beth and Lily both went outside.

Willa caught up with them at her van. "What appointment?"

"Don't you remember? Sex Piston made a hair appointment for you at her shop during your bachelorette party."

"I don't remember that. I'll call and cancel. I told Evie I would be gone an hour. I can't leave her babysitting while I get my hair done."

"She already knows." Lily opened the van door, climbing into the back, and Beth sat down in the passenger seat.

"This is going to be bad," Willa muttered, getting in behind the steering wheel.

"What did you say?" Beth's curious eyes stared at her as she started the van.

"This is going to be fun."

&#8270; &#8270;

Lucky disconnected the call. If Train called him one more time, he was going to drive to Ohio and kick his ass. Shade had won the bet, and none of the other brothers wanted to leave town. He also hadn't talked to Willa about the club, fulfilling his own side of the bet. He needed to tell her before Sissy did; leaving her without the information made Willa vulnerable.

He punched in Willa's number, and it took several rings before she answered.

"Hello?"

"We need to have a talk. Are you doing anything tonight?"

"I'm busy tonight. How about tomorrow? We could meet at my house at one. Leanne and Charlie will be at school, and the girls will be taking a nap."

"I'll see you then."

"All right."

Lucky hung up, already dreading the meeting. Willa was too innocent to understand the sexual side of the club. Worse still, she was going to be disgusted and angry that Sissy had found out. It was a good thing their engagement wasn't for real, because he had a feeling she was going to throw that cheap-ass ring at him.

When his cell phone rang again, he promised himself, if it was Train again, he was going to change his fucking number. Looking at the caller ID, however, he saw it was Knox.

"What's up, brother?"

"I have some good news. One of the investigators found the kids' relative, and he's flying in from Texas. I'm going to meet his plane in Lexington in the morning. We'll be in Treepoint by noon."

"He's willing to take the kids?"

"Yes, he owns a ranch and has a housekeeper. I checked him out, and the state will, too, before they give him custody of the children, but I don't see a problem. He's a bounty hunter who works his ranch until he's called out on a job. He said he'll take a couple of months off to get them settled before he goes back to work. He's used to catching felons on the run and has staff working on his ranch, so he doesn't think the kids are going to give him any trouble. Your ass is off the line."

"Willa's going to take it hard. She's grown attached to them."

"I agree. You want to tell her before I bring him by to meet them?"

"I'm meeting her tomorrow at one. Give me an hour to tell her."

"Will do. What about you? You still going to keep your bet with Shade?"

"Yes, I made the bet, and I'm going to keep it. Besides, I don't trust Sissy. She'll find a way to hurt Willa."

"I'll see you around two."

Lucky set the cell phone down before he was tempted to break it like he had the last one. He sat down on his chair, expecting to feel relief that the engagement would be broken, and Willa's conscience would be off the line for caring for the children. Instead, he was hurting so badly it was everything he could do not to find out where Willa was and go to her, check into the nearest motel, and show her exactly how he felt about her. He buried his head in his hands, breaking out in a cold sweat.

He couldn't listen to his heart and take the chance Willa would be hurt. He would tell Willa tomorrow. He would also check out the relative himself. It should only take a couple of days, and then he could finally tell Train he could come home as soon as he found a new pastor to take over.

Everyone would be happier in the long run—everyone but him.

# CHAPTER
# SEVENTEEN

"You're early," Willa stated, opening the door at Lucky's knock. Her hand went to Ria's head as the dog sat down next to her.

"I wanted to get it over with," Lucky stated coldly.

Her smile slipped when she saw the grim look on his face, and she opened the door wider for him to come inside. He walked into the living room then waited for her to join him, but her footsteps lagged. She could tell whatever he was going to tell her was bad.

Yesterday had been one of the best days of her life, losing herself with Beth and Lily by pretending for a short time that Lucky would marry her, help her keep the children, and in time fall in love with her. *Miracles happen every day, so it could happen*, she had told herself while Sex Piston had worked on her hair.

*"Bitch, who's been working on your hair?"*

*"I've gone to a couple of different beauty shops, and I experimented with color myself a few times," Willa apologized, brushing her hair away from her face.*

*Sex Piston ran her hands through her long hair, surveying it critically. "Can you fix it?"*

*"I can try. I'm good, but some of it's going to have to be cut. It's all different lengths from you going short too long."*

*"Cutting it is fine," Willa said miserably, knowing she kept it in a bun most of the time, anyway.*

*"We'll see what I can do. What color were you trying for?"*

*"I wanted blonde, but it washed me out and was hard to keep up. My brown is boring."*

*"I'm going to give you a mix of the two. It'll look hot when I'm done."*

Willa had been skeptical, but Sex Piston had come as close to hot as she was going to get. Her newfound confidence was sinking fast under Lucky's gaze, though.

"You cut your hair?"

"Some. Sex Piston evened it and layered it for me." She didn't constantly have to brush it back from her face.

Lucky didn't remark that he liked it like a normal fiancé would. Of course, there wasn't anything between them, so why should he be considerate of her feelings?

"What did you want to talk about?" Willa prompted him, beginning to think he disliked her hair.

Lucky cleared his throat before taking a seat on her couch. Willa felt tactless for not asking him to sit immediately. Her mother would criticize her lack of manners, like she criticized most things she did.

"Would you like something to drink? A cup of coffee?"

"Coffee would be good."

Willa went into the kitchen with Ria following behind her. She poured Lucky his coffee then went back into the living room, setting it down on the coffee table in front of him. Then she sank down on the couch with Ria sitting on her haunches next to her knees, and Willa absently rubbed the tense dog's back.

"Knox told me you found a dog."

"The kids have fallen in love with her. Leanne hasn't been feeling well. I think she may be allergic. It's going to be hard if we have to give her up."

*"We?"*

"I've grown attached to her. It's hard not to since she follows me everywhere. I've even started to let her go in the van when I make deliveries. She sits in the front seat. I never thought about owning a dog—"

"Knox found the children's uncle. His name is Travis Russell, his mother's second husband adopted him and gave Clay his name."

Willa's hand kept stroking the dog despite the shock of the bomb Lucky had just thrown at her.

The children would be taken from her. She had known deep down their relative would be located sooner or later, but she had hoped it would be after the kids were grown and in college. She had told herself not to become attached, yet each day that passed had made her love them more.

"When will he be here?"

Lucky looked down at his watch. "In forty-five minutes."

"He won't just take them, will he? Chrissy and Caroline will be frightened. Charlie and Leanne will be, too. They'll pretend they're not, but they will be."

"The transition will be gradual. Travis has taken off two months so the children can become comfortable with him. Knox has checked him out, and the state will, too, before they give him custody."

"What about Sissy?" Willa hadn't seen the girl since she had gone to live with Knox and Diamond.

"Sissy turns eighteen in a few months, but I assume she'll want to go to Tyler, Texas with her sister and cousins. If she doesn't decide to live with them, she may decide to live nearby."

"Tyler, Texas?"

Lucky nodded his head.

"Texas will be good for Sissy." Willa bit her lip, deciding she would wait until tonight to cry. "There isn't a reason for our engagement to continue. You must be relieved."

"Let me know how much the dress you bought yesterday cost, and I'll give you back your money."

"It wasn't expensive. I don't need you to pay for the dress."

"If that's what you want."

Willa could tell he wanted to keep arguing about the dress, but he had decided not to press her into accepting his money.

After Willa took the diamond ring off, handing it to Lucky, he placed it in his suit pocket. It seemed almost business-like the way he was talking to her, while her heart was being shredded by the second.

Willa wished he would leave. It would be easier to put up a front in front of Knox and Travis Russell.

"Willa, despite our engagement ending, I feel there's something I need to tell you."

What more was there to explain beyond the fact that she was losing the children and Lucky? Was he going to throw in her face again that he knew she was secretly in love with him and he didn't return her feelings? Willa didn't think she was strong enough to maintain her composure if he showed her any pity. Then another fear of hers struck.

"Did Knox find Ria's owner?" Was she going to lose the only thing she had left to love?

"No, I wasn't talking about the dog." His lips firmed. "I want to tell you the truth about the night Sissy ran away."

She stared at him in surprise. "The truth?"

"She made it to Rosey's, but Mick didn't find her in his car. He found her hiding in one of the back rooms. Jenna had let her in the back door and served her beer. Mick's a friend, and we didn't want him to lose his license."

The bar's owner attended the church, and Willa had sat with him several times. Mick was a nice man. She couldn't imagine he would deliberately serve a minor.

"I won't say anything. I like Mick."

"It's not you I'm worried about talking; it's Sissy."

Willa frowned. "If she's not said anything before now, why would she?"

"To hurt you. She's not going to open her mouth to the authorities about the liquor, but she hates you."

Willa winced. "She's told me several times, but how can she hurt me now? I don't have custody of her any longer."

"By telling you what Jenna told her and what she overheard the brothers talking about that night." Lucky started to touch her hand but pulled back, shoving his hands into his jacket pockets. "Willa, The Last Riders allow women to become members."

"Lily, Beth, Winter, Evie, Jewell, Bliss, and the other women are all members, I know."

"Do you know how they become members?"

"No. Is there a process?"

"Yes, there is. Our club is different. There are eight original members of The Last Riders who formed the club and decided to let the women join. We use votes to make our decision if they will fit into the club, and there are three different ways to gain votes." Lucky paused, his expression cautious as he waited for her reaction. "The women have sex with six out of the eight to become members. Each of the six counts as a vote. They don't have to have sex. If the men come from watching them having sex, that counts as a vote. The third way is to earn markers from the original members. Each marker counts as a vote."

Willa tried to comprehend what he was telling her. As she repeated his words in her mind, she began laughing. Leaning over, Willa buried her face in Ria's dark fur.

"Willa?" Lucky's hand touched her shoulder.

She raised her head, jerking away from his touch.

"Who are the eight original members?" She stifled her laughter, waiting for his answer.

"We don't disclose that information to non-members, but Sissy found out, so I'm going to tell you. Razer, Viper, Knox, Shade, Rider, Train, Cash, and me. Viper's brother was one, but he died. We recently voted for Crash to have voting rights."

"Jenna told Sissy this?" Willa wanted to scream at Lucky. Thankfully, her emotions were becoming numb.

"Yes. Jenna knew because she had tried to become a member, but she couldn't get enough votes."

"She had your vote, didn't she?"

Lucky didn't look away from her. "Yes."

Willa bit back the hysterical laughter that threatened to break loose again.

"There's more."

Willa held her hand up. "Please, don't."

Lucky ignored her, continuing. Willa wanted to cover her ears; instead, she listened to Lucky as he finished ripping the veil away from her eyes, exposing his and the club's secrets.

"The club has parties on Friday nights. The best way to describe them is they are sex parties where everyone has sex and watches others. Moon and Rider had gone to Rosey's, and Sissy overheard them talking about watching me have sex with Raci, Story, and Ember. They were also discussing how I use knives on the women."

Willa paled. "You cut them?"

"I'm a master at knife play. I don't cut. I use the knives to stimulate the women, not hurt them."

Willa couldn't hold back her laughter any longer, falling back against the couch. "Oh, my God. I was so jealous of Beth and Jenna when I wasn't even competing against just one woman, but dozens."

"You were jealous of Beth and Jenna? There was no reason for you to—"

"You're exactly right. You have made it obvious you aren't attracted to me. Our pretend engagement gave me no rights. You have been openly honest about your feelings for me. I was the one who fell in love with you, not the other way around."

"Don't." Lucky tried to touch her again but she stood up, moving away from his touch.

Ria moved to stand next to her, and a warning growl had Willa glancing down at the dog. However, the sharp command that came from Lucky had the dog sitting again, relaxing against her.

"What did you do?"

"I told her to sit. Ria's a protection dog. I bought her so you would be protected when we became engaged. Willa, I have enemies. I'm a—"

"How much did she cost? I'll pay you back for her." Willa skirted around him, going to the entry table to take out her checkbook.

"I don't want your fucking money. I bought her so you would be protected—"

"I don't need your protection; I can take care of myself. How much?" Willa practically screamed at him.

"Twenty thousand."

A sob had her clutching her checkbook. "You paid twenty thousand dollars for a dog?"

"Ria is highly trained. Colt gave me a discount because we served together."

"I'm surprised he's not a member of The Last Riders. Maybe you should have let him in so he would give you a better discount." Willa stared down blankly at her checkbook.

"I don't want the money, and the dog is yours. I want to explain why—"

Willa set the checkbook down on the table. "Lucky, I've had more explanations than I can take in one day. I can't give you the dog immediately; the children will want to say good-bye—"

"I'm not going to take the fucking dog." He started toward her, but a knock sounded on the door, startling them both.

"That will be Knox and Mr. Russell. I would appreciate it if you left. I don't need your help."

"I'll go. I know you're upset, and I don't want to make it worse by staying."

Willa moved to answer the door. Her hand was on the doorknob when Lucky stopped her.

"I won't take Ria back."

"It's not your decision to make. This time, it's my choice that matters." Willa had grown attached to the dog, but did she really want the constant reminder that Lucky had given her Ria every time she looked at her? Whichever choice she made, Willa worried it was going to be painful. After all, it was going to be difficult enough seeing Lucky around town.

Who would pay twenty thousand dollars for a dog? Obviously a man who wouldn't know a good deal when it bit him on the butt.

Willa looked at the dog hopefully. "Would you bite him on the butt if I asked you to?"

# Chapter Eighteen

Travis Russell was a rugged man and nothing like his half-sister and brother. He was always polite and respectful and handled the children sternly yet fairly. Over the last month and a half, the younger girls had already fallen in love with him, and even Leanne and Charlie, though slower to accept him, were growing more comfortable in his presence. Charlie was especially excited when he found out his uncle was an adept video game player. They spent thirty minutes a day playing before Travis would grab the football he had bought Charlie and take him and the rest of the kids to the park. She would remain behind, giving them their alone time.

Each day, she felt them growing farther away from her as they began looking for their uncle when they woke up. Willa had, after the second day he had visited, invited him to stay at her house. He learned their schedules, and the last two mornings, she had awoken to find breakfast cooked and Caroline and Chrissy eating their oatmeal and toast.

Since he was at her house, Flora had gained permission for Sissy to return until their departure in two weeks. The girl wasn't happy about it, but her attitude was checked by Travis, who would tell her to go to her room and then deny her the use of her electronics. The first time, she had smarted off to him, and he had given her a warning, telling her ladies her age should know how to behave. The second time, Sissy had smarted off to Willa, and he had picked her phone up, which had been sitting next to her at the kitchen table, and tossed it into the garbage disposal. Sissy's mouth had fallen open, but she had been polite since, at least in front of Travis.

ༀ ༃

Willa pushed the buggy down the grocery aisle, looking sideways at the lean cowboy walking next to her, pushing the grocery cart that resembled a fire truck. The girls were buckled in, taking turns tugging on the rope to ring the plastic bell. Leanne and Charlie had remained at home after returning from having lunch with their uncle.

With Travis's help with the children, it didn't take long before they were checked out and rolling the carts filled with groceries to her van.

Willa turned her head when she recognized a truck that had pulled in and parked a few spaces from her.

Shade, Lucky, and Lily got out. There was no way to avoid them. It wouldn't have bothered her not speaking to Lucky, but she couldn't bring herself to be rude to Lily and Shade.

"Hi, Lily, Shade."

"Hi, Willa," Lily responded while Shade gave her a nod.

"Willa."

"Lucky," she returned his greeting without looking at him.

The three didn't move on, and Willa was forced to introduce Travis.

Lily's eyes didn't budge from the tall Texan, who was wearing faded jeans, scuffed boots, a T-shirt, and a cowboy hat.

"Where are you from?"

"Tyler, Texas, ma'am."

Lily's eyes widened.

"He owns a ranch where the children will be moving with him in a couple of weeks. He's staying with me and the children until they leave," Willa explained.

"In your house?"

Lucky's sharp question had Travis raising a brow in his direction.

"Yes. That way, he can get to know the kids better, and it won't be as traumatic when they leave." Willa was angry at herself for caring that he might get the wrong impression of Travis staying with her.

"Do you have horses?" Lily asked, breaking the tense silence.

"Wouldn't be called a ranch if I didn't."

"We need to hurry, Lily. We don't want to leave John alone for long with Raci babysitting."

"It was nice—" Lily was tugged away before she could finish her sentence.

Willa started to push the buggy forward, but was blocked by Lucky.

"If you need any help packing their things, I could come by."

"No, thanks. Travis and I have it under control." Willa shoved the buggy forward, leaving Lucky to decide whether to get run over or move. Wisely, he moved out of the way, walking into the store.

Travis helped her buckle the girls into their car seats then load the groceries into the van before opening the passenger door for her then getting in on the driver's side. As he pulled out of the parking lot, Willa saw Lucky staring out the window of the grocery store.

"He an old boyfriend?"

"No," Willa choked out.

"Want me to go back and punch him for you?"

Willa had to think about it for a minute then decided the good, Christian girl couldn't see Lucky get hurt.

"You think it would be that easy?" she teased.

"Ma'am, I chase criminals for a living, so he would be a piece of cake. No pun intended."

Willa laughed, thankful he was sticking around for a while. He was good company, and while she still missed Lucky, at least Travis had kept her from moping around all day. By the time Travis left, she probably wouldn't miss Lucky anymore. Unconsciously, she crossed her fingers in her lap.

ᘔ ᘓ

Willa placed the cake carefully into the cake box just as the doorbell rang. Closing the box, she hurried to her door.

"Hi, Douglas. Come on in."

"The cake's ready? I can come back later if it isn't."

"I just finished." Willa shut the door, motioning him toward the kitchen. "How are Angus and Myrtle doing this afternoon?"

"They're so excited. I told Myrtle to take an extra blood pressure pill and gave Angus a beer. Their daughter is visiting and bringing her kids, and it has them excited. Myrtle said thanks for fitting her in on short notice."

"They've been keeping you busy?"

"Myrtle always finds something to keep me busy." Douglas was the older couple's handyman, and he kept an eye on them since their children all lived out of town.

Willa pointed at the pink box on the counter. "Would you like a cup of coffee before you go?"

She didn't give him time to answer, going behind the counter to pour him a cup.

"I really don't have the time."

Willa turned to glance over her shoulder as Douglas started to reach into his back pocket.

"No charge. It's my present to them."

"They gave me the money…" Again, he reached for his back pocket.

"Then you can give it back." She gave him an unconsciously sad smile. "Are you sure you can't stay for coffee? I could use the company."

177

Douglas opened his mouth to say something, but was interrupted by a scratching at the back door.

"Excuse me." Willa opened the back door, letting Ria inside.

The dog sniffed the air and began growling.

"Halt."

Ria sat down on her haunches without taking her eyes off her.

"Did you just call her off?" Douglas's eyes narrowed on the dog.

"Yes. Isn't she smart?"

He stared at the dog warily, taking a seat at her counter. "I'll take that coffee."

"I'm glad." Willa placed the coffee in front of him.

"When did you get a dog? You didn't have one the last time I stopped by and picked up Angus's and Myrtle's anniversary cake."

"I've only had her a few weeks." Willa poured herself a cup of coffee then, standing on the opposite side of the counter, facing Douglas.

"Pretty dog," he stated, taking a drink of his coffee.

Tears blurred her vision, but Willa blinked to get rid of them.

"Are you all right?" The man sat stupefied as she burst into tears.

"I'm sorry. I didn't mean to start crying. I have to give Ria back to Lucky, and my kids are going out to dinner tonight with their uncle." Willa began to cry harder. "They really like him."

"That isn't a good thing?" He set his cup down on the counter.

"It is." Willa nodded her head, crying harder. "I want them to like him, but I don't want to lose them, either. He's going to take them back to Tyler, Texas with him next week. I thought it would take longer, like maybe six months." Willa brushed the tears away from her cheeks.

"Where are they now?" Douglas glanced around the kitchen, as if hoping someone would rescue him.

"Travis, their uncle, took Caroline and Chrissy to the park." The tears began again. "I tried to get him to stay here with them and play, but he thought it would be a good idea to spend some alone time with them."

"I bet he did," Douglas muttered. "Your upcoming wedding will give you something—" His coffee cup paused halfway to his mouth when a sob escaped Willa's mouth.

She waved her empty ring finger in front of his face. "I'm not engaged anymore."

"I'm sorry to hear that."

"Don't be. He's a jerk…" Willa began hiccupping while tearing a paper towel off the roll. Then she wiped her face, finally catching her breath.

Seeing the expression on his face, she began laughing.

"I'm so sorry, Douglas. I didn't mean to fall apart in front of you. Here." Willa turned to the side of her counter, easily putting together a cupcake box and slipping a cupcake inside. "I hope this makes up for all the crying." She gave him a sweet smile that had him pausing as he stood.

"Depends on what flavor it is…"

"S'more." Willa set the smaller box on top of the larger one.

"That'll do it." He lifted the boxes, going to the front door. "See you around, Willa, and you can tell that ex-fiancé of yours for me that he's an idiot."

She smiled up at him. Then, before she could change her mind, placed a brief kiss on his cheek. "Thanks. I needed that."

He gave her a stunned look before smiling back. "I did, too."

# Chapter Nineteen

The time for Travis and the children to leave came much sooner than Willa anticipated. They were loading the children's suitcase into the van when Curt Dawkins pulled up at Jenna's house, which was now his since the sale had gone through the week before. He didn't look in their direction as he went inside his new home.

"Be careful of him," Travis warned. "I don't like the way he looks at you when you're in your backyard."

"I know exactly what kind of man Curt is, and I'm as close to him as I want to be."

Willa climbed into the van, trying hard not to cry on the ride to the airport. It was going to be gut-wrenching to let the children go, but deep inside, Willa acknowledged that the children would be happier. They could leave Treepoint behind and all the gossip they would have to face about their parents. With them gone, maybe Georgia and Lewis would become a part of the past.

"Do you think you'll ever come back to Treepoint?" Willa just had to ask.

"Doubtful. I would be willing to send you a plane ticket any time you want to visit, though."

His bluntness was hard, but she would rather have it then promises that wouldn't be kept.

"I may take you up on that."

"I hope so. If you come, try to talk Lily into coming with you. Tell her I'll teach her how to ride a horse."

"I can't." Willa leaned her head back on the headrest. "I don't want to make the kids orphans again."

‰ ‰

Lucky entered the crowded diner. Searching the tables, he saw Viper and Shade sitting at one of the back ones. He strode forward, sitting down at the table across from Shade.

"You're late."

Lucky's mouth twisted at Shade's impatience. "What's the hurry? Lily's still at the church store."

"Had to leave John with Raci."

"What's wrong with that?"

"Last time I let her babysit, she lost his paci and his blanket. I'm worried she'll lose my kid."

He waved the waitress away. "What did you need?" He glanced at Viper.

"I'm sending Moon back to Ohio. It's either bring Train back or kill the fucker."

"I'm looking for someone to take my place at the church, but no one's biting. It's taking longer than I anticipated."

"If you weren't being so picky, it would have been done and you gone. What the fuck is taking so long?"

"I don't know. It could be the fact that there's only a little over a hundred attending church or the fact that the pastor salary we can offer is for shit. Or it could be that the only mall is a three-hour drive away," Lucky said sarcastically.

"What does a mall matter to a pastor?" Viper asked.

"It doesn't, but it usually does to his wife. I'll make some more calls when I get back to the church, schedule a few more on-calls."

"The women are missing having you around with Train gone."

"I miss the club, too."

"How's that vow of chastity going?" Shade sneered.

"Shut up, Shade."

"You could sneak out to the clubhouse every now and then. No one would know."

"I would," Lucky stated. As long as he was the church pastor, he would not break the vow he had retaken when he had returned to the church to help Willa.

"I've always been curious about something." Shade leaned across the table. "Does your vow mean no hand jobs?" The bastard's snicker was the last straw.

Lucky came out of his chair and Viper rose, pushing him back down.

"Cut it out, Shade."

Shade shrugged. "He's too sensitive. Must be those blue balls of his."

Lucky gave Shade a saccharine smile. "Lily made my lunch for me today."

Shade's blue eyes darkened, his relaxed air disappearing.

"Lucky..." Viper warned.

"She even put extra sugar in my coffee, just the way I like it."

Lucky's chair fell backward as he escaped before Shade could punch him, nearly knocking Knox over as he was coming into the diner.

"What the fuck?"

"Sorry, Knox. Glad to see you, brother." He slapped Knox on the back then placed his arm over the brother's shoulder, which wasn't easy. Lucky gave Shade a shit-eating grin as he came outside with Viper trying to hold him back.

"One of these days, you're going to push me too far, and I'll catch your ass before you can get away."

"Ain't gonna happen," Lucky gloated, his expression turning serious once he saw Willa walking from the church parking lot and crossing the street toward him with Ria following next to her.

The expression on Willa's face was neutral, but the wounded pain in her eyes had him stiffening, his arm dropping from Knox's shoulder.

"I was about to go inside the church when I saw you."

Lucky remained silent.

"Hello, Willa," the other three men greeted.

She nodded her head in their direction.

"Did Travis and the children's plane get off all right?" Knox questioned.

Willa's face broke into a pain-filled mask. "Yes, thank you. I just got back." Her hand holding Ria's leash thrust toward Lucky. "Here."

Lucky refused to take the leash from her hand. "She's your dog."

Willa dropped the leash. "I told you that it wasn't your choice. Stay, Ria." A lone tear slid down her cheek as she began to cross the street.

Lucky started to go after her, but Shade pulled him back. "She'll come back. Wait."

Lucky held his breath as Willa stepped up onto the curb on the other side of the road. When she reached her van, her hand was on the door handle before she turned around, coming back toward them.

"I told you I knew Willa," Shade said softly, his hand dropping from his arm.

She had just stepped off the sidewalk, brushing her tears away, when the sound of a loud motor resonated through the air. Everyone froze except Ria as Lyle's tow truck came flying down the street.

Lucky and Shade began running but he knew they wouldn't be able to reach Willa in time. Willa screamed in terror as the tow truck headed straight for her.

"Willa!" Lucky screamed in agony, desperately trying to reach her in time.

Ria ran out in the street her four legs easily out distancing the men racing to save Willa.

Willa screamed out the command for the dog to stop but Ria kept running, jumping up she knocked Willa backwards onto the sidewalk. The tow truck struck the brave dog before hitting the pole coming to a crashing stop.

"God, please let her be okay…please…" Lucky was unaware of the agony in the prayers falling from his lips as he and Shade ran to the other side of the tow truck. Seeing Willa laying on the ground took twenty years off his life, as he fell to his knees beside her.

Lyle began moving inside the truck, trying to open the truck door.

"Don't move, Lyle!" Viper shouted to no avail.

The door came open and the town drunk fell out onto the road.

"Go take care of him, before I decide to kill him myself." Lucky ordered Shade.

Willa's frightened eyes opened, staring up into his.

"Is Lyle alright?" She asked shakily.

"For now." Lucky gritted out helping Willa to her feet.

"Ria!" Willa screamed, trying to get to the dog laying pinned underneath the tow truck.

He swept her up, backing away as fast as he could. "Don't look, I've got you."

Willa wound her arms tightly around his neck, screaming out Ria's name. Her hysterical cries brought tears to his own eyes, seeing the dog couldn't be helped.

Sirens filled the air as the ambulance arrived. Lucky ignored the pandemonium, carrying Willa inside the church while she sobbed, each one like a lash against his soul.

He talked softly to her as he walked through the church, carrying her to the part that was his home. Lucky laid her down on the bed then lay next to her, pulling her into his arms. He rocked her as she cried, his hands smoothing over her body to soothe her while checking to make sure she was all right.

"Sh…You're going to make yourself sick," Lucky whispered.

"Is…Ria dead?"

He knew Willa already knew the answer, but when you loved something, any chance was worth the pain of the answer.

"Yes, Willa, she's gone. I'm so sorry, baby."

She lay against his side, crying until she gradually quieted, falling asleep. Lucky continued to hold her as he stared up at the ceiling.

Some choices in life you made for yourself, and some choices were made for you. Seeing Willa nearly killed in the split-second before Ria had saved her had helped him finally make the choice he had been struggling with since the day he had stared down from the pulpit and seen Willa.

That day, the sunlight had made a halo over her, and he had imagined for a moment one of the angels from the paintings on the walls had become real and was sitting a few feet away. Although she had glanced away when her shy gaze had been caught by his, Lucky had felt as if her soul was calling to him, trying to capture his soul without words.

"Thank you." Lucky closed his eyes, giving thanks for the life saved and for the soul that had returned from the dead.

# CHAPTER TWENTY

Willa blinked her swollen eyes as she woke, finding Lucky's hand cupping her cheek, his thumb caressing the smooth flesh.

"You okay?"

She nodded her head against his hand before sitting up on the mattress, looking around the room.

"Where am I?" Her throat felt raw.

"My bedroom." He sat up on the side of the bed.

Her eyes turned to the side as he stood and stretched. He glanced over his shoulder. He had taken off his suit jacket and was wearing only his pants and white shirt. He had unbuttoned the top buttons, exposing his gleaming skin. At the base of his throat was a tattoo that she couldn't make out.

She slid across the bed. "I need to go home."

He slid his feet into his shoes before holding his hand out to her. "I'll take you."

Willa slipped her hand into his, and he helped her rise to her feet. He steadied her while she slipped her shoes on. Then she followed him from his bedroom, down the hallway, and to the door that led outside.

She pulled back when he would have opened the door. He placed his arm around her shoulder, pulling her close to his side.

"The wreck has been cleaned up," he said, letting the words silently tell her Ria's body had been removed.

"Where is she...?" Willa's voice broke, but she managed to keep from shedding any more tears. Her aching heart felt as though she didn't have any more to give.

"Knox buried her in Cash's family cemetery."

Willa liked the thought of her dog not being alone. She saw the sun in the sky. "What time is it?" Her voice broke despite her best efforts.

"It's morning. You slept through the night. Do you want to go to the diner and get some breakfast?"

"No." The thought of food made her stomach heave.

Lucky led her to his SUV.

"I can take my van," Willa protested as Lucky opened the passenger door.

"Get in. I'll see that your van's at your house by lunch."

She sat down, letting him shut the door. When Lucky had gotten behind the steering wheel and pulled out onto the main street, Willa closed her eyes tightly.

His hand took hers in a tight clasp. "We're past the spot." His low voice gave her the courage to open her eyes.

"I saw Lily and Rachel at the church store yesterday before…"

Lucky's mouth tightened. "They heard the crash. Thank God Rachel was there. She wouldn't let Lily out the door. Rachel had to push her back. She said they didn't see anything."

"I'm glad. I wouldn't want Lily and Rachel to have that in their head."

Lucky pulled into her driveway, bringing the Yukon to a stop. "Like it's in yours?"

"I keep seeing Ria, she saved my life." She was wrong; she did have more tears left. As another one found its way down her cheek, Lucky wiped it away with a tender smile.

"Yes, she did."

"Do you think she knew I was coming back for her?" Willa's voice broke.

"Yes, I do."

"What do I tell the kids when they call and ask about her?"

"Tell them she found a better home."

Willa agreed it would be kinder to not tell them. Besides, the dog would eventually slip from their memories as they made new ones.

"She was the only dog I ever had."

"I can get you another—"

Willa vehemently shook her head. "I don't ever want another one. She can't be replaced."

Lucky stared down at her with a look she didn't understand. "No, she can't."

Willa didn't think he was talking about Ria anymore. Taking a deep breath, she reached for the door handle.

"Willa?" She turned back to him. "Will you go out with me tonight? We can go to dinner at King's."

Willa's heart gave a lurch before she made herself calm down. "I'll be fine, Lucky. I don't need you to take me out to dinner to make me feel better."

"Ria isn't the reason I'm asking you out. I want to go out like a normal couple."

"I don't know…"

"Willa, you almost died yesterday, and there wasn't a fucking thing I could do to prevent it. Please just give me a chance. That's all I'm asking for now. Can you do that?"

"I can do that," she said softly, unable to resist his husky entreaty.

"Good. I'll pick you up at six."

"Okay." Willa slid out of the SUV then watched as he pulled out until he turned the corner back to the church.

She might be making a mistake by going out with Lucky, but she was done running. This time, she was going to stand still and see what happened.

ಬಿ ಲಿ

Lucky walked through the front of the clubhouse. He had called Viper after he had dropped Willa off to ask for the club meeting, and now the members were waiting for him in the packed kitchen.

Viper was standing in the TV area with the other six original members as Lucky walked up to them, coming to a stop. He reached into his pant pocket, pulling out two sets of bike keys, handing one set to his president.

"Lucky..." Viper's eyes went to his hand.

"My cut is in the saddlebag."

"Brother, don't."

"I can't be a brother and have Willa, too. I love her, Viper. I always have."

The club members were silent, listening to every word.

"It doesn't have to be either. You could choose both," Shade spoke up.

"Yes, it does. For me to have Willa, it does."

Lucky heard the women in the background crying.

"I don't give a fuck if you wear our cut or not; you'll always be a brother. I love you, man." Viper took the keys from him then pulled him in for a tight hug before releasing him. The other brothers crowded around him, each saying their good-byes. However, Shade stood still with his arms crossed against his chest.

Lucky gave Rider the second set of keys when it was his turn, but the man refused at first to take them back.

"We both know I cheated in the first place. I was never going to let Moon have her."

"Brother, the only one who didn't know was you."

Lucky slapped Train on the shoulder. "Glad you're back. The women were having a hard time without you."

Train's dark eyes held the emotions that the former Seal would never reveal. They had been together since the service, and their bond would last until death. "Wasn't the same without you guys."

Lucky nodded then smacked Knox on the shoulder, grinning up at the brother wearing the police uniform. "I'm never going to get used to seeing you in that get-up."

"I'm getting used to it. You'll have to borrow one of the deputies' uniforms some time. Makes Diamond hornier than hell."

Lucky laughed. "I'll keep that in mind."

Cash and Razer both gave him grins before nearly breaking his ribs with their hugs. When he managed to break their grips, he turned to the women giving each a brief hug. Lucky went to the door where he stopped and looked back at Shade, who had made no move to tell him good-bye.

"Lucky, I told you that you don't know shit about Willa."

He stopped, turning back to Shade. "It's myself I finally figured out. It's what I want, too."

"Yeah?"

"Yes," Lucky said truthfully.

"You're sure?"

"I'm sure."

"What about Bridge?"

"I'm going to deal with him. You made your promise, and I expect you to keep it," Lucky reminded the enforcer.

"I made that promise to a brother."

# CHAPTER
# TWENTY-ONE

"I am not going swimming." Willa stared ahead mutinously.

"Yes, you are. It's hot as hell today, and where I'm taking you is private."

"Just because I've been seeing you for three months, it doesn't mean I have to listen to you."

*Until Lucky sees me naked, I'm not giving him any rights over me,* Willa thought to herself.

She cast a quick glance at his hard profile as he drove. The most intimate thing they had done during the time they spent together was the kiss he would place on her lips as he was leaving. It was respectful and chaste, but it was also darn frustrating. Her mother and father would have been happy at his courtly behavior. Her, not so much since she couldn't figure out if it was because he cared for her or if it was because he wasn't attracted to her.

She didn't have any other dating experiences to compare it to, so she would often dissect their dates for hours after he had left as she lay in her lonely bed. They saw each other almost every day, spending hours in each other's company. They would go for walks and watch television, but during all the time they spent together, he had never tried to take their relationship to a more intimate level.

A few times, she had even tried to tempt him, though she was ashamed to admit it. She would part her lips when he kissed her, but he would pull back. One time, she had even been brazen enough to sit down next to him on the couch close enough that the side of her breast had brushed his arm. She had hoped he would turn and give her a passionate kiss. However, he had merely scooted over so he was no longer touching her.

She had begun to believe he was going to The Last Riders' clubhouse to see the women there, but he hadn't. She knew this because Lily and Beth, whom she saw at the church store when she stopped in, had told her that he had left the club. When she had mentioned it to him, he had told her that he still saw the men in town and frequently hung out at the diner with them.

She had asked him, "Why did you stop being a Last Rider?"

And he had answered, "If I were to hang out at the clubhouse, would you believe I wasn't with any of the women?"

Willa couldn't answer without lying, so she had remained quiet.

"That's why I didn't want that in your head." He had taken her hand. "The clubhouse isn't about the sex, Willa. It's about the brothers having your back when you need them. That's why people in the military have such a hard time adjusting when they get out. They're used to that camaraderie, being up each other's ass all the time. We're loners, and we respect each other's privacy when we need it, but it's nice to be able to walk into a room and be surrounded by friends just sitting around, shooting the shit, drinking a beer."

"I don't want you to give that up because of me," Willa had protested.

"I didn't give it up just for you. I gave it up for the church, too. Do you see the parishioners letting me be pastor while belonging to The Last Riders?"

"But they all know you lived there when you gave the church up."

"That was different. They love to forgive a reformed sinner as long as the sinner doesn't go back for their fix."

Willa had wondered if Lucky knew how telling his statement had been by comparing The Last Riders to an addiction.

Like an addict, Lucky was trying to stay away from the worst part of his addiction—the clubhouse. It was what drew them together and made them whole. It gave them their bonds that would be hard to break. Then again, Lucky seemed to be happy with his choice, and Willa didn't want to keep dwelling on his decision if it was truly what he wanted.

He still spent time with them, and when she saw them around town, they were all friendly, asking how she was doing since the children had left. During the holidays, they had even had a big party at King's restaurant to celebrate, saying it was much easier to cook and fit everyone in there. However, Willa thought it was because they didn't want to leave Lucky out.

Willa blinked back tears, turning her head to look out the window at the passing scenery, trying to shake the thoughts from her head.

"What are you thinking?"

Willa gathered her composure before turning back to him. "I was just thinking it's a beautiful day."

Lucky parked his SUV on the private land near the lake. Getting out, he took out the picnic basket she had placed in the backseat before opening her door.

"Are you going to sit there all day?"

His good mood was beginning to get on her nerves.

"I'm thinking about it." She was too embarrassed to tell him she didn't want him to see her in her swimsuit.

"While you're thinking about it, I'm going swimming."

Lucky set the basket down on the picnic table before taking off his T-shirt, already wearing his swim trunks. He walked into the cool water until it was deep enough to dive underneath. When he came up, he shook his hair out of his face.

"What kind of freaking pastor has tattoos?" she said to herself as she slid out of the SUV, tempted to start it with the keys he had left in the ignition and leave his butt in the lake. She almost giggled to herself, imagining his expression if she did.

She sat down at the picnic table, taking a bottled water out of the basket. She began to get hot sitting in the sun, wishing the table was in the shade. It was only April, but a hot spell had fallen over Kentucky, and the temperature was reaching the nineties.

Looking at the water, she saw Lucky floating lazily with his face turned up to the sky.

"I hope his nose gets burned." She had plastered a whole bottle of sun block on herself before he had picked her up.

She saw the tats on his shoulder and back as he began swimming. Darn it, was she ever going to be able to see them closely? It was always a flash here or there. He would catch her looking at them and lift a brow, and she would look away quickly, but the jerk knew she had been staring.

"I'm melting." Willa brushed the dampness off her forehead. Glancing back at the water, she was determined to tell Lucky she'd had enough, only to see his body gone. Willa stood up, her eyes searching the lake. When she didn't see him, she yelled out.

"Lucky?"

Willa didn't hear a sound. Becoming more frightened, she began walking closer to the water.

"LUCKY?"

The silence made her even more frightened. She began running into the water, searching frantically for him, going deeper and deeper. How long did it take someone to drown? Wouldn't he have called out if he had a leg cramp? Could he have hit his head when he had gone under water?

A hand wrapped around her ankle, pulling her under the water before letting go. Willa gasped when she came up, seeing the mischievous look on Lucky's face.

"You ass!" She hit him on his chest with her fists. "You scared me to death! I thought you drowned!" Furiously, she put her hands on his head, pushing him back underneath. If the asshole wanted to pretend to drown, she would freaking help him.

Arms circled her waist, lifting her up into the air before tossing her backward. Her squeal was cut short when her mouth filled with water. She came up, sputtering water, her eyes narrowed in determination.

Her hands gripped his shoulders, and she used all her weight to sink him to the bottom of the lake. Lucky's body twined with hers, his mouth finding hers in a passionate kiss that had her not caring if she drowned. Finally, he pulled them to the surface, releasing her mouth.

"Are you trying to kill me?" she sputtered.

"I'm trying to get you to have some fun."

Willa slung her wet hair back from her face. "You seriously think this is fun? Is our next date at the dentist's office?"

Willa couldn't help joining in with his laughter as he pulled her closer to him. His hands went to her waist, tugging at the large T-shirt she had put over her swimsuit.

"What are you doing?" She tried to wiggle away yet was unable to before she found her T-shirt swimming away.

"Taking off that raft."

"Are you insulting my clothes?"

"Just that T-shirt. It's ugly as shit."

Willa hadn't thought the bright yellow shirt was that bad. She had found it on the clearance rack at a high-end store. She hadn't believed her luck when she had found one in her size. *Well, it might have been a little too large*, she thought to herself, seeing it float away.

"Aren't you going to get it for me?"

"Hell no. Just think of how many lives it will save," Lucky replied with a grin.

"It's a good thing I'm a good Christian, or I would let you have it," she said, not liking the fixed gleam in his eyes as he moved closer. "Don't you dare."

As his hands went to her waist, tugging at her shorts, she screamed in frustration.

"I'm going to kick your butt, and I'm big enough to do it," she threatened to no avail, seeing her black shorts float away seconds later.

His laughter was cut short when she splashed water into his face. Before he could react, she began swimming toward the bank.

"I'm going to see your ass when you get out of the water," Lucky yelled at her back.

She quit swimming.

"Darn it." Her fist hit the water angrily, spraying it into her face.

Lucky's arms circled her waist from behind, pressing his chest against her back. His hand flattened against her stomach. Then she felt it curve around the bulge that several hours on her treadmill wouldn't get rid of, making her self-conscious.

She felt his lips exploring the side of her neck as he pressed even closer to her backside, and her hands clutched his at the wrists, trying to pull them away.

"Siren... You're so beautiful."

Weakly, her head fell back against his shoulder, wondering which was burning her worse—the sun or Lucky. Both were going to burn her alive and leave their mark if she didn't move away from his touch.

"Lucky…"

The tips of his fingers slid under the band of her swimsuit, not moving farther. The small intimacy made her shake in the shallow water as he tugged her back into the deeper part of the lake before turning her around to face him. His hand glided around to her back, his fingertips brushing at the top of her butt.

Her nails dug into the flesh of his shoulder. "I can't—"

"Sh…Siren, trust me." His lips took hers gently, letting her set the pace of the first kiss they'd shared since the night of her bachelorette party.

The peace of the lake made her feel as if they were the only two people in existence as she parted her lips, letting him explore her mouth with the glide of his tongue. Her own traced his bottom lip, nipping it softly, and a groan sounded from deep within his chest.

"Did I hurt you?"

"Siren, the only thing that hurts is how badly I want you."

"Why do you call me siren?"

"Because your soul calls to mine."

"What does it say?" Willa teased.

"It says, I love you." Revealing that he was more then aware that she was in love with him.

As her face turned serious, she started to turn away from his intent gaze.

"My soul calls to yours, too," he continued.

"It does?"

Lucky nodded his head.

"What does it say?" Willa whispered, her breath catching in her throat.

"It says, I love you, too."

"Lucky…" She didn't know how to respond to his admission, too afraid to believe he really loved her. Doubt began to rear its head, making her believe he couldn't love her...a woman so different from the other women he had been with.

"Don't, siren. I know exactly what my soul is telling me. My stomach, too."

"What's your stomach saying?"

"Feed me."

"That one, I believe." Willa laughed as Lucky waded out of the water.

She stopped in her tracks, seeing the tats covering his back all the way down to his feet. She swallowed hard as he bent down to pick up his T-shirt, sliding it over his head.

"Dammit." She had missed another opportunity to get a good look at the tats on his chest.

Lucky pulled his cross necklace out from under his T-shirt. "What did you say?"

"I'm hungry, too." Willa consoled herself with the fact that it wasn't technically a lie as she came out of the water, only then remembering her clothes were gone.

She picked up one of the towels she had brought, drying off. When she would have wrapped it around herself, Lucky stopped her.

"Let the air dry you. Come and help me move the table to the shade."

Willa placed the towel on the bench before picking up one end of the table as Lucky picked up the other side. When they set it down, she noticed it fit down into four perfect grooves of dried earth.

"Does it usually sit over here?"

He sat down on the bench, pulling a sandwich out of the basket. "Yep."

"Then how did it get by the water?"

"I have no idea," he said, taking a large bite of sandwich.

"Are your fingers crossed?" Willa asked suspiciously, staring at his fingers.

"Nope," he said, unwinding them.

Willa sat down on the bench across from him, taking a sandwich for herself. She took a bite, chewing thoughtfully while Lucky demolished his then another.

"What are you thinking about so hard?"

"I was wondering if God counts it as a lie if you cross your fingers. I'm going to add it to my list."

Lucky stopped chewing. "What list?"

"I have a list of questions I'm going to ask Him someday. Like, do more women or men go to Heaven? Does He really love all the creatures He created? I don't think I could love a bat. Could you?"

"No, I don't think I could," Lucky admitted, his lips twitching. "What else are you going to ask?"

"Who's the worst sinner in history? Who's the worst sinner in our church?"

"I can answer those two."

"Okay, who?"

"Shade is the worst sinner in history. I'm the worst in our church." Lucky tried to make a joke out of his answer, but his hazel eyes held a pain that Willa wondered at as she stared at the cross necklace around his darkly tanned skin.

"I don't believe that."

"Believe it." Lucky laid his hands down on the picnic table. "Since I was a child, I've always wanted to be a pastor. I would watch my father behind the pulpit and knew that was where I belonged. I became a youth minister then became a pastor over my father's church by the time I was nineteen. I believed I would spend the rest of my life there in that small town. I even had a high school sweetheart I intended to propose to when the time was right."

Willa didn't interrupt, imagining him as a young man with all his dreams coming true.

"One night after service, I was putting up the Bibles that had been left on the pews. At first, I thought the voice I heard was a parishioner who had come back. It wasn't. I heard His voice as clearly as if He was standing next to me."

"What did He say?"

"He said, 'There is more.'" Lucky stared down at his hands. "I was being called. A month later, I joined the service. Then I finished my degree before I was shipped out.

"It took one week before I realized I didn't know shit about life. I ran around, trying to save as many souls as I could before the enemies took them, but I lost more than I saved, mine included. I told them we could get out of there, go home. They placed their faith in me, and I let them down."

"No."

"I did, Willa. I rode back on the plane with their bodies and informed the families, watched their hearts break, and knew they would never be the same again.

"I married Knox and Sunshine. I still see them together that day. Knox was so happy, and Sunshine looked beautiful. A week later, I was telling Knox that she was gone." A tear slid down his cheek. "I'll never forget his face. Knox is as big as a mountain, and he fell to his knees, crying. After that, I couldn't do it anymore.

"I took the Seal training, left being a pastor behind. I didn't lose my faith in Him, though; I lost faith in myself. I had to learn differently—to take a life instead of saving them. I began to enjoy the adrenaline rush when we were in combat. This way, I was making a difference. I was saving the brothers I served with, giving them a chance to make it another day.

"I became tight with Bridge. We had gone through training together, spent vacations together. I got to know his family. Mine were all gone, but his took me in and made me one of their own. When his younger brother joined, Bridge called and asked me to watch out for him, and I swore I would. I made another promise I couldn't keep. I promised he would make it home, but he died his second week there."

"You can't blame yourself."

"Yes, I can. I left him behind."

"You had to have a reason."

"The reason doesn't matter. He's dead, and Bridge wants payback."

"Payback?"

"He wants me to lose something I love, to feel what it's like."

"Is that why you bought Ria when we pretended to be engaged?"

"Yes. I wanted you to be protected when I couldn't be with you. That's why I only went out with women who would be able to move on when Bridge grew tired of me waiting to fall in love. He doesn't know that I found what I was searching for. I found that out when you nearly died, when Ria gave her life for yours."

"What did you find?"

"I found home. You were what I had been searching for all along. I didn't want you hurt because of me, yet you almost died. None of us know how long we have on this earth."

Lucky stood up, coming to sit down next to her with his back to the table. Reaching into the picnic basket, he took out a ring box.

"I love you, Willa. Will you marry me?"

"Am I dreaming? I'm afraid, if I say yes, I'll wake up."

Lucky opened the ring box, showing her the large, pink diamond in the rose gold setting that she had fallen in love with all those months ago. The tiny diamonds twinkled up at her in a starburst of color as he slid the ring onto her finger, closing his hand around hers.

"No. This is as real as it gets." He kissed her with a passion that was able to convince her that her body wasn't asleep.

"I guess this is my lucky day," she teased.

He winced at her pun, looking up at the bright blue sky. "I have another question to ask God when you see Him."

"What?"

"How many times I've heard that before."

# Chapter
# Twenty-Two

"Bitch, you didn't just carry those cupcakes in here?" Sex Piston paused while blow-drying a pretty blonde whom Willa once would have been envious of as she set a bright pink box on Sex Piston's reception desk.

"Is it me or does this box get a brighter shade of pink every time I see one?" Killyama asked, opening the box to take out one of the cupcakes.

"I keep experimenting with the color. I thought you girls could use a treat while Sex Piston does my hair." Willa smiled.

Killyama stared down at the box as she ate her cupcake. "You chose this shade of pink deliberately? Pink is pink, bitch."

The comment didn't hurt her feelings. She knew she was a little OCD over her boxes. She was in search of the perfect shade of pink; therefore, she ordered a different color each time she ordered boxes.

"Do you know how many shades of pink there are? It's hard to pick just one."

"My ass doesn't need another cupcake!" Crazy Bitch wailed as she teased a woman's hair.

Willa laughed. "I say that all the time."

"Give me five, and I'll be with you," Sex Piston told her.

"Take your time." Willa started to take a seat, nearly tripping when she saw Sissy sweeping the floor. The girl had stopped to glare at her.

"What are you doing here? I thought you left with Travis." Willa started to give the girl a hug then stopped when she saw the reaction on her face.

Killyama took a chair that was near where Sissy was sweeping.

"I turned eighteen. I can do what the hell I want to now."

"She showed up here last week, asking to work here, so I hired her to run errands." Sex Piston frowned at the girl.

Willa had seen enough instances of kindness from Sex Piston to not be surprised. She watched over her biker bitches like a sister, and as a result, she would have recognized, like Willa, that Sissy was crying silently for help. Sissy wouldn't take it from her, but maybe she would from Sex Piston.

"What about Leanne and your cousins; don't you miss them?"

"Miss all the tantrums and snotty noses? No, I don't." Sissy started sweeping again.

Willa bit her lip. She should ignore the girl and go sit down, but Willa couldn't stop the need within her to somehow reach the girl.

"I miss them all the time. Caroline and Chrissy are getting bigger every day. Leanne has a crush on one of the work hands—"

Sissy laughed at her, leaning on the broom. "Do you really think you're going to fool me? You may fool all of them"—she waved her hand at the women in the shop—"but I know what kind of woman you really are. You're a murderer and a slut!" the young woman spat at her.

As Willa gasped at the hatred on Sissy's face, Killyama jumped up to stand in front of Willa, but she stepped around her.

"I wish every day I wasn't responsible for taking your uncle's life, but I'm not a slut," Willa said firmly.

"I saw the text messages you sent. My uncle would get me to babysit when he went out to meet you at a hotel."

Willa shook her head. "I never met your uncle at a hotel once."

"You're lying!"

"Why would I lie? If I were sleeping with someone, I wouldn't care who knew. It's not like a woman gets in trouble for that."

"You want to keep your image up in town."

"What image?" Willa gave a bark of sarcastic laughter. "I was made fun of in high school. I never had a date until Lucky asked me out a few months ago. I never had friends until Lily, Beth, and Rachel felt sorry enough to include me. People never even talked to me in church unless they wanted me to bake them something."

"Lewis was in love with you!"

"Lewis wanted me to be his babysitter, and he wanted the money my business brought in." Willa sighed. "You want the truth, Sissy, but the thing about the truth is it can be twisted to anyone's advantage. I don't know whose text messages you read, but they weren't mine. I never texted Lewis." Willa paused then admitted, "I hated him. I was so afraid of him I bought the gun to protect myself. He managed to almost rape me, and if a customer hadn't shown up to pick up a cake, he would have."

"No!"

Willa stared at her in sympathy. "If you don't believe me, ask Angus Berry. I don't know how he managed it, but he did. I was so embarrassed and afraid of Lewis that I asked him not to tell anyone. I bought a gun the next day."

"Why would Lewis lie to me?" Doubt was beginning to show in Sissy's eyes.

"I don't know. Maybe he wanted to keep who he was really having an affair with secret. Only Lewis knows the answer to that question."

"And he's dead."

"That, I accept responsibility for. I don't know if I would have been able to pull the trigger to save myself, but I couldn't let him kill Rachel."

"My mom hated you."

"Yes, she did, from the time we were in grade school."

"Why?"

Willa looked away from Sissy. She had never admitted to a living soul why Georgia hated her so much, but she remembered it as if it had happened yesterday.

"We were in second grade homeroom together, and it was Valentine's Day. I had stayed up the night before to make a Valentine box. It was very pretty," Willa said modestly. "The teacher placed mine next to Georgia's, and the children in the class weren't very nice. They made fun of hers." Willa blinked back tears at the cruelty of the other children. "When we came back from lunch, my box was lying in pieces. The teacher tried to blame Georgia, but I told her I had done it, that I wanted to count my valentines."

"Did my mom do it?"

"I don't know," Willa lied, crossing her fingers behind her back. "But I'm sure it was embarrassing for her, anyway."

Georgia hadn't been embarrassed; she had been furious. After school, Georgia had followed her home and had ripped out half of her hair before Drake had pulled her away.

"That's not much of a reason," Sissy scoffed.

"For Georgia, it was." Willa had thought about it over the years. "She knew I was afraid of her, and it made her feel powerful. She liked the feeling it gave her. That's why people bully others." Willa stared at Sissy.

The young girl turned red, looking down at the floor.

"I'm ready for you," Sex Piston said as the pretty blonde left the shop.

Once Willa crossed the floor and sat down in the chair, Sissy began sweeping again. Then Willa felt a tug on her hair. Thinking Sex Piston was being unusually rough, she glanced upward, and their eyes met in silence. With the flick of her wrist, Sex Piston flipped her top up, showing a scar on her abdomen. Then she felt Sex Piston's finger touch the bald spot on her scalp which she always kept hidden.

Sex Piston was one of the strongest women Willa knew, and she was telling her she had also been a victim of bullying. Ever since the day Georgia had attacked her, she had felt like a scared child who was too afraid to strike back. However, right in that instant, a burgeoning of confidence began to grow inside of her.

"Damn, bitch, look at that rock on her finger!" Sex Piston grabbed her hand, lifting it so the other women in the shop could see.

"Lucky and I are engaged." Willa smiled. She couldn't contain all the joy she was feeling.

"I don't talk to Lily and Beth one day, and I miss all the gossip," Sex Piston fussed.

"I asked them not to. I wanted to tell you all today."

"Does this mean we get to have another bachelorette party?" Crazy Bitch asked.

"Fuck no. The last one almost killed me," Killyama complained.

"I'm with Killyama; one was more than enough." Willa still had problems with recalling certain parts of that night.

"I heard one is never enough for Lucky." Willa's smile slipped at Sissy's snide comment. "For none of The Last Riders, either. I don't know why anyone would want to pick one when you can have them all. Viper promised, as soon as I turn nineteen, I can join the club. Don't worry, Willa; I only need six of the eight votes."

Willa gasped, not at what Sissy said, but at Killyama's reaction.

The woman moved like a pouncing tigress, jerking the broom away from Sissy, and began hitting the girl with it.

"Shit!" Crazy Bitch ran toward Killyama, but she couldn't get close because the broom was moving so fast.

Willa tried to get up to stop the crazed woman, but Sex Piston pushed her back down on the chair.

"Sit your ass down. Killyama won't hurt her too bad. It's a plastic broom."

Willa could only sit and gawk as Killyama hit the girl several times across her butt and thighs. Sissy curled into a ball on the floor with her hands over her head.

"If I see your ass near The Last Riders, I'll fucking rip those tits of yours off! You want a man, you find him in Texas, because that's where I'm taking you when I get done. I see you back in Treepoint or Jamestown again, and I'll make fucking sure the only man who wants to fuck you is a blind one!" Killyama threw the broom down on the floor then reached down and jerked Sissy to her feet by her hair.

Sissy screamed in pain, tears pouring down her face while Killyama threw her in Willa's direction at the same time the shop door opened as T.A. came inside.

"Tell Willa you're sorry," Killyama ordered.

"I'm...I'm sorry." Sissy was crying so hard she could barely talk.

"It's all right—"

"Shut up," snarled Killyama. "That bitch should be kissing your ass. Talking about babies' snotty noses when she's an ungrateful little snot. Quit crying! I took a worse beating when I was in fifth grade." Killyama threw one of the shop towels at Sissy. "Get your ass in my car. I'll be there in a minute."

Sissy ran past T.A. and out the door.

"What did I miss?"

"Killyama beat the shit out of Sissy," Crazy Bitch told her, reaching for a cupcake when her client practically ran outside after throwing some cash down on the reception desk.

"Oh." T.A. went to the counter, taking a cupcake while Killyama went to the door.

"Is it just me or is this box—" T.A. began.

"Make up your fucking mind about what color pink to use," Killyama said as she shot a glare at Willa.

Willa opened and closed her mouth. Killyama in a temper was scarier than Georgia ever had been.

"I guess that one then. Everyone noticed it."

"What shade is it?" T.A. asked dubiously.

"That one is Pink Flamingo."

"I'd pick another one," Sex Piston offered her own business advice. "And she's not the only one who needs to make up her mind."

Killyama threw her friend a glare of rage before going out the door and slamming it shut behind her.

Willa turned back to face Sex Piston.

"Don't worry about Sissy. Killyama's calmed down. She just has STS."

"STS?"

"Sudden Train Syndrome. She freaks the fuck out when she thinks about Train and a clubhouse of women."

"She likes Train?" Willa asked, grateful for the change in topic.

After all, Lucky had told her he had given up his cut, which Willa took to mean that he was no longer a Last Rider. He had told her all her friends' husbands remained faithful to their wives, and she was happy for them, but she was much more comfortable with the quiet life she envisioned for herself and Lucky.

"She hates Train, but that doesn't stop her from wanting him."

Killyama was the complete opposite of herself. She was filled with confidence. The clothes she wore clung to her body yet weren't as suggestive as her friends. They fit along the lines of her body so that, when she walked, it was like a cat about to spring on you if you made the wrong movement.

Willa had talked briefly with Train at Winter's wedding and Lily's shower. His low voice had sent her scurrying to her friends. He had been polite, but in his dark eyes she had seen swirling emotions.

"She should go for Rider. He's much friendlier."

"Rider would piss himself. He's afraid of Killyama." Crazy Bitch threw herself down in the shop chair next to hers, eating a cupcake.

Sex Piston began pasting Willa's hair with the hair color, lifting the sections as she worked.

"I noticed last time that you don't have your ears pierced. How come?"

"I just haven't ever done it." Willa brought her hand to her ear, but it was slapped away by Sex Piston.

"Why not?" T.A. pressed.

Willa sighed. "I'm afraid of needles."

All three women burst into laughter, and Crazy Bitch even had to wipe tears away.

"How do you feel about knives?"

ॐ ଔ

Willa knocked on Lucky's office door.

"Come in."

She opened the door, seeing her fiancé sitting behind his desk, working, and he was wearing one of her favorite suits. The charcoal-grey color did things to his skin that made Willa get a warm feeling in her stomach.

His face broke into a welcoming smile when he saw her.

"I see your appointment went well. You look fantastic."

Willa blushed at his compliment, coming to a stop on the other side of his desk. "Thanks. Are you busy?"

"For you? No."

"I wanted to ask a quick question."

"In a minute." Lucky leaned back in his chair. "Come here."

Willa tilted her head to the side. "Why?"

"Because my future wife needs to give me a hello kiss."

"Oh." Willa turned red as she moved around the desk to bend down and kiss Lucky briefly on the lips. When she would have risen up, his hand went to the nape of her neck, holding her in place.

"Like this." His seductive voice had her stomach clenching tighter. Then his tongue thrust demandingly into her mouth until her hands plastered against the front of his shirt, and she kissed him back. "That's the way I want you to tell me hello."

"I can do that," Willa whispered.

"Good. Now what was the question you wanted to ask?"

Willa stared helplessly in his eyes, unable to return to reason as quickly as him.

"You said you had a question to ask me."

"Oh." Willa straightened, reluctantly taking her hands away. "Did Viper promise Sissy that she could join The Last Riders?"

"Moon did, not Viper," Lucky admitted.

"You're joking, right? Moon promised an underage girl that she could join a sex club?"

"Relax, Willa. Moon told her she had to be nineteen." Lucky held his hand up. "The promise is one that Viper has no intention of honoring, though. You have nothing to worry about," Lucky assured her.

"I don't?" Willa was having a hard time retaining her temper. "Did you know that Sissy ran away from Texas? Sex Piston gave her a job...well, she *did*. I think she's been fired. Killyama is driving her back."

"She is?"

Willa nodded.

Lucky laughed. "We won't have to deal with her again."

She decided to change the subject before she became angry at his attitude toward Sissy. Willa traced a paper on his desk. "You have several appointments today."

"I schedule couples' counseling on Wednesdays. In the morning, I spend my time with couples about to be married. In the afternoon, with those already married."

"Why haven't we done that?" Willa asked with interest.

"Because it would be hard to counsel myself," Lucky replied with a grin.

Once the idea took hold, Willa didn't want to give it up. "What kinds of things do you counsel the ones getting married on?"

Lucky leaned back in his leather chair, rocking it back and forth casually with his hands laced together across his flat stomach. Willa swallowed hard. Lucky made her want to touch him, yet she couldn't work up the courage to.

"I discuss their expectations of each other, their finances, if they want a Christian marriage."

"We could get counseling from the pastor in Jamestown. He's very nice."

"Yes, he is. I've met him several times. I'm more than willing if that's really what you want. I'll call and make an appointment."

Willa smiled happily until Lucky's next words had her rethinking bringing in a third party to discuss their relationship.

"I'm surprised. I thought you would balk at talking with someone. You usually try to avoid personal topics…"

Lucky had the phone in his hand, but Willa put her hand over his.

"Personal topics?" she questioned.

"Yes. He will talk briefly about sex and—"

"Maybe we should wait."

"We're getting married in two weeks," Lucky reminded her.

"I know that," she snapped. "Now that I think of it, I really don't have the time. I have several orders scheduled, and Beth and Lily still haven't picked their bridesmaids dresses. It was just a thought, anyway."

"Sit down, Willa." When Lucky motioned her over to the chair by the window, she crossed the room and gingerly sat down. "Perhaps it would be better if we just have an open discussion between us. Will that make you feel more comfortable?"

Willa gave a relieved sigh. "Yes."

"All right." Lucky sat down in the chair across from her, and Willa looked at him expectantly. "What do you envision for our marriage?"

Willa took a second to think, dreams filling her head of the years ahead. "I see us living a happy, fulfilled life with you as pastor and me helping you however I can. Maybe have...I don't know, two children?" She looked at him from underneath her lashes. She really wanted four, but she didn't want to scare him away before she could get a ring on his finger.

Lucky frowned. "Two?"

"One?" Willa bit her lip. How was she going to talk him into four if he only wanted one? Fear that he didn't want any had her wanting to change the subject. "We can talk about that later. What's next?"

"We should discuss this now. Children are an important part of a marriage."

"Can we talk about them later?" Willa twisted her hands together nervously.

His gaze dropped to her lap. "Okay. Then we should talk about finances. What is your credit rating?"

"I'm not sure."

His frown deepened. "You're not sure? You've been looking at properties to expand your business, so you should be familiar with your credit score."

"I figured I would check on it when I found a place."

Lucky ran his hand through his hair. "I could look over your finances—"

"That's not necessary. I have an accountant."

"Who?" Lucky asked in a way that made Willa think he believed she wasn't the best judge of character.

"Dustin Porter."

Lucky looked horror-stricken. "You let Dustin manage your books? He's a kid."

"He's my age." That choice of words didn't seem to make him any happier.

"He doesn't even have a high school diploma." Lucky's voice had risen to the extent that Willa was becoming angry.

"Yes, he does. He earned it over the internet like he did his accounting degree."

"What was the college? DegreeMart?" Lucky snapped.

"No...Why are you becoming so angry?"

Lucky took a deep breath. "I'm not angry. We'll come back to that question later."

"I think that would be a good idea."

His eyes narrowed at her self-righteous expression.

"What are your expectations of me as your husband?"

Willa gave him a reassuring smile. This one was easy. "I expect you to be faithful, make me happy, and to be a good provider, and faithful." Willa stressed the last one.

"You mentioned the last one twice."

"I did?"

"Yes."

"It's important to me."

"I can see that. Can I ask you a question?"

"Go ahead," Willa said apprehensively.

"Do you believe that I love you?"

Willa didn't immediately answer.

"Willa?"

"I believe that you love me."

"If you really believe that, then you will trust that I will be faithful."

Willa's hands began to twist tighter. "It's not that I don't believe you love me. I do, but..."

"What?"

"What if I don't make you happy? There's a difference between us—"

"Thank God for that."

Willa didn't take that as a compliment. "I meant you're more experienced than I am. You've been with several"—she looked at him askance, but the man was smart enough to remain quiet— "while I haven't been with anyone. I will only have you, while you'll be able to compare me to..." Willa cleared her throat. "Do you have a number?"

"No, I don't have a number. I didn't keep track."

She frowned, unsure if that was a good or a bad thing. "Are your fingers crossed?"

Lucky raised his hands, wiggling his fingers. "When you're in my bed, I can promise I won't be comparing you to anyone," he said gently.

"But how can you help it? I compare cupcakes. I compared vans before I bought one..." Her voice trailed off. "What if I'm not any good? What if you don't enjoy sex with me?"

Lucky was staring at her indulgently while she expressed her fears. Willa had seen the women he had slept with, though. They were freaking gorgeous.

"What if I don't enjoy sex with you?"

Lucky's smile slipped.

"Maybe all those women didn't want to hurt your feelings." Willa smiled smugly, seeing he hadn't liked that sentence.

"There's one way to find out."

"That's o—"

"I could fuck you, and you could give me your opinion."

Lucky hid his smile at Willa's shocked expression. He had been courting Willa, trying to be respectful of her upbringing in the church and her beliefs. He wanted her to have a courtship she would look back on without regrets or guilt. However, he had failed to take into consideration her lack of self-confidence. As a result, he might have gone too far and given her the misguided belief that he wasn't attracted to her or didn't feel the same desire for her that he had for other women. Truthfully, he didn't; what he felt for her was so much more.

He had never been more conscious of his body's needs and wants as when he was with Willa. He had even been reduced to mentally quoting scripture when he was tempted to lean her backward on the couch and make love to her instead of watching television. Other times, he had wanted to pin her against the door as he was about to leave and fuck her until she would remember what it felt like to have him in her until he returned.

There wasn't a day that he didn't want to return to The Last Riders, yet all he had to do was be in her presence, and it would pass until the next day. Even the fear of Bridge hurting her wouldn't change his mind. The accident had shown life could end in an instant, that Willa could get killed at any moment without any effort from Bridge. And, after she was gone, would it hurt any less? No. All he would have was the regret of not being with her when he'd had the chance. Therefore, it was the only decision he could make because he couldn't live without Willa.

It would serve no purpose to try to talk to Bridge again. It would only reinforce in Bridge's mind how much Willa meant to Lucky and make her an even bigger target. He was simply going to place his faith in God as he had when he had seen Ria reach Willa before he could, believing she would be kept protected by God's love and by the precautions he had taken. He was going to roll the dice and pray his luck held out.

Giving Willa up was no longer an option. He couldn't walk away from her. Even if he was damned for eternity, burning in the fires of Hell, he was going to take his chance of Heaven on Earth and make Willa his wife. It was time he showed his fiancée just how much he wanted her by giving her the part of himself he had held back.

He hadn't touched her, wanting to show her his respect and love before introducing her to the physical side. Instead, he sensed she had seen it as a lack of passion on his part. Willa needed to feel some of the fire he had been dealing with over the past few months. He only hoped he could keep it from consuming them both. By the time he was finished, she was going to be able to judge for herself exactly how good he was.

"That's all right. I think this is something we can talk about during another session." Willa stood up, looking at the clock on Lucky's side table. "Your next appointment will be coming."

Lucky took her hand, tugging her down onto his lap. "I have a few minutes. This won't take long. Kiss me, siren."

Willa expected him to be the one to initiate the kiss like he always did. She lowered her mouth, touching her lips to his. Parting her lips, she waited for his tongue to enter her mouth; instead, he only parted his lips. Her tongue entered, tasting the sweet coffee he always drank. Then her arms wound around his neck as his hands went to her back, pressing her breasts against his chest. Her eyes closed as she lost herself to the sensations of being close to him, savoring the kiss as it gradually escalated to him taking control from her.

When Lucky's hands went to her hips, settling her more firmly on his lap, she felt the bulge of his cock against her butt. It didn't frighten her as she expected; instead, she unconsciously wiggled on his lap as a feeling of wetness dampened her panties.

His hand went to her thigh under the thin, rose-colored dress. She pressed her breasts harder against his chest, enjoying the pressure against their sensitivity. Her hand went to his shirt, unbuttoning the first three buttons before sliding her hand underneath, and Lucky's hand went higher, touching the band at the leg opening of her panties.

Willa's hand floated over his chest in a fluttering movement, not knowing where to settle. She wanted to touch all of him. Her head fell to his shoulder as the kiss became heated from Lucky pushing her boundaries with his fingers.

She jumped when she felt his fingers on her clit for the first time, but she couldn't prevent the whimpering moan when his finger rubbed the nub, making her wetter, his finger sliding easily against her. Her nails dug into his chest as she turned her mouth, trying to catch her breath.

"Lucky…"

"Hmmm…" His mouth went to her neck, opening her up to sensations she had never dreamed possible.

"That feels so…good…" Willa moaned, rubbing her bottom against the bulge underneath her.

Lucky moved his finger faster as she raised her head, trying to catch his mouth. He denied her, teasing her until Willa grabbed handfuls of his hair, bringing his mouth back to hers. She nipped at his lips, traced his firm jawline, and then explored his throat, biting a small piece of his flesh.

Lucky's groan filled her with a sense of triumph because she could excite him as much as he was exciting her.

"Spread your legs wider."

Willa mindlessly obeyed his command, letting her clenched thighs relax as they fell apart. Lucky traced the opening to her pussy, and then she began shaking as he entered her a tiny amount.

"Do you want more, siren?"

"Yes." Willa moaned in need, the fire in her driving her insane. Her hips wanted to thrust down on the finger that was entering her with exquisite slowness.

His other hand held her still as he worked his finger into her then stopped, pulling it back to the beginning of her opening. She arched, shuddering when he thrust it back in farther than he had gone before. Her thighs splayed wider as he stroked his finger inside of her until it began to hurt. Willa tried to adjust her hips so it wouldn't hurt as badly, but the pressure inside of her was building at the same time. She wanted to escape the pain, yet at the same time, she craved it.

Lucky eased his finger down her pussy until the pain eased, but the fire didn't. Then he curled his finger upward at the same time a series of explosions hit her pussy, releasing a scream from her that he stifled with his mouth.

Afterward, she lay shuddering against his chest as she wiped the tears from her face on his shirt.

"Willa? Do you want to stay a virgin until our wedding night?"

She thought it over carefully before nodding against his chest.

"Then I suggest you get your pretty ass up before I fuck you on this chair with your legs wrapped around my waist."

Willa got up so fast she almost tripped, straightening her dress back down her legs. Lucky winced when he stood up, adjusting his pants to a more comfortable position, and she turned bright red when he looked up and caught her staring.

"Did that answer your question?"

"My question?" Bewildered, Willa stared at him.

"On whether or not I can satisfy you."

Her face flamed angrily as she went to his desk to pick up her purse. Lucky followed nonchalantly behind her, retaking the chair behind his desk and pulling his schedule toward him.

"That was an excellent start. Since we're getting married in two weeks, I think we should have three sessions a week until we're married."

Willa's mouth dropped open.

"You do want to continue with our pre-marital sessions, don't you?"

Willa shook her head. "I think we're good." She started backing away toward his office door.

"Are you sure? I have an hour free Friday morning," Lucky taunted smugly.

"I'm sure." Willa gritted her teeth. Just once, she wanted to shut the arrogant pastor up.

"Willa, aren't you forgetting something?"

"What?" She looked down at the purse in her hand.

"My good-bye kiss."

"Are you for real?" She stormed back across the room, bending down to place a hard kiss against his lips, then charged back to the door, slinging it open and nearly running into the Wests.

"Excuse me." Willa forced a smile to her lips. She hadn't liked the snooty couple before she had almost lost custody of the children, and she disliked them even more now.

"Good afternoon, Willa," Lisa greeted her, moving to the side to let her husband enter.

"Lisa, Dalton, I was just leaving."

"No rush. Congratulations on becoming engaged again." Her eyes flicked down over her simple flower dress then traveled up to her hair. "I see you've changed your hair color again." She gave a tinkling, fake laugh that was like nails grating a chalkboard. "You have a hard time picking colors, don't you? The next time you go to a hair appointment, I could go with you." Lisa patted her gleaming black locks. "I have some color swabs from when I decorated. I could bring them over and lay them on top of your boxes. I think a pretty shade of aqua would pop."

Willa brushed past them.

"Or a light shade of pink. You know, the shade they usually paint piggy banks."

"Bitch," Willa muttered.

"What did you say?" Lisa's eyes widened, while her husband began to look angry. Willa refused to look at Lucky to see his reaction.

"I said watch. Lucky's carpet is bunched up. I wouldn't want you to trip," Willa said, practically running outside, her steps loud on the gleaming, hardwood floor.

She floored her van as she drove home, pummeling her steering wheel in fury. Slamming the car in park, she went to her door, almost breaking the key off in the lock.

She still hadn't calmed down thirty minutes later when her doorbell rang.

"Hello, Willa. How are you this afternoon?"

"Hi, Douglas. I'm fine. You?"

"Good." His smile slipped a notch when he saw her puffy eyes and the tissues in her hand.

Willa opened the door, taking a step back for him to enter.

"Would you like a cup of coffee?" she asked, her bottom lip wobbling.

"No!" Douglas cleared his throat, lowering his voice. "I just stopped by to see if you still wanted me to build that deck for you. The weather is finally getting dry enough to work outside."

"Yes. Even if I don't live here, it will add value to the house."

"You're moving away? You shouldn't let a break-up run you out of Treepoint."

"What?" Willa gave a smothered sob. "I'm not leaving Treepoint. Lucky and I are engaged again. I was talking about the fact that we haven't decided yet if we'll be living in my house or the church."

"That's good news, isn't it?" he asked when her eyes filled with tears.

"Yes."

"I went ahead and made the invoice." Douglas was reaching behind his back when her cell phone rang.

"Excuse me."

"This will only take a min—"

Willa turned her back on Douglas, reaching for her cell phone on the entry table.

"Hello? Knox?"

"Willa, have you seen Sissy?"

"No, I haven't seen her since this morning in Jamestown. I thought Killyama was taking her back to Texas."

"She snuck off the plane before it could take off."

"Oh." Willa hated to admit it, but she was glad the girl had been heading back to Texas.

"She's not in any trouble. Her uncle called and wanted me to check to make sure she was okay and to help her find a place to stay since she's so determined to be near Treepoint."

"I can make a list of her friends if you want."

"That would be a help. This time, I'll keep it in my files. It will save time. I'll be there in a minute."

"I'll be waiting." Willa disconnected the call, seeing Douglas's frustrated expression. "I need to take care of something for Knox. Can this wait until after he leaves?"

"That's okay. I can stop by another day. I'll go ahead and buy the materials, and you can reimburse me."

"I appreciate it."

Douglas left before she could offer him coffee again. Shrugging, Willa sat at the table, making out the list of names Knox wanted. It didn't take long since Sissy only had a handful of friends.

After Knox left, Willa took a shower, making sure she didn't get her hair wet. She took time pampering herself. She even lit her favorite scented candles and placed her waterproof speaker in the shower so she could listen to the music. She was listening to "Jar of Hearts," her face turned up to the spray of water after giving up on keeping her hair dry, when she saw movement at the door.

A startled scream was caught in her throat when she recognized it was Lucky standing in the doorway. Her eyes widened, and she covered her breasts with her arms.

"Did you forget we're having dinner tonight?"

"I'll be right out," Willa managed to croak out.

She stepped back against the shower stall when Lucky strode forward, sliding the glass door open.

"Why have you been crying?"

"Lucky! I'm naked!"

His eyes darkened. "I can see that. Why have you been crying?"

Willa turned her face away from him.

"Because of Lisa?"

Willa nodded her head, but Lucky wouldn't let her escape his eyes.

"Don't you dare let that bitch upset you. Your body is a gift from God." His eyes focused on her breasts, and her nipples peaked as if he was actually touching them.

Lucky unbuttoned his shirt, and then she licked the water away from her lip as he took off his pants and shoes, stepping into the shower with her. Willa's eyes feasted on the sight of his body. It was a thing of muscular beauty, gleaming a golden hue as the water created rivulets while it fell.

Her eyes and fingertips investigated each tattoo from the top of his chest, reading '*Only God Can Judge Me,*' to the inked guardian angel and cross that led down to his cock where two roses weaved through the cross. His tattoos were fascinating and revealing, used to express his faith. She had to blink the water out of her eyes to see the ones on his cock. Even his feet had tattoos, and Willa couldn't imagine the hours he had been under a needle to cover his body.

Lucky's hand took hers, laying it on his cock and showing her how to glide her hand along its length.

"Do you know what I do every time I see you?"

"No." Willa gripped him harder.

He moved his hand to her breasts. "I thank God I'm a man." He began teasing her nipples with swipes of his tongue as her thumb slid over the crown of his cock. "I think about what our wedding night is going to be like: how I'm going to sink my dick into that tight pussy; how you're going to walk the next day, remembering me inside of you because I'm going to fuck you so hard you'll hurt." Lucky bit down on the tip of a nipple, releasing it after a brief second before lifting her other breast to his mouth.

As he sucked the nipple into his mouth again, she released cries of need, wanting to please him and wipe the memory of every woman from his mind.

"I think about how soft your skin is, how you're sweeter than those cupcakes you make, and how you can't stand to hurt anyone's feelings, even at the cost of your own. You're beautiful soul shines from your eyes and makes me hard as a rock."

His hand covering hers tightened until Willa was afraid she was hurting him. Then she saw that he was shuddering while his other hand braced him against the wall of the shower, and then he came in her hand.

Afterward, Willa self-consciously dried off in front of Lucky who refused to leave and give her privacy.

"You might as well get used to me seeing you naked."

"I won't ever get used to that." Willa turned to leave then spun around in shock when she felt the snap of a towel on her buttock. She glanced back over her shoulder to see him smiling at her innocently.

She giggled. She hadn't seen this playful side of Lucky, and it made her fall in love with him even more.

"Be careful. Those expensive shoes of yours are getting wet."

When he turned to use his foot to scoot the shoes onto the bathroom rug, Willa returned the small bite of pain to his own butt. Lucky's shocked gaze turned back to her.

"Stop!" Willa giggled. Once she saw he was going to get retribution, she immediately sobered. "I'm sorry."

"You don't seem very sorry." Lucky shook his head, still advancing on her.

"I am." Instead of trying to run away, Willa ran into his arms, kissing his cheek and lips. "I'm sorry."

Lucky's hand went to her hair, tugging until she stared up at him. "I love you, siren."

"I love you, Lucky."

# CHAPTER
# TWENTY-THREE

"You look beautiful," Beth told Willa as she straightened the veil down her back.

Willa felt beautiful when she stared at herself in the full-length mirror in Lucky's guest bedroom.

"Thank you both for being my bridesmaids."

Willa gave each of them a small jewelry box, and Lily and Beth both opened them to find exquisite pearl bracelets that Willa had chosen because the meaning behind them touched her soul.

It was said that they were made from angels passing through the clouds in Heaven. They meant love, and Willa wanted Beth and Lily to know how much they meant to her.

"I wanted to thank you for my dress." Willa straightened her shoulders, staring at the women who had tried to be her friends over the years. "Both of my parents are dead. I was an only child, I used to beg my mother for a sister or brother. I accepted the dress because, if I had a sister, I would buy her one. I'm not explaining it right." Willa tried to make another attempt, but Lily caught her hand.

"That's why we bought it, because we felt like your sisters, too."

Beth nodded at her sister's words, and then they hugged each other. Lily was the first to break away.

"It's almost time." Lily handed Willa her red rose bouquet, pushing her toward the door.

"We have fifteen more minutes before I have to be downstairs." Willa tried to pull back.

"I told Lucky that I would bring you to the side door."

"It's bad luck to see the groom before the ceremony," Willa protested.

"He'll be careful. Come on. We're losing time," Lily encouraged.

Beth picked up the bottom of her dress and veil as she followed Lily's pale rose figure down the steps. She opened the side door that was an extra exit from the entry of the church.

"Stand here." Lily positioned her next to it, facing sideways.

After Lily opened the other door and held out Willa's hand, Lucky's hand grasped hers from the other side. It was the most romantic touch Willa could have ever dreamed of. She could see no part of his body, only feel the loving clasp of his hand from the other side of the door.

"Will you pray with me, Willa?"

"Yes." Tears clogged her throat as she lowered her head.

"Dear Father, thank You for this beautiful day, fulfilling Willa's and my desire to join our two souls together with Your holy blessing. Hand in hand, we come before You, giving our hearts to You, and in return, we trust our faith to guide us through the journey You have set forth for us.

"Make our marriage as flexible as this cord I wrap around our wrists so that our love will continue to grow through the years. Make our marriage as strong as the diamond I placed on her hand. I promise to give Willa a smile for every smile, a kiss for every kiss, to hurt every time she hurts until our bond is as unbreakable as our devotion to You. Amen."

Willa almost went around the door to Lucky. Placing her free hand on the door, she felt his love coming through as though she could actually touch him.

"Amen," she whispered back.

"I love you, Willa. I've never felt luckier than I do at this moment."

Her hand tightened in his. "This isn't luck; this is a blessing from God. When He created you, He created a man who serves Him, a man who brings joy to my heart and a love that I will always cherish. Today, I give to you all that I am: body, heart, and soul."

In the background, they heard the cellist begin to play.

"You have to go. The ceremony is beginning."

"I'll be waiting." Lucky released her hand.

She heard him walking away to the side of the church that would put him at the front of the podium.

Willa turned back to Lily and Beth who were standing by the door that led into the chapel. Both were wearing their pearl bracelets as she was wearing the same one around her own wrist.

The saleswoman who had "helped" her and Lucky previously at the jewelry store had glowered at her angrily when she had asked for someone else to wait on her. Willa didn't feel guilty giving the commission to someone else for the expensive bracelets while the saleswoman had stood, watching enviously.

"Are you ready?" Beth asked with tears of happiness that were mirrored in Willa's own eyes.

"I'm ready." Willa smoothed down her dress for the final time.

"Pastor Sparks is already up front," Lily told her.

The pastor from Jamestown had agreed to perform the ceremony for them.

The ushers opened the door.

"Here we go," Lily said softly, stepping forward.

Beth followed behind her sister.

"He's there," Willa whispered, seeing Lucky waiting for her beside the podium.

"Was there any doubt?" Angus asked.

Curling her arm through his, she didn't take her eyes off Lucky. "None at all." She crossed two of her fingers that were holding the bouquet. "None at all."

&#8253; &#8278;

Willa paced back and forth in the small bathroom, knowing Lucky had to be wondering what was taking her so long. She sat down on the edge of the tub, feeling as if she were hyperventilating.

"He wouldn't use his knives on our wedding night," Willa whispered out loud to give herself courage.

"Did you say something, Willa?" Lucky's voice from the other side of the door had her jumping to her feet, double-checking that the door was locked.

"I said I'll be right out!"

They had decided to stay at her house tonight then leave for their honeymoon to Jamaica tomorrow afternoon.

She took another glance at herself in the mirror. The black, baby doll gown came to her knees, and the bodice dipped between her breasts, giving a generous view. The gown was daring for her, but it didn't scream 'come and get me', either. Willa wished she had been more adventuresome when she had picked her lingerie for her honeymoon. The prices on those flimsy bits of material had been hard to talk herself into, though. She thought the one she had on was seductive, and the best part was she had found it for thirty percent off in the expensive store.

The most expensive one had been a present from Sex Piston, and she had packed it in her suitcase, but she was seriously debating taking it back for a refund. There was no way she could ever envision herself wearing the minuscule bra and panty set.

Her hand went to the doorknob. She could do this. Lucky had shown her twice what kind of pleasure came from being with him.

He wasn't going to hurt her. She wanted him so badly her mother would be ashamed of her, because a good, Christian girl never let her body's needs control her.

She turned the lock, twisting the door handle then gradually opening the door. She didn't know what she had expected, but seeing Lucky sitting on her bed, playing PS4 wasn't one of them.

Travis had left Charlie's behind, explaining he had several at his ranch for the ranch hands to use and that Charlie would have it here for when he visited.

"Wanna play?" Lucky threw her a quick glance. "I'm winning."

"That's a real shocker." Willa tentatively sat down on the bed next to him.

He was only wearing a pair of shorts, and her eyes traced down the tattoos on his legs. Most of them were religious. The one on his thigh made her want to trace the outline of Mary to give her the courage she had always wanted. The sad look on her face and the tear rolling down her cheek touched Willa. She wondered what had made Lucky pick the ones he had inked on his body.

She placed her pillow against the headboard, giving herself an unrestricted view of the ones on his back without him knowing she was staring. They were different, not religious. They were symbols of violence and destruction.

The center was a Navy Seal insignia with a snake wrapped around it from the bottom up, leaving the face of the snake glaring back. Objects surrounded the insignia: two revolvers with a metal chain wrapped around the barrels of the gun, linking them together; brass knuckles; a hand of cards; and a razor knife. The whole tattoo had a layer of shadows, giving it an eerie effect.

She didn't want to know why he had chosen those. She shivered as she reached out to trace the hand of cards. Then her eyes went to the horseshoe on his shoulder, seeing the scarred flesh beneath, the ridges giving the horseshoe a more realistic appearance. The four leaf clover hid what looked like another scar. The largest scar was covered by an elephant with its trunk up. Her fingers traced each of the symbols.

"Why did you get the rainbow?"

"Because of God's promise in the Old Testament after the flood."

"Oh."

Lucky threw down the controller and, picking up the remote, he turned the television off. He turned, scooting down slightly on the bed, and then flipped onto his stomach with his head at her waist.

"The dolphin?"

"Protection."

"Is that one a cricket?"

"Yes, crickets alert you to danger. They stop chirping when someone gets near."

"Good luck symbols don't go against your religious beliefs?"

"God created them all," he said simply. "Besides, I don't put my faith in them; I put my faith in Him."

"A little extra luck never hurts." Willa smiled, running her hand over his shoulder.

"Exactly." His hands went to her hips, scooting her down in the bed to lie next to him.

Willa stared up into his hazel eyes. "How did you get those scars?"

"I was shot a few times."

"More than a few. I counted six."

Lucky wiped a tear away from her cheek. "Siren, I don't want to see any tears from you on our wedding night."

Willa turned her face to the side, unable to bear looking at his beautiful face. "I could have never met you."

His hand turned her back to face him. "I'm here, exactly where I was meant to be." Lucky touched the corner of her mouth with his.

"I can't believe I started laughing when Pastor Sparks read your first name."

Lucky smiled against her lips. "What's so funny about Lucky David Dean?"

"I thought Lucky was your nickname."

"My mother named me when I was born three months premature, and the doctors told my parents I wouldn't make it. She always said I started life with a lucky star in the sky, but my father gave all the credit to God. He named me David because he said I had to fight giant obstacles to live. Each week, they said something would go wrong: my lungs, my kidneys, and then my liver. The doctors said I was a miracle," he finished wryly.

Her arms wound around his neck. "I believe that, too." Her hand went to his face. "You're so beautiful."

"Men aren't beautiful." His mouth went to the cleft of her breasts. "You want to know a secret? Your breasts are sexy as fuck."

"You like my breasts?" They were the only part of her anatomy that she wasn't embarrassed by.

"Siren, 'like' isn't the word I would use." He rose slightly, pulling the spaghetti straps down until her breasts were uncovered, and her rosy nipples were peaked. Then Lucky took one into his mouth.

Willa buried her hands in his hair. "Lucky, there's something you should know. I don't take pain very well."

His tongue began playing with the tip of her nipple. "Siren, there is pain…" His teeth latched onto her nipple. The tiny pain didn't hurt, but the fear had her center melting. "Then there's pain." His hand slid under the hem of her gown, finding the tiny, black panties, and he slipped his hand underneath.

His fingers found her clit, rubbing the nub until she tried to twist to escape his torment. However, Lucky didn't allow her to flee his torture, plunging a finger inside to stroke her pussy into grinding back against the palm of his hand.

Willa moaned. "I can't catch my breath."

"Take a deep breath and hold on. It gets better," Lucky taunted, adjusting his body.

He slid down the length of her body, tugging her gown up and exposing the lace panties with the tiny red bows that were tied at the side.

"Isn't that convenient." He untied the panties, easily removing them. "You need to buy those in every color."

"I'll watch for them to go on sale."

"Buy them, anyway. I'll give you my credit card." Lucky kissed the smooth flesh he exposed.

"I'll still wait for the sale. I don't believe in throwing money away."

Lucky chuckled against her. "This is a surprise."

"That I'm thrifty?"

"That you shaved."

"I read magazines," Willa retorted primly.

"I have to admit, I'm kind of disappointed."

"Really?"

"I was looking forward to doing it."

The thought of Lucky shaving her had her thankful that she had taken care of that herself. Lucky with anything sharp in his hand made her nervous. She wouldn't even cook him anything that required him cutting since Killyama and the biker bitches had her spooked. She had even debated giving her knife block to the church store.

Her thoughts were diverted when his tongue touched her clit. She jumped, nearly knocking Lucky off her. He pinned her down to the bed with his muscular body while he explored her damp flesh, showing her a pain of need that had her fighting against the climax that was consuming her pussy. His hard hands parted her thighs wider before his tongue slid inside of her, pressing high as he rubbed against her walls.

The heels of her feet tried to find traction on the mattress but Lucky forestalled her, hooking his arms under her knees and lifting them to her chest. Then his mouth went to her neck as he rose above her, and she felt the touch of his cock against her opening.

"Do you want me to stop?"

"No!" Willa whimpered.

His cock slid inside her, pushing against the barrier within her pussy as he went deeper.

"Does it hurt?"

"Yes!" Willa hit his shoulders. "You're taking too long."

She felt his body shaking in laughter. "Then hold on, and I'll see what I can do about going faster." Lucky lifted her thighs higher.

Willa was concentrating so hard on the pull of her muscles in her legs that she barely felt it when Lucky surged inside of her, thrusting his cock home. A gasp escaped her lips at the feeling of him stretching her, his pelvis flush against hers.

"Does it hurt?" he breathed into her mouth, licking her bottom lip.

"It feels wonderful." Willa's body shook as Lucky slid out then thrust back inside with a powerful stroke.

"I don't want to hurt you," he groaned.

"I never expected it to feel this good." Willa wanted desperately to move, but Lucky's hold kept him in control of her and the climax that was just out of her reach. "Can we do this all the time?"

Lucky groaned again. "Can we finish this time first?"

"I don't want it to end," Willa said fervently.

"You won't be saying that in five minutes," Lucky promised.

She was so glad she had gone to her doctor to get birth control so they could have their wedding night with nothing between them.

When he had begun making love to her, it had been a gentle breeze floating across her body, escalating to the beginning of a storm that began lifting her away until she only felt what he was doing to her body. She felt like she was being tossed about in the whirlwind of desire to the point that she was afraid she wouldn't come out the same as when she had gone in, losing a part of herself in the eye of the storm that she would only find again when she returned.

Lucky's movements sped up, his body moving over hers hard enough to shake the bed. Her body was at the mercy of the storm that had built until it couldn't be contained any longer.

Willa could have sworn she saw white lightning when her body couldn't take it anymore, and then it burst into a myriad of colors that flashed before her eyes. She blinked rapidly, wanting to see Lucky's eyes clenched in a desire so painful only she could give him the relief he needed.

She couldn't move, but she did have use of her mouth. Instinctively, she turned her head, gently biting into his bicep. He stiffened over her, a deep groan coming from his chest as he stroked his climax inside of her. He then released her legs, moving carefully to her side.

"Is it normal that I can't move my legs?" Willa gave her own groan as she tried to lower them back to the mattress.

Lucky laughed, raising up to massage her legs then helping her to lay them on the bed. Even then, he stroked her, telling her how beautiful she was, how special making her his wife was.

Willa placed her hand over his mouth. "I don't need to hear you say all that." Lucky stared down at her with his heart in his eyes. "You told me all that when you married me." Willa waved her hand at the rumpled bed. "This is just icing on the cake."

Lucky fell back on the bed. "In that case, let's get you in a hot shower so you won't be too sore."

Willa winced when she sat up on the side of the bed. "I can manage that on my own."

Lucky started to protest, but then a cunning look crossed his face before he sat up on the bed, reaching for the remote control. "That's cool. I'll play another game. The last one only took an hour and a half."

"It didn't take that long." She must have stayed in the bathroom longer than she had thought.

She went to the bathroom door, hearing him start the PS4. Holding the door open, she turned back to him.

"All right, you can shower with me, but no hogging the water."

Lucky jumped out of the bed. "Don't worry. I always share."

# CHAPTER
# TWENTY-FOUR

Willa rolled over in the bed, her hand searching for Lucky in the rumpled sheets. Her eyes opened in the dark bedroom. He was gone again. She didn't have to search for him, knowing he was in the backyard of the church. It was where he went every night when she fell asleep after they made love.

On their honeymoon, she had believed he had risen to watch the sun rise from the beach. However, when they had returned home, it didn't take long to realize something was wrong. She had tried to talk to him several times, but he maintained that it was the time he used for his prayers. She believed that, but the prayers weren't ones of mediation. Willa feared it was much more than that, and he wouldn't confide in her.

She climbed out of bed, picking up her robe from the chair beside the bed. The hardwood floors were cool underneath her feet.

They had only been married for a little over a two months; therefore, she was aware it would take time for him to unburden what was bothering him. Willa was deathly afraid she might be what he was praying about, though. Had he discovered he didn't love her as much as he had believed? Was she doing something wrong, and he was praying about the best way to tell her?

She walked down the hallway in the dark, comfortable in the silence and the stillness. They had moved into the pastor's quarters when they had returned from their honeymoon. They were having her bedroom at her house enlarged into a suite with a sunken bathtub. She was also enlarging her kitchen and putting in new carpet throughout the house. Douglas had given her such good quotes it had been hard to resist the upgrades.

Lucky had wanted to find a different contractor, complaining that, whenever he had stopped by to check on the work, Douglas had been nowhere around.

"He's busy. He works for several people in town. I can't fire him when he's doing a great job."

Lucky had lost that argument and the one where he had wanted to install new wiring into the house so that everything was controlled by one system.

"Do you have any idea how much that would cost?" She had fought against it until Lucky had offered to pay for it. Seeing that he really wanted it, she caved yet did an internet search for the cheapest system.

She opened the door to the church's backyard, seeing Lucky standing with only a pair of shorts on, his skin gleaming with sweat.

"Lucky?" she spoke softly, not wanting to interrupt, but she was concerned for her husband.

"Go inside, Willa. I'll be there in a little while."

Although she thought about refusing to be sent away again, the tense way he was holding himself made her wary.

"Okay. Take your time." Willa bit her lip, tempted to try again. She wanted to say something that would reach him so he would talk to her, tell her anything.

"I love you."

"I love you, Willa." The tone in his voice brought tears to her eyes.

Since moving into the church, she had taken over the huge kitchen. Because the women provided meals for seniors, it had already been approved for food preparation, and Lucky had gained permission from the church deacons for her to do her baking there. She finally had the space she needed, which had almost tripled the desserts she made each week. Willa was ecstatic to be able to produce more without the added cost of overhead. He had even bought her two display cases that he had put in the church store. She was able to sell her desserts and give the church a percentage of the profits.

Her life was falling neatly into place. She took over Bible studies, baked in her free time, and was able to support Lucky as pastor when he needed her by his side.

She looked over her shoulder before going inside, torn to go to him.

Pain and loneliness shrouded him in the morning mist.

"God, please help him find what he's searching for."

&#2766; &#2771;

Lucky heard the door close as Willa went back inside. He had heard her when she had come outside, but he hadn't turned to face her. He couldn't. The nightmare that awakened him still had him in its grip. He had prayed when they had married that he would be able to sleep next to Willa, that his love for her would keep the nightmare at bay. He had realized his mistake when he woke up in the middle of the night, drenched in sweat and shaking. The strange hotel hadn't helped, either. He had jerked clumsily out of bed, but thankfully, Willa had been too exhausted to feel him leave.

Each night for the first two weeks, he had tried to fall asleep next to her yet had woken with the same fear churning in his gut. Since then, he had dozed at night, making sure to schedule two hours in the morning to sleep in his office. In the evening, he would tell Willa he had sermons to write and would sleep another two then.

The smell of bacon lured him from the early morning sun rising. Going inside, he bypassed the kitchen to go upstairs to shower and change. He came out of the shower to find a suit neatly pressed, lying on the bed. She had even shined his shoes and laid a matching pair of socks and tie perfectly positioned on the bed.

She did the same thing every morning, making his breakfast and laying out his clothes. She worked to anticipate his every need. She would fix his lunch, keep a pot of coffee warming, and even his favorite oatmeal raisin cookies sat in a container on the kitchen counter.

She was driving him nuts.

He wasn't used to being waited on. Despite his objections, she would find something else he liked and make sure it was readily available.

As he began to go out the bedroom door, he picked up the starched handkerchief he had begun wearing in the front pocket. This was one of two habits he hadn't tried to break. Inevitably, by the end of the day, he would be wiping Willa's tears with it. His wife was too tenderhearted, and everyone in Treepoint was taking advantage of it. If he didn't put a stop to it soon, the woman was going to work herself into an early grave.

He smiled when walked into the kitchen, wrapping his arms around Willa from behind.

"Good morning, husband."

"Good morning, siren." He slid one hand inside the front of her robe, cupping her breast in his hand.

She swatted his hand away. "Go sit down; breakfast is ready. I need to get changed. I invited Dustin to bring my accounts by so you'll quit worrying."

"I'm only concerned because you let your customers run up big bills or don't pay you at all. From what I can tell from what paperwork you have shown me, King and about five other customers are paying you." Lucky sneaked one of the oatmeal raisin cookies as she placed his plate on the table.

"I told you I love baking, and my customers pay me when they get paid."

"Why does the restaurant of Charles's father owe such a large bill, then?"

Lucky was aware Lily's old boyfriend had gone to school with Willa, also.

"Oh, he's behind in taxes, but he's going to get caught up with me after they're paid."

"Owing taxes didn't keep him from buying Charles that new truck."

Willa poured him a cup of coffee. Bending down, she placed a kiss on his cheek. "You worry too much."

"I'm going to talk to them," Lucky said firmly.

"Don't you dare." She placed the coffee pot back on the burner. "You'll hurt their feelings."

Thankfully, Lucky had just swallowed the bite of bacon he had taken, or he would have choked on that choice of words.

"I've got to go get changed. Promise me you won't be mean to Dustin if he comes before I get back."

When Lucky took another bite of his bacon, remaining silent, Willa went to the cookie jar, taking out a cookie that Lucky saw as she paused by the table.

"I'll try." He took the cookie she handed him, chewing it thoughtfully.

He needed to start exercising more, or Willa was going to make him fat. He missed the exercise equipment at the clubhouse. He and the brothers would compete to see who could lift the most weights. Missing the time they hung out together grew worse each day.

He looked up when he saw Dustin standing in the doorway.

"Willa texted me and told me to come on in."

If Lucky hadn't known Dustin for years, he would have never recognized the young man standing in the doorway. He was wearing a grey suit that was not only clean, but pressed, and his dress shoes were more expensive than the ones on Lucky's own feet.

"Fix yourself a plate. Willa left plenty on the counter."

"I'll just pour myself some coffee." Dustin placed his briefcase on the table before going to the counter.

Lucky finished his breakfast while Dustin drank his coffee as he opened his briefcase.

"How long have you been Willa's accountant?"

"Since I gained custody of my son. I had gone by Willa's house to pick up a cake for his birthday. I was a dollar fifty short, but she wouldn't take the money. I had just earned my high school diploma, and she asked what interested me. I told her money, just joking around, but she offered me a scholarship and wouldn't take no for an answer.

"I thought she was crazier than shit, but I worked hard in college and discovered that I have a head for numbers. Then she offered me the job because her accountant wanted to retire. I almost shit myself when he showed me all this, though." Dustin looked down at the papers in his hand before handing them to him.

Lucky moved his dirty dishes aside as he began going through the paperwork.

"Willa's great-grandfather founded a company that made millions. When her father and his wife passed, Willa inherited as their only child.

"I didn't start taking a salary from Willa until she began making money on my investments." Dustin pointed at one of the columns. "This is the normal commission a broker would make."

Dustin began going over the paperwork, intermittently pausing to answer a text.

"Have you built up other clients?"

"Rachel and Cash, even though I didn't want to. Cash threatened to kick my ass if I didn't. Shade, Angus Berry, Drake, and a couple of investments of King's." Dustin paused, answering another text.

Lucky went through the paperwork for over an hour before he leaned back in his chair, dismayed at what he had found out about his wife. The numbers were so large they were beginning to run together.

"Exactly how rich is my wife?"

"I would say richer than God, but I don't think you would appreciate the analogy," Dustin joked, getting up to refill his coffee. He sat back down then handed Lucky a lone paper that he had kept to the side. "I need you to sign this."

"What is...?" Lucky picked up the paper, going pale as he read over it.

"It makes you beneficiary of her estate."

Lucky tossed the paper to him. "I'm not going to sign that."

"It doesn't matter if you do or not. I just wanted to witness for Diamond that you received a copy."

"Diamond?"

"Knox's wife is Willa's attorney. My office is next to hers, and Diamond had to be in court this morning with Tate, so she asked if I would take care of it for her. Willa asked Diamond to explain the way her estate will be split, but since she couldn't be here, she gave me permission."

"Who was the beneficiary before she changed it?" Lucky asked hoarsely.

"I'm familiar with the details because I was in the meetings with Diamond when she was writing the will. She wanted my advice on how to split her estate.

"Willa has several beneficiaries. Seventy percent of her fortune goes to you, but that's subject to change depending on the number of children you have. It decreases with each child. She wants her children taken care of, but doesn't want to leave them enough to spoil them." Dustin's mouth twitched. "She keeps going back and forth between five and ten percent."

"The other thirty percent?"

"The children she fostered split ten percent, and Lily, Beth, Rachel, Angus Berry, and last week she added Killyama—though I couldn't understand why, something about a broom—will split the remaining twenty percent." Dustin's phone dinged with another incoming text. "This doesn't include her house and two other investments. The house is paid for and, upon Willa's death, remains in the direct family, unable to be sold."

"Why?"

"Willa wants a home for her children in case they ever need it. The two investment profits go to various charities that she decides on each year."

"You can tell Willa to come back down now." Lucky nodded toward the cell phone in Dustin's hand when it dinged.

"How did—"

"It doesn't usually take my wife two hours to get changed," he said wryly.

"Willa is very sensitive," Dustin confided.

Unless Lucky was mistaken, the youngest Porter brother had a crush on Willa.

Lucky burst out laughing. "My wife is a tightwad. Did you know she won't buy anything unless it's on sale? I settled for an ugly green tile in her bathroom shower because it was twenty percent cheaper per tile. I thought she was broke. I didn't even think to check her finances out before we married."

"It could be emasculating for a man to have a wife as rich as Willa is."

"I think my masculinity will survive."

Lucky caught his wife's apprehensive look as she came into the room. As she drew nearer, he put his arm around her waist.

"We're changing the tile color."

When she started to argue, Lucky forestalled her. "I think we can afford those two children you want, but I was hoping to sweet-talk you into four."

Happiness filled her face. "Really?"

"Yep. On one condition. You have to talk Dustin into becoming my accountant."

# CHAPTER
# TWENTY-FIVE

"I can't believe it!" Willa closed her computer, so excited she wanted to tell Lucky the good news. She had entered a contest to win a state-of-the-art smart home computer system and won.

Knowing Lucky was in his office, working, she decided to peek in and tell him. She practically skipped to his office, wanting to gloat that she wasn't going to have to pay a penny for the system he wanted. She was so excited she forgot to knock. Opening the door, she saw him sitting in the chair by his window and Willa stopped, looking at the tired lines of his sleeping face.

She wanted to wake him and tell him to come to bed. If she did, though, he would do what he did every night—make love to her then disappear until morning. As a result, Willa quietly left his office without waking him.

Going to her bedroom, she sat down on the side of her bed. She stared at the clock on the nightstand, seeing it was only seven in the evening.

Picking up her cell phone, she made a call she should have made two weeks ago.

"Hello? Willa?"

"Hi, Lily. I hope I'm not disturbing you."

"No, I'm just feeding John. What can I do for you?"

"I was wondering, if it's not too much trouble, could I borrow that cookbook of your mother's? I'm bored, and nighttime is my favorite time to cook."

Lily paused. "I could bring it to you."

"No! Like I said, I'm bored, and I could use the fresh air."

Again she was met with silence, although she thought she heard voices in the background.

"That's fine, Willa. I'll see you when you get here."

"Thanks, Lily. I'll be there in ten minutes."

Willa put on her tennis shoes then ran a brush through her hair and tugged it up into a ponytail. Grabbing her purse and keys, she left Lucky a quick note, placing it on the mirror of the dresser so he would see it when he entered the bedroom. He usually didn't come upstairs until nine, and she expected to be back long before that, but she didn't want him to worry if he finished his work early.

It was getting dark when she pulled into The Last Riders' parking lot. It was filled with motorcycles and several club members were standing around, shooting her curious glances as she got out of her van.

She went up the side walkway that led to Lily's house. As she passed the clubhouse, Willa heard loud music and saw the kitchen filled with people. Before she could get to Lily's house, Lily came out the front door with the cookbook in her hand. Willa was disappointed. She had hoped to find Shade alone with Lily in their house.

"Here you go, Willa." Lily handed her the cookbook.

Willa took it. "I didn't mean to bring you out," Willa apologized.

She was about to ask if she could speak to Shade when Lily shook her head.

"I needed to escape for a moment. Beth and Diamond are playing cards. Shade had already left to get some beer for the clubhouse, or he could have dropped it off to you."

"That's okay. It's such a pretty night that I wanted to get out." Willa turned to go back down the path. "Thanks, Lily."

She left Lily, walking back toward the parking lot. Willa wanted to confide in Lily and ask her advice. However, Lucky wouldn't be happy if he found out she had discussed him with her friend. It was a good thing Shade wasn't home. There was only one person she needed to talk to, and that was her husband.

The parking lot was even fuller as she made her way to her van with her head down, only looking up when she reached her vehicle

"Evening, Willa."

Shade was sitting on his bike. She could have sworn there was a black one parked there when she pulled up, not the cherry red he was sitting on. Rider was standing next to him with two twelve-packs of beer under his arms.

"Shade, Rider." She gave them a nod.

Rider gave her a wink.

"They're waiting for the beer," Shade reminded him with a frown.

"Oh, yeah. Later, Willa."

"Good night, Rider."

Shade remained sitting on the motorcycle with his blue eyes on her. She was about to get into her van when she looked at the bike he was sitting on again.

"That looks like Lucky's bike."

"It used to be. It's a club bike now until someone claims it."

Willa froze. "A club bike?"

"It's a rule—when you leave the Last Rider's, you give up the bike you joined with."

"That's not fair."

"I hate to tell you this, Willa, but biker clubs aren't known to be fair."

Willa swallowed hard. She should get back in her van and drive into town, but she didn't.

Her hand holding her keys dropped to her side. "Do you know what's bothering Lucky?"

Shade stared back at her, his expression impassive. It was the only one she saw him wear unless Lily was there. Several times, she had been brave enough to look into his eyes and seen...nothing— no emotion, no soul—and she was terrified that, unless she found a way to reach Lucky one day, she would wake and see the same thing in his eyes.

"Yeah."

Willa licked her dry lips. "He's dying inside, isn't he?"

"He died a long time ago and doesn't want to admit it. That's his problem."

"What's wrong with him?" she whispered.

"How bad do you want to know?"

Willa blinked back tears. "Please, Shade...help me."

"He'll hate me if I tell you...Not that I care a rat's ass, but what I tell you could just as easily destroy your marriage as save it. Are you willing to take the risk?"

"I love Lucky, Shade. Nothing you tell me is going to change that."

"We'll see." Shade stood up from the bike, motioning her up the steps to the clubhouse.

Willa went up the steep steps in front of Shade, and two bikers she didn't recognize were standing in front of the front door when she reached the top. Both looked intimidating, blocking the doorway.

"It's cool, RIP, Fang."

The two men moved out of the way.

"They're recruits from Ohio," Shade explained.

Willa didn't ever want to visit Ohio if that's where they lived. She hoped they went home soon.

Shade moved to stand in front of the door. The music was even louder than when she had arrived.

"Lucky tell you about the Friday parties?"

Willa nodded her head.

Shade opened the door, motioning for her to go inside. From what she could see, she didn't want to go in any farther, even though no one in the hallway paid her any attention. They were too busy having sex.

She recognized Jewell with her legs wrapped around Train's hips as he bucked against her. Jewell was holding onto the rails of the steps with her T-shirt pulled up over her breasts, and she wasn't wearing anything from the waist down. Train wasn't wearing a shirt, and his jeans were unzipped as his cock thrust into Jewell.

"You coming in?" Shade asked.

Willa stared at him wildly, her face going pale at what else she could see in the room.

"No one will touch you," Shade promised, Willa didn't doubt his assurance.

She stepped hesitantly inside, and Shade closed the door behind her.

"This way." Shade made a path for her through the crowded room that she imagined was what Sodom and Gomorrah would have looked like. She was afraid lightning would strike any second as she walked across the room.

She was almost at the kitchen when her eyes were caught by a couple on the couch. Winter was sitting on Viper's lap with his hand under her skirt. You couldn't see anything, but from both their expressions, you could tell what was going on between the married couple.

Willa almost fell as she rushed into the kitchen behind Shade where it went from bad to worse. Raci was on Crash's lap, bouncing up and down on his cock. Her back was to the door, but Willa easily recognized her face because it was turned to the side, giving Rider a blowjob. Several members were standing around in the other room in various stages of undress.

Shade opened a door on the wall of the kitchen. When she would have rushed through it, Shade caught her arm.

"Be careful."

She made herself slow down as she went down the wooden steps. Downstairs, she saw several different exercise machines and weights against one wall, and there was also a couch and chair. The room was large with a metal pole in the center. Thankfully, this part of the house was empty, and she was able to catch her breath.

"This way." Shade walked across the room, going through a door into a hallway. He went to the door at the end, opening it after a brief knock.

Willa's mouth dropped open when she went in after Shade.

Rachel was on her knees on the bed, giving Cash a blowjob.

"Dammit, Shade," Cash snapped.

Rachel's mouth came off Cash's cock with a pop. Then her friend frantically began pulling a cover over her, burying herself beneath it.

"I need the room."

Willa could have sworn she heard amusement in Shade's voice. She glanced away while Cash pulled on his shoes and boots, picking up his shirt from the bottom of the bed.

"I don't think Lucky would be happy to hear you say that," Cash commented.

Shade didn't respond, forcing Willa to clear up the misconception. "We're just going to talk."

Both men laughed at her expression.

"Willa, I knew that." Cash went to the bed. "Let's go, Rachel."

"No, I'm not coming out. Ever. Tell them to go talk at Lily's house."

"I need this room," Shade stressed.

"I don't care. I'm not—" A loud squeal filled the room when Cash reached under the cover to pull his wife out. Rachel didn't release the covers when Cash tossed her over his shoulder, going to the door.

"It's all yours."

"Thanks, brother, Rachel."

"You freaking bast—!" Shade slammed the door on Rachel's insult.

"She's pretty mad at you," Willa observed.

"She'll get over it."

As Shade went to a large, wooden cabinet against the wall, Willa stared around the room. The bed was huge with a black sheet. It was masculine-looking and...sexy. Willa was ashamed of the sinful feelings rising in her body, knowing her mother would be mortified she had even thought the word.

Shade opened one door of the cabinet then took a set of keys out of his pocket, unlocking the other side. Curious, Willa wandered over to look inside.

There were several drawers inside the cabinet. Some were half-drawers; others were whole; all had keyholes. One at the bottom was twice as large as the rest, and Shade slid a smaller key inside then opened the drawer, revealing leather books. There was also a glass-framed display.

"Have a seat on the couch," Shade ordered.

Willa took a seat while Shade removed the items from the drawer, setting them down next to her. Then he sat down on top of the coffee table in front of her.

Picking up the display case, she was able to see several medals and a flag.

"Lucky tell you anything about when he was in the service?"

"He told me that a friend's brother was killed, and he felt responsible."

"He wasn't responsible. I've told him that, his superiors have told him that, and this tells him he wasn't responsible"—he gestured at the case—"but he can't let himself off the hook because he made that promise to Bridge."

Shade's face twisted. "The Last Riders met when we were overseas, and we've remained friends even after we were discharged. I've thought over the years about what has kept our friendship strong, what made the difference between us to keep us from splitting up and just talking occasionally." Shade shrugged. "We work well together as a unit. We watch each other's back, and we trust each other. I came to the conclusion that each of us has a code that we live by that makes us the men we are."

"What's Lucky's?" Willa stared down at the picture frame in her hands.

"You tell me."

"Honor."

"Yes. I met Lucky when he was still a pastor in the service. I was in and out of camps during different times, and I never had much contact with him then, but even from what little I saw of him, I saw the war taking its toll on him. After Knox's wife Sunshine died, he couldn't do it anymore. He couldn't tell one more brother that someone they loved wasn't coming home. I thought he would leave the service then, but he re-upped, went into Seal training, and came out at the top of his class. If Lucky couldn't save them with the Bible, he had made his mind up to do it with a rifle. His sense of honor had him wanting to make sure he could bring as many brothers home as he could, even if he had to sacrifice all his beliefs, even if it was his own life he had to forfeit."

"John 15:13: '*Greater love hath no man than this, that a man lay down his life for his friends*,'" Willa quoted softly.

"He went on all the dangerous missions in the worst areas. Then Bridge asked Lucky to watch over his kid brother when they were told to empty a village before the enemy attacked, and Lucky promised he would.

"Willa, what I'm about to tell you is classified."

"I swear to God I won't repeat what you tell me," Willa said earnestly.

"I know you won't, or I wouldn't have told you as much as I have."

Shade leaned forward, putting his forearms on his thighs as he recounted Lucky's past.

"We were given six hours to evacuate a village of sixteen hundred. I was in place on a ridge to alert them if any enemy approached, but I was ordered not to make my presence known. There was intel that a target the government wanted taken out would be present when the enemy forces attacked, and the government wanted that target bad.

"Two squads went in. Lucky, Kale, Razer, and four others were in one. They would get the refugees out. The other squad would take them to safety. The evacuation was going well until one of the refugees didn't like being rushed and turned on the soldiers. He grabbed Kale's gun and turned it on him. He was shot in his leg and arm.

"The rest of the soldiers continued with the evac while Razer and Lucky worked on Kale. It took time, and the enemy was getting there sooner than the intel had predicted. Lucky called for air evac for Kale, so Train and his team were on the way to get them out. At that point, everyone had been evaced except Lucky's squad, and it was those ten men who were left to face the Hell that was about to open up.

"Keep in mind, I wasn't allowed to break cover and give them any support. The target I was after was too important. I had to watch those men fight one of the dirtiest fights I've ever witnessed.

Lucky brought down soldier after soldier, but they needed a break so Train could land the helicopter and get the men out."

"What did Lucky do?"

Shade's mouth twisted. "The crazy bastard went and found a break in the enemy line then sneaked out of the part of town that wasn't covered. He sneaked behind enemy lines. It was a suicide mission. He set off explosives that gave Train time to land and get the squad on board."

"How did Kale die?" Willa whispered, barely able to talk without bursting into tears.

"He bled out. He died when Lucky was setting off the explosives. The men tried to get his body to the transport. Two men were shot trying. Razer still tried, risking his own life until the command was given to leave him."

Willa bit down on her hand, realizing it must have been torture for the men to leave one of their own behind.

"The helicopter took off without Kale and Lucky. Both were irretrievable."

"Lucky was left behind?" Willa cried out.

"The squad had no choice; he was behind enemy lines. Train had his orders, and he had to think of the lives on that helicopter. He had his own team to protect, plus the remaining squad members."

"What happened to Lucky?"

"The lucky bastard kept them chasing him for an hour. They got close enough to shoot him three times, yet he kept managing to find hiding places for short periods of time. The last one got him in the back, but he managed to find cover between two rocks."

"How did he get out?"

"Train defied orders and came back for him alone. He wasn't allowed to fly for six months and was demoted for that stunt." Shade's hand tapped the glass that covered the medals. "He received these for saving those lives that day, but he won't even look at them. I had them framed for him, though, because he deserved every damn one of them."

Shade reached for the other medals, and he flicked one open and laid it on her lap. "He received this for saving a village when he was a pastor. He stayed behind because there were children he refused to leave. The children were sick and couldn't be moved. The squad left him behind. The only one who stayed was Razer. He received a medal also."

Shade laid another, bigger leather book on her lap which he flipped open. "He was given this for saving a U.S. envoy that was escorting food to a town that was slowly being starved to death. Only five men have been given this medal since it was made."

The last leather book was set on her lap and contained nine different medals of various sizes with a larger one at the top. "Lucky was awarded the one at the top from the president. The rest are from the different states that contained the drug and firearms pipeline that Lucky busted while undercover as Pastor Dean."

"Undercover?"

"Lucky was an ATF Special Agent."

"He never told me."

"Again, this is all confidential. Several of the sources he used could be killed if the wrong people found out where the information came from to make the arrests. He also was instrumental in finding several women who were kidnapped by a sex ring, and Lucky saved Lily's life.

"What you are looking at, Willa, is Lucky's life. He's saved hundreds of lives and has made a difference in hundreds of others. He's a fucking hero, but he can't live with one fact."

"What?" Willa choked out.

"That he can't save them all."

"He can't honestly believe...No one has that power. Only God." Willa's fingers trembled as she held the proof that Lucky had tried, nearly at the cost of his own life, to do just that.

"Logically, Lucky knows that, but that's what PTSD does to you—it fucks you up."

"That's why he can't sleep."

Shade stared directly at her. "Yes. It was better here at the clubhouse, but it's becoming worse."

"Because of me," she stated, staring back at him. "Why?"

"I don't know. You'd have to ask Lucky that question."

"Why do you believe the PTSD is becoming worse?"

"The brothers and I kept Lucky physically active. We aggravated him so he'd come down to the gym to work out his aggression. We kept him busy with paperwork and errands. We also have initiations for the recruits, and we made sure he was always one picked to fight."

"The women, also." Willa bit her lip. "He used knives on them."

"Not like you're thinking, Willa. It's not about cutting; it's about trust. Lucky is a master with those things. He never makes a mistake with them."

"You'd have to trust someone a lot to let them put a knife to your throat," Willa said ruefully.

Shade pointed at the medals still sitting on her lap. "Do you really believe that the man who earned those medals could hurt a woman, especially one he loves enough to risk his sanity?"

"Do you think he knew it was going to be hard leaving The Last Riders?"

"Yes, it was hard for him when he was undercover, but building the cases kept him busy, and the parishioners."

"He doesn't have that now, and he walked away from the club."

"Exactly."

"I didn't ask him to leave."

Shade stood, taking the medals away from her and stacking them back into the cabinet before locking the drawer closed then locking the cabinet.

"I would like those, please."

"They aren't mine to give." Shade put his hands in his pockets, going to stand by the door. "You may not have asked him to leave, but you knew he was leaving because of you. He already feels guilty because Bridge wants to hurt you. Do you know he always said he was going to marry a slut?"

"What?" Willa gasped. She didn't know if she should be happy or upset that she didn't fit Lucky's image of a perfect wife.

She thought Shade's mouth twitched, but she couldn't be sure.

"He'll tell you it was because of Bridge, that he didn't want to leave a wife behind who couldn't move on, but I believe he knew it would be difficult to leave The Last Riders. A slut would fit into the club."

"That's true," Willa snapped then frowned. "There's something I don't understand. I thought Bridge threatened to kill the woman Lucky loves, not Lucky."

"He did, but if Lucky finds out Bridge got anywhere next to you, he'll kill Bridge. Lucky is a Christian, but he won't mind going to prison if he thinks anyone he cares about is in danger."

Willa stood, walking to the large bed before turning to face Shade. "Lucky needs The Last Riders to heal."

"Yes and no. He needs you, too."

Willa dropped her head. "I can't share him, and I really don't want to let someone else touch me." She looked up to see his reaction.

Shade's arms crossed over his chest. "Do Lily and Beth seem happy to you?"

"You mean...I thought because they lived..."

"Rachel and Cash have their own home, too. Lucky laid the foundation for his home a few feet from Razer's."

"He didn't tell me..." Willa didn't know what to do. To help Lucky, she was going to have to let go of the ideal of the kind of marriage she and Lucky should have. It was going to be up to her to make most of the changes and accept a group of people as family.

"Can I ask you one more thing?" she asked hesitantly.

"Go ahead." This time, there was no mistaking his amusement.

She pointed to the upstairs. "Is it always like that, or was it just a wild night?"

"It gets worse."

Willa paled.

"I know you, Willa. You're strong enough to make a place for yourself in the club. Lucky will help you find the parts you like and keep you from the rest. It can work if you want it to."

Willa nodded, walking toward him, and Shade opened the door for her.

"Something you said about when Lucky was behind enemy lines...You said he had crawled between two rocks. How did he get from there to the helicopter?"

"That's another question." He moved aside so she could pass. Instead, she stopped in front of him with tears coursing down her cheeks, barely able to see him as she tried to blink them back.

"You broke cover, didn't you? You saved his life, and it wasn't the last time, was it?" She went to her toes, reaching up to kiss Shade on his cheek. "Thank you."

"You're welcome."

# CHAPTER
# TWENTY-SIX

Willa let herself in the church, relieved when she heard Lucky in the shower. Smiling mischievously to herself, she took her clothes off and slipped on the bra and panty set Sex Piston had given her. She barely had time to throw her clothes in the hamper and arrange herself on the bed. With no time to spare, she found the remote on the nightstand.

Lucky was drying his hair with a towel with another knotted casually on his hips when he came to a stop in front of the bed, his mouth dropping open.

"How was the progress going at your house?"

"Good." Willa didn't cross her fingers. She was sure the house was progressing fine. She raised the remote in her hand. "Want to play?"

"Yeah, I want to play." He threw the towel in his hand on the chair then jerked the one around his hips off, tossing it on top of the other one.

Willa giggled when Lucky jumped onto the bed. Before he could touch her, though, she scooted away.

"I love you so much, Lucky."

"I love you, too, siren. Come here."

Willa shook her head teasingly. "Ask me how much."

"How much?"

"Ask me how much I love you."

Lucky's expression turned serious. "How much do you love me?"

Willa held her arms apart as far as they would go. "This much."
She crawled forward, wrapping her arms around him.

Lucky twisted his body until she was lying underneath him.
"Siren, there are no words to describe what I feel for you."

"There aren't?"

"No, but I can show you."

Lucky proved it to her with each brush of his mouth against her
body. When his hand took hers, placing it on his cock, he showed
the desire he had for her. Willa took his hand, showing him her
body's response.

She brushed her mouth against his nipple. "I have something to
confess. I like your tattoos."

"Thank you."

"A lot." She pushed him back on the bed, rising over him, her
breasts brushing his chest. The bra she had on barely contained
them. Willa placed one knee on the other side of his hip, straddling
him. "Am I too heavy?"

Lucky's hand smacked her butt, and Willa's hand went back to
soothe the slight sting while she pouted down at him.

"You could have just said no."

"I thought that answer would be more effective."

"Kind of puts me out of the mood," she said.

"Let me see if I can help you find it again." Lucky grinned unrepentantly up at her, each hand sliding up a thigh until they met at
her pussy with his thumbs resting on her clit.

Willa ground herself down on him.

"Nope." Lucky took his hands away.

"You do want to make love, don't you?"

"Yeah." Lucky arched his hips underneath her, pressing his cock
against her mound. Then his hands went to her breasts, tugging
them out of the bra cups until they were pushed up and framed by
the leopard material. "Lord have mercy," Lucky breathed.

Willa placed her hands on his chest, exploring the ridges of his muscles. "I say that every time you touch me," she confessed.

She kissed the firm jaw that made her melt. Then she licked the groove of his throat, feeling him swallow hard.

The women at her bachelorette party had all shared the particular trigger that made them horny. Just looking at Lucky made her feel that way: each time he stood next to her when church released, when he winked at her, when he swiped another oatmeal cookie, or even when he became angry because she insisted on serving him at the table. There was nothing about her husband that she didn't like...except for one thing.

"Quit teasing me," she moaned when he put his hands behind his head.

"Whatcha gonna do about it?" He smirked up at her.

Willa's eyes narrowed on her arrogant husband, believing he needed to be taken down a peg or two. Having been observant long enough to know what Lucky's trigger was, Willa gave her husband a saccharine sweet smile that brought a worried frown to his brow.

She scooted down his body, bringing her breasts to his eye-level, then unclasped the front closure, letting her tits swing free. Lucky's eyes widened. He leaned forward, but before he could trap a nipple in his mouth, she slid down farther, placing butterfly kisses on his flat stomach. When she heard his groan, she slipped her legs between his. Taking his cock in her hand, she adjusted her body then seductively—she hoped—rubbed his cock against her breast, using the crown of his dick to tease her nipple. When his hands clenched the sheets, she knew she had him.

She lowered her head, flicking the tip with her tongue to make it wet, and then pressed it against her nipple. His eyes glazed over when he saw the moisture clinging to her nipple.

Her head lowered again, and this time, she twirled her tongue over the entire head before rising and placing the tip against her other nipple.

"Siren…" He didn't have to tell her; she could tell from his expression he was about to lose control.

Quickly, she pressed his cock in the cleft between her breasts. Using her hand, she stroked him as fast as she could, and he practically ripped the sheets off the bed he came so hard. Willa waited until he quit shuddering before releasing him and crawling back up to lie next to him.

Lucky turned to his side. "Remind me never to get you mad at me."

"I will."

"It's going to take me a few minutes to recover."

"We have all night."

"I know what will make me hard again in a second." His trying to be helpful didn't fool her.

"What?" she said, feeling his hand slide under her panties.

"Do that again."

∞ ∞

Lucky jerked awake, breathing heavily. He sat on the side of the bed, angry at himself for falling asleep. He had been so careful not to fall asleep next to Willa, but tonight, there had been a newfound confidence in her that had made her initiate their intimacy, and they had spent most of the night making love. Regardless, he had meant to only lie beside her long enough for her to fall asleep.

Standing, he went to his dresser and pulled out a pair of jeans. Unable to bear the thought of anything else on his body, he soundlessly left the bedroom. The wooden floor under his feet reminded him he was home and not back overseas, trying to figure out how to save Kale's life.

He took a deep breath of air as soon as he stepped outside. Running a hand through his damp hair, he came to the realization he was going to have to take the medication he had been avoiding since he had been let out of the service. Willa was already worried, and he wasn't going to have her concerned that him being unable to sleep with her was her fault.

"Lucky…"

Startled, he almost turned around at her voice.

"Go inside." He clenched his fists at the unintentional harshness in his voice. "Please, go inside." This time, he was successful in making his voice appear normal.

"Let me help you."

Composing his expression, he turned his back to the sun just as it was beginning to rise in the sky.

Willa was standing five feet away, holding her hand out to him.

"I don't want to hurt you, Willa. You're not safe with me. Go—"

She took a step closer, not dropping her hand. "John 1:5 *'The light shines in the darkness and the darkness has not overcome it.'*"

"You didn't know you were taking on a fucked-up mess when you married me." He took a step back.

"You're fighting a cruel war you can't win, Lucky. You're not responsible for Kale or any of those men's deaths. You're a hero."

He grimaced. "I'm not a hero."

"Yes, you are," she insisted. "You left The Last Riders because you love me, and I'm asking you to go back to them for the same reason."

"You would hate it there. I might be happier there, but you would be unhappy."

"Romans 12:18. *'If possible, so far as it depends on you, live peaceably with all.'* As long as we're together, I don't care where we live." Her sincerity began to sink into the darkness that had been clouding his nightmares.

"You're too tenderhearted. The men won't be polite all the time. In fact, they're usually assholes, and the women can be bitchy."

"Proverbs 27:17. *'As iron sharpens iron, so one person sharpens another.'* I'll learn how to give as good as I get."

"I would be the vice-president. There would be things that I do that go against the church's beliefs."

Matthew 22:21. *'Render therefore unto Caesar the things that are Caesar's; and unto God the things that are God's.'* I know that, even if you leave the church, God will dwell in our home," she said with certainty.

Willa took another step forward, standing directly in front of him, still holding her hand out to him. Her love and faith shined clearly from her eyes as the sun glistened down on her at the beginning of a new day, a new life they were about to begin.

"You were meant to be a pastor's wife," he said achingly.

"I was meant to be *your* wife." Her whispered vow released him from his last doubt.

Lucky reached out, taking her hand. Stepping forward, he grabbed on to the future that God and Willa both held for him.

# CHAPTER TWENTY-SEVEN

"Hi, Douglas, come in. I wasn't expecting you." Willa held the door open as the handyman entered.

"I wanted to stop by to go over the kitchen costs with you one more time before I took out the cabinets."

"That's fine. Lucky's at the hospital visiting Angus. He's doing much better. I stopped by at lunch today."

"I know. He told me you stopped by, and Lucky was coming by this evening."

"Hopefully, they'll get his blood pressure down and release him tomorrow. Let's go in the kitchen, and you can show me...You didn't bring the spreadsheet?" She glanced over her shoulder curiously, looking at his empty hands.

"No..."

When they walked into the large church kitchen, Douglas came to a stop as Dustin turned around, and a moment's frustration crossed Douglas's face.

"Don't worry; Dustin won't mind if we take a short break on our meeting. He's stuffing his face with a new cupcake I'm working on."

"I should have called first. I don't want to interrupt—"

Willa waved away his concern. "Don't be silly. Take a seat. I have a fresh pot of coffee, and you can give me your opinion on the cupcake."

Douglas's shoulders slumped as he gave in, taking a chair.

Willa introduced the two men while she poured Douglas's coffee and picked him out the largest cupcake on the platter, placing it on a pretty saucer with a paper doily. Humming, she set them in front of him then sat down at the table next to him while Douglas stared at the cupcake and coffee making no move to touch either.

Scooting her chair closer to the table, she placed her elbow on the table, propping her cheek on her hand, wanting to see his reaction when he bit into the cupcake. He hesitated until he looked up and saw she was waiting expectantly.

"I've been working on tweaking a recipe I found in an old cookbook for two days."

"It looks delicious." He didn't sound as if he thought it was going to be good.

Willa frowned then smiled when he took a large bite.

"It's great. It's even better than your chocolate lava." He licked a dollop of frosting off his lip. "Do I taste bourbon?"

Willa nodded. "Did I use too much? I don't drink, so I couldn't taste-test."

"You might cut back on it some," he advised, taking a drink of his coffee.

"I told her she should use some more," Dustin said, getting up to get another one.

"That's your last one," Willa threatened. "I don't think you'll be able to drive if you eat any more."

Dustin sat down, already biting into another cupcake. "I can just see Knox's face if he pulls me over, and I tell him I've been eating drunken cupcakes."

"They aren't drunk; they're tipsy," Willa countered.

"They're drunk off their ass," Douglas muttered, taking another bite.

"I'll adjust the recipe." She put her full attention on Douglas. "So, you wanted to talk about the costs?"

"What? Oh, yeah. I emailed you the cost of the new cabinets."

Willa picked up her cell phone, pulling up her email, and then she started getting heart palpations at the figure she was staring at.

"I just wanted ordinary white cabinets."

"You already have those. For the same price, you can get those. They're on sale, and with my discount, it's a good deal."

"Are the white ones on sale? If they are, they would be cheaper. I could save—"

"They aren't on sale," Douglas cut her off.

Willa stared down at the figure, her mind running the total cost of the project.

"Get the cabinets. Kitchen upgrades always increase the value of the home."

"I know, but…"

They went back and forth. She was finally satisfied when Douglas promised to check a competitor's price. She also showed him a sale ad for the carpet she had picked out, telling him she would give him a check to go ahead and make the purchase.

"I told you it would be better to wait. They always run sales on the first of the month. I saved eighty-nine dollars," Willa said proudly.

"I'll take care of it tomorrow," Douglas said, getting up and carrying his dirty cup to the sink. "I need to get going."

"I'll see you later this week. Lucky wanted to stop by yesterday, but we didn't get time. We're packing—"

"You're moving?" Douglas asked sharply.

"Don't worry; I'm not moving back into my house. We're moving just outside of town. Lucky wants to build his own home."

"What about the one you're working on?"

"I'll probably rent it out. I want to save it for my children."

"I see."

From his frown, she didn't think he did, but she didn't pry. Douglas was a nice man who liked his privacy and didn't pry into other's business, so she saw nothing wrong with extending the same courtesy.

He was almost out the front door when she caught up with him. "I boxed you up a couple of cupcakes."

"Oh, thanks." He nodded at Dustin who had followed Willa into the hallway. "It was nice meeting you."

"You, too," Dustin said, holding out his hand. "I wouldn't eat any more of those if you're driving," he joked.

Willa thought she heard Douglas say, "No shit."

After the door was closed, she turned to Dustin. "Did he say…?"

"He said they were a little too sweet."

"Really? Then maybe I should cut back some on the sugar," Willa mused aloud as they walked back into the kitchen.

"You do that, add a touch more bourbon, and you'll have a winner."

"You think so?"

"Yeah. When you make them, text me. I'll taste-test them for you again."

Willa smiled, refilling his coffee cup. "You didn't wear your suit I bought you today."

Dustin lost his happy expression. "No, you said Lucky wasn't going to be here today. I still don't see what would have been wrong with jeans and a T-shirt." He smoothed down his T-shirt with '*I Dig*' and a picture of a plant. Willa thought it might be a picture of cannabis, but she couldn't be sure.

"It's not exactly professional," she said delicately, not wanting to hurt his feelings. "Lucky is my husband. I want him to have confidence in you."

"Did it work?"

"Oh, yes." Willa nodded happily. "You were amazing. I knew you would be."

Dustin flushed, staring up at her, and she went to put the coffee pot up then turned when she heard Dustin greet Lucky.

Once Lucky came to the counter, pulling her into his arms and kissing her breathless, she had to hold onto the counter as he released her.

"How are you doing tonight, Dustin?" Lucky asked, pouring himself a cup of coffee.

"I've been better," he said, picking up his briefcase.

"Did you eat too many cupcakes?" Willa asked in concern.

"No, I skipped dinner. Too many sweets on an empty stomach, I guess." His expression was downcast.

"I should have asked. I'm so sorry. I could make you a sandwich if you want." She placed her hand on his arm in sympathy.

He seemed about to accept then changed his mind, looking at Lucky over her shoulder. "That's okay. It's Greer's turn to cook. I'm sure there are plenty of leftovers."

"It wouldn't take me long."

"No, don't bother. I'll see you in a couple of days, Willa."

She started to follow him out but Lucky walked by her, following him, so Willa began doing the dishes. She didn't have many, because she liked to do them as she used them.

"Why don't you use the dishwasher?" Lucky asked, coming back into the room.

"I didn't have enough dishes to do a full load."

He pulled her into his arms. "You could just stack them in the dishwasher until you have a full load."

"I don't like dirty dishes sitting around. My mother always told me a wife is supposed to keep a clean house."

"Willa, I've told you that's an old-fashioned concept. I can help with the chores. When we move into the clubhouse in two days, you'll have to get used to the chores being split up among the members."

Her eyes darkened in worry. "Does that mean I can't cook you breakfast every morning?"

Lucky sighed. "Siren, what is it with you cooking breakfast every morning? I do know how to make myself a bowl of cereal."

"I want you to be healthy, and breakfast is the most important meal of the day."

Lucky slid his hands to her butt. "I know one that's more important." He lifted her up until her legs wrapped around his waist. Then he turned, setting her on the metal counter.

"What?"

"Snack time."

Willa laughed. "Snack time isn't a meal."

"Oh, yes, it is." His mouth kissed the base of her throat as he unbuttoned her faded pink blouse, pulling it off.

She was wearing a new lace bra that she had found on sale, and the cups barely covered her nipples.

"I could come just from staring at your tits." He pulled her breasts out of the bra before laying her back on the counter next to the cupcakes. He tugged off her jeans and tennis shoes.

"Someone could come in," Willa whispered.

"I locked the door when Dustin left."

She heard him opening a drawer next to her where the utensils were kept, and her heart stopped beating when she saw a butter knife in his hands.

"Lucky...?"

"I haven't had a chance to try your new flavor. Did Dustin like them?"

Willa didn't like the look in his eyes. It was making her nervous. She would have jumped down off the counter if Lucky hadn't pressed a hand down on her stomach, holding her still. He used the butter knife to scoop a small amount of frosting then smeared it across one nipple. She wiggled unsuccessfully while he repeated the same to the other then tossed the knife into the sink.

The cold metal at her back made her shiver as her hands curled over the edge of the counter. Lucky unzipped his jeans, pulling out his hard cock. Then he gave a satisfied smile as he swiped his thumb over her clit, and she knew her arrogant husband was gloating to himself that she was already damp.

She was anticipating him to build her desire higher. As a result, the shock of his sudden entry had her arching as she adjusted to him taking her. His hard body pressed her back as he took her nipple into his mouth, licking the frosting off.

His cock felt as hard as the steel she was trembling on, and the sensations were almost more than she could bear.

Her small scream was cut off when he caught her mouth with his. She tasted the chocolate icing on his tongue.

"Wow, I did use too much bourbon. It tastes like…" Willa lost her train of thought when he surged inside her again.

"Fire," Lucky said, licking the frosting off her other nipple.

"Fire," she murmured in agreement.

"Siren?"

"Hmm?" She lifted her glazed eyes to his.

"Do you know that Dustin's in love with you?"

Astonished, she shook her head.

Lucky nodded his head back at her. "I don't want you alone with him anymore."

His firm tone had her hackles rising. "He's not in love with me. We're friends. You're being ridiculous. He would never—"

"It will be easier on him to get over you if he's not alone with you. It's hard to be around you and not fantasize about these tits."

"You're crude and wrong," Willa snapped. If she wasn't so darn close to coming, she would get down and show her husband that he couldn't tell her…Another small scream pasted her lips shut when he bit down on the nipple in his mouth.

"Do you want to make me jealous?"

She gaped at him in dismay. The thought that Lucky could possibly be jealous of Dustin had to be a joke.

"Willa?" Lucky's cock slid to a stop inside of her.

"I'm thinking," she snapped. "Truthfully, the thought that you could be jealous of another man over me…" Willa began giggling. "It's kind of cool."

"Willa, did you like it the last time I spanked that ass?"

"No…You know I don't deal well with pain."

"Then I suggest I don't find you alone with Dustin again."

"Okay…There's no reason to become angry."

"Willa, shut up and fuck me."

"Are you going to stay mad at me?"

"I'm not mad," he ground out, clenching his teeth.

"You look mad," she said dubiously.

"I'm not. It's just kind of hard to carry on a conversation when I'm trying not to come."

"Oh." Her hands slid to his shoulder as she thrust her hips up at him. "Is that better?" she cooed playfully before going pale when she heard him open the utensil drawer again. Her pussy clenched on Lucky's cock while she tried to remember if the knives were within his reach.

"What are you do-doing?"

"My damn belt is caught in the drawer," Lucky told her, finally jerking his belt free.

Willa gave a sigh of relief. Darn it, Killyama had made her paranoid with her snarky comment on *Saw*.

Willa froze on the counter. "How did Killyama know you used knives when you had sex with women?"

Lucky stiffened on top of her.

"Get off." Willa pounded her fists on his chest.

Lucky grabbed her hands, pulling them over her head. "Listen to me!"

"You had sex with Killyama!"

"God, no!"

She stopped struggling at his horrified reaction.

"Then how did she know?"

"Do we have to talk about this now?"

"Yes."

"A while back, Fat Louise got herself into some trouble in Mexico. Killyama asked for The Last Riders' help to get her out, and we agreed."

"I love Fat Louise. I'm so glad you offered to help."

"It was my idea."

"That's so sweet." Willa wrapped her arms back around him.

"I thought so," he agreed arrogantly. "Anyway, it was decided we were going to leave early in the morning, and to save time, Killyama spent the night at the clubhouse while we went over the plans. My part was mainly getting the approval of both governments and doing recon.

"After our meeting, Rider was supposed to keep an eye on her." His expression became pained as he confessed what happened next. "She was supposed to sleep in the main clubroom on the couch, but apparently, if the noises are loud enough, they can be heard downstairs in the clubroom. Killyama heard some"—Lucky cleared his throat—"and came upstairs to investigate with her fucking pistol in her hand. I still say she did it deliberately just to see what was going on and make sure it wasn't Train."

"I don't have to guess what she saw, do I?"

"No," Lucky admitted. "She went psycho on me. That bitch didn't need our help to get Fat Louise out; she could have done it herself. She damn near broke my hand before Jewell could scream at her that we were doing a scene."

Willa maliciously enjoyed seeing Lucky's face turn a bright red as he struggled to find the right words to give her an explanation.

"A scene or play is where you can enjoy fantasies in a safe environment with limits."

"Limits?"

"Yes. Like, I use knives, but don't cut. It's about erotic play."

"Oh." Willa still couldn't imagine becoming aroused with someone holding a knife to her, but she could understand how each person had their own fantasies. Lucky had figured prominently in most of hers. With that thought, her own face blushed a betraying red.

Lucky stared down at her, his interest caught. "Want to tell me what your fantasy is?"

Willa laughed, shaking her head. "Maybe after we've been married a few years. Finish telling me what happened with Killyama."

"There's nothing else to tell. I was mad as hell at being interrupted at gunpoint, and my hand hurt like fuck. I told her to get out or sit on the couch and watch. It wasn't one of my better moments." He winced when she hit him on his shoulder. "Don't worry; Killyama paid me back. She told me to shove my knife up my ass, and if she heard another scream coming from my room, she would shoot and ask questions later."

Willa tried not to grin. "She was a little harsh," she lied, crossing her fingers at the same time she wrapped her legs around his waist then ran her hands down his back soothingly. The woman had probably hurt Lucky's feelings when she had threatened him.

"I didn't blame her. I shouldn't have been a smartass. But it was a big knife."

She kissed his jawline. "She still didn't need to be so…graphic." She began wiggling her hips again to make him move.

"I don't think I'm in the mood anymore," Lucky said grumpily.

"Let me see if I can help you find it again."

# CHAPTER
# TWENTY-EIGHT

Lucky parked his SUV in The Last Riders' parking lot. "We're here."

Willa held her cookie jar tighter against her chest, pasting a smile on her face.

Lucky turned to her, taking her hand in his. "We don't have to do this, siren. We can live in your house." It was the thousandth time he had made sure that she was willing to move. Even after he had told the deacons that he was leaving and had found a new pastor for the church, he had wanted to make sure she wasn't having second thoughts.

"I want to give it a try. Besides, it's only until your house is built. As soon as Douglas is finished with my house, he can start on our new house."

"Douglas isn't going to be doing our house."

"Why not? He's an excellent contractor."

"I'm not disagreeing with you. When I texted him to set up a meeting to discuss him taking the job, he told me he already has another job lined up. I thought you would prefer to find someone who could start right away."

"I would," Willa admitted.

The sound of someone banging on her window had her jumping. She rolled her glass down.

"You two going to sit here all day, or are you going to get out?" Rider gave her a welcoming smile as he opened the door for her.

Willa climbed out, seeing most of the clubhouse had come out to greet them.

After Lucky went to the back of the SUV, raising the hatch, everyone reached in to help pack the last of their belongings up to the clubhouse. The men had moved everything else the day before.

Razer and Viper took the larger boxes, and Knox took Lucky's two large suitcases. Willa went to pick up her make-up bag, but Jewell took it from her hand.

"Let me help." She shook the travel case gently. "That perfume you always wear in here?"

"Yes," Willa answered, not liking the gleam in the other woman's eyes.

"Cool." She left before Willa could ask why she wanted to know.

"There any cookies in that jar?" Rider asked.

"Yes. I made them this morning."

"I'll pack it up the steps for you."

"Be careful. That's my grandmother's jar."

"I'll be careful," he promised, passing Lucky and Train who were struggling to get a shelving unit out.

"Aren't you going to help?" Lucky asked.

"I am," Rider responded, lifting the lid of the cookie jar to take out a cookie then taking a large bite. "Oatmeal raisin, my favorite." He went up the steps, shoving the rest of the cookie in his mouth.

"I'm going to kick his ass," Lucky threatened.

"Don't worry. We've got all this," Train grunted.

"He's going to eat all the cookies before I can get up there," Lucky complained.

Willa watched as the men unloaded the rest of their belongings, not knowing what to do. Lucky and Train were walking up the pathway to the side of the clubhouse where they would go down the side door into the basement. Lucky had told her they would be taking the large bedroom in the basement until their house could be built.

She decided not to tag along with the men. Going up the steps, she braced herself before opening the door. They didn't have sex out in the open during the day, did they? Willa wished she had asked Lucky that question before she came in by herself, but thankfully, the front room was empty.

"Thank you, Lord. If you could give me a couple of days before…" Willa trailed off, unsure whether it was appropriate to ask God not to let her see any of the members have sex until she grew used to living in the house. Then she worried that God could hear her thoughts. She decided to add that question to her list—if He could hear their thoughts.

Hearing voices in the kitchen, she went in that direction then remembered when she had come in the clubhouse with Shade. Slowly opening the door, she peeked around the corner, seeing the room filled with the members.

Lily and Beth were putting food on the counter, Raci and Stori were cooking, and Rider was setting out drinks. Willa went through the door, enjoying the smell coming from the kitchen. The platter of fried chicken looked mouthwatering and doomed the diet she had promised to start today. Fried chicken was her weakness. She made sure she never went into the diner the day it was on special.

"Hi, Willa."

Both Lily and Beth came from behind the counter to welcome her. Then Winter stood from the table, handing her a vase of flowers without meeting her eyes.

"Thank you." Willa blushed, remembering the last time she had seen her.

"We all wanted you to know how much you're welcomed and that we're looking forward to having you live here," Lily enthused.

"It's going to be really nice when we add her name to the chore list," Rider said then winced as Ember elbowed him in the ribs.

"What? It's the truth. One less week I have to do the dishes. It's not like we aren't all thinking the same thing."

"I'm not thinking that," Lily protested.

Beth glared at Rider. "Me, either."

"I am. I hate the fucking dishes." Jewell picked up a chicken leg, biting into it.

"I hate clothes," Raci admitted, "but I'm still glad you're here."

Willa laughed. "I don't mind chores."

Lucky came up from behind her, placing his arm around her shoulder. "Just make sure that you don't do everyone else's."

"I'll try." Willa didn't want to make promises she couldn't keep.

"Let's eat before it gets cold." Viper walked around them, taking a plate from the large stack.

Willa got in line with Lucky, filling her plate sparingly with only a chicken thigh and a scoop of potatoes.

Before she could move down the line, Lucky placed a chicken breast on her plate. "I know it's your favorite."

She was doomed to have a big ass until she died. She tried to remember how many carbs green beans had then didn't think it mattered, considering the fried chicken. While Lucky lagged behind at the apple cobbler, Willa steered clear, going through to the dining room after seeing the kitchen table was full.

Searching for a place to sit, she saw Viper and Winter sitting at a large, round table where Bliss and Raci were also sitting. There were two empty chairs, so Willa set her plate at the table. She was pulling the chair out when Bliss rose, carrying her plate away without a word and sitting down at another table.

"Did I do something wrong?"

Winter cast Bliss an angry frown. "No, have a seat."

Lucky came up next to her, taking the other empty chair.

"Something wrong?" Lucky asked when she didn't sit down.

"No." Willa would ask Bliss later if there was a problem. She had always been friendly with the woman and couldn't understand why she had left the table.

Willa observed her laughing and joking with Train and Rider who shared her table.

"What do you think?" When he placed his hand on her arm, she realized her husband was talking to her.

"What about?"

"Viper and the brothers are going for a ride after dinner; want to go with them?"

Willa knew he was anxious to be back on his motorcycle.

"I want to get unpacked. You go ahead." The memory of Bliss's butt on the back of his bike would forever be ingrained in her memory, so there was no way she was getting on a bike with him. After all, she didn't want the person who came up behind her on Lucky's bike to have nightmares.

When she finished, she carried her dishes into the kitchen and washed them off, not wanting to interrupt the others talking at the table.

Raci placed her dishes in the sink on top of hers. "It's Ember's turn to do the dishes."

"Oh…okay." Willa dried her hands on the towel rack before self-consciously going to the door that led to the basement.

Once in the room that was going to be her new home for the time being, she set about getting comfortable before she started unpacking. She lifted her suitcase to the bed, opening it and taking out a pair of jeans and a loose top. Carrying them into the bathroom, she changed out of her dress. She zipped up the jeans, surprised to find they were loose. She then went back into the bedroom and searched through her clothes, finding her favorite pair of size eighteen jeans. Knowing her weight was like an escalator, she kept two different sizes of clothes. Next week, she would be back in her twenties.

Going back in the bathroom, she slid on the jeans then the cotton top and felt more comfortable as she moved around the room.

She had finished unpacking one suitcase and was about to unpack another when Lucky walked in the bedroom.

"You ready?"

Willa gaped at him. "I'm still unpacking."

"I'll help when we get back. Come on." He took her hand, dragging her out of the bedroom.

She tried to tug against him. "I don't want to go," she protested shrilly.

Lucky stopped. "Why? And don't tell me you want to unpack when we can easily do that after we come back."

"I don't want to go," she mumbled, looking down at her shoes.

"Look at me and tell me the truth."

Willa lifted her lashes. "I'm too heavy. I'll make you wreck."

"I don't know which pisses me off more—you insulting yourself or me."

Willa gasped. "I didn't insult you."

"So, you admit you insulted yourself after I have told you repeatedly not to? You think I can't handle my bike with my woman on it?"

"No." She was aghast that he thought she was putting down his skill.

"Good, then let's go."

Willa didn't know what to do, but she darn sure didn't want to embarrass herself with her ass half hanging off the motorcycle. .

He was pulling her up the side steps when she broke and began crying helplessly. "I don't want to go."

Her husband stopped on the top step, staring down at her with a frown. "I know what's going on here, Willa, and it's really pissing me off."

"No, you don't—"

"You're comparing yourself to other women you've seen on my bike."

Well, hell, maybe he did.

"Willa, do you think you're the only woman I could marry or fuck?" His stern expression demanded her answer.

"Of course not. Most of the women in town would leave their husbands for you, and there's not a single woman at church who wouldn't give her soul to be with you," Willa said dejectedly.

"So when I married you, didn't that tell you anything?" he asked angrily.

Willa's eyes widened as she stared at him. "I thought you fell in love with my personality."

Lucky's hand tightened on the banister. "That was a part of it. I fell in love with each part of you: your tits, your ass, your thighs, especially when you clench them around me when I'm fucking you."

"Shh...I get the message."

"Can we go for a ride now?"

"Yes, but I've never ridden before," Willa said apprehensively.

Lucky gave her a smile that no pastor should ever give. "Don't worry, siren. It's not the first time I've taught you to ride."

෴ ෴

The motorcycle ride tonight turned out to be beyond her wildest dreams. They rode through the mountains then headed toward Jamestown. At first, Lucky drove conservatively, riding in the middle of the other bikers. As she began to get more comfortable on the back of his bike, he increased his speed, and the other bikers matched him.

She noticed the men with women at their backs rode in the middle of the large group, the lone bikers taking the front and back, except for Viper, who led the group with Winter at his back.

When they reached Jamestown, Viper motioned for them to stop at a gas station. Lucky pulled to a gas pump at the end, and as he pumped, she couldn't help watching the smooth way his body moved.

He placed the cap back onto the gas tank. "Like what you see?"

"Did anyone ever tell you that you're a little conceited?" she asked with a grin.

"My wife does every now and then." He smiled, bending down to give her a quick kiss before getting back on the bike.

"How come the women ride in the middle?" Willa asked curiously.

"Protection. The bikes in the back stay a certain distance from the bikes in the middle, keeping cars off our tail. The bikes in the front alert us to the danger ahead."

"Viper and Winter are up front."

"Because Viper's the president, and Winter's his old lady."

"Winter doesn't mind being called an old lady?"

"It's not meant as an insult; it's a sign of respect. You're an old lady now."

"What do you call an old lady that's old?"

Lucky grinned at her over his shoulder. "A real fucking old lady."

Willa laughed, wrapping her arms around his waist.

Lucky's expression turned serious. "Are you having fun?"

"Yes. I can see how it can be addicting. There's nothing like it, is there?"

"No, there isn't."

When Viper and the others began lining up to pull back onto the road, Lucky tapped the helmet she had taken off while he fueled his bike. "Back on."

Willa made a face. "Can't I just hold it on the way back? You aren't wearing one."

"Your ass isn't on my bike unless you have one on."

"Maybe Rider will let me ride with him to see what it's like without one," she joked then wished she hadn't when Lucky's expression went cold.

"You never ride on anyone's bike but mine."

"Why? The women switched bikes when we stopped. I don't—"

"Did you see any of the old ladies switch?"

Now that she thought about it, she hadn't. "I was just joking."

"Riding on another brother's bike is considered cheating unless you have my permission."

Willa started to get upset at the chauvinistic attitude. "Do other women members get to ride with men who have old ladies?"

"It depends on if he wants her to."

"That doesn't sound very fair to me."

"Biker clubs aren't—"

"Fair. I know. I've been told that before by someone else," she snapped, putting on her helmet. "Asshole."

"Did you say something?"

"They're waiting," she yelled out over the sound of his motor.

The ride back was even more fun. The sky had grown darker, and she didn't feel as if she were going to fall off. The hum of the powerful motor and the wind whipping at her clothes made her feel as if she were flying. She was disappointed when they arrived back at the clubhouse.

Lucky stayed upstairs with the men while she went downstairs to shower and get ready for bed. When she heard the music from above her head, she tried not to think about Lucky being up there with all the women. Then she opened the bathroom door and almost dropped her hairbrush when she saw Lucky undressing.

"Dammit. I was hoping to join you before you got out."

Willa unwound the towel she had knotted at her breasts, letting it drop to the floor. "I missed my back."

ഇൗ ഌ

Willa rolled over in bed, stretching her hand and hitting Lucky's shoulder. Rising up, she peered at him in the darkness, seeing him sleeping deeply. She lay back down, curling against his side and placing a hand on his flat abdomen.

A tear slid out of the corner of her eye, landing on his shoulder. Seeing her husband sleeping soundly was worth any price she had to pay. After all, he had been willing to live a life that was driving him crazy for her, so the least she could do was be willing to try to adjust to a different way of life for him.

# CHAPTER
# TWENTY-NINE

Willa poured herself another cup of coffee, trying to wake up. She had another forty-five minutes before she had to leave for the church. The deacons had agreed to let her rent the church kitchen after Lucky had left as pastor. She was happy with the way it had worked out. She still had all the space she needed to make her desserts to supply her growing customer base. Plus, she was able to sell in the church store. She had even been able to call Ginny and offer her a job. The girl had been thrilled about quitting her job at the theatre and had started two days ago.

"Would you like some help?" Willa offered Ember who was flipping bacon.

"No, thanks. I have it under control." The woman flinched when bacon grease popped up. It was the second pan she had watched the woman fry.

*Keep your mouth shut, keep it shut*, Willa kept telling herself.

Ember flinched again when a bubble of hot grease landed on her hand.

"Damn." Ember shook her hand in pain.

Willa couldn't take it anymore. "It's easier if you bake it in the oven. You can cook twice the amount and no popping grease."

"You can bake it in the oven?" Ember looked at her questioningly.

"Yes. Do you need to make more, or is that the last of it?"

"With the way the men eat, I have two more packs to fry."

"Where are the baking pans?" Willa turned the oven on to pre-heat then set her coffee cup down when Ember pointed to a lower cabinet.

Ember and Raci both watched as she pulled out two baking sheets then went to the refrigerator and pulled out the bacon. It took Willa no time to spread out the bacon on the baking sheets then slide them in the oven.

"Is it going to taste the same? The men can be picky."

Willa stared down at the fatty mess that Ember had cooked. "The men won't notice the difference," she lied. Her own name wasn't on the chore list for four weeks, and it was going to be hell for her. She had only been there three days, and each morning, she had watched instead of helping the way she wanted.

Winter stood up from the table to pour herself another cup of coffee.

"I'm on kitchen duty next week."

Willa nodded her head absently, watching as Raci filled a kettle with boiling water.

Willa couldn't help herself. "Are you going to boil eggs with that?"

"Yes. Why?"

"If you have a muffin tin, you can bake them in the oven, too."

As Raci dumped the water back into the sink, going for the cabinet, Winter cleared her throat, drawing Willa's attention back to her.

"Because I have to be at school so early, I have to get up at four-thirty to cook breakfast before I leave. I saw you down for laundry in three weeks. We can switch if you want. I can do that when I get home from work," she said.

"Are we allowed to switch?"

Winter frowned. "Allowed?"

"We don't get in trouble?"

Ember and Raci both stopped what they were doing to stare at her.

"We don't get in trouble," Winter explained. "We're not children, and we're not in boot camp. If you don't do a chore, someone else usually steps up and takes care of it. The only time someone gets in trouble here is if you hurt someone within the club or show disrespect."

"Disrespect?"

"Like, for example, you can't tell Viper to go fuck himself. Only I can do that." Winter smiled. "Seriously, Willa, we're pretty laidback. So, do you want to switch?"

"I would love to."

"You just made my day. I get to keep my regular schedule next week."

Willa didn't notice Raci and Ember rolling their eyes behind her back.

"Is there any way to bake oatmeal in the oven?" Ember asked.

"Sorry, no, but you can do it in a crockpot. It's too late to do it today, but you can start it tonight when you go to bed, and it will be ready in the morning."

Ember's disappointed expression brightened. "I'll do that."

The side door opened, and Lucky came into the kitchen at the same time several of the other members came to eat. The kitchen became crowded, so Willa moved out of the way, watching as her husband fixed his plate. When he sat down, she poured him a cup of coffee and placed it in front of him.

"Thank you." Lucky tugged her down for his morning kiss.

Willa straightened when he was done, blushing at the show of affection in front of the other men and women.

"You have a busy schedule today?" he asked, beginning to eat.

"Yes," Willa answered, moving to lean against the refrigerator as Winter, Viper, and Rider sat down to eat.

Shade and Lily came in the backdoor, and Willa melted when she saw Shade carrying his son. She and Lily had started driving in to the church together in the morning.

When Raci took the bacon out of the oven, Willa took two pieces for Lucky, setting them on his plate. Winter, who was chewing her own piece, lifted her brow as Jewell sat down at the table next to Winter.

"Aren't you eating?" her husband asked, looking over his shoulder at her.

"I already ate." She had eaten an apple while she had watched the women cook.

Willa poured Lucky a glass of orange juice, setting it down next to his plate.

"Do you always wait on Lucky?" Winter asked, her toast poised at her mouth.

Willa smiled down at her husband. "A wife serves her husband's needs."

The room went silent.

Jewell put her fork down on the table. "You're kidding, right? Do you know what century this is?"

"I know it's old-fashioned, but I like to make sure Lucky has a good breakfast. It's the most important meal of the day. My mother would get up every morning and fix my father's breakfast, and they were married thirty-seven years," Willa boasted. "They never spent a night apart, and they were very much in love. They were so much so that they never planned on having children, content with each other."

"That must have been very lonely for you." Lucky reached out, taking her hand then pulling her closer to side, wrapping an arm around her waist. Willa leaned against him, placing her arm across his broad shoulders.

"Sometimes, but I would use the time to read my Bible or bake once I was old enough. I spent summers with my grandmother since she was a teacher and had summers off. She was the one who taught me to cook and bake." Willa smiled, reminiscing.

"Your mother didn't let you cook?" Winter asked sharply.

"Oh, no. My mother was the only one allowed to serve my father. She would feed me my food before he went to work and before he came home. Then she would wait at the door twenty minutes before he came home."

"That must have been difficult for you," Lily said.

"No, it was very structured. I would spend two hours with my father every evening doing my homework. My father was very intelligent."

"Yes, he was." Jewell's sarcastic voice didn't make it seem like a compliment, and Willa frowned.

"Don't misunderstand. My father and mother were very much in love. They were enough for each other. I was the accident. I was the one in the way."

"They actually told you this?" Lucky snarled, pulling her closer to him.

"My mother did when I misbehaved or didn't do my Bible lessons."

"Your Bible lessons?"

"Yes, every good, Christian girl should know her Bible. She used to say a quote, and I would tell her what scripture it was. Or she would reverse it and tell me the scripture, and I would tell her the quote. I would study my Bible every night after dinner while my mother and father watched television. She would sit on the floor and lay her head on his knee while he sat on the couch. It was beautiful watching them together."

Willa's attention was diverted when Winter made gagging noises, which she stopped when Viper sent her a stern look.

"My father would look at my mother like that all the time. I miss them when I think back on my childhood." Willa glanced down at her watch. "Ready, Lily?"

"Yes." Lily gave her husband a kiss before taking her son who had been sitting on Shade's lap while Lily ate her breakfast.

"Have a good day, angel."

Willa smiled, thinking her friend blushed as much as she did.

Willa started to leave, but Lucky kept her pinned to his side. "I don't get a kiss?"

Willa bent, giving him his kiss.

"You going to be at the church all day?"

"Yes. I'm filling orders today, and Carl will be making the deliveries."

"Call me when you're on your way home."

"All right," Willa agreed, rushing after Lily out the backdoor.

Lily wouldn't carry the baby down the front steps; she always used the side path to the parking lot.

Driving into work with Lily and John was one aspect of the club she was enjoying. Lily would let her pack the baby into the church store and hold him while she set up the register. She missed being around Lucky during the day and worried constantly about him being alone with the women members until Lily told her they worked in the factory until five. As a result, Willa always made sure she was home by four-thirty. She didn't want anyone fulfilling any of her husband's needs except her.

⅋ ⅏

"That woman needs to grow a backbone," Winter said, glaring accusingly at Lucky.

"I've told her not to wait on me. She's getting better. When we first married, she wouldn't let me get my own plate." Whenever he had told her he could do something for himself, she would give him a wounded look that had him backing off.

Therefore, Lucky had gone slowly, not wanting to hurt Willa's feelings.

Shade stood, going to the kitchen counter to fix himself a plate of food. "Is it me or did her mom and dad's relationship sound like a Dom/sub relationship?"

"It sounded fucked-up to me," Jewel said, pushing her plate back angrily. "I wish that bitch was still alive so I could shove that book up her ass."

"Me, too," Lucky said. "Her father was wealthy as shit, but he only gave Willa's mother a small allowance. Willa won't buy dish soap unless it's on sale. She works her ass off baking, gives most of it away, and still manages to live on the income she has left. Meanwhile, she has enough money that she wouldn't have to work for six lifetimes. She's already made her will, leaving almost everyone in town money, but she won't buy herself a fucking pair of panties unless they're on sale."

Rider perked up. "She leave me anything?"

"I made her take you out. I told her you had a motorcycle collection that was worth a fourth of what she had."

Rider's face dropped. "A man never has enough pussy or bikes."

"A fourth? How rich is she?" A glint of interest sparkled in Winter's eyes.

"Don't even think of asking her for donations for that school of yours. Who do you think paid for the new roof when the tornado hit?"

"An educational foundation I applied to that Willa told me about..."

Lucky nodded his head. "From what little Dustin told me, her great-grandfather invented a new method of treating rubber. He started a company in the 1800s that lasted until Willa sold controlling interest after her parents died."

"What's the company's name? Maybe I should invest if it has that kind of longevity," Viper questioned.

"I saw the paperwork. DB Rubber is the company. I've meant to Google and see what they do."

Rider burst out laughing. "Don't bother." He rose up and took out his wallet, taking out a rubber and tossing it on the table. "Look at the back."

Lucky reached for the condom like the one he had in his own back pocket, looking over the back of the small package. He couldn't prevent his own laughter when he saw the company name at the bottom.

"She told me they made tires and toys."

"I'm sure they do." Jewell, usually the most serious of the women, was even laughing until tears came out of her eyes.

"We can't tell her we know; it would embarrass her to death," Winter warned, wiping her own tears away.

"Maybe she doesn't know," Viper said, trying to hold back his own laughter.

"She knows. She's the reason I haven't Googled it yet. Every time I start to, she distracts me."

"What, with a rubber?" Jewell wisecracked, smacking the table with her hand when she couldn't stop laughing.

"Viper, don't worry about investing." Lucky tried to choke back his laughter. "Looks like we all already own stock."

# CHAPTER THIRTY

"Are they having a party tonight?" Willa watched Lily's reaction as she filled the display with cupcakes.

Lily looked up from a notebook she was writing inside as she sat on a stool behind the counter. "Yes, The Last Riders have one every Friday night."

"Are you going to be there?" Willa tried to pretend she only had a casual interest.

"No, I don't have a sitter for John. Shade and I only go about once every month or two." Lily looked back down at the notebook she was writing in, a blush stinging her cheeks.

"Oh." Willa took her time putting the cupcakes in the display, trying to figure out a delicate way to phrase her question, but Lily saved her the trouble.

"When Shade and I go to the parties, we stay down in the basement, and only a few people come downstairs. They don't...We mainly hang out and dance."

"That sounds like fun." Willa thought she could handle a night like Lily described. "Do you think Lucky would miss being upstairs during the parties?" Willa closed the display case, sick to her stomach as she waited for Lily's answer.

"No, I don't know of him ever attending the parties. Maybe he goes for a bike ride."

"I would like that, too." Willa gave a relieved laugh. "I was dreading tonight. I'm happy I was worried about nothing."

Lily turned sideways on her stool to face her. "Willa, Shade's always been sensitive to my feelings, and I can't imagine Lucky doing any less as much as he loves you."

"I know he loves me," Willa said, meticulously cleaning the glass.

"I can hear you thinking from over here."

Willa looked up. "Lily, I don't feel comfortable talking about sex. My mother always told me good, Christian girls don't."

"Beth and I were raised the same way," Lily acknowledged, looking down again. "Both of us are married with children, and we don't discuss sex unless Sex Piston and her crew are around. Even then, it's usually just making jokes."

"I wish I were more like Killyama."

Lily nodded her head. "I wish I were more like Sex Piston."

"Maybe we could pay them to teach us," Willa joked.

"They would do it for free," Lily replied with a grin.

"I want to give Lucky what he needs, but I'm…worried that I can't," Willa said in all seriousness.

"You should talk to Lucky. He's really easy to talk to. When I'm…worried, he always makes me feel better."

"Me, too."

Lily tilted her head curiously. "Then why haven't you talked to him?"

"Because I'm afraid of the answer," Willa admitted.

"Well"—Lily stood up and took a five out of her wallet, placed it in the register, and then reached in the display case, taking out two vanilla cupcakes and handing one to Willa—"you might get the answer you don't want, or you might find out there was nothing to be afraid of."

"I'm afraid it will be the former," Willa said, taking a bite of the cupcake.

"I was, too. Once, I asked Shade a question I was afraid of the answer to. It took me a long time to work my courage up, and I got the answer I didn't want."

"What happened?"

Lily stared her directly in the eye. "I realized I wasn't as afraid of the answer as I thought I would be. The most important part of marriage is trust, and if I give Shade that, then any answer he gives me doesn't matter."

Willa licked frosting off her bottom lip. "How did it work out?"

Lily gave her a mysterious smile. "It was the best decision I ever made."

ॐ ✦

Willa walked into the clubhouse at four-twenty. Her hesitation evaporated when she found the room empty. She was about to go in search of Lucky in the kitchen when she heard someone coming down the steps.

"Lucky's upstairs in my room. We've been working on getting payroll taxes done," Viper told her.

"Okay." Willa started toward the kitchen.

"You can go on up if you want. I'm leaving to meet Winter. She's having a get-together for new students who are entering school in the fall."

"I don't want to disturb him if he's working."

"He'll be glad for the break. We've been at it since this morning."

Willa frowned. "Did he eat lunch?"

"Yes, ma'am. Stori made us lunch."

That statement didn't make her any happier.

"I'll go up and check if he needs anything." Willa moved hesitantly around Viper. Next to Shade, he made her the most nervous. He was better humored than Shade, but some deep sense of caution within her warned that it could change as suddenly as the weather.

"You do that. It's the last door at the end of the hall." Viper left while she was mentally debating if she should start coming home for lunch.

As she was going up the stairs, Bliss was coming down in a little black skirt that was bouncy. She also wore only a tiny, black bra that had a dangling charm that swung against her tiny stomach. Therefore, Willa was able to see more of the blonde bombshell than she ever wanted to see.

"Hello, Bliss." Willa moved to the side of the staircase so she could pass.

Bliss shot her a hateful glance, brushing past her without a word. Willa didn't understand the mean looks Bliss had been treating her to. The woman had always been friendly to her in the past. However, ever since she had moved in, she had either avoided her or left it unspoken that Willa had done something to offend her.

Willa went down the hallway to the open bedroom door, seeing Lucky sitting at a desk against the wall.

"Hey, siren."

"Does Bliss not like my coffee?"

"I don't know, why?"

"Because, from the way she treats me, I'm beginning to believe she thinks I spit in it," Willa remarked, trying not to show her feelings had been hurt.

Lucky frowned, leaning back in his chair. "I'll talk to her."

"No, I don't need you to. I'll ask myself when I get the chance."

"Fine, but if I see her treat you rudely, then I'll deal with her."

"Don't you dare. It will just make it worse."

Lucky's frown deepened. "Has she said anything to you?"

"No! She just gives me dirty looks, so what can you say to her? 'Willa doesn't like the way you're looking at her'?"

"No, I'd say cut it out, or your ass is out the door." Lucky's firm tone told her he would do just that.

"You can't do that. The club is her home more than it's mine." Willa was unaware of what she had revealed with her hasty response.

Lucky turned his chair to the side, tugging her down onto his lap. "This is your home just as much as Bliss's."

"I know that." Smiling, she patted his chest when she saw he was becoming angry with her. She wiggled on his lap so she could see what he had been working on, seeing the tax forms and a business credit card sitting next to the computer.

"Did it hurt?" she asked mischievously.

"Not too bad," Lucky replied. "You have a habit of changing the subject to keep from having an argument."

"I don't like to get in arguments; someone always gets their feelings hurt."

Lucky's hand went to the nape of her neck. "You mean you usually get your feelings hurt?"

"Yes."

"Siren, sometimes arguments can be good. I need to introduce you to make-up sex."

"That only works if I get in a fight with you," Willa teased. "What if I get in a fight with someone else?"

"Depends on who it is."

Willa hit Lucky on his chest and started to jump off his lap.

"Settle down. I was only teasing you back." Lucky pinned her legs by trapping them between his. He reached on the desk for the credit card, twirling it in his fingers. "I see you had a busy day."

Willa looked down at her top where his eyes had dropped. She had made chocolate-covered strawberries for a client's girlfriend, and the chocolate had managed to become splattered across her top and the flesh above.

"I made two dozen chocolate strawberries."

"Did any make it onto the strawberries?"

"I only taste-tested a few."

"Umm-hmm."

Lucky turned the credit card to the side, and Willa trembled as he pressed the edge of the card to her skin. When he slid it under the chocolate speck, removing it from her flesh, the blunt edge stirred a sudden passion in her she hadn't experience yet. Then Lucky slid the card to the base of her throat, holding it against her strumming pulse.

Lucky put his mouth against her ear. "Are you wet, siren?"

Her pussy clenched in need. "The door's open."

"Do you know what that means around here?"

Willa didn't shake her head with the card pressing against her. "No." She licked her bottom lip.

"It means anyone can come in and watch."

As her eyes widened at his answer, the card glided along her skin, down the cleft of her breasts. Lucky used the card to flip her top back, showing the curve of her breasts before he moved it toward the sensitive pink areola that the tiny bra didn't cover. Willa shivered as the blunt edge pressed down, and then she wiggled her ass down on the bulge that was becoming hard under her.

"Raise your dress and show me your pussy," Lucky ordered.

The tone in his voice had her wanting to deny him just to see what he would do, and the thought shocked Willa to her core. Her fantasies that she rarely let escape during the middle of the night were trying to do exactly that during the light of day.

"Do you want to serve my needs? I need to see your pussy." The aching desire in his voice had her hands going to her dress, inching the hem upward inch by inch.

"That's my siren. I can see you're wet. Do you want me to touch you?"

"Yes," Willa moaned.

Lucky flicked the credit card onto the desk as his hand slid under the top of her panties. He found her wet pussy, sinking a finger deep inside of her as his other finger rubbed along her slit.

"This is another reason I call you siren—because you're always wet for me. Your pussy calls to me. Do you want to know what it says?"

Willa arched as he finger fucked her into a frenzy, escalating the fire inside of her without quenching the need that was taking her over.

"It's says, fuck me."

Voices in the hallway snapped Willa out of her lust-induced haze and she wiggled off Lucky's lap, nearly crying out at the emptiness. Before he could stop her, she ran out of the bedroom, coming to a stop at the head of the steps, panting as if she had run a mile instead of a few feet.

The party had begun while she was upstairs with Lucky, but she had been so under his spell she hadn't even heard someone turn the music on. Several members were dancing, others were standing around drinking, and a few were having sex.

Willa gripped the handrail, her nails digging into the wood. She felt the dampness between her thighs increase as she watched the uninhibited way Stori pulled off Moon's T-shirt, showing his tanned skin that had several tattoos. He reached out to play with Stori's nipple as a hand on her stomach pushed her backward into Rider, and then all three of them moved seductively to the music.

Madness was how she felt right now, as if she had fallen into a pit of desire she didn't know how to escape from. Good girls didn't stand and watch as two men began having sex with a woman whose face showed she was ecstatic at being pressed between them.

She felt Lucky's hard arm circle her waist, his body pressing against her back as he began swaying them seductively to the beat of the music. Her ass pressed against his cock, trying to find the satisfaction she wasn't going to be able to reach through their layers of clothing. Her head fell back on his broad shoulder before turning so she could keep watching the trio down below.

Moon's hand took Stori's swaying hips, pressing them to his as Rider's hands circled her, grasping her breasts, lifting them to Moon's mouth, but he didn't take them. His eyes lifted to the head of the steps, catching Willa's gaze as "Sail" by AwolNation began playing while his hands went to his jeans. He flipped Stori's skirt up, pulling out his cock and sliding a leg between hers. He then tore a rubber open, rolling it on before he rammed himself inside the small woman, fucking her to the beat of the music.

Rider's mouth went to her neck as his hand went to his jeans, unzipping them, and Willa found herself thinking the woman couldn't possibly take two men at once. However, then Moon moved their bodies so she could see his cock sliding in and out of the woman who was lifting herself up on her tip-toes so Rider could press his cock into her ass.

Willa closed her eyes, unable to watch anymore without climaxing. She felt herself lifted and turned then pinned against the wall. A large, rubber tree had been placed in front of a nook she hadn't noticed when she came upstairs. She could see the downstairs, but anyone looking upstairs would only see shadows as the darkness fell outside.

"Marriage is give and take. I'm going to take what's mine; you gonna give it to me?"

"Yes." Willa opened her thighs to his urging, lifting herself up after he ripped away her panties.

His frantic hands lifted her, sliding easily in her to the hilt. She buried her face in his shoulder, biting down in ecstasy as he fucked her harder than he had ever done before. He had always made love to her with exquisite gentleness, but there was nothing gentle about the way he fucked her now. It was hard, frantic, and she could swear she felt the beat of his heart against her breasts.

Wanting him to touch the bare flesh of her breasts, she rubbed them against his chest, trying to give him the hint that she was too shy to tell him.

"Later. I can't touch them without Moon seeing. No one is going to see or touch you but me."

*Marriage is about trust*, Lily had told her, and now she understood in a way she hadn't before. She could trust Lucky with her body and soul. He wouldn't take her past her limits. Although he might push them, he wouldn't let her cross the invisible line that weakened her willpower.

"You're really my husband."

Lucky stopped moving, staring into her eyes. "Yes."

"You won't cheat on me," Willa stated with certainty.

"God, no."

"You wouldn't hurt me with your knives."

"When you hurt, I hurt," Lucky vowed then picked up the pace again, hammering into her while he stared into her eyes.

Willa used his T-shirt to stifle her scream while he braced his arm on the wall above her head as he came with her climax. Their panting breaths mingled together as they gazed into each other's eyes, each finding the part of their soul they had lost to each other when they had made love.

"One of these days, I won't give it back," Willa murmured, lost in what she was experiencing at that moment.

"What?" His lips twitched.

"Nothing." She wasn't about to tell him what she was thinking.

"Siren, it drives me crazy when you do that. Maybe I'm thinking the same thing."

She smiled as she straightened her dress. "I doubt that."

He cupped her face, making her look at him. "That, for a moment, our souls touched."

Willa's smile slipped. "I thought it was just me," she whispered in awe.

Lucky shook his head. "No, Willa, it's not just you." His other hand took hers, placing it on the cross at his throat. "It's a gift."

# CHAPTER THIRTY-ONE

Willa closed the refrigerator door before going to the oven where she took out one tray of bacon then slid another inside. Then she went to the table and sat down to enjoy her own breakfast. It was her first day of kitchen duty, and she had looked forward to it all weekend. That was, until she had looked at the list and seen who shared the chore with her—Bliss. She was also thirty minutes late, which had left Willa's nerves on end, dreading her arrival. She would prefer to do it by herself than be stuck with a woman who was becoming more and more obvious about her dislike.

She took a bite of her fruit parfait as the door to the basement opened. Lucky came in, looking like he had just gone to bed.

"Can't sleep?" she said, slowly taking the spoon out of her mouth.

"No," he grumbled. "I couldn't fall back to sleep after you left."

"I shouldn't have woken you. Have a seat and I'll get your breakfast," she said, getting up.

"I'm going to let you since you wore me out by waking me up after having your way with me all night. I need to refuel. Just so you know, my dick is off-limits for the next twenty-four hours. He's on strike."

Willa giggled as she placed a large omelet onto his plate and scooped him a large helping of hash brown casserole. She set the plate down in front of him before going to get his coffee. She handed it to him before kissing his upturned mouth.

"Even my lips hurt," Lucky complained, wincing when he took a sip of his hot coffee.

"I told you when you…" Willa paused, unable to bring herself to say the word out loud. "That it makes me…"

"Horny? Siren, that makes any woman horny," he boasted, wincing again when she hit him on his shoulder before she sat back down.

The kitchen door opened and Bliss came in, yawning. She was wearing a short pair of lavender pajama shorts that barely covered her butt and a matching top that dipped between her breasts and was only held up by spaghetti straps. From the way her nipples poked through the thin top, Willa discerned she wasn't wearing a bra. Willa was worried that was why Lucky was staring at the blonde woman whose body was perfectly proportioned.

"You're late," Lucky snapped at her, relieving Willa of her misconception.

Bliss shrugged as she went to the refrigerator. "I knew Willa would have it under control." She waved her hand at the food laid out on the counter. "And I was right."

"Tomorrow, be on time or your name's going in the punishment bag."

"What's the punishment bag?" Willa asked.

"It's a bag where they make you draw a punishment when you've been bad. Isn't that right, Lucky?" Bliss poured herself a glass of orange juice, leaving the bottle out on the counter.

Willa itched to get up and put it back in the refrigerator but she made herself sit still, not liking the provocative way Bliss was talking to Lucky.

"Yes," Lucky ground out, his eyes narrowing on Bliss.

Willa stood up, going to the oven where she took out the last tray of bacon then turning to set it on an empty burner on the stove.

"Careful, you almost burned me."

Willa hadn't been near enough to burn her, but Bliss's harsh comment rattled her. Regardless, she couldn't think on it long, because right then, several club members began trailing in one after the other.

She saw Shade come in with Razer. Lily had called her last night to tell her that she was off today and that Rachel was working the church store. Winter, Viper, and Moon came in as she placed toast in the toaster. Bliss merely moved to lean against another counter without trying to help.

Going back to the double oven, she leaned over to pull out the tray of biscuits.

"That's not a sight I want to see first thing in the morning," Bliss said nastily from behind her.

Willa's face flamed at the insult, aware the whole room had heard the comment.

Willa heard Lucky's chair scrape back. "Bliss, I want to talk to you upstairs in Viper's room."

Willa turned carefully to place the baking sheet on the stove. "Lucky, it's all right."

"No, it's not—"

Before Lucky could complete his sentence, Willa watched in horror as Bliss's hand went to set down her orange juice, deliberately sliding it forward and knocking over the cookie jar that Willa had filled an hour ago with Lucky's cookies. It shattered on the floor in a thousand pieces, which was exactly how many pieces her heart broke into.

Willa's already frayed nerves snapped.

"Why did you do that? Why have you been so mad at me? I thought we were friends."

"Friends!" Bliss yelled at her. "Friends don't stab each other in the back."

"How did I stab you in the back?" Willa asked, thoroughly confused.

"You fucked Shade! I saw you go downstairs with him! You stayed down there a long time in the bedroom. Does Lucky know you fucked Shade on the same bed you do him every night?"

When Lucky and Viper approached Bliss angrily, Willa held her hand up to stop them, wanting to hear the rest of the filth spewing from her mouth.

"Does Lily know?" Bliss gave a bitter laugh. "He wouldn't cheat on Lily with me, but he did with you. Do you want to know the funniest part? The night before Lucky was supposed to leave for Ohio, he wanted me to fuck him, and I didn't! I turned him down because you made me that fucking candy. He fucked Raci, Ember, and Stori all night, instead. I won't make that mistake again. If you want me to go upstairs with you, Lucky, let's go." Her voice had turned sultry, her wanton insinuation like a slap in Willa's face.

Willa turned around, giving the room her back as she battled her rising temper. "God, give me strength."

"What did you say? If you've got something to say—"

Willa turned around sharply. "I said shut up!" Willa yelled, going toward Bliss angrily. "I didn't have sex with Shade. We talked! That's all! He showed me Lucky's medals and talked to me about their time in the service. That was all we did!"

Lucky, Viper, and Bliss all took a step back at the fury on Willa's face. All the anger she had been holding in for days, weeks, and years came spilling out at the woman who had broken a cookie jar she had cherished.

"Why is it that you felt like you had the right to talk to me like that? You wouldn't have talked to anyone else that way, just me!"

Bliss started trembling. "I don't know."

"It stops now! Do you hear me?" This time, Willa yelled at the whole room of onlookers.

They all nodded in unison.

"That chore list sucks! If I want to cook and manage this kitchen, then I'm damn sure going to do it! Okay?" She glared at Viper.

"Knock yourself out." Viper's concession didn't slow her down.

"If I want to do it, I will," she snarled at her husband who was about to protest. "If it gets to be too much, I'll tell you."

"One person can't do it all. You can't handle this kitchen and your baking business—"

Willa cut him off. "I don't plan do to it alone. I plan to hire someone. Ginny can quit the diner. She hates it. Everyone can keep their freaking clothes on while she's in the house for a few hours a day. Everybody should pick the chores they want to be responsible for. If they don't get done, dock their pay and give it to Ginny to pay her for doing them."

"We usually vote on…" Viper began then stopped at her glare. "We'll try it on a trial basis."

Willa went to the pantry, taking out the broom and dust pan, angrily sweeping the broken glass and cookies up jerkily.

She pointed the handle of the broom at Raci. "If I want to wash dishes by hand, I will. It relaxes me."

Raci jerked back as the broom handle nearly tapped her nose. "Okay."

Willa dumped the glass into the trash can before turning her heated glance toward Winter. "And if I want to fix my husband breakfast and wait on him because it makes *me* feel good, then I will!"

"But, it's archaic—" Her teeth snapped together at Willa's glare. "All right."

Stori moved out of Willa's way as she put the broom and pan back in the pantry. Willa shut the pantry door then stopped in front of Stori, pointing her finger at her chest. "If anyone is going to make my husband's lunch, it's going to be me. If I'm not here, then he can fix it his own damn self."

"Okay."

Willa looked at her watch, realizing she was going to be late for work, and she hated being off schedule. She was almost out the kitchen door when she turned around.

"And, Rider, put down the freaking toilet lid in the half bath when you're done, dammit."

"I'll remember that."

Her tirade wasn't over as her gaze focused on Jewell. "Do you see a nose on my face?"

Jewell gave her a strange look, nodding her head.

When Willa slammed her hand against the kitchen door, sending it flying the rest of the way open, Jewell hastily moved out of the way so it wouldn't hit her when it swung back.

"I want my perfume back. It's been missing since the day I moved in, and I smell it on you."

She stormed out the kitchen door, still yelling her angry volleys over her shoulder as she headed toward the front door. She was going to get The Last Riders under control, and if not for good, then it would at least be until her and Lucky's house was built.

୬୦ ୯୪

The kitchen was silent as they all listened to Willa's shouts from the other room as she left.

Lucky saw Moon open his mouth to reply when he heard Willa yell at him to get his boots picked up off the floor.

"Don't say anything. She might come back," Winter whispered.

Moon closed his mouth, flinching at the sound of his boot hitting a wall, which had them all staring at each other in trepidation that she would come storming back into the kitchen. The slam of the front door had more than one member giving a sigh of relief.

Raci went to stand by the back door. "Do you think she's really gone, and she's not faking us out?"

After several seconds, Viper opened the kitchen door, looking into the other room. "She's gone."

"Thank fuck." Jewell sat down shakily at the kitchen table. "I thought she was going to kick my ass."

"Mine, too." Winter's hand was trembling as she lifted her coffee cup to her lips.

The tension in the room didn't dissipate with Willa leaving, though.

"Bliss, that's the last time you hurt a member." Viper's cold voice was directed at the cause of the unexpected showdown which Willa had won.

"Willa's not a member." Bliss's defiance had disappeared when Willa's rant had begun. Now she stood in the middle of the members who had gathered in a circle around her.

"I wasn't talking about Willa. I was talking about Lucky. She's his wife, so anything you do to hurt her hurts him."

Lucky saw Bliss's eyes move in his direction. Coldly, he stared back as Viper began stripping Bliss of her rights as a Last Rider.

"A member has to have eight out of eight votes from the original members to be voted out. When you mouthed off to Lily, you had six out of eight. Two members voted to give you another chance—Lucky and Rider. I'm taking another vote." Viper glanced at Shade. "Call Knox and get his vote."

Viper continued talking as Shade moved to the side, making the call.

"I vote out." Viper looked at Razer. "In or out?

Razer didn't hesitate. "Out."

"Train?"

"Out."

"Lucky?"

Bliss's tears didn't affect his vote.

"Out."

"Shade?"

"Out and Knox votes out." Shade placed his cell phone back in his pocket.

"Cash?"

"Out."

All eyes in the room were on Rider when Viper called his name.

"Rider?"

Rider, who had saved Bliss from expulsion three times before, was Bliss's final hope.

"Please don't, Rider. I promise—"

"Out." Rider's curt vote sealed Bliss's fate.

Bliss's shoulders began shaking while she stood as an outcast among them, but Viper showed her no mercy.

"Since I know you don't have a place to go, you have until the end of the month to get your shit packed and find somewhere else to live, preferably not in Treepoint. You could go back to Ohio."

"If I don't belong to The Last Riders, I don't have anything to go back to there."

"You don't belong to The Last Riders anymore, so there's nothing waiting for you there," Viper agreed harshly.

Bliss wiped away her tears with the back of her hands, walking through the room of angry members to leave.

None of the members were happy Bliss was being forced to leave. They all knew her feelings for Shade were hard for her to get over. They had all hoped the woman would be able to move past her love for him.

Lucky glared at Shade. "You brought Willa inside the club-house without me?"

"She wanted to know what was wrong with you. I told you to tell her about your PTSD before you were married."

"I was going to tell her."

Shade crossed his arms over his chest. "I saved you the trouble."

Lucky's hands clenched into fists. "When did you take her downstairs?"

"The night she came to borrow Lily's cookbook."

"That was a Friday night."

"Yes, it was." Shade's cavalier attitude pissed him off even further.

"What did you tell her?"

"All of it." Shade gave a laconic shrug. "I showed her all those fancy medals of yours, told her how Kale died, and how you nearly got your ass killed—all of it."

"I was—"

"I know, you were going to tell her. I saved you the trouble. Plus, she gave me a kiss for saving your sorry ass." Shade pointed to his cheek. "Right here."

"Let me show you my gratitude." Lucky punched Shade's smug face, making him stumble backward into the counter, knocking the platter of omelets to the floor.

"Watch the food!" Rider yelled.

Shade gave him a triumphant look before swinging his fist back and nailing him in the stomach. Lucky launched himself at Shade and both of them barreled into the kitchen table, crashing it to the floor and sending Winter and Jewell scrambling to get out of the way.

Moon pulled Lucky to his feet while Viper and Train yanked Shade back.

Lucky struggled against Moon's grip.

"Take it easy, brother."

Lucky knocked him back with an elbow to his face.

"What the fuck was that for?"

"I saw you looking at Willa's tits when she was sweeping up the cookie jar."

Moon gave him a shit-eating grin. "Can you blame a brother?"

"When I get finished with you, you'll be riding back to Ohio in a hearse." Lucky picked up one of the kitchen chairs, throwing it at Moon who ducked out of the way. It hit one of the crockpots sitting on the counter, tumbling it off the edge and sending oatmeal oozing onto the floor.

"I said to watch the food." Rider pushed Lucky back before he could attack Moon again.

Moon was pissed off enough to shove Train when he tried to keep Moon from attacking Lucky. Train's mercurial temper rose and he struck Moon in the eye, sending the two men into a fist fight while Lucky went at Rider.

"Why in the fuck are you hitting me?"

"Leave my fucking cookies alone."

Rider began hitting him back in defense, the two barreling into Viper who was still trying to contain Shade.

"What in the fuck is going on in here?" Knox barked out, coming into the room and then tossing the brothers apart.

Lucky managed to catch himself on the kitchen counter, holding his jaw that Rider had managed to land a blow on. Straightening, he angrily started at Knox then stopped. He hadn't lost what sense he had left to go for him.

Taking a deep breath, he managed to get control of his temper, and the other men quit fighting, looking around the destroyed kitchen.

"I'm hungry. Is there any food left?" Knox went behind the counter, searching for an unbroken plate.

"There are some paper plates in the pantry," Raci said helpfully, snagging one of the last biscuits.

"After Knox eats, there won't be anything left," Rider complained, glaring at Lucky. "You already ate that big plate Willa fixed you." He stomped to the refrigerator, pulling it open, and staring him in the face were rows of breakfast parfaits.

Lucky couldn't help laughing at Rider's face when he turned around, slamming the fridge shut then pointing his finger at him.

"Will someone fucking tell me how that fucking lucky bastard managed to catch the best cook in Kentucky who actually wants to wait on him hand and foot, is rich as shit, has the best tits I've ever seen, and from the sounds coming from downstairs, is fucking his brains out?"

Lucky gave praise to the one responsible. "I give thanks every day for her."

Shade gave him an unnerving grin. "You're welcome."

# Chapter Thirty-Two

"Did I do something wrong?" Ginny asked tentatively.

Willa set the decorating bag down. "No, I'm sorry. I'm not in the best of tempers today." She apologized for the silence that had continued throughout the day.

"That's okay. I just wanted to make sure I hadn't screwed something up." Ginny stacked another pink box of cupcakes she had finished filling. "I'm excited about being able to cook full-time. When do you want me to start at the clubhouse?"

Willa had offered her the job as soon as she had arrived that morning before her temper cooled, and now she was regretting it. Firming her resolve, she stuck to her guns, though. "Give notice at the diner and let me know when would be good for you."

"I'll tell them this afternoon when I go in." Ginny began filling another box with cupcakes. "I'm renting an efficiency apartment because I can't afford anything bigger right now. I don't make much waitressing, so once I start working full-time for you, I'm hoping to rent a one bedroom."

Her chattering dissolved the rest of Willa's ill humor.

"Can I ask you a personal question?"

"Shoot." Ginny neatly folded the ends of the box closed.

"Why don't you like the Wests? I mean, you lived there for several years, but you avoid them when you see them at church."

A guarded look crossed Ginny's face as she reached for another box.

"I was just wondering since they have custody of Darcy. Her older brother Cal is living with a friend of mine, Drake Hall."

"They never laid a hand on me or did anything inappropriate, if that's what you're thinking."

"Is she safe?"

Ginny paused then began placing cupcakes into a box. "Is your husband leaving Treepoint, or is he here for good?"

Willa felt a chill go down her back at Ginny's words.

"We're not going anywhere."

"Then she's safe," she said with a nod of her head.

"Did Lucky…?"

"Lucky saved my life. I'll never be able to repay him for what he did. They aren't bad people; they just have very high standards that I couldn't measure up to."

"I know what that's like. I never measured up to my mother's standards."

"You? I can't believe that. You're perfect. You're sweet, kind, and you try to help everyone. I wish I could be more like you."

Willa felt humbled by the compliments. "Go get us some lunch at the diner while I finish the order. I'll take a chicken sandwich and a salad." Willa handed her a twenty. "Buy yourself lunch, too. I noticed you didn't eat any yesterday." Willa gave her a wink. "You can give notice while you're there."

Ginny grinned back. "I'll wait until I get our food then tell them."

Willa turned her back to the door as she left to count the boxes that had been finished, deciding she would call Carl after lunch.

When her cell phone rang, making her lose count, she frowned at the number she didn't recognize.

"Hello?"

"Willa! I need your help!" Sissy's frantic voice on the other end of the line had Willa's hand tightening on the phone.

"What's wrong?" Willa could barely understand her for her crying. "Slow down so I can understand you."

"Can you come and pick me up at the lookout? I was dropped off here, and I don't have a way back to the place I've been staying. Can I stay with you?" The girl began crying harder.

"Yes, give me ten minutes to get there. I'm on my way." Willa grabbed her purse as she walked to the door.

"Hurry, please!" The phone went dead.

Willa started running out of the church to her van. Her fingers were trembling so badly she barely managed to put the key into the ignition. Finally starting the van, she peeled out of the church parking lot, driving toward Lookout Mountain. Thank God it wasn't far away.

It was actually the mountain that sat above Rosey's bar, and it was where the local teenagers hung out. Willa had never been there herself to party, but she had been there as a volunteer to clean the area when the church had become concerned it was being filled with trash and becoming overgrown. It was one of the few visitor sites the town had, giving a spectacular view of the other mountains and the valley below.

Willa made the turn onto the side road that led up the steep mountain, going slow as she looked for Sissy. She was almost to the top when she pulled over as close to the edge of the road as she dared so she could call Sissy back to find out where she was waiting.

When she couldn't make a connection, she looked at her phone to find there were no bars. Her cell phone couldn't get a signal through the heavy trees and mountains.

"Darn it." She was going to have to turn around. Sissy couldn't have called her from this high up; she wouldn't have a signal. The only place to turn around was at the top, though.

As she got to the top and turned her van around, she saw Sissy sitting on a picnic table by the chained-off cliff.

Willa slammed on her brakes, throwing the gear shift into park. Getting out of the car, she ran toward Sissy then slowed down when she saw the triumphant look on her face.

"Sissy, is everything okay?"

Sissy ignored her question. "See? I told you she would be stupid enough to come, didn't I?"

"Yes, you did."

Willa saw a man she didn't recognize step out from behind a tree, pointing a gun at her, and she paled. She didn't have to guess who he was.

"Hello, Bridge. I've been waiting for you."

ॐ ୧

"What in the hell happened in here?" Dustin was standing in the doorway with his briefcase.

Lucky set down his end of the new table that Train had helped him carry into the clubhouse. "Who let you in?"

"I did." Shade came in the door behind him, carrying a chair in each hand.

"Move," Viper ordered Dustin, packing in two more.

Lucky had been dodging Dustin. He had liked life better before he had found out about Willa's money. It was becoming a pain in his ass since Dustin had become his accountant, and Willa had decided that he needed to save more money.

She never approached him directly, sending Dustin to do her dirty work. When he had told Dustin to pay for a load of lumber so a delivery date could be set up, Willa had Dustin try to talk him into waiting until she could do a price comparison. It was only when he had threatened to go with a more expensive wood that she had backed off.

Rider came in, packing a box containing the new crockpot.

"I thought you were helping Razer."

"Nope, he had it." Rider set the box down like it weighed fifty fucking pounds while Razer came in, struggling under the weight of the middle section of the new table.

Lucky sprang forward, helping him before he dropped it.

Razer bent over, putting his hands on his thighs and panting for breath. "I'm going to kick that fucker's ass as soon as I can catch my breath."

"I have a question: why didn't you just pack it around on the path instead of up all those steps?" Dustin snickered at their expressions. "You all are a bunch of dumb fucks."

Lucky placed a hand on Shade's chest, holding him back.

"What do you want, Dustin?"

"I wanted to pick up your receipts from the donation you made for the football field. Diamond also asked me to drop off the latest copy of Willa's new will." He set his briefcase on the table, opening it to pull out a thick sheath of papers. "Diamond said she wished you would quit pissing Willa off. This is the fourth time she's had to change it since you've been married. Personally, I would have told her to stop after the third time."

"I'll tell Willa you said that," Lucky said, glancing through the papers absently, not really giving a flip who she gave her money to.

Dustin lost the cocky expression on his face. "I meant that she should take her time to come to a decision she'll be happy with. That way, she wouldn't need to make as many changes." Dustin nodded, trying to cover his ass. "It'll save her the money she has to pay Diamond to change it each time." Seeing Lucky wasn't buying his bullshit, Dustin pointed at the paperwork. "Diamond said to explain that Willa took down the amount she was leaving you to fifty percent." Dustin couldn't hide his satisfaction at that change.

"She didn't take my inheritance down because she was pissed; it was because she admitted she wants four children." Lucky gave him a gloating grin. "I told her I would be happy to give her as many kids as she wanted."

Dustin's crestfallen expression had Lucky chuckling as he tossed the papers on the table. "You can pass on the bad news to Diamond, though. She'll probably call her tonight and change it again. Willa's pissed at a lot of people right now."

"Dammit, I knew when she told me that you two were getting married, and she had drawn up a will, that she should do a prenup, too, but she refused."

"We're not getting divorced." Lucky frowned. "Wait a minute, when did Willa draw up her first will? I thought she's been doing this for years. She's had control of her money since her parents' deaths."

Dustin looked back through the paperwork. "She called me the day after you became engaged to tell me she was having the will drawn up." Dustin pointed to the date on Willa's original will.

Lucky gripped the table, staring down at the legal document. Willa didn't want to leave this world without leaving everyone left behind something to remember her by.

"Lucky?" Viper placed his hand on his arm.

"I told her about Bridge the night before."

"Who's Bridge?" Dustin stiffened, his face becoming concerned at Lucky's tormented expression.

"A man who promised to kill the woman I fell in love with."

"What the fuck!"

"She doesn't know. She thinks she's going to die. All these weeks, she's been living with this fear, and she never said one word, never asked me. She doesn't know."

"Know what?" Dustin asked, staring at the group of silent men.

"That I've been protecting her. I never left her safety to chance."

"Who's been protecting her?"

Lucky was about to answer Dustin's question when his cell phone rang. After he answered it with a curt hello, Lucky's face paled at the voice giving him instructions.

"We're on our way." Lucky disconnected the call. "Tell the brothers to get their weapons. Alec called; Willa took off in her van."

"Who in the hell is Alec?"

"Willa's bodyguard," Lucky answered, running to his room where he unlocked the bottom of his nightstand and pulled out his service revolver then ran outside.

Lucky didn't question how Shade had beaten him to the parking lot as he saw him jumping into the back of Rider's truck. Lucky climbed on his bike as the other brothers arrived.

"Where are we heading?"

"Lookout Mountain. Dustin, call Knox and tell him to get there."

The motorcycles were roaring out of the parking lot before Dustin could get his cell phone out.

Lucky had taken every precaution with Willa's safety, but he had been prepared for Bridge to try to snatch Willa, not for Willa to make it easy on the bastard and deliver herself to him. It didn't matter, though. Lucky wasn't going to take another chance with Willa's safety. The time had come to end Bridge's vendetta. One way or another, either Bridge or Lucky wasn't going to live to see another day.

# CHAPTER
# THIRTY-THREE

"You know who I am?"

Willa watched cautiously as Bridge walked closer to her.

"Yes, Lucky told me that you hated him, that you wanted to hurt him by taking away someone he loves."

"Like he took my brother."

"Lucky tried to *save* your brother."

"Shut up. You don't know anything about what happened to my brother."

"I know what Shade told me."

"Shade? That cold bastard doesn't know what it's like to lose someone he loves."

Willa didn't know enough about Shade to give an opinion, so she remained silent, turning her attention back to Sissy. "Are you all right? Did he hurt you?"

Sissy stood up gracefully. "Why would Bridge hurt me? I've been living with him."

Willa threw a disgusted look at the man who appeared to be Shade's age.

"Don't get your panties in a twist. I don't do kids. Besides, she doesn't have enough tits for my taste. You, on the other hand...If I had time, I could show you what Lucky only wishes he had."

"Don't be vulgar in front of Sissy," Willa snapped.

"You've got to be kidding me. When are you going to get it out of your head that I'm not a child? I wasn't one before I turned eighteen," Sissy gloated.

"Sissy, I know you think you're an adult, but you're not. You grew up too fast, and Lewis put too much responsibility on you. You've done nothing the last few months except show you're still a child."

Sissy snorted in disbelief. "How?"

"You've been screaming for attention like a child does. I think you've been screaming for help for a long time, and no one was listening," Willa said softly. "You were so hurt and angry when your mom went to prison. When she died, you had to live with Lewis, and then he died. You don't know who you can trust, who won't leave you. That's why you won't trust anyone. That's why you wanted in The Last Riders so badly. They watch each other's backs, and they protect their women."

"They've done a shitty job watching out for you," Bridge interrupted. "Sorry, but I have to hurry this along. It's not going to take Lucky long to get here with that bodyguard he has watching every move you make. Get your ass over here."

"What are you doing, Bridge? You said you were only going to scare her." Sissy went to stand next to him, tugging at the arm with the gun. He lifted her off her feet, holding her around the waist.

Willa ran to help her then stopped when he pointed the gun at the girl's head.

"You have two choices: either jump or I shoot her. You've got ten seconds before I make up your mind for you."

From the callous way he talked, the man wanted his revenge. Therefore, Willa was left with no choice, and she stepped toward the edge of the cliff.

"Drop the gun, Bridge!"

Willa spun around at the shout from behind her. Douglas and four other men Willa recognized from doing various jobs at her house during the remodeling ran from the cover of the trees and spread out, covering Bridge from different positions.

"Willa, come here," Douglas ordered.

Willa took a step toward him.

"Take another step and I'll blow her brains out."

As Sissy began crying, Willa couldn't leave the girl. She stopped moving, listening as the roar of motorcycles could be heard in the distance.

"Your husband is going to get to see if you can fly."

Willa didn't show any trace of her fear, unwilling for the last image Lucky had to be of her crying and begging. She wanted him to remember their last night together and how much she loved him.

The motorcycles came to a stop and Lucky got off his bike, his fury palpable. The other men got off their bikes, trailing behind him.

"Bridge, let Sissy go. This is between us. Neither Willa nor the girl has anything to do with us. You want me. I'm here." Lucky spread his arms open. "Take your fucking shot."

"I don't want you. I want to see your face when she goes flying," Bridge snarled then turned with the gun to Sissy's head. "Jump, bitch!"

Willa watched as Sissy turned her head to the side, biting into Bridge's shoulder. The man tossed her into the air at the same time a shot rang out.

"Sissy!" Willa barely managed to grab Sissy's hand, losing her own balance on the edge of the cliff.

"No!" Lucky yelled as another shot rang out.

Willa felt herself tumbling over the edge, her body twisting sideways from the force of catching Sissy's weight with her hand.

Willa screamed in agony at the pain radiating from her arm. Her free hand clawed to catch the edge of the cliff before grabbing onto the safety chain that Bridge had unhooked from the edge, holding on with what strength she could.

Sissy's screams sounded from beside her as the girl held on.

"Hang on, Willa. Don't you fucking let go!" Lucky's hand grabbed her forearm as Viper fell down on the ground next to him, reaching for Sissy.

Willa was unaware of the whimpers of pain escaping her as Viper and Train lifted Sissy, taking her weight off Willa. As soon as they moved away, Cash bent to help Lucky pull her up.

"Don't pull her up from her arm; it's out of its socket!" Lucky ordered.

Cash reached down farther, taking the waistband of her jeans and lifting her straight up into Lucky's arms. Then his hands went to her arm, holding it steady as Lucky carried her away from the edge of the cliff, sinking down on the ground with her on his lap.

"An ambulance is on the way," Viper said from next to them.

Lucky held her arm still, telling her not to move, while Willa looked through blurry eyes at the man bleeding on the ground a few feet from where she was lying. Douglas was standing over Bridge with a gun pointed at his head.

When a truck came to a screeching stop, Willa watched as Shade jumped lithely from the bed with a rifle strapped to his back. His blue eyes ran detachedly over Willa and Lucky as he walked by Sissy sitting on the ground, crying helplessly, not stopping until he came to Bridge's side. He crouched down next to Bridge, and his deadly, cold gaze had Willa shivering in the late summer heat.

"You missed."

"I don't miss. I hit where I was aiming."

Bridge laughed, wincing in pain. "You should have killed me. I won't stop coming after him."

"Bridge, I'm done pussyfooting around with you. The only man responsible for Kale being dead is *you*."

Bridge tried to rise up and go for Shade, but Shade reacted with lightning speed, grabbing the man's shirt where blood was pouring out and pressing him back onto the ground.

"You were the one your brother followed into the service, not Lucky. You were the one who should have taught the dumbass to keep his safety on. You were the one who should have knocked some sense in him the first time he was reprimanded for not keeping his weapon close to his side. He was fucking careless with not only his life, but the other men on the mission. Kale was a goof-off, and everyone in the squad fucking knew it. That was why you asked Lucky to watch out for him.

"Lucky did everything he could do to save him, and I'm done watching you blame him for something he couldn't prevent. If you go near him and Willa again, I'll take out every family member you've got left breathing *and* those dogs of yours. When I'm done, there won't be a person living to cry over the grave I bury you in. You got me?"

Bridge turned his face away, unable to meet Shade's gaze. "I got you."

"Good." Shade released him, rising to his feet.

The ambulance pulled to a stop and the EMTs got out, grabbing their equipment. When they would have gone to Bridge, Shade snarled at them.

"You fucking treat her first. I didn't shoot any vitals. He'll wait."

One EMT broke off, dropping to Willa's side.

"Her shoulder's dislocated."

Lucky's hoarse voice helped Willa bear the brief examination. Then she bit back her cries of pain as they immobilized her arm.

"Willa, stop." Lucky buried his face in her hair. "Quit telling me you're all right. I know it hurts like hell. I dislocated mine when I played high school football."

"Oh." Willa buried her face in his T-shirt. "Will you make sure Sissy's okay?"

"I'll take care of her," Lucky promised.

Willa didn't like the tone in his voice, but she was in too much pain to argue.

Knox and another ambulance arrived, quickly loading her onto the stretcher. Lucky held her hand as the stretcher rolled her toward the ambulance. As she passed Shade, she looked up at him.

"Don't you dare thank him. He has a big enough head, anyway."

Willa managed to laugh at her husband's wry comment.

"You going to write me in your will?" Shade joked.

Willa stared up at him. "I already have. Didn't Lucky tell you?"

Shade gave Lucky a mocking smile. "No, he must have forgotten."

"I think I've finally figured you out," Willa told him softly.

His smile disappeared, and an inscrutable look crossed his features.

"You told me each of The Last Riders has a code. Lucky's is honor." A lone tear slipped from the corner of her eye. "Yours is loyalty."

Shade reached out a gentle hand, wiping her tear away. "Go get your arm taken care of. I'll keep an eye on Lucky for you."

"I know you will," Willa softly replied. "I know you all will."

# CHAPTER THIRTY-FOUR

"Sit down and I'll get you some juice to take your medication with before we go downstairs."

Willa sat down at the kitchen table, feeling self-conscious with the other members standing around.

Lily and Beth both sat down at the table on opposite sides of her.

"Are you in any pain?" Lily asked with concern in her violet eyes.

"Surprisingly, no. They put me to sleep to put my shoulder back in socket and repair the torn ligaments. I'll be good as new in about eight weeks." Willa took the juice from her husband and the pain pill he held out.

"She has to have physical therapy. I've already called Donna."

"The Last Riders keep her in business," Beth joked.

"I have to admit, I did like Conner." Winter sat down at the end of the table with a fond smile of remembrance.

"He's not an option," Lucky said.

"Why? Maybe I should meet him."

"No, he had to leave town." Lucky glared at Winter.

"I don't know, Lucky. There were a lot of benefits to having him around," Shade commented, taking a seat next to his wife and placing his arm over her shoulders.

"Don't you all have somewhere else to be, like taking care of your kids?" Lucky asked grumpily.

JAMIE BEGLEY

Beth laughed. "Evie and King have them for the day."

Willa stood up, going into the fridge to refill her glass. When she came back to the table, Lucky had taken her chair, and the rest of the table was full. Lucky's arm went around her waist, tugging her down onto his lap, his hand resting casually on her denim-covered thigh. Lucky grinned unrepentantly at her faint flush.

"Is this the same table and chairs?" Willa asked, studying the table.

"Yes," Lucky answered, rubbing her thigh.

She could have sworn the table had been a darker shade of oak.

"Did Sissy get on the plane?" Winter asked as she stood up to let Viper sit down and then sat down on his lap, wrapping her arm around his shoulder.

"Yes, Knox drove her to Lexington. She didn't argue, from what Knox said. She was ready to go live with her family," Lucky said. "She finally realized being young doesn't make you invincible."

"She almost got herself and Willa killed. She's fortunate her ass isn't sitting in a jail cell. I bet she wouldn't be throwing around how she's fucking eighteen if she was in front of a judge."

Willa sent Shade a reproachful look.

"She came by the hospital after I came out of surgery, and we had a long talk while Lucky was there with Knox. She finally believes I wasn't having an affair with Lewis. I still can't believe it was Brooke. She didn't seem like the type."

"Sluts never do."

Shade jerked his leg back, giving Lucky a glare.

"Did you just kick Shade under the table?" Willa frowned at her husband.

"No."

Rider came through the kitchen door. "Alec's here to see you, Willa."

330

Douglas came in the door, wearing an expensive suit. Willa still couldn't grasp the fact that Angus's handyman was a bodyguard, no matter how much Lucky had explained it to her. Apparently, Alec was usually on the road with Mouth2Mouth. He had rented out Evie's house because he'd thought it would be a quiet place to relax. With Angus living next door, he would help him out occasionally, and Willa had simply assumed he was Angus's handyman, which had provided Alec with the perfect cover.

"Hello, Doug—Alec."

"Hi, Willa. I stopped by the hospital to see you, and they said you had been released early."

"She wanted out before she was charged for another day," Lucky griped. "If you had picked a better insurance policy, you wouldn't have had to worry."

"I'm young and healthy. I'll buy a better plan when we're ready to start a family." Willa started to get up. "Let me get—"

"No!" Alec cleared his throat then lowered his voice. "I have something to confess now that I'm not working for Lucky. I hate coffee, and I don't eat sweets. I'm kind of a health nut."

Willa's face dropped. "You should have told me. I could have made you some tea."

"I didn't want to hurt your feelings," he said gently. "With Bridge in jail, I can lose the six pounds I've put on. My men will miss all the freebies, though."

"I still think you should have told me you hired a bodyguard," Willa chastised her husband.

"I should have," Lucky agreed. "But like I told you, Alec only stays in Treepoint when he's not on a security job. Besides, it worked. If Alec hadn't followed you that day..." Lucky pulled her closer to him.

"It shouldn't have gone down the way it did. I was watching for Bridge to take her, not for Willa to go to him. When I followed her, I thought at first she was rushing to make a delivery, but then she turned off at the lookout, and I knew something was wrong. Then she stopped at the side of the road, and I thought she was turning around, so I backed up to give her room, but when she didn't come back down, I knew I had screwed up. Thank fuck I called you and my men when she made the turn."

"At least we won't have to worry about Bridge anymore," Willa said, rubbing Lucky's tense shoulders.

"At least until he gets out of prison," Lucky agreed grimly.

"He won't be giving you any more trouble, regardless," Shade said.

Willa saw the silent battle between the men then found her attention diverted again.

"Is that my cookie jar?" Willa rose from Lucky's lap, going to the counter to gently touch the glass cookie jar.

"Bliss found it on eBay and bought it for you."

"I'll have to thank her." Willa blinked back tears of happiness. It wasn't the same one, but it would bring back the same memories, and it was the memories she cherished, not the jar.

Willa noticed the sad looks on the women's faces and the grim ones on the men.

"What's wrong?" Willa looked around the crowded room. "Where is Bliss?"

"She's out looking for an apartment," Lucky finally answered when no one else spoke up.

"Why?"

"She was voted out of the club. Her behavior toward you was the last straw."

Willa adjusted her sling carefully. "Then vote her back in. I don't want to be the reason she has to leave."

Viper shook his head. "It wasn't because of you. It was because she showed disrespect to Lucky by hurting you. She's also hurt several of the women who are members."

"Was it the women members who voted her out?"

"No, it was the same men who voted her in."

Willa blushed at his reminder of how the women were admitted to the club.

She could see why Viper had been made president. He showed no remorse for the decision the club had made. His stern expression also showed that the decision was written in stone and wouldn't be changed.

"I was hoping she would decide to leave Treepoint and make a fresh start, but she wants to stay here."

"Because all her friends are here," Willa dared to take up for Bliss. The woman might have hurt her feelings, but she had ended up being the loser. Willa felt terrible for Bliss. "When Lucky left the club, you remained friends; he didn't stop being your brother. Bliss deserves the same as a former member. She can still be your friend." She looked at Jewell, Ember, Stori, and Raci.

"Maybe you're right, Willa. We can keep an eye on her and still put enough distance between her and Shade so she can move on." Viper brought out the elephant in the room—the real reason Bliss couldn't remain.

Willa looked at Lily who was twisting her hands together until Shade took them in his. Lily looked up at her husband, but from his expression, he wasn't going to give in to her silent pleas.

Willa sighed. Beth didn't seem any happier with the decision. None of the women did. However, Willa could see in some ways that Viper was right. When Lucky had been seeing other women in town, she had been miserable, and she hadn't even been with Lucky. He hadn't even noticed her. As a result, Bliss must be in agony watching Shade and Lily together. Maybe she would stand a chance of finding what the other couples had when she moved into town.

"She's going to be lonely living by herself after living with so many people..." Willa said, touching the cookie jar.

Bliss regretted her actions, or she wouldn't have gone to the trouble of replacing the jar. Willa lifted the lid, deciding she would make—her eyes watered when she saw it was filled with oatmeal raisin cookies.

The baker in her had her lifting one out and taking a bite. Then Willa started laughing.

"What's so funny?" Lucky came up behind her, wrapping his arms around her waist.

"Those are mine. She must have bought them from the church store."

"Bliss is going to be fine," Lucky assured her.

"I know she will." Willa leaned back tiredly on her husband, and her eyes caught something else on the counter. "Is that a new crockpot?"

"No."

৯০ ০৪

Willa pulled her jeans up, snapping them closed. She looked across the room at Lucky, who was standing in the bathroom, drying his hair with a towel.

"What's wrong?" He stopped his hand. "Did we hurt your arm in the shower? Maybe you should call Donna back and tell her it's too soon to release you."

"I'm wearing a size sixteen," she said in awe. "I haven't worn a sixteen since I was in high school and had a crush on Drake. I starved myself all summer—"

"You used to have a crush on Drake? He's a lot older than you," Lucky snapped.

"Calm down. He didn't even know." Willa giggled as she went to the dresser mirror, twirling around.

She'd had these jeans in the bottom of her drawer. They were the size she had aspired to get into every single time she had started a new diet. Her eighteens had been loose, so she had taken the chance to try them on.

"I can't believe it. I haven't even really changed my eating habits. I'm working out with you, but we both know I only last twenty minutes. I wonder how…" Willa turned to look at her husband who hadn't bothered to wrap a towel around his hips, and his perfect body still had droplets of water clinging to his tanned skin.

"What?" Lucky asked warily.

"I think I've finally found a way to lose weight that I enjoy." Willa smiled at her husband seductively.

"I thought you had to get to work. Isn't Lily waiting to drive in with you?" Lucky narrowed his eyes on his wife as she slowly began to unbutton her pink blouse.

"She can drive in with Ginny."

Ginny had been working for The Last Riders for three weeks, and it had worked out surprisingly well. The women didn't fuss as much about the other chores, each picking the ones they could live with.

Willa let her blouse slip to the floor.

"I'm going to need a nap. You kept me awake most of the night." Lucky tossed the towel toward the hamper.

Willa shivered when he walked toward her like a predator stalking his prey. She took a teasing step backward toward the doorway as she slid her bra straps down her arms. Her fingers found the doorknob and she twisted it, opening the door.

"Where are you going?" Lucky's voice dropped.

Willa felt herself get damp. Whenever he used that lethal voice on her, it made her—Willa refused to think of the word.

She put her finger in her mouth then glided it down the curve of her breast tauntingly.

"That does it!" he growled.

Willa spun around, throwing the door open, laughing as she ran down the hallway where she came to an abrupt halt.

Moon was sitting at one of the exercise machines, lifting weights. Willa didn't see him that often, but Lucky had told her that he liked going back and forth between the two clubhouses.

Willa's face flamed as the biker's gaze dropped to her breasts that were barely contained by her bra. None of the men ever came downstairs before noon. That was why she had playfully run from Lucky. It did something to her insides when he chased after her.

Willa turned on her heel, intending to run back into her bedroom, but she crashed into Lucky's chest, instead.

"Caught you." He grinned, taking in her embarrassment and Moon sitting there, gaping.

"Anything I can do to help?" Moon's gruff voice had Willa pressing her breasts harder against Lucky.

She leaned back against the wall next to the washer and dryer so her back was to Moon.

"Yeah, you can tell Lily to ride into town with Ginny. Willa's going to be late."

"Anything else?"

Willa's eyes widened when Lucky's hand went to the washer where clothes were neatly stacked. Willa had seen Winter folding them last night. She had bought a new outfit and was washing it, and the scissors she had used to cut the tags off were still sitting there. He grasped the scissors and Willa swallowed hard, wondering what he was—

The sudden release of her bra answered her question. He had cut her bra off.

Willa opened her mouth to yell at him then found his mouth on hers, and the passionate kiss had her hands going to his hair.

Lucky leaned his head back, taking his mouth away. "No, that's all I need from you, brother."

As Lucky turned, keeping his arms around her so she was out of Moon's sight in the hallway, Willa stared at her husband, trying to catch her breath. The feel of the cold metal on her back and Lucky's mouth on hers had awakened a primitive reaction to danger. His naked body covered in tattoos combined with the ruthlessness on his face made Willa run without caring who watched.

Lucky's laugh didn't sound good-natured; it sounded sinister, strumming her already-spiked desire. She ran into the bedroom, tossing her ruined bra onto the floor. Then she turned around, gasping as Lucky slammed the bedroom door.

"You're going to buy me a new bra!"

"Okay." He took a step closer.

The bathroom was only a few feet away, and her feet edged in that direction.

"It's not going to be on sale, either. I'm going to buy the most expensive one in the store," Willa taunted.

"I don't give a fuck how expensive it is. Just make sure it's red. It's my favorite color."

When Lucky's body tautened, as if he was about to spring at her, Willa felt like a rabbit in front of a panther.

"Good girls don't wear red." Willa shook her head. "It raises lust in men."

"It sure as fuck does in me."

She pretended to run to the bathroom, but she immediately felt Lucky's breath on the back of her neck since he was so close. Feinting left, she ran to the bed and jumped on it then sat on her knees as she laughed up at Lucky.

"Got ya!"

Lucky reached out, pushing her until she toppled over.

"Nope, I've got you." Lucky unsnapped her jeans, tugging them off. "When I get done fucking you, you'll be a size fourteen," he boasted.

"Your dick doesn't have that kind of staying power!" Willa's laughter was released in a gasp as Lucky threw himself on her.

"My wife said her first dirty joke."

"I did not!" Willa yelled

"You said dick! That's a bad word! I'm telling." Lucky rolled off her to lie on his back, staring up at the ceiling.

"Oh, Lord, forgive her. She spoke a four-letter wor—"

Willa rose over him, placing a hand over his mouth. "Are you going to be good? I'm not letting you go until you prom-ise—" Willa's teasing broke off at the narrowed-eye stare focused on her. In the next instant, she was flipped onto her stomach with his hands on her wrists, pinning them to the pillows beside her head.

With his mouth to her ear, he said, "Are you going to be good for me?"

Willa's humor disappeared as Lucky used his knee to spread her legs. Then his naked stomach pressed into her ass, and her hands clenched the pillows.

"Yes."

"Lift your ass."

Lucky lifted himself off her, releasing her wrists. When she started to lift herself on to her elbows, his hand on her back stopped her.

"Just that ass."

Willa burrowed her face in the pillow, wanting to scream at him to hurry up. Lucky was merciless in making her wait for his cock.

He placed tender kisses against her back. "One day, when you're being really bad, I'm going to spank you with my knife." His hand smoothed over the flesh of one of her ass cheeks.

The thought sent a tingle of anticipation through her. Every now and then when they were having sex, he would smack her ass. At first, it would always startle her out of the mood, but then she had gradually grown to like the sting of pain.

Willa was a firm believer in fulfilling her husband's needs, especially if she benefited with the mind-numbing pleasure he gave her in return.

Lucky reached over to the nightstand. Willa turned her head to the side to see what he was reaching for, and her heart skipped a beat when she saw him pull a leather case out of the drawer. Once he untied the leather cord, flipping the pouch open, she watched as his finger played over the different assortment of knives, going for the least dangerous one in the pouch. It didn't even look like a knife; it looked like a pearl-handled letter opener.

"Trust, trust, trust," Willa murmured into the pillow.

"What did you say?"

"Nothing," Willa muttered.

She felt the smooth, pearl handle trace a line down her back, glide over her butt cheek, and then she felt the handle rub against her clit. Gently, he rotated it against her clit until she was begging him to make love to her.

"What did you say? I can't hear you," he taunted.

"Lucky, please, I need you inside me."

Lucky laid the letter opener back on the nightstand before placing his cock at her opening. At the same time he thrust his dick inside of her, the palm of his hand came down on her ass. Willa bit her fist to keep from screaming, not wanting Moon to hear if he was still in the other room.

She wanted Lucky to go faster, his movements so slow she felt every ridge on his cock. Unable to take it any longer, she thrust her ass back at him, only to have his hand smack her other ass cheek.

"I need you to go faster," Willa mumbled.

"Then ask me nicely."

"Please, please..."

His cock plunged to the hilt in one stroke then slid back out of her pussy. Then he began moving so fast his movements started to ignite her into a frenzy.

She rocked back and forth as he moved, driving him higher inside of her. If she slowed down, his hand would give another smack. Her skin began to get sensitive, so each time his stomach brushed her ass, it made her pussy clench on his cock.

It wasn't long before her pussy began to spasm as her orgasm hit her in a rush. She wasn't even aware she was screaming his name until he placed his lips at her ear.

"Siren, you're calling me." He buried his face in her neck as his own climax hit.

Willa collapsed on the bed with his weight on top of her. "Lucky?"

"Yes?"

"I can't breathe. Is that normal?"

Lucky chuckled, rolling off her. His hand gently massaged her back, brushing her damp hair away from her face while he looked down at her, his smile widening.

"What's so funny?"

His humor was beginning to mess with her confidence.

He rose up, leaned over her, and placed a gentle kiss on the curve of her ass. "Good girls do wear red."

# CHAPTER
# THIRTY-FIVE

"Is that a new dress you're wearing?"

Willa twirled. The black dress that came to her knees was made out of a slinky material that made her feel sexy.

"Yes, do you like it? I've been waiting for it to go on sale forever. I got it for half off." Willa stood still so her husband could get a good look.

"I like it." He came up behind her, staring back at her in the mirror.

The black dress was simple. The most exciting thing about it was where the top of the dress crossed in the front, leaving a deep V. With her golden cross necklace, it gave the contradictory appearance of both saint and sinner. She was about to take sinner out of the equation.

Reaching into a drawer, she pulled out a black lace handkerchief, tucking it between her breasts.

"Siren, you just ruined it, but that's okay since I won't be going with you and the other women." He stepped closer to her back, his hand touching her neck then sliding forward to the deep V.

"Are you sure you don't want to go?" Willa asked.

"Go to Crazy Bitch's graduation party? Hell no."

"I won't have anyone to dance with," Willa complained.

"I'll dance with you when you get home. If I danced in front of those women, I might not get out alive. I still have nightmares from Beth's wedding reception."

Willa laughed at his expression.

"It's Friday night. Are you sure you want to leave me alone with the women?"

"I trust you." Willa tucked the handkerchief in more securely.

"You're a cruel, cruel woman. Are you wearing my new, red bra?" Lucky tried to snatch the handkerchief but Willa smacked his hand away, stepping quickly out of his reach.

"Technically, it's *my* new, red bra, and yes, I'm wearing it…and the panties that match," she teased.

"If I didn't know Shade was going to be watching you…"

Willa narrowed her eyes in a mock threat.

"I would go," he finished lamely.

"Shade is so sweet to drive us."

"He's only doing it because Lily wants to go, and I picked you up the last time you all went out drinking," he reminded her. "I didn't hear you calling me sweet then," he said grumpily.

"The next time it's your turn to pick us up, I'll make a note to remind myself. Besides, I don't drink, and neither does Lily. I only got drunk during my bachelorette party because Penni spiked the lemonade, and she's not going to be there tonight."

"Praise God," Lucky muttered.

"I heard that, and it wasn't nice, but I agree. I don't ever want to feel the way I did that next morning. It was horrible."

When her cell phone dinged with a text message, Willa picked it up, reading it.

"Shade said to shake my ass; they're all waiting."

"Since when did Shade start texting you?" Lucky tried to take the cell phone, but Willa slipped it inside her purse.

"Gotta go. I love you, husband."

Lucky pulled his cell phone out of his pocket.

"What are you doing?"

"Telling Shade you're on your way."

Willa shook her head at her husband's disgruntlement. "Are your fingers crossed?"

She was still laughing when she went upstairs to see Winter, Beth, Lily, and Rachel were all waiting for her in the kitchen. They were picking Diamond up at her house in town on their way.

Shade's expression was impassive as he put his phone back in his pocket.

"Sorry about that," Willa apologized, knowing Lucky had sent a nasty message.

"No problem."

She followed the group out of the kitchen, wanting to apologize again, but she decided to let it go. Shade and Lucky shared a complicated relationship. They antagonized each other half the time and took each other's back the other half.

She wished Lucky would figure out that most of Shade's aggravation toward him had to do with helping Lucky release the stress of his PTSD. If it was directed at Shade, it wasn't directed at himself—which, in some twisted way, worked for Lucky— and Shade had recognized the calming effect it had on him. On a psychological level, Lucky needed The Last Riders; his sanity depended on them.

Since he had moved back in with The Last Riders, he slept better, and the nights he didn't, he kept her busy by making love until he was exhausted enough to sleep. It wasn't perfect, though.

Sometimes, when they were watching television or each reading, she would catch a sad look on his face and knew he was missing the church, despite the fact that they both attended regularly. The new pastor was good, if a little standoffish, but she got the feeling that Lucky would rather be the one behind the pulpit.

Diamond was waiting for them when Shade pulled up in Lucky's Yukon. The women chatted all the way to Jamestown. Lily sat in the front with Shade, their hands clasped on the console.

Her marriage to Lucky was good. She couldn't ask for more from a husband or be happier, but Lily's and Shade's relationship, she had to admit, made her envious. From the looks of the other women in the vehicle, she wasn't the only one.

By the time they arrived, the party at the Destructor's clubhouse was in full swing. Willa was never good at parties, but with such few men there, she relaxed, especially being surrounded by so many of her friends.

Stud and another man who bore a resemblance to him were at the bar, drinking beer. Shade joined them while Willa, Lily, and Beth found room at the table Sex Piston, Crazy Bitch, and Killyama were sitting at.

"About time you all got your asses here." Crazy Bitch slung back the beer in her hand.

"Sorry, I was late finishing a cake, and I took a long time getting dressed," Willa admitted.

Crazy Bitch waved away her excuses. "That's okay. You're rockin' that dress. Want a beer?"

"No, thanks. I'll take a diet soda."

Killyama's chair scraped back as she took the drink orders.

Willa reached into her pocketbook for some cash.

"Forget it. It's a club bar; we don't pay unless it's the expensive shit. Then it's B.Y.O.B. Since we're celebrating tonight, Stud volunteered to splurge and even buy that." Sex Piston waved her empty beer bottle at Killyama.

"Does Stud know?" Crazy Bitch joked.

"Not yet." Sex Piston stood up, taking Lily's hand, and the two went onto the dance floor.

Willa watched, surprised at the natural way Lily moved on the dance floor, although Sex Piston danced exactly how she imagined she would. Her sensuality made her glad Lucky had stayed home.

The other women gradually began going to the dance floor until Willa was sitting at the table alone.

"Why aren't you dancing?" Killyama asked, setting the drinks down on the table.

The woman trailing behind her set the rest on the table. Willa thought she looked familiar in the dim light. When she straightened, Willa wanted to leave.

"Hello, Jenna."

Jenna walked off without acknowledging her.

"What bee crawled up her ass?" Killyama's angry frown made Willa even more uncomfortable.

"She doesn't like me. She's Lucky's ex-girlfriend."

"Don't let that club whore ruin your night. Get your ass up," she ordered.

Willa wasn't left with a choice. She rose at the woman's demand and found herself dragged to the middle of the dance floor.

Willa had one of the best times of her life. The biker women were such vivacious dancers that it was easy not to feel self-conscious. Eventually she relaxed, forgetting Jenna was in the clubhouse.

After an hour, she managed to escape Killyama and Crazy Bitch, who were both dancing with her, to return to the table to rest and take a drink of her soda.

"You want another one?" Crazy Bitch asked, sitting down at the table and fanning herself.

"No, thanks."

"You should have what I'm having." Crazy Bitch pushed her drink toward her.

"What is it? I don't drink alcohol."

"It's a Long Island Iced Tea," Crazy Bitch said, starting to take it back.

"I like tea."

Willa was hot and thirsty, and her diet soda was hot and tasted terrible. Before Crazy Bitch could take it back, she took a drink of the icy beverage.

"This is delicious," Willa said.

Crazy Bitch started to say something, but the man coming toward their table distracted both women.

"You going to dance with me tonight, Crazy Bitch?"

The woman leaned back in her seat, critically surveying the good-looking man who was confidently waiting for her reply.

"Calder, I'm never going to be drunk enough to dance with you. Why don't you ask that whore behind the bar to dance with you?"

"Why do you always have to be a fucking bitch to me?" The man's face grew angry at her rejection.

"Three reasons, Calder." Crazy Bitch raised one finger. "Because you're a dick." Another finger went up. "Because you fuck anything that moves with that dick." A third finger went up. "Because I already got rid of one dick and don't need another to replace him."

The man spun on his booted heel.

Crazy Bitch waved her fingers at his departing back. "Bye, dick."

Willa took another long drink of the tea, not wanting to laugh at the man's injured pride.

"I wish I could do come-backs that good. I get tongue-tied and cry."

"Fuck crying. It's never solved a fucking thing. My boot up someone's ass, on the other hand, has solved several problems of mine." Crazy Bitch stood up. "Want another?"

"Yes, please. I need to get the recipe and make a pitcher for the clubhouse. I'm sure they'll like it."

"I am, too, since it has—"

"Bitch, what's taking you so long?" Killyama asked, motioning for her to come back onto the dance floor.

Willa jumped up, going back to dance with her.

Three songs later, they all groaned when someone slipped a slow song into the playlist. The floor emptied out. Willa sank back on her chair, picking up her tea as Lily and Beth both sat down. It didn't take Shade long to take a seat next to his wife, bringing her a glass of the tea she was drinking.

"It tastes good, doesn't it?" she asked Lily after she took a drink.

"I love tea. Sex Piston makes sure she stocks it behind the bar when she knows I'm coming."

"I hope it's all right that Crazy Bitch gave me some, too."

Lily looked at her strangely. "That's not—"

Jenna set down beers in front of Sex Piston, Killyama, and Diamond who flopped down next to Willa. When she finished, she started to leave then paused, staring down at Willa with a fake smile of friendliness that didn't fool her.

"Thought I'd save Crazy Bitch the hassle of going to the bar for refills. How's business going, Willa?"

"Fine," Willa answered warily, taking another drink of her tea nervously. She had been the victim of bullying too many times not to see it coming. Jenna wasn't the type to do anyone a favor. Her sole intention of coming to the table had been to get in her face.

"If you want, I can write down my recipe for frosting."

"Why would she want your fucking recipe? How hard is it to open a can?" Crazy Bitch snickered, which only made Jenna angrier.

"It must be pretty damn good for Lucky to say it tasted better than Willa's when he licked it off my tits."

All the smiles at the table disappeared.

Willa tried to keep her face impassive so Jenna wouldn't know the hurt she had inflicted, but the woman wasn't done.

"Lucky enjoying riding that bike he won off Rider?"

Although Willa had noticed that Lucky was riding a bike other than his red one, she had assumed it was a club bike.

"I think it's hilarious as shit that he's riding a bike he won betting Moon he would ride you first."

"He made a bet with Moon that he would have sex with me first?"

"Yes. Of course, both agreed to let the other fuck you when they got you in the club."

Willa looked across the table at Shade and knew Jenna was telling the truth. Her perfect world tilted off its axis.

Over the span of her life, Willa had been the recipient of many hurtful comments, too many to count. However, none had ever hurt to the degree that Jenna had just inflicted.

Shade started to say something, but Willa shook her head. She didn't need him to defend her nor the women who had heard the insult. She didn't need anyone to defend her, not anymore.

"Lucky may have gotten the motorcycle, but I got the ring." Willa lifted up her hand, flashing the big, pink diamond that was on her wedding finger.

Jenna's face flushed angrily.

"The only thing you ended up with was another club to wait on. This time, without getting paid, and the men certainly don't have to make a bet to have you. They don't even have to ask, do they?"

Jenna's hand went to her hair, nearly jerking her out of her chair, but Willa had been prepared for her reaction. It wasn't the first time her hair had been used as a weapon against her.

Willa braced herself, taking the pain before her hands went to Jenna's, finding her thumb and bending it back mercilessly.

The woman screamed in pain, dropping to her knees.

"At least you didn't call me fat this time. I appreciate that." Willa bent her thumb back farther.

"You're going to break my hand," Jenna sobbed.

"All it takes to make me stop is one word," Willa said heartlessly.

"Sorry! I'm sorry."

Her cries made Willa sick. She didn't want to hurt her, but she was done being treated like a dog from the pound who expected nothing except torture. The confidence in herself that her parents had never instilled in her had developed since her marriage to Lucky. He may not love her, but he had given her one gift—the ability to face fear and to stand up for herself. It was something he was going to regret as soon as she got home.

Willa released Jenna, watching as she lurched to her feet.

"I'm going to be sick," she mumbled, putting her hand over her mouth then running toward the restrooms.

"I guess she couldn't handle the pain. It does hurt like a mother." Sex Piston laughed.

"Thank you for showing me that move," Willa toasted Killyama.

"I told you it would work when Sex Piston showed me that bald spot on your head," she toasted her back.

"Do you want to dance some more?" Willa drained her glass, motioning to a pale Jenna coming out of the bathroom to bring her another one.

"Hell yes, but do you think it'll be safe to drink anything she brings you."

"I don't plan to drink it. I just wanted to piss her off some more."

Willa went to follow Killyama to the dance floor, pausing only long enough to give Shade a firm glance when she saw he had pulled out his cell phone.

"Don't even think of giving my husband a heads-up. He told me that you're really a big softie under that exterior of yours. He told me you cried when you asked him for Lily's hand in marriage." Willa crossed her fingers behind her back.

Lily looked at her husband with tears in her eyes. "You did?" she gushed. "He never told me that. That's so sweet."

Willa had noticed, the madder Shade became, the more impassive he became, and she smiled in satisfaction when he slid the phone back in his pocket. Some of Lucky's luck was beginning to rub off on her.

# CHAPTER THIRTY-SIX

Lucky looked up from his hand of cards for the fourth time. "Winter text you back yet?"

"Not yet," Viper answered impatiently. "I just texted her. Give her time."

"They should have been home an hour ago. Willa's not answered my texts for the last two hours. Shade hasn't answered…I'm getting worried."

"I'm sure they're fine," Viper said, throwing a twenty into the pot.

Lucky absently threw in a twenty then another to raise the stakes.

"If I had a woman, she would answer my texts." Rider threw in his money. "She'd know there would be hell to pay if she didn't."

Lucky threw the brother a disgusted look. "How in the fuck do you ever get laid?"

"The women love me." Rider's smug face was nothing but a challenge to Lucky.

"Tell me one woman who loves you," Lucky said sarcastically.

"Willa, she loves me. She told me so, and she wrote me into her will." Rider flipped him off.

"Don't get cocky. She'll write you out of it next month." At least she had settled down about changing her will weekly since Diamond had gone up on her rates. Now she only did it every month.

"Maybe, maybe not. She said she thinks I'm special."

"You are. You only have one brain cell left from that weed you smoke, and it's struggling to survive. She thinks of you like a kid brother," Lucky mocked.

"No, she doesn't. Besides, I'm older than her."

"Chronologically, not mentally."

Rider looked at him suspiciously. "What in the fuck does that mean?"

Lucky rolled his eyes. "I rest my case." He laid his hand of cards on the table, leaning back to gloat a little himself as he raked in his winnings then looked at his cell phone again.

"Want me to text her?" Rider offered, taking out his cell.

"If she won't text me, why would she text you?"

Rider ignored him, texting Willa.

A sudden thought came to Lucky's mind.

"Why do you have Willa's number?"

Rider didn't look up from texting. "I text her a couple of times a day."

"What in the fuck do you text Willa for during the day?"

"I don't always text her. Sometimes, she texts me."

Lucky decided he was going to have a long talk with his wife when she arrived home.

"She text anyone else here?" Lucky gazed around the table at the brothers who refused to look at him. He barely looked at the cards that Viper dealt him. Turning in his seat, he looked at Train sitting at the bar, playing with Jewel's nipple.

"Does Willa text you?"

"She has a couple of times."

Lucky turned back around, staring down at his cards and frowning. Not paying attention, he bet too much on the hand. Showing his cards, he drank the rest of his beer as Rider smirked, gathering his winnings.

"Relax, brother, we're just fucking with you. Guess I'm not as stupid as you thought." He waved the cash he had just won under his nose.

The sound of the front door opening was the only thing that saved Rider from the ass-whipping he was about to get.

Shade walked in with Lily, Winter came in slightly weaving, Beth wasn't in much better shape, and Diamond and Rachel each seemed sober yet had a glazed look to their eyes. Willa was the last to come in. She had left looking sleek and elegant, but coming back, she looked like a holy mess. Her hair was messed up, one side higher than the other. The handkerchief that had been placed between her breasts was missing, leaving her cleavage on display, and her beauties were barely held in place by the red bra that was showing.

The other wives went to their husbands, while Willa totally ignored him.

Winter tugged Viper's arm. "I'm tired. Let's go to bed."

"You drink some beer?" Viper teased.

"Yeah, that's it. Let's go," she hissed, nodding her head toward the stairs.

"O…kay." Viper went toward the steps with his wife who couldn't leave the room fast enough.

"Let's go, Shade. Stori's waiting for us, and I need to feed John." Lily tried to tug her husband along.

"You go along. I want to drink a beer. You don't need me to feed John."

Lily threw her husband a wild look before fleeing the room.

Lucky was beginning to have a suspicion that something wasn't right when Willa, instead of greeting him, went to Moon who was sitting on a chair with Ember sitting on the arm, rubbing her hand under his T-shirt.

Willa leaned over the chair, placing a hand on each arm. Moon's eyes lowered, his mouth dropping open.

"Knox, I'm ready to leave," Diamond tried to coax her husband up from the card table.

He tugged her down onto his lap. "I'm not."

"Cash…" Rachel began.

Cash threw his arm over her shoulder. "Vixen, I've lost two hundred dollars tonight, and I'm not leaving until I get my money's worth."

Lucky stood up, wanting to hear what his wife was saying to Moon.

"Did you or did you not make a bet with my husband?"

"He wasn't your husband when we made the bet," Moon replied, unable to raise his eyes to meet hers.

"I see." Willa turned to face Lucky with her hands on her hips.

"Siren…If you have something you want to know, ask me."

"Don't 'siren' me." He heard the barest trace of a tremble in her voice. "You were going to share me with Moon, and he wasn't the only one you were going to share me with."

Not one tear glistened in his wife's eyes. The only thing he could see there was hurt.

"Willa, let me explain."

"Is that new bike you've been riding the one you won in the bet?"

"Yes, but—"

"Did you tell Jenna you liked her frosting better than mine?"

Lucky's face paled when he saw her hand unconsciously go to her breast. He knew she had been told he had done the same thing to Jenna that he had done to her.

"Yes…Please, listen to me—"

"Smiling or hurting, which one am I doing now, Lucky?" she whispered.

He took a step forward. "I only bet Moon to make him stay away from you. Hell, Willa, half the town's in love with you. Dustin can't stay away from you, Alec ate junk food for you, Rider wants to know what you're doing all the time, and Moon's been driving back and forth between Ohio and Kentucky just to get a glance of you. So, yeah, I bet him before we were engaged. I kept telling myself that I was doing it to protect you from him, but I lied to myself. God knows I lied to myself from the moment I looked up from reading my sermon and saw you sitting in the church with the sun shining down on you. I was going to marry Beth just so I could keep you safe from Bridge."

"What?" Beth gasped.

"I wouldn't have let him hurt her any more than I would have you," Lucky explained, "but I was so close to breaking that I was afraid, if I didn't marry Beth, I would seduce you. I kept telling myself what I felt for you was a figment of my imagination, because I was undercover for so long. But I couldn't do it. I didn't want my ring on anyone's finger but yours, despite the lies I told myself.

"I took the bike and have been riding it, yes, because I paid Rider for it. He finally agreed to sell it to me." He ran his hand through his hair. This was going to be the hardest part to explain.

"Yes, I told Jenna her frosting tasted better than yours. I lied, and you know I did, but that's not what has you so pissed. What has you so mad is that I did the taste-test the same way."

His voice went achingly soft. "I'm going to tell you something that's not easy for a man to admit. The only way I could touch that woman or any woman was to pretend it was you under me. That doesn't make it right, and it's pretty shitty, I know, but it's the truth. I fucked up with how I treated you from the beginning. I should have realized what I felt for you wasn't going away. I should have dealt with Bridge a long time ago. I didn't want another man's death on my conscience. But the hardest part was what God was trying to tell me all along."

"What?" Willa whispered.

Lucky took a step forward. "When I heard His voice that day in church, I misunderstood. I thought He was telling me to do more, to give of myself more."

"He wasn't?"

"No, He was trying to tell me I would *have* more. He wanted me to see that I would have more brothers than I could count, that I would have a town I would be more than content in, that I would have one I'd love. But most of all, He showed me that I would have more than a wife by my side. I would find a woman who would take my soul and give me hers. I would have more, much more, than I ever expected and much more than I damn sure deserve.

"Ask me how much I love you," he choked out, praying she would ask.

"How much do you love me?" she repeated.

Lucky held his arms open as wide as he could. "This much."

Willa gave him a watery smile, stepping into his arms, which he closed tightly around her.

"Do you really think her frosting tastes better than mine?"

Lucky came to the conclusion that he was never going to understand his wife if she was too shy to ask the real question.

"No, siren, no one makes better frosting than you," Lucky said truthfully.

"Let me see your hands."

# CHAPTER
# THIRTY-SEVEN

"Are you sure about this?"

Willa jumped when she heard Lucky's question from the other side of the bathroom door.

"I'm sure." Willa made her voice sound firm, but inside, she was trembling with nerves. She wasn't afraid of Lucky; she just didn't want to disappoint him. She didn't want to come up short compared to the other women he had played with before.

"If you're not afraid, why aren't you coming out?"

"I'm just finishing up what you told me to do," Willa lied. She had finished showering and wiping herself down with alcohol ten minutes ago.

Her hand went to the doorknob. So help her God, if she opened the door and he bore any resemblance to Jack Nicholson in *The Shining*, she was going to lock herself in the bathroom, screaming the safe word he had made her pick.

She slowly opened the door to see Lucky leaning against the bedroom wall with his arms crossed in front of his chest. He was only wearing a pair of jeans, his face hidden in the shadows of the bedroom, giving him a dangerous appearance she wasn't so sure was merely an illusion.

Her heart stuttered when she saw the selection of knives laid out on the nightstand with a pitcher of ice water and a glass. What was that for? To throw on her if she passed out?

The bedroom lights had been turned out with candles providing dim lighting. The bed had been turned down, and he had even changed the sheets to red silk.

Willa's hands tightened on the belt of her robe. "What do you want me to do?" She bit her lip, unable to take her eyes off the bed.

Lucky's loud sigh drew her attention from the wanton sight that was beginning to have an effect on her body.

"Willa, let's forget it. We can try it another night. The purpose of a scene is to heighten your arousal, not frighten you to death."

"No, I want to do this, Lucky. You promised."

Lucky straightened from the wall, walking toward her. His masculine beauty never failed to make her pussy quiver in need, overriding her fear.

Lucky reached out, curving his hand around the back of her neck and pulling her toward his body.

"If we're going to do this, you have to give me something to help you."

Willa eagerly nodded her head.

"What's your fantasy, Willa? The one in the back of your mind that you think about when you're daydreaming or I'm fucking you?"

Willa shook her head. "I don't..."

Lucky reached down, raising her hand and showing the crossed fingers.

"Tell me, siren." Lucky's voice deepened, going from a request to a command.

Willa turned her head so she couldn't see his reaction. "Pirates."

"Pirates?"

She nodded. "You know, they wear leather pants and vests, have tattoos—"

"I know what they wear." Lucky's gentle voice had her chancing a glance at him. "You never stood a chance, did you?"

She shook her head, understanding what he meant. Lucky resembled a modern-day pirate with his sharp features and tattoo-covered body.

"I'll be right back." Abruptly, he left the bedroom door, closing it behind him.

Willa stared at the floor in consternation. He could have just told her he wanted to laugh in her face; he didn't need to leave the room to do it.

She was about to turn to go back into the bathroom when the bedroom door was flung open and Lucky came in carrying a plain, leather vest.

"Mine has patches. I took one that Viper bought for a new recruit. I'll buy him another one. Don't you dare tell me you'll find one on sale, or I'll smack that ass of yours."

"Don't forget to shut the door." Willa usually checked to make sure the door was locked when Lucky wasn't looking. She was paranoid a gust of wind would blow the door open and she would look up when Lucky was making love to her and find a couple of The Last Riders watching.

"In a minute, I'm waiting for—"

Willa nearly ran to the bathroom, but Lucky caught her. "Trust, siren. Remember that, okay?"

"Okaaaay."

Lucky turned her back to the doorway where Rider was standing, wearing black leather pants and no shirt. He was also holding a gleaming sword, that was held confidently in his hand.

"Why did I have to put these on? I almost couldn't fit in them anymore. I have to quit eating so many cookies or start working out more." He gave Willa a wink, grinning.

"You have a sword?"

"I like to collect different objects. I had it hanging on my bedroom wall."

"It's scary-looking." Willa stared at the long, thin sword.

"Yeah, it is, isn't it?" Rider appeared happy at what he thought was a compliment. It wasn't.

"I'll be right back."

Willa watched as her husband went to the dresser where he kept his clothes, opening the bottom drawer and pulling out a pair of black leather pants. Without saying a word, he went into the bathroom to get changed.

Willa spun back to face Rider.

"Dinner was good tonight," he said casually.

"Th-Thank you."

"Next time, could you fry more chicken breasts? Razer ate three of them, Shade two, and I only got one. Stingy bastards."

"I saw you get three chicken legs," Willa reminded him.

"I like more meat. There isn't enough on a leg."

Willa took a step back. "I'll remember that."

"All right, let's get started," Lucky announced, coming out of the bathroom in the leather pants. "Shut the door, Rider."

Willa expected Rider to go out the door and close it behind him; instead, he closed the door and turned to face them expectantly.

"Willa, go stand by the bed for a minute while I talk to Rider."

She was about to argue, but then she remembered she had her safe word if she began to feel uncomfortable. Of course, she had no problem screaming it at the top of her lungs, either.

Warily, she watched the men as they talked. She looked down, rubbing her toes through the thick carpet, trying to overhear what they were saying.

"Ready?"

Willa was proud of herself; she only hesitated for a second or two before she answered, "Yes, I'm ready."

Lucky's expression changed in an instant, becoming the man she had always sensed was hidden behind his sophisticated appearance. More surprising and frightening was the change in Rider.

His expression became cold and aloof, as if she was only there to please him. The look really suited the spoiled biker. Willa didn't know which man to look at first, as both were compelling.

Rider's easygoing nature was gone as he walked a circle around her, stopping once again by Lucky's side.

"Your ship is now my property, just as you are."

"No, I'm not," Willa muttered.

"What did you say?" Lucky's voice dropped to a lethal level that literally had goose bumps going up her arms, and if she wasn't mistaken, he had a decidedly French accent. "My name is Captain Francois Le Danc. This is my quarter master, John Donnelly."

Willa couldn't resist another quick glance at Rider. She had never really paid much attention to the man's body before. He was only slighter shorter than her husband, but he was heavier. There was no sign of the easygoing friend she was used to cutting up with.

"Did you hear me?"

"Um, yes. I said, no, I'm not your property."

"Do. Not. Move."

Lucky took the sword from Rider, easily cutting through the belt of Willa's robe. As her robe parted, exposing her pajamas, Lucky lowered the sword, going behind her back. He slid the robe off, first one shoulder then the other, and the loosened robe fell to the floor.

Willa felt Rider's eyes drop to her red satin pajama shorts and her red cami. Neither showed any more skin than if she were wearing a tank top and shorts. Regardless, Willa was self-conscious of her plump curves in front of Rider. She forced herself to look at him, seeing him give her a wink, and Willa relaxed.

Rider was her friend, and his casual attitude made her feel comfortable in a strange way.

"What's your name, lass?" Rider's voice was gruff as his molten silver eyes glided over her body.

"Willa."

Lucky raised a brow.

Willa shrugged. What fun was a fantasy if she couldn't be herself, albeit more sultry and trampy? She firmly kicked her mother's voice out of her head.

"Are you denying you're my property?"

"Yes."

"You leave me no choice but to show you I am your master."

Before Willa could blink, she was tossed over Lucky's shoulder and carried across the bedroom floor, placing her against the wall. He grabbed one of her hands, raising it above her head where two paintings had hung. Now there were two hooks that looked like they had been drilled in the wall.

Lucky went to the cabinet and opened a drawer, pulling out two chains with cuffs on one end. He handed one to Rider, and then both men cuffed a wrist and raised it above her head, chaining her against the wall.

Lucky and Rider took a step back, surveying their handiwork.

"Who is your master?" Lucky asked again.

This time, Willa remained stubbornly silent. No good would come out of it if she answered him the way she was tempted to.

Lucky read the stubborn determination in her eyes.

"She's a fiery lass, isn't she?"

"Break her, Captain," Rider said, turning on his heel and going to the nightstand to pick up two scarves and a wicked-looking knife that looked sharper than anything she would have in her kitchen.

Rider strode back, handing Lucky one of the scarves and taking the sword from him before handing him the knife.

Willa watched as Lucky, with a flick of his wrist, used the knife to cut the scarf in two pieces that floated softly to the floor.

Rider then handed Lucky the other scarf that looked thicker and was black. He tied it around her eyes, blocking them from her sight.

"I have her under control now. Go swab the deck," she heard him order Rider.

The room went silent. She thought she might have heard a shuffle then a loud grunt before the door was slammed shut. Then she heard the distinct sound of a lock clicking into place.

Willa relaxed against the wall, sensing Rider was gone.

Lucky's French-accented voice whispered in her ear, "Don't look so pleased with yourself. How do you know he's really gone? Maybe he's standing beside the door to guard it from my crewmembers who want to steal away the beautiful woman I captured." His words cast doubt on whether Rider had left. Only knowing her husband as well as she did calmed her fears. Plus, he won points for calling her beautiful.

"Don't move. Stay completely still," he ordered again.

Willa held her breath. She was rapidly learning that, when he ordered her not to move, something was getting cut. She felt the blunt side of the knife on her skin as he cut upward, severing the strap on her shoulder. A second later, she felt the other one cut, and the top slipped to her waist. The blunt side of the knife ran along the length of her leg before then cutting the shorts off her body. Her stomach quivered when she felt the blade against her as the remains of her top fell away. Willa released her pent-up breath.

"Captain Francois, you're going to owe me a new pair of pajamas and a robe."

☙ ❧

Lucky grinned, glad she couldn't see his amusement. Quietly, he turned, going to the nightstand and replacing the sharp knife before taking out one he had spent hours sharpening when he had bought a new set of knives. He had thrown away the set he had used on other women. No equipment he had used on another woman would ever touch the skin of his wife.

He slid out another knife that was an exact match to the one he had just replaced except for one difference. He had used a scouring pad to blunt the blade. He had checked it a dozen times before, but he still slid it across the palm of his hand to make sure it was completely dull and there were no nicks in the metal to scratch her skin.

He picked up a cigarette lighter, placing it in his tight leather pants. Rider wasn't the only one who needed to quit eating Willa's cookies.

He silently walked back toward Willa, releasing the blindfold. Willa gasped as he took out the lighter, holding it underneath the blade for several minutes, then turned it over, doing the same on the other side, repeatedly flipping the knife. Then Lucky tucked the lighter back into his pocket before using his free hand to tug the blindfold back up.

Silently, he moved away again. Reaching into the glass of ice water, he took out a couple of the melting ice cubes, placing them in his mouth. Before placing the knife in the ice water, he took out another blunted knife that he had placed in there before Willa had come out of the bathroom. Running the knife across the palm of his hand, he felt the cold metal then crossed the floor to Willa and began to show his wife just how sensual his knife play could be.

"Don't move."

Willa tensed. He heard her breath catch again as he pressed the blunted edge of the knife against the side of her breast, watching as the water that had been clinging to the blade caressed her flesh while it slid downward, making a path toward her stomach to cling to the mound of her pussy.

"You're wet for me, aren't you, siren?"

"Yes."

Lucky slid his finger through the damp lips of her pussy, rubbing her moist clit before removing his hand. He then bent his head, taking her peaked nipple into his mouth and rubbing it with his cold tongue. Her breath hissed when he sucked it in again, and Lucky ran the edge of his teeth against her cold nipple.

His finger returned to her pussy, rubbing through her slit again, letting his palm press down on her clit. He switched breasts, sucking her other nipple in his mouth, teasing the tip until it stood out in a hard nub. Using his tongue, he pressed it against the roof of his mouth until he felt her knees buckle. Then he stepped back.

Using the blunt tip of the knife, he traced the line of her thigh and then across her belly, watching as goose bumps rose on her flesh.

"Is that with desire or fear?"

Willa licked her bottom lip. "Desire."

"Who's your master?"

"You are," Willa moaned, arching her hips, showing that she wanted his hands back.

He was going to give her more than she anticipated.

Unbuttoning his pants, he released his aching cock then nudged her feet apart with his booted foot and placed his cock at her wet opening, thrusting hard inside of her. He buried his face against her breasts as his cock slid into her as if begging for more. He gave her every inch he had, rising onto the toes of his boots to give her more than he had ever before.

Her legs lifted, wrapping around his waist as he fucked her like the pirate she wanted him to be. He wasn't rough with her, but neither was he gentle, making sure the leather of his pants rubbed against the inside of her thighs, and the leather vest scraped against her tender nipples.

"Come with me, siren. Show me you can keep my bed warm on the cold nights at sea and serve all the needs I desire from you."

"Francois!" Willa screamed as her orgasm hit, her body stretched from the metal chains.

As the erotic intensity on her face captured his lust, Lucky came, grinding his orgasm out in his wife as her cries filled the room.

When they both quit shaking and Lucky didn't feel as if his own knees were going to buckle from the ecstasy he had just experienced, he unchained Willa, removing her blindfold.

He pointed the knife at her. "I'm only releasing you because of the pleasure you've given me. Anger me and I'll chain you back up until you plead for me to release you."

"Is that a threat or a promise?" Willa teased, letting him pull her to him then laying her head on his shoulder.

"It's a promise."

"I love you, husband."

"I love you, wife. Let's go take a shower. By then, I'll be able to show you how those sheets feel on a tender ass."

Willa walked to the bathroom then turned back as he was replacing his knife in the leather pouch.

"The next time I make frosting, I might let you have some."

ಬ ೞ

"Is Willa all right?" Lily asked as she and Shade walked through the backdoor with a wiggling John held securely in his father's arms. "She almost ran us down with those boxes she was carrying."

Lucky's lips twitched. "She's fine. She was late to help Genny set up for the Forrester's wedding, and she hates being late."

"That wasn't what it sounded like to me." Shade bent over, placing John in a highchair. It should seem out of place in the motorcycle club, but strangely, it wasn't. Lucky prayed one of his children would be the next to use it.

"She was muttering something about freaking pirates."

Lucky felt Shade's quizzical gaze as Shade poured himself and Lily both coffee. Lucky was able to keep his expression impassive, but Rider sat, glowering from his chair at the table.

"Everyone must be having a bad day." Shade sat down at the table, observing Rider. "What's wrong with you? Someone steal one of your motorcycles?"

"Is Rider angry he couldn't have one of those cupcakes Willa was carrying?" Lily asked.

"That's it, exactly." Lucky laughed at the glowering brother.

"I'm going to go find Jewell. Tell Willa I better see some peanut butter candy when I come down to dinner." Rider stood up in a huff and was about to leave the room when Shade's voice stopped him.

"Jewell's at work and so are the rest of the women. Not everyone took a long lunch today like you and Lucky did. Whatever you're packing will have to wait until they get off this afternoon."

Lucky braced himself at the expression on Rider's face. It wasn't often the brother's temper came out, but when it did, it made Willa's look like a tornado in a bottle, while Rider's were of hurricane proportion, leaving a path of destruction that took days to clean up.

"Tell Willa she better put extra peanut butter on my candy," Rider snarled, leaving the kitchen with the door swinging angrily behind him.

Lucky didn't have time to relax, and Lily was still sitting with her mouth open when Rider barged back into the kitchen, going to the counter and picking up the sword he had left behind, shooting

Lucky a vindictive look before leaving the room with another swoosh of the kitchen door.

"Was that a sword?" Lily's voice trembled in fear.

"No," both Shade and Lucky answered at the same time.

The room grew quiet except for John playing with the small motorcycle that Shade had given him.

Lucky cleared his throat, broaching the subject that had been tearing at his conscious. "I talked to Beth a couple of days ago, but I haven't had a chance to talk with you yet. I would have never married Beth unless—"

Lily raised her hand, stopping his next words. "I was going to leave Shade when Brooke threatened him. I can't imagine you living with Bridge's threats for years. You're the one who guided Razer toward Beth. I know you, and you would never have done anything to make Beth unhappy, just like I always knew you would be my pastor again," Lily said happily.

"Really? And how did you know that? I didn't even know it myself," he said wryly.

"I never lost faith," she said simply. "You were always there for me, even when you left the church. You gave of yourself to everyone in town. You started a donation drive to fix the football field, went to the hospital twice a week to visit the sick patients, and if anyone lost a relative, you were the first one there by their side. You were also the one who organized the clean-up in town to help when homes were destroyed during the storm. Being a pastor is being more than standing behind a pulpit; it's standing beside the parishioners in their time of need. You were always there anytime I needed you, not only as a pastor, but as a friend."

Lucky lowered his head, looking down at the floor. "Lily, when I stepped away from the church, I did things no pastor should do…"

"Romans 12:2 'Do not conform to the pattern of this world, but be transformed by the renewing of your mind.' You needed time to find out what God's will was for you."

Lucky's hand went to the bridge of his nose, pressing hard to regain his composure. Lily, with one quote, had healed the last open, raw wound in his soul.

When he was sure he wouldn't break in front of Shade, he walked forward to Lily's chair, crouching down and taking her hand in his.

"You have the soul of an angel; do you know that?"

Lily stared down at him, her eyes brimming with tears. "Shade tells me that all the time." Her impish smile was a thing of beauty.

Lucky said a silent prayer that he was fortunate enough to have this beautiful woman as a part of his life.

"Your faith gave you strength when you needed it most, Lily. I don't know anyone who has a more beautiful, loving soul."

Lily reached out to cup his cheek gently. "I do."

Lucky saw Shade tense, but before he could say anything, he heard a sound at the door, and he turned, seeing Willa.

"I forgot my keys."

Lucky rose as Willa went to the counter, avoiding his eyes.

"I'll walk you to your van," he said huskily, following her out the door.

They were halfway down the path before he took her arm and brought her to a stop.

"Willa, what I said to Lily—"

"Stop, don't you dare take away from what I was just blessed to witness because you think my feelings are hurt. It was beautiful." Willa swiped away a tear clinging to her lashes. "I don't want to know what Lily's had to endure in her life. I went to school with her, and there wasn't a day that I didn't see the pain in her eyes." She leaned her head on his chest. "I honestly don't know if I could have kept my faith like her. I pray to God I never find out. She's stronger than I could ever be."

"That's not true," Lucky replied.

"It is true. I'm weak, Lucky."

"I don't want to hear that come out of your mouth again. You're strong, Willa." Lucky couldn't help letting his laughter escape. "Siren, you managed to scare The Last Riders into doing exactly what you want. We haven't had to do the punishment bag in weeks because no one wants to piss you off."

"That's just because they don't want to be written out of my will."

"No, it's because they don't want you to whip their ass."

Willa smiled, shaking her head up at him. "I can't believe I used to be so afraid of them."

"You're not anymore?"

"No, I can't imagine my life without them now."

"Good, because Viper wanted me to ask you for a favor."

She gazed up at him happily. "What?"

"He wanted to know if your company could give him a discount on a set of tires."

Willa's expression turned pained. "There's something I needed to confess. We don't make tires."

Lucky plucked her up into his arms, twirling her in a circle, his heart filled with joy. He was no longer watching everyone else live their lives while he was trapped, merely watching. Instead, he had his own piece of Heaven. He was exactly where he was meant to be in this moment in time with this woman in his arms. The loneliness and sorrow were a fading memory. From the time he had looked up from his Bible and seen Willa, he hadn't had a choice but to love her. No choice at all.

# CHAPTER
# THIRTY-EIGHT

"Explain to me why you wanted to make cupcakes tonight."

Willa shot him a frazzled look. "Because I was in the mood to bake."

"You don't seem to be in the mood to bake. You seem more in the mood to punch someone." Lucky leaned against the kitchen counter, drinking his coffee and watching as his wife carefully placed her creations on a cupcake tower.

"After I get this finished, I can relax." She placed the last cupcake at the top, taking a step back to survey her accomplishment critically.

"Want me to taste-test your frosting for you?" Lucky teased.

"No, you're not allowed to taste my frosting until I'm not mad at you any longer."

"I could have sworn you didn't seem mad last night when you were coming on my cock."

She gave him a vindictive smile. "I told Shade you said he cried when he asked for permission to marry Lily."

Lucky straightened. "You didn't."

"I did." Willa wiped her hands on the dishtowel then folded it neatly. "He's going to pay you back. You know that, don't you?"

"You're taking the imminent demise of your husband pretty well."

"He won't kill you." She went to the oven, pulling out the huge tray of meatloaf she had made and setting it on the stove. "At least, I don't think so."

Lucky watched her go to the two crockpots she had sitting out, stirring the contents of each.

"Siren, I know the club eats a lot, but you've made enough to feed an army." Lucky stared at the huge amount of food sitting on the counter. Beth had also helped by making a fruit salad, which she was sliding on the counter.

"That's it. We're done." Willa stared down at her watch. "With three minutes to spare."

"What—" The sound of the front doorbell ringing had Lucky raising a brow at the two women's expectant faces.

Viper opened the kitchen door. "You have company."

Lucky shot his wife a curious look, as it was obvious she knew who was there to see him. "It better not be Diamond. You promised me no more wills for at least six months."

"It's not Diamond," she said, pushing him through the door.

Lucky walked farther into the club room, seeing a crowd of people he had never expected. The room was filled to capacity with the church members. It was so crowded people were lined up on the steps to the upstairs, and all the members of The Last Riders were lined up against all four walls, wearing their cuts.

"What's going on?" Lucky asked.

Angus Berry moved to stand in front of him, and the rest of the deacons lined up behind him.

"We're here to ask you to return as our pastor."

Lucky had felt the loss of the church to his being, but he couldn't return to the life that would take his sanity.

Lucky cleared his throat. "I can't—"

Before he could continue, Angus raised his hand.

"Hear us out before you make your mind up. When you returned to the church, you told us you loved being a pastor, is that true?"

"Yes. I never lied about my love for the church or God, only my inability to walk the narrow path a pastor must walk."

"A nondenominational church doesn't have a path that narrow. They make their own, don't they?" Angus Berry's white eyebrows rose.

"Yes…" Lucky agreed, staring at the faces surrounding him.

"We voted to give up the Baptist church and become a nondenominational church. It's time you quit fighting that war with yourself and come home."

Lucky battled back the tight feeling in his chest. "What are you saying?"

"We're telling you that we can't sit through another long-winded sermon from a self-righteous pastor who wouldn't understand the scriptures of God if the Almighty came down and explained it to him. We wouldn't expect anything from you except what you've done the last few years, and that's to be there when one of us is in need and give us a better understanding of God two nights and one morning a week. In return, we promise not to care if you want to drink a beer or ride that bike up and down the streets."

"It isn't anything we aren't doing," Myrtle muttered. "Well, except for the motorcycle. We're too old for that."

Lucky laughed. "You're all sure?"

"Yes. We already told the windbag he's done. Wasn't too Christian the way he took it, but like we said, we're not going to judge another man, even though I have to admit, it's hard to do when I see him taking a twenty out of the collection tray every Sunday."

"We would love to welcome both you and Willa back, Pastor Dean," Myrtle spoke up, handing him his Bible that Willa must have brought upstairs.

His wife had known what the church was going to ask him and had made a feast for celebration. His wife had also known the answer he would give in return.

Reaching behind his back for Willa's hand, he pulled her to his side as he and everyone in the room bowed their heads.

"Heavenly Father, thank You for allowing me to serve you, for giving me not only Willa, who I will spend my life cherishing as my wife, but a holy home where we can share our love of You with others.

"John 4:18: *'There is no fear in love.'* You have shown me that I do not need to fear losing my way. Your love will always light my path, carry me when I stumble, and You gave me Willa to walk it with until we find our way home to You. Amen."

Lucky gazed at the room filled with everyone he loved, his hand tightening on the worn Bible in his hand that his father had passed down to him, and he would pass on to his son.

Willa wiped a tear away as she leaned against him, sharing her love and happiness for him without words. He had never been more thankful than he was at this moment in time.

Lucky stiffened, turning around to make sure Shade wasn't standing behind him. He could have sworn he heard, "You're welcome."

# Epilogue One

"Why am I not surprised to see you?"

Lucky turned at Bridge's snide comment as he was escorted into Knox's office. Knox shoved his prisoner forward into the office, slamming the door closed behind him and leaving Lucky alone with the man it took all his control not to kill.

"If you're expecting me to—"

"Shut up, Bridge. I'm done listening to the shit coming out of your mouth. I came by for only one reason, and it's to tell you that Willa's refusing to press charges. Sissy won't, either; she thinks she's in love with you."

At Lucky's disgusted expression, Bridge went on the defensive. "I didn't touch that girl. I only gave her a room to sleep in while she hid out from everyone. I only wanted to use her to get to Willa. I didn't intend to throw her, but she was biting the hell out of me. Her family's already fucked her up enough."

"She needs counseling, which Willa tried to get for her, but she refused. She's ready now, so hopefully it can help her. If not, she'll walk the same road as her mother and uncle, and she won't have anyone to blame but herself."

"Why isn't Willa pressing charges? I figured she'd be pissed off with Sissy almost taking a nose dive off that cliff." Lucky saw the regret in Bridge's eyes that he would never voice. The man he had once loved like a brother had saved countless lives; therefore, to almost take one unintentionally must be a bitter pill to swallow.

"Because she has faith that you'll realize your actions almost cost them their lives. She's praying that almost succeeding opened your eyes to the price your revenge could take."

"I see you're not thinking the same way."

"No, I don't, which is why I'm here." Lucky turned his back on Bridge, no longer able to look at him. Talking about almost losing Willa without beating Bridge to a bloody pulp was testing his resolve.

"During our last tour, Evie was hurt, and the men responsible not only nearly killed her, but got in a fight with Levi, Evie's fiancé. When they were up for court martial, it looked like they were going to walk. Shade and the rest of the squad were ready to kill the fuckers before the trial was halfway over. One of the main attackers was a general who was using his rank. It was Evie's word against four men. Levi's death had already been ruled an accident, so the brothers were out for blood. I knew it was only a matter of time before Shade killed them, lost his career, and then spent the rest of his life in a military prison.

"I pretended to be drunk and started a fight in the barracks, and they threw me in a cell for a week that was next to the men who had attacked Evie. It took three days before the arrogant pricks started bragging. They gave every fucking detail, and I remembered it all.

"I testified against them, and with my record and past as a pastor, it was no longer just Evie's word against theirs. They'll be sitting in that prison until they need Viagra to get a hard-on, and even then, they probably won't be saved from Shade.

"All the men gave me their markers. Each promised to repay me for putting those fuckers away. I didn't do it for their markers; I did it for Evie and Shade." Lucky turned back to face Bridge.

"I didn't know anything happened to Evie." Bridge's face had gone pale, his body taut with anger.

"No one did. It was kept quiet. They said it was out of respect for Evie, but everyone knew it was to protect General Lander and his son's reputation. It happened two weeks after Kale died. You were stateside with your family."

"I served with Evie."

Lucky continued as if Bridge hadn't spoken. "I never took any of them up on their markers until Viper and I returned from Kale's memorial service, and Viper told me Shade was coming after you."

Lucky still remembered how harshly Bridge had told him to leave when he and Viper had arrived. Viper had heard every threat.

"I called in his marker not to kill you, and he has kept it all these years. You were like a brother, and it's not easy to kill a brother, even when Willa's life hung in the balance. When Willa was in surgery, repairing her shoulder, I released him from that promise. Willa and I are trying to start a family. She could have been pregnant, and you could have succeeded in killing Willa and my child. I thought I could protect her from you, but I won't take that chance again.

"What it comes down to is a choice between you and Willa, and she will win every time, so I'm done fucking around with you. I have a better use for Shade's and the rest of the brothers' markers now, and it doesn't involve you.

"I'm giving you a last chance to move on, Bridge." Lucky tossed a set of keys to Bridge who caught them in his hand. "Move on, leave Treepoint, and don't come back. Kale is dead and gone, and there is nothing either of us can do to bring him back. If you ever try to come near Treepoint again, Shade will make sure it's the last time you suck air." Lucky went toward the office door, brushing past Bridge to open it.

He paused without looking back. "Ride as far as you can, Bridge, and find a place that you can call home." Lucky's voice became choked, remembering all the times they had spent together when they were in the service. "I was fucked up when I came out of the service, too. The difference is I became a member of The Last Riders, and they helped me keep my sanity. You turned them down, and you've been lost ever since.

"Goodbye, brother. I pray you find peace. I already have."

Lucky walked out of the office, coming to a stop at seeing all the brothers waiting outside the door. They were there to support him, just as they always had and always would.

☜ ☞

Willa had lunch waiting for them when they arrived home. The men ate while sitting around and talking when Shade went to the counter, taking a cupcake.

Lucky was eating his own meal as he looked up to see Shade take a bite. An expression of complete ecstasy came over his face as he took another bite.

He turned to Willa who was sitting next to Lucky with Lily and John sitting on her other side. "What flavor are these?"

Willa broke off her conversation with Lily to answer his question. "Oh, those are chocolate bourbon. The recipe was giving me trouble. I thought they would be a big seller during the Derby festival. I think I've finally got it right."

"You sure as fuck have. Willa, I love my wife, but woman, if I had never met Lily, that asshole husband of yours wouldn't have caught you. I would have put a ring on your finger after the first bite."

Willa blushed, smiling in pride at her accomplishment.

"Willa, I'm going to need that recipe." Lily laughed, not at all upset by Shade's comment.

Lucky couldn't say the same. He saw red.

Why did the brothers all think Willa would have succumbed to them over him?

"Willa wouldn't have given you the fucking time of day."

Shade finished eating his cupcake. "It wouldn't even have been a competition."

The last word wasn't out of his mouth before Lucky was out of his chair and lunging toward Shade who dodged his first blow. Lucky, unable to stop his momentum, fell against the counter, sending a Crockpot full of macaroni and cheese crashing to the floor. This time, as Lucky twisted, going after Shade again, he managed to send Shade backward against the counter, nearly toppling the cupcake tray.

"Watch the fucking food!" Rider said, jumping up from his chair to break the men apart with Train's help.

"Lucky, there are children in the room!" Willa yelled at him angrily.

Lucky glanced at Beth's boys and Shade's son who were too busy eating the vanilla cupcakes that Willa had made to notice what the adults were doing.

Lucky shoved Rider off him, retaking his seat. Guiltily, he let Shade clean up the mess. Damn bastard deserved it for aggravating him.

"You should be ashamed of yourself," Willa snapped.

"I'm sorry," he apologized to the women.

"I don't know what you became so jealous for." Willa placed her hand over his.

"I don't, either," Lucky said, picking up his fork.

"Willa, after dinner, I brought those papers for you to sign," Diamond said, handing Knox a cupcake before taking one for herself. The brother took it then reached for another before retaking his chair.

"You promised me no more changes to your will for at least a year." Lucky frowned. He had hoped telling her that she would save money would be an added incentive.

"Oh, it's not a will."

The room went quiet as the members eavesdropped on their conversation.

"I signed over my house to Ginny."

"You gave your house to Ginny?" Lucky was surprised Willa hadn't mentioned that she was thinking of doing it. She had told him that she was keeping it for their future children. "Why?"

"Because she can't afford an apartment and pay for college, too. Bliss is going to be her roommate. It will help her afford the bills."

"She's going to share the house with Ginny?"

"Yes, that way, Ginny can afford it until she gets her degree, and Bliss won't be lonely," Willa explained, waiting for his reaction.

"I thought you wanted to keep your home for our children?"

"They'll have a home. The home you're building is where they'll grow up. You can only have one home."

Lucky couldn't resist placing a kiss on his wife's lips.

"There can only be one home—the one we'll make," Lucky agreed.

"Ginny deserves it. She finally opened up to me what her issues were with the West's. I was worried about Cal's sister Darcy living with them, so she told me to keep me from being worried about her. It gave me another reason to love you." She looked up at the men in the room. "All of you."

"We're glad you think that since you're our newest member." Viper grinned. "You're going through the initiation tonight."

When Willa went white, Lucky almost laughed, knowing she was thinking about how he had told her the votes were given.

"Siren, I told you that votes could also be given by markers, and I called all mine in to make you a member."

Willa still didn't seem to be jumping with joy. "Exactly what's the initiation?"

Lucky waited for Viper to answer, having already noticed that Shade was boxing up the last of the cupcakes before they could be eaten.

"You have to make another batch of those cupcakes," Viper stated, wincing when Winter hit his arm.

"And a batch of peanut butter candy," Rider added quickly.

"And a batch of oatmeal raisin cookies," Lucky joked.

"I thought you wanted me to stop making them until you lost some weight?" Willa teased.

Lucky bent down to whisper in her ear, "How do you feel about bandits?"

# EPILOGUE TWO

"Dad, Becky said I'm going to Hell."

Willa gasped, looking up from playing with the one-month-old infant in her arms when her son repeated her daughter's angry statement. Then she and Lucky both stared up from where they sat on a blanket in the front yard, watching their children as they played outside.

"Why did you tell your brother he's going to Hell?"

Willa threw Lucky a chastising look at the amusement she heard in his voice.

"He said dammit." Becky's voice rose as she told on Kale.

Kale turned a bright red. "Uncle Rider says it all the time."

"Just because Rider says it, that doesn't mean you can." She was going to let Rider have it the next time he came over to investigate what she was cooking, which was daily. "I've told you that before."

Becky and Kale were as different as night and day. Becky was older than Kale with an angelic personality. Her son, on the other hand, had a bit of a hellion inside of him. He was definitely his father's son. He was constantly in trouble, and despite his five years, he was already begging for a miniature bike. Every time Rider showed him his motorcycle collection, the little boy would spend the next three days asking for one. The boy was definitely stubborn and had a temper when his older brother and sister pushed him. She didn't know where that came from because Lucky rarely lost his temper.

"Why did you say it?"

Kale remained silent, but Becky spoke up, answering her father's question.

"He said it after he asked Mama for a dog and she told him no."

"Kale." Willa had noticed her son becoming angrily silent and walking away after she had told him he couldn't have a puppy like the one Razer had given his children.

"Go play," Lucky ordered. "Kale, we will discuss how to control your temper and your language tonight."

"Yes, sir." Both children ran off to play with their older brother.

Lucky waited until they were out of earshot before chuckling.

"It's not funny," Willa snapped. "He needs to control his temper."

"Siren, he can't help it. He takes after his mother." Lucky leaned toward her, giving her a kiss that melted her indignation. When he straightened, she could tell he wanted to get something off his mind. Unfortunately, she knew what it was. They'd had the same conversation many times before.

"He wants a dog. All the kids do."

"I know, but I can't," she said, her expression filled with pain. The passing years hadn't taken away the pain or the guilt of losing Ria.

"She was trained to be a protector from the time she was a pup. She wanted to save your life. She would have been proud. If you hadn't survived, our children would have never been born."

Willa wiped the tear sliding down her cheek away, cuddling her son closer to her chest.

"I gave her away." Willa sobbed, revealing her secret anguish. "I was so hurt I couldn't look at her and not think about you. I didn't care if she cost twenty thousand dollars. I thought, if she wasn't there, I wouldn't think about you so much."

"I know it wasn't about the money," Lucky spoke soothingly. "You're the most generous woman I know. The whole town depends on your foundations from the schools to the women's abuse shelter. You turned around; you were coming back for her. You weren't able to leave her. You're not capable of giving up someone you love." Lucky nuzzled her neck as he reached out to stroke his baby's soft cheek.

Willa regained her composure, not wanting the children to see her cry.

She gave a hiccupping laugh. "I don't know about that. I didn't like you very much when Jenna was your girlfriend."

Lucky straightened up, staring into her eyes. "Jenna was never my girlfriend. I've only had three girlfriends my whole life. One was Ava, whom I dated in high school and thought I was going to marry. Beth was the second, and you were my third and still are the only one I ever loved."

"Your fingers are crossed." Willa looked down at his hands. "I'm not the only one you loved."

Lucky stared at her seriously, his eyes hurt. "I can prove it."

He shifted, reaching into his back pocket and pulling out his wallet. Willa watched curiously as he opened it and pulled out a thin strip of paper before he showed it to her.

Willa's mouth dropped open in surprise. She had wondered on and off for years what had happened to the pictures from the photo booth.

"You've had them?"

"Yes, I took them because I didn't want you to see them." Lucky's voice was filled with emotion.

She stared at the pictures, barely glancing at herself. Instead, she was focused on the raw emotion on Lucky's face that she had been too shy to recognize when they had been in the photo booth.

His face was filled with hunger, which was what she had remembered from that night, but one captured the love that he couldn't hide for a split second.

"Lucky…"

"You have been and always will be my only love," Lucky choked out, sliding the pictures back inside his wallet.

"I want those."

"Nope, they're mine, just like you are." He grinned, leaning forward to brush back her hair then placing a possessive kiss behind her ear on the micro tattoo of a swan.

Willa gazed up at his perfect face that grew more handsome each year they were married. Her husband would always be beautiful, both inside and out.

"Tonight at dinner, we'll tell the children they can have a puppy," Willa relented then quickly added, "a normal dog from the pound."

"All right, but I'm still going to get her trained by Colt."

Willa liked the thought of the children having a canine protector watching over them. It would be painful at first, but it was time to let the children have one to bond with and grow alongside them.

"Here, let me hold him for a while."

Willa handed Lucky his child.

"He's as heavy as a couple of bricks already," Lucky boasted proudly, gazing down at his son like he had all his children, filled with love.

This child, she could tell, already held a special place in his heart. They had named him Hunter. Lucky swore his name would make him a mighty hunter for the Lord, but Willa knew exactly who their son was named after.

"My lucky number seven."

# Books By Jamie Begley:

## The Last Riders Series:
Razer's Ride
Viper's Run
Knox's Stand
Shade's Fall
Cash's Fight
Shade
Lucky's Choice

## Biker Bitches Series:
Sex Piston
Fat Louise

## The VIP Room Series:
Teased
Tainted
King

## Predators MC Series:
Riot
Stand Off

## The Dark Souls Series:
Soul Of A Man
Soul Of A Woman

.

Made in the USA
Monee, IL
23 August 2020